JANE AUSTEN'S BUSINESS

Jane Austen's Business

Her World and Her Profession

Edited by

Juliet McMaster

and

Bruce Stovel

First published in Great Britain 1996 by
MACMILLAN PRESS LTD
Houndmills, Basingstoke, Hampshire RG21 6XS
and London
Companies and representatives
throughout the world

A catalogue record for this book is available
from the British Library.

ISBN 0–333–62920–5

First published in the United States of America 1996 by
ST. MARTIN'S PRESS, INC.,
Scholarly and Reference Division,
175 Fifth Avenue,
New York, N.Y. 10010

ISBN 0–312–15835–1

Library of Congress Cataloging-in-Publication Data
Jane Austen's business : her world and her profession / edited by
Juliet McMaster and Bruce Stovel.
p.   cm.
Includes bibliographical references and index.
ISBN 0–312–15835–1 (cloth)
1. Austen, Jane, 1775–1817—Criticism and interpretation.
2. Women and literature—England—History—19th century.
I. McMaster, Juliet.   II. Stovel, Bruce.
PR4037.J36   1996
823'.7—dc20   95–35817
                                                           CIP

10   9   8   7   6   5   4   3   2   1
05   04   03   02   01   00   99   98   97   96

Printed and bound in Great Britain by
Antony Rowe Ltd, Chippenham, Wiltshire

In memory of
Jack
(J. David Grey)
Co-Founder of
the Jane Austen Society of North America
and friend

Contents

viii   *Contents*

List of Illustrations

Texts and Abbreviations

References to Jane Austen's works are to R. W. Chapman's editions:

The Novels of Jane Austen, ed. R. W. Chapman, 5 vols, 3rd edition (London: Oxford University Press, 1933), reprinted with revisions 1969.

Minor Works, ed. R. W. Chapman (London: Oxford University Press, 1954), reprinted with revisions 1963.

Jane Austen's Letters to her Sister Cassandra and Others, ed. R. W. Chapman, 2nd edition (London: Oxford University Press, 1952).

Abbreviations

E   *Emma*
L   *Jane Austen's Letters to her Sister Cassandra and Others*
MP   *Mansfield Park*
MW   *Minor Works*
NA   *Northanger Abbey*
P   *Persuasion*
PP   *Pride and Prejudice*
SS   *Sense and Sensibility*

Notes on the Contributors

Julia Prewitt Brown is an Associate Professor of English at Boston University and author of *Jane Austen's Novels: Social Change and Literary Form* (Harvard, 1979) and *A Reader's Guide to the Nineteenth-Century English Novel* (Macmillan, 1985). She is currently working on a book on Oscar Wilde.

George Butte is Professor of English at Colorado College, where he teaches the nineteenth-century novel and film studies. He has published articles on Trollope, Thackeray, Conrad and Nietzsche. He is working on a book about intersubjectivity in the novel and film.

Lorrie Clark is Associate Professor of English at Trent University in Peterborough, Ontario. She has recently published *Blake, Kierkegaard, and the Spectre of Dialectic* (Cambridge, 1991), and is currently working on a book project entitled *Romanticism and the Politics of Sympathy* involving Rousseau, Wordsworth, Burke, Austen, George Eliot, Conrad and Nietzsche.

Edward Copeland teaches eighteenth-century English literature, including a course on Jane Austen's novels, at Pomona College in Claremont, California. He is the author of *Women Writing about Money, 1790–1820*, published by Cambridge University Press (1995), and he is now co-editing, along with Juliet McMaster, *The Cambridge Companion to Jane Austen*.

Margaret Drabble has written twelve novels and has written or edited many books of literary criticism, most notably the new and revised *Oxford Companion to English Literature* (1985). She has published many essays and reviews on Jane Austen, including introductions to the six novels in the recent Virago Press edition and to the Penguin edition of *Lady Susan, The Watsons, Sanditon*.

Jan Fergus, Professor of English at Lehigh University, has published *Jane Austen and the Didactic Novel* (Barnes and Noble, 1983) and *Jane Austen: A Literary Life* (Macmillan, 1991). She is Book Review Editor for *Eighteenth-Century Studies* and is completing a study of the audience for prose fiction in eighteenth-century England entitled *Readers and Fictions*.

Isobel Grundy is Henry Marshall Tory Professor at the University of Alberta. Her publications include *Samuel Johnson and the Scale* *of Greatness* (Georgia, 1986); with Patricia Clements and Virginia Blain, *The Feminist Companion to Literature in English: Women Writers from the Middle Ages to the Present* (Yale, 1990); and an edition of Eliza Fenwick's novel of 1795, *Secresy, or The Ruin on the Rock* (Broadview, 1994). She is currently working on a biography of Lady Mary Wortley Montagu.

Gary Kelly is Head of the Department of English at the University of Keele. He has degrees from Toronto and Oxford Universities and was for many years Professor of English at the University of Alberta. He has published books on Mary Wollstonecraft, the French Revolution and the novel, women writers, and popular literature. He is the General Editor of Longman's eleven-volume *History of Women's Writing in English*.

Juliet McMaster, University Professor of English at the University of Alberta, is the author of *Jane Austen on Love* and of books on Thackeray, Trollope, and Dickens, and editor/illustrator of *The Beautiful Cassandra*, a youthful story of Austen's, adapted as a picture book for children. She has also written *Jane Austen the Novelist: Essays Past and Present*, published by Macmillan, and is co-editing with Edward Copeland *The Cambridge Companion to Jane Austen*.

Jane Millgate is Professor of English at the University of Toronto. She is the author of *Macaulay* (Routledge, 1973), *Walter Scott: The Making of the Novelist* (Toronto, 1984), *Scott's Last Edition: A Study in Publishing History* (Edinburgh, 1987), and of numerous articles on nineteenth-century literature and the history of the book.

Douglas Murray, Associate Professor of English at Belmont University in Nashville, Tennessee, is the co-editor (with Margaret Doody) of Jane Austen's *Catharine and Other Writings* (Oxford, 1993) and the author of essays on Dryden, Richardson, Pope, and other authors of the eighteenth century as well as on English vocal music. He is at work on a study of the visual culture of Jane Austen's era.

Peter Sabor is Professor at the Université Laval, Quebec. He has recently edited *The Complete Plays of Frances Burney* (Pickering and Chatto, 1995). Other publications include *Horace Walpole: A Reference Guide, Horace Walpole: The Critical Heritage*, and editions of Richardson's *Pamela*, Cleland's *Memoirs of a Woman of Pleasure*, Sarah Fielding's *Remarks on Clarissa*, and (in collaboration) Burney's *Cecilia* and *The Wanderer* and Carlyle's *Sartor Resartus*.

Elaine Showalter, Professor of English at Princeton University, is the author of several books on women's writing: *A Literature of Their Own: Women Writers from Brontë to Lessing* (1977); *The Female Malady: Women, Madness, and English Culture, 1830–1980* (1985); *Sexual Anarchy: Gender and Culture at the Fin de Siècle* (1991); and *Sister's Choice: Tradition and Change in American Women's Writing* (1991).

Bruce Stovel is a member of the English Department at the University of Alberta. He has written many essays and reviews on Jane Austen, as well as essays on Richardson, Fielding, Swift, Sterne, Charlotte Lennox, Frances Burney, Scott, Evelyn Waugh, Kingsley Amis, Brian Moore, and Margaret Laurence.

Judith Terry teaches English at the University of Victoria, Canada, and is the author of *Miss Abigail's Part, or Version and Diversion* (1986), which tells the tale of *Mansfield Park* from a servant's point of view. She has edited and written an introduction to the new Everyman edition of *Persuasion*.

Inger Sigrun Thomsen received her PhD from the Committee on Social Thought at the University of Chicago. She is an Assistant Professor of English at the University of Puget Sound in Tacoma, Washington, and is currently completing *A Rhetoric of Silence*, which explores the effect on the novel of late-eighteenth-century attitudes to language.

Acknowledgements

Figures 11.1 to 11.4 are all from George Hepplewhite, *The Cabinet-Maker and Upholsterer's Guide*, 1788. Courtesy of the Henry E. Huntington Library. Fig. 11.5 is reproduced courtesy of the Pierpont Morgan Library.

See the captions to the plates for further acknowledgements.

Introduction

> Her business is not half so much with the human heart as with
> the human eyes, mouth, hands and feet; what sees keenly, speaks
> aptly, moves flexibly, it suits her to study, but what throbs fast
> and full, though hidden, what the blood rushes through, what is
> the unseen seat of Life and the sentient target of death – this Miss
> Austen ignores.[1]
>
> Charlotte Brontë of Jane Austen,
> Letter of 12 April 1850

Charlotte Brontë's strictures on Jane Austen's lack of passion are
well known, and frequently quoted. Rather than disputing them,
we have decided for the purposes of this collection to embrace
them – to show that the study of 'what sees keenly, speaks aptly,
moves flexibly', which Brontë so impatiently dismisses, is strikingly
fit to be the proper business of the novelist.

Austen's characters are able to perform each of these activities
with transcendent aplomb, with virtually professional accomplish-
ment. Their stylish mastery of language, or equally stylish abuse of
it, their penetrating vision or impenetrable blindness, are among
those attributes that keep us reading from page to page, that
compel our attention and reward our observation. As they 'move
flexibly' in the dance, that emblem of the graceful achievement of
balanced relationship, they prompt us to enthuse, as Fanny Price
does of the measured motions of the stars, 'Here's harmony! . . .
Here's repose!' (*MP*, 113).

But lest the reader succumb too languorously to repose and embrace, we throw down the gauntlet to Charlotte Brontë too. Some
of these papers challenge the contention that Austen ignores affairs
of the heart, that she lacks 'poetry' and a spiritual dimension, that
she is without passion.

We have grouped the following essays, then, under four heads:
'What Sees Keenly', 'What Speaks Aptly', 'What Moves Flexibly',
and, of course, 'What Throbs Fast and Full'.

Under 'What Sees Keenly' comes a cluster of essays on looking
and seeing as a deliberate and skilled activity, and sometimes an
aggressive one. Isobel Grundy shows Austen as 'writing of business,

pleasure, and humour', and in the process taking up the challenge of her formidable senior, Anna Laetitia Barbauld, who had suggested that humour was the province of male writers. Anne Elliot, herself marginalised, becomes the spectator who often sees more of the game than the participants; though deeply feeling, she is acutely observant, and often as amused by human folly and human vagaries as her more vivacious predecessor, Elizabeth Bennet.

Peter Sabor and Lorrie Clark, in two complementary essays, engage paintings and other pictures described in Austen's novels, and in *Persuasion* particularly, exploring the verbal representations of visual representations. Sabor analyses Austen's use of ekphrasis, the verbal description of visual projections, and demonstrates the rich significance of the portraits and prints. Clark focuses on a single fictional painting, the Turneresque seascape that depicts what Admiral Croft calls 'a shapeless old cockleshell' (*P*, 169), and interrogates it as a commentary on the fashion for the sublime in art. Douglas Murray explores the gaze as an exchange between aggressor and passive recipient, and the power dynamic that is represented by the panopticon, and examines Austen's own sensitivity to looking and being looked at in her life as well as in her fiction. 'A watcher watches another watcher in pursuit of the tell-tale look', writes George Butte, in an essay that explores intersubjectivity in *Emma*, and Austen's innovative layering of characters as one responds to being perceived by another.

The characters' powers of representation and manipulation by speech is a common concern in the three essays on 'What Speaks Aptly'. Mary Musgrove in *Persuasion*, as Jan Fergus engagingly shows, has developed the whine to a fine art: between casting herself as put-upon victim, and accusing others of calculated and unmerited neglect, she has discovered a rhetorical strategy by which she can't lose; everyone else must always be in the wrong. Juliet McMaster, in exploring the characters' critical sensitivity to each other's verbal practices in *Pride and Prejudice*, illuminates the different relations each character's speech bears to reality. And Inger Thomsen demonstrates how even the silences in the novels are eloquent with unspoken meaning.

In grouping the three essays in the section on 'What Moves Flexibly', we have allowed ourselves a margin of flexibility. It is less the characters' motions here than the *author's* that emerge as supple and effective. The writers of these essays engage Austen as professional artist, plying her trade with a developed expertise. Jane

Millgate examines the literary relation between Austen and her more famous contemporary Sir Walter Scott, and shows how there was a two-way exchange, a 'partly explicit, largely implicit, literary dialogue' between them, in which Austen exercises a limber professionalism in a business where the women novelists had as much prominence as the men. Judith Terry presents the narrator of *Persuasion* as maintaining a cool hand on the wheel, steering the reader among competing interests, releasing and withholding information in such a way as to control and direct reader interest and reader sympathy with the correct balance of identification and distance.

In the same group of essays, Edward Copeland engages Austen's relation to material culture. His fascinating study of the accounts of Ring Brothers, a retail furniture house in Basingstoke, connects the actual historical retrenchments and conspicuous consumption of Austen family members and their associates with Sir Walter Elliot's fictional extravagances in *Persuasion*, in the process showing how Austen formidably knew her business.

Gary Kelly usurps the title of this volume in a wide-ranging cultural study which he heads 'Jane Austen's *Real* Business'. Austen, as he shows, was shrewd in developing a means 'to transform the hitherto sub-literary form of the novel into Literature as a particular form of cultural capital'. As part of this project, she created novels that would be amply re-readable, that would last as 'classics' in a reading culture that had hitherto treated fiction as ephemeral matter for brief circulation. Julia Prewitt Brown extends the exploration of Austen as a professional in examining the relation of her 'private and personal life and her public ambition as an artist'. Brown focuses on the relation of private to public in the moral and philosophical positions in Austen's fiction as well as in her life.

These essays present an author who was more than the quiet spinster who hid her writing under the blotter when the door-hinge creaked, restricted herself to those three or four families in a country village, and left the politics to the men. *This* Austen is professionally astute, however circumscribed her circumstances, sensitive and assured in artistic decisions, and alert to the large economic and cultural movements in the world around her.

The essays grouped under 'What Throbs Fast and Full' shift from affairs of the head to affairs of the heart. Elaine Showalter provides a fine transition from the one to the other in a moving study of economies of feeling. Her essay on 'Retrenchments' connects the heart with the purse, and Anne Elliot's time with ours. And in a

1 Logo for the Lake Louise conference of the Jane Austen Society of
North America

study of an often overlooked group of Austen's writings, the prayers,
Bruce Stovel explores a spiritual dimension of her work.

To wind up the volume, we provide a *new* love story. In a piece
of fiction that updates *Persuasion* and brings Austen's Somerset
and the Elliot family into the twentieth century, Margaret Drabble
presents a heroine deeply and irreversibly in love. With whom, or
what? Ah, that would be telling. But in developing her 'Somerset
Romance', Drabble lingers lovingly over every local detail, and loads
every rift with ore.

The 'Somerset Romance', the chronicles of Ring Brothers of
Basingstoke, the analyses of fictional events at Bath and Lyme, and
many of these other papers, were first delivered a very long way
from those places. But there was nevertheless sufficient reason to
linger lovingly over local detail. Most of these papers were part of
the programme of the Jane Austen conference[2] held at Lake Louise,
a magnificent setting in the heart of the Canadian Rockies. The
annual conference of the Jane Austen Society of North America

takes place in a different venue each year, usually a major city. This was the first time the membership gathered in a rural setting, rather far from the amenities of airports, taxis, galleries and corner restaurants. It was fitting that the programme featured *Persuasion*, the most Romantic of Austen's novels, and the one that evokes most poetically 'the sweet scenes of autumn' and 'the very beautiful line of cliffs stretching to the east' (*P*, 85, 95).

It was no doubt the splendid scenery of Lake Louise that enabled us to attract this outstanding group of speakers, and that drew (along with our impressive programme) an unprecedented number of 600 delegates to the conference. Besides attending the papers and watching the world première of *An Accident at Lyme*,[3] a musical based on *Persuasion*, they went on hikes, had encounters with porcupines and rutting elk, and walked on glaciers: not everyone's idea of activities appropriate to the celebration of the quiet rural novelist of the home counties. Yet it turns out that one of the two spectacular mountains in the panorama, Mt Lefroy, was named after – who else? – a collateral descendant, John Henry Lefroy.[4] Jane Austen still has influence in high places.

Such a gathering of Jane Austen specialists, both lay and academic – people who travelled thousands of miles to get there, who bought books, tapes and videos, who gave papers and listened to them, who thronged souvenir shops and restaurants, who attended or performed in the musical production, who turned out in Regency dress to dance the country dances of Austen's time – such a gathering testifies to Jane Austen's Business in ways both direct and indirect. Her artistry and her place in our culture were discussed at length, and exuberantly celebrated. Clearly she not only *has* business; nowadays she *is* business.

A collection such as this affords occasion to ponder over the intricate interrelatedness of Jane Austen's concerns, and to marvel at it. In one sense this book is highly specialised, focused not just on a single author of one period, but on one whose *oeuvre* has been slender, and who, moreover, has been famous for her 'limitation'. We have all heard about the little bit of ivory two inches wide, about how Jane Austen never presents a scene between men where there is no woman present (since by definition she had never witnessed one herself), and never mentions the Napoleonic wars although she wrote in the midst of them. There is a large body of criticism that celebrates her limitation, as well as another large body that insists she isn't so limited after all.

But the intensity of our focus on this one 'limited' novelist, even the concentration, notable though not exclusive, on her last and shortest novel, itself produces an unexpected scope of vision, as we discover the world that is reflected in the water-drop. These essays together suggest the extraordinary extent to which Austen's work is an intricate web that touches and connects the multiple movements of her culture. Just as the bumbling commentary of Admiral Croft at a print-shop window (as Lorrie Clark shows) takes us to the heart of the aesthetic debate on the sublime, so Austen's light and familiar touches make her novels vibrate with the major economic, social and cultural issues of her time.

It is a long way from Hampshire to Lake Louise, Alberta, Canada; but not so long a way as that quiet country spinster has come, in fame and fortune, since she wielded that fine brush over her little bit of ivory, creating a world which two centuries later has become part of the shared culture of three continents.

J.M., B.S.

Notes

1. From Charlotte Brontë's letter to W. S. Williams of 12 April 1850. *The Brontës: Their Lives, Friendships and Correspondence in Four Volumes*, ed. Thomas James Wise, The Shakespeare Head Brontë (Oxford: Basil Blackwell, 1932), III, 99.
2. The essays in this collection have largely been selected from the thirty papers delivered at the Lake Louise conference of the Jane Austen Society of North America (JASNA) on 7–10 October 1993. The present editors were also the co-convenors of that conference. While the particular occasion must be left behind in a published collection such as this, it accounts in large measure for the shape of this book, including the visible concentration on *Persuasion*. Essays added, for the sake of greater range among Jane Austen's works, are those by the editors, Juliet McMaster and Bruce Stovel, and by George Butte and Inger Thomsen (who substituted her essay on the narrator's language in a range of the novels for the paper she had delivered on *Persuasion*).
3. *An Accident at Lyme*, with libretto by Paula Schwartz and music by Neil Moyer, is a lively and engaging piece of theatre that will no doubt find other production. This production was directed by Stephen Heatley. A review of it by Judith Terry can be found in *Persuasions* (the annual journal of JASNA), 15 (1993), 21–2.
4. See Bruce Stovel, '*Persuasion* is 1993 AGM topic at Lake Louise', *JASNA News*, 8:1 (Spring 1992), 8.

Part I
What Sees Keenly

1

Persuasion: or, The Triumph of Cheerfulness

Isobel Grundy

As I discovered midway in writing this essay, I was preparing for it fifty years ago. An aunt of mine remembers me as a small child rushing up and down the Cobb at Lyme Regis, tearing around, enjoying myself. She remembers thinking, 'If that child doesn't look out, she's going to fall and get hurt.'

Later I became one of many readers of *Persuasion* to be bothered by the scene where Louisa does just that – and by what it seems to convey about the author's attitude to enjoying oneself. It suggests a tabloid headline: 'GIRL PLAYS ON STEPS, DIES'. Most first-time readers assume, at least for a moment, that 'taken up lifeless!' (109) means Louisa is dead. As penalty for enjoying oneself (no matter how illicit the idea of female enjoyment, no matter what the connotations of the word 'fall'), even as penalty for stealing the hero from the heroine, capital punishment strikes the modern reader as excessive.

Jane Austen's earliest readers might find this apparent fatality less startling. It would be well within the range of many of her fiction-writing peers: of those bent on improving adults as well as girls. They regularly deploy poetic justice to punish female characters for infringing rules of conduct; and those rules include a prohibition of displays of physical energy: particularly displays put on for men. Fictional women who are careless of decorum, or forward with men, are quite likely to have the gravity of their offence hammered home by its causing a death.[1] And Louisa is guilty not of sheer physical exuberance but of calculated flirtation: she wants, not to jump, but to 'be jumped' by Captain Wentworth, and it is to 'shew' her enjoyment that she insists on jumping again.

Readers discover two pages later (as do her companions) that she isn't dead at all. The reversal left me not relieved, but on the contrary feeling I had been tricked. And the trick has a second part. It emerges that Louisa's punishment, like her death, is only apparent: in the long term her fall turns out well. Readers have a devious and complex joke played on them: not sudden death but anti-climax, not a savage didactic condemnation but (after long-drawn-out, painful suspense) a comic resolution.

Austen has carefully planned a complex effect.[2] The misleading word 'lifeless' serves as tip-off to her larger joke. Louisa is not being punished for physical or sexual exuberance; she is being cleared from Anne's path with a kind of jovial ruthlessness. This trick exploits the reader's melodramatic expectations from plot, and punitive expectations from morality. Contrary to fictional models, Louisa's fall, not to her death but to eventual marriage and happiness, in the end will be seen by Anne as amusing (167).

In *Persuasion*, that is to say, suspense and horror intrude only to be ousted by cheerfulness. In the same way, the 'declining year' attempts to impose 'poetical despondence', but is frustrated by the forward-looking farmer, ploughing and repairing the footpath, 'meaning to have spring again' (85). Austen calls attention to her novel's debate between melancholy and cheerfulness by balancing them here, and letting the scales swing towards cheerfulness.

There is, however, a reading of *Persuasion* in which melancholy or wistfulness prevails, perhaps because the author was already suffering from the disease that was to kill her almost exactly a year after she finished its first draft (Fergus, 164, 170). Anne can be seen either as standing out among Austen heroines because of her suffering, or as representative in this of her sex. As Anne herself maintains, women's generalised 'fate' is to be preyed on by their feelings and subjected, more than men are, to emotional pain and despair (232).

Anne attributes this susceptibility to society, not biology. Women 'live at home, quiet, confined'; they are not 'forced on exertion' by 'a profession, pursuits, business of some sort or other' (232). Generalising from her own experience, she says what most of her contemporaries would accept. Maria Edgeworth scribbled her agreement in the margins of *Persuasion* at this passage: 'our mind is continually fixt on one object', she wrote.[3] But Edgeworth's conservative, didactic works urge women to stay at home. The women in *Persuasion*, on the contrary, are permitted a number of pursuits, exertions, and variations on the 'quiet, confined' home.

They represent a great variety, too, in innate, biological temperament or 'spirits'. The single vignette of Anne as a girl shows her at boarding-school after her mother's death: 'of strong sensibility and not high spirits' (152). The level of spirits is often measured. Much is made of the high spirits of the Musgrove family, the low spirits of Mary. High spirits are the gift of nature. The Musgrove high spirits go with their clannishness, their enjoyment of a family crowd, while Mary's low spirits are fostered by loneliness. Anne, who combats low spirits on principle, longs to have a place in the community.

Mrs Smith, as sociable by nature as the Musgroves, has an inexhaustible 'spring of felicity' in 'the glow of her spirits' (252). Even when bereaved, alone, and crippled, in dark, noisy, cramped accommodation, she has 'a disposition to converse and be cheerful beyond [Anne's] expectation'. She has 'moments only of languor and depression, to hours of occupation and enjoyment', not from fortitude or resignation only, but from 'that elasticity of mind, that disposition to be comforted, that power of turning readily from evil to good, and of finding employment which carried her out of herself, which was from Nature alone' (153–4; cf. Showalter in this collection). She shares Anne's appetite for amusement, for hearing 'something that makes one know one's species better . . . the newest modes of being trifling and silly' (155). Unlike the more vulnerable Anne, she finds cheerfulness too easy to be the protagonist of a triumph-of-cheerfulness story.

Anne must learn, *without* natural high spirits, to be happy or cheerful. These words are not synonymous: 'happy' and 'happiness' cluster about Anne as soon as she and her lover are reunited; but they cluster also about Sir Walter and Elizabeth once the two are established at Bath. They are happy about their superior furniture, the number of visiting cards they receive, and Mr Elliot's flattery (137–8). Happiness, it seems, is capable of being devalued; urgently as women need 'pursuits, business of some sort or another', such pursuits can be debased, and produce a debased kind of happiness. I have not found 'cheerfulness' being subjected to such debasement.

Anne's remarks on women's social circumstances and women's feelings, addressed to the brotherly and sympathetic Captain Harville, have become perhaps the most familiar passage in *Persuasion*. They speak to so many pressing late-twentieth-century concerns. Are women different from men, and how? Can we safely believe what male-authored texts say about them? Are women more prone to emotional suffering? If so, is this tendency innate or socially constructed? This debate at the White Hart in Bath, which now seems so inevitable, arose only on second thoughts. It comes from the one section in *Persuasion* which illness allowed Austen to subject to revision. But it would have sounded familiar to many readers even at its first appearance, for it reviews and refashions some influential remarks about women and fiction which date from the outset of Austen's publishing career.

As Anne is debating with Captain Harville, Austen is debating with Anna Laetitia Barbauld, who had become the leading critic of fiction with her groundbreaking edition of *The British Novelists* (1810). This was the first standard or canonical set of English fiction. It survives in the literary time-capsules of country-house libraries: a handsome, uniform, 50-volume set conferring on Austen's male and female fictional predecessors an authorised status out of reach of her heterogeneous, cheaply produced contemporaries.

A commercial venture with status-raising intent, this edition sought to promote the novel from a circulating-library milieu to that of the lady's or gentleman's specially bound, book-plated collection. It included Barbauld's introduction, 'On the Origin and Progress of Novel-Writing', and her 'Prefaces, Biographical and Critical' on the novelists. 'Prefaces, Biographical and Critical' was, of course, the original title of what later became known as Samuel Johnson's *Lives of the English Poets*. Barbauld was doing for novelists what Johnson had done for poets: placing them in the great tradition of literature. But unlike Johnson she was swimming against the current in hoping to prove that 'this species of composition is entitled to a higher rank than has been generally assigned it'.[4]

Barbauld presents a gradual feminisation of the novel: eight of her 21 novelists are women, and they cluster towards the more modern end of the span. *Clarissa*, that paradoxically female text, stands first in the collection, which, chronologically, begins with *Robinson Crusoe*. Five novels by men follow before the earliest woman's novel, *The Female Quixote*, 33 years after *Crusoe*. Out of seven novelists who are twice selected, the first three are all men, ending with Henry Mackenzie, and the last four all women, beginning with Frances Burney. The first selection from a canonised woman dates from the very year after the final selection from a canonised man. From after 1790 Barbauld includes seven novels by women and only one by a man. She remarks explicitly, and with approval, that the baton has passed from male to largely female hands.[5]

The feminine novel which Barbauld admires, however, is the sentimental novel of 'distress'. Men, she says, prefer to read and write fictional action, satire, or humour; women prefer sentiment. As she speculates as to why this might be, she sounds, very briefly, almost like Anne Elliot talking to Captain Harville. Do women, she wonders, 'suffer more'? Because they are barred from 'mixing at large in society' like men, have they 'fewer resources against melancholy'? And does all this qualify them by their gender to become sentimental novelists?

> Is it that women nurse those feelings in secrecy and silence, and diversify the expression of them with endless shades of sentiment, which are more transiently felt, and with fewer modifications of delicacy, by the other sex? (44)

But between her comments on women feeling distress and her comments on their expressing these feelings in fiction, Barbauld inserts two sentences sounding very unlike Anne and totally unlike Austen. She seems to suspect that men's mixing in society gives them an advantage as novelists; that they write not just a different but a better kind of novel. Do they, she wonders,

> have a brisker flow of ideas, and, seeing a greater variety of characters, introduce more of the business and pleasure of life into their productions? Is it that humour is a scarcer product of the mind than sentiment, and more congenial to the stronger powers of man? (44)

Barbauld's speculations do not separate nature from nurture, but elide the two; though she connects men's 'brisker flow of ideas' with the variety of their lives, she seems to see their 'stronger powers of mind' as innate.

When this was published, in 1810, Jane Austen was newly settled at Chawton Cottage, on the brink of her most productive years as a novelist. She was probably reworking *Sense and Sensibility* for print (Fergus, 1991, 127); if so, the relation of humour to sentiment in her stories was much in her mind. She was striving to become a published novelist, and here was *the* editor of *the* prestigious collection of novelists, a woman like herself, attributing all Austen's own specialities – humour, flow of ideas, variety of characters, the business and pleasure of life – to 'the stronger powers of man', and leaving for the woman novelist nothing but diversifying the expression of feeling with endless shades of sentiment!

Austen could not have read that passage without indignation and resistance. It seems safe to assume that she did read it, not long after it appeared. *The British Novelists*, though beyond her own means, was highly suitable for her brother Edward's library at Godmersham Hall, which she used on her visits there (Honan, 332-3). One might regard her entire literary career as an answer to Barbauld, designed to prove that she could do humour, flow of ideas, and so on, and refuse to do the endlessly diversified shades of sentiment, and still write like a woman, not like a man. Her writing of business, pleasure, and humour carries her dissent from Barbauld into every cranny of her *oeuvre*.

Aside from such general reply, *Persuasion* in particular (written when one might expect failing health to make humour harder and sentiment more tempting) attacks the binary 'male humour, female sentiment' in the very bones of its plot. It demonstrates that Anne, a woman, stands to benefit by that mixing in society which men enjoy, that her lover's male emotions are *not* more transiently felt than hers, and especially that humour is highly congenial to the feminine mind. This novel poises itself on the edge of that sentimental situation which Barbauld evokes (sensitive, suffering woman, lacking external resources; man mixing at large in society) while simultaneously contradicting Barbauld's dichotomies through its depiction of woman's humour, woman's strength, and woman's creative power. Woman indeed has sentiment – or the heroine has – but no more than the hero.

The most specific reply to Barbauld, Anne's speech to Captain Harville (the speech of a keen reader who knows *The British Novelists*), comes as culmination to this argument. Anne there assents to the notions that women have fewer resources against melancholy and that mixing at large in society gives a brisker flow of ideas. But she denies the hint of biology-as-destiny which those notions carry in Barbauld.

In short, what Austen shares with Barbauld is the idea of gender difference as having social causes; what she challenges is the idea of it as innate. Barbauld's tentative question-marks reassuringly prevent the divergence of these two opposing possibilities. The latter alternative – the received idea of men's creative power, women's feeling and absence of humour – was deeply embedded in the ideology of the day, and indispensable to a consensus-seeking publication like

The British Novelists. Anne's words to Captain Harville attribute gender differences wholly to social causes; Anne's whole story claims humour, a quality capable of healing the ravages of sentiment, as natural to the female mind.

Anne, despite her suffering and sensitivity, is virtually an anti-sentimental heroine. As the story opens, she is alone with the memory of her broken love affair, isolated in her unloving family; she is shut away from resources outside herself, never 'forced on exertion' since her father and sister deny her any role. Her escape from this situation is measured by her growing capacity for humour. Humour, I believe, is not the cause of her recovery, but it is the gauge of it. It must be the Musgroves' mirth, not Anne's, which Mr Elliot hears through the walls at Lyme. Yet Anne is more alert to find amusement in the spectacle presented by her fellow-creatures than any Austen heroine since Elizabeth Bennet. She does not wait to be loved and happy before she can feel amused; she begins to feel this way as soon as she begins to mix at large in society. Indeed, for lifting her melancholy and offering her resources, being anxiously in love seems almost as effective as being happily in love.[6]

Barbauld's ideas are the starting-point from which Austen widely diverges. A woman lacking 'resources against melancholy' is transformed by access to such resources; she excels not only in sentiment, but also in the rarer and stronger quality of humour. Lest the implications of this should be missed, Austen supplies a background of proliferating role-reversal. Throughout this novel, men and women repeatedly contradict the stereotypes of what male and female ought to be. We begin with Sir Walter Elliot's vanity about his beauty: the kind of vanity women are supposed to have. We end with Anne speaking up for her sex while Wentworth perforce listens in silence, with no voice, but only suspense and concealment. He even hides his writing under the blotter, as we are told his creator did herself.

In between, Mrs Clay declaims against any kind of gainful employment for a man lest it should spoil his looks (20): a favourite argument of conduct-books against either jobs *or* study for a woman. Anne's mother possesses solid judgement except for a 'youthful infatuation' (so natural in a heroine's father, like Mr Bennet; so unheard-of in a heroine's mother!); it is agonising for her to relinquish parental responsibility to the 'authority and guidance of a conceited, silly father' (4–5). Not only is Admiral Croft a rotten driver and his wife a good one; it is she who 'asked more questions about the house, and terms, and taxes, than the admiral himself, and seemed more conversant with business' (22). Captain Benwick pines away for love, and damages his spirits by romantic reading, like a girl.[7] Anne lectures him about moral duties, emboldened by 'feeling in herself the right of seniority of mind' (101), which reverses the whole conduct-book tradition of men advising women.[8]

Amusement for Anne begins as something rather tepid and wholly orthodox. After the loss of Kellynch, her sister Mary's children will provide 'interest, amusement, and wholesome exertion' (43). Here the beneficial effects of amusement and of being 'forced on exertion' sound distinctly medicinal. The reader knows those children will be hard work. But *any* prospective amusement for Anne is a novelty: her other sister, this paragraph reminds us, is 'repulsive', 'unsisterly' and 'inaccessible'. It is almost fair to say that Mary's tendency to be *distressed*[9] actually makes Anne feel better: Anne embraces cheerfully the task of cheering Mary up (38).

More active sources of amusement appear once Anne has digested her distress at meeting the now apparently indifferent Frederick Wentworth. Her new amusement (most unlike that of child-minding) results from seeing other people as comic – and therefore, unavoidably, herself as superior to them. Austen daringly or riskily ascribes this highly anti-sentimental attitude to her heroine in the context of the elder Musgroves' reminiscences about their dead son. Whatever one thinks of this chapter,[10] Anne is *not* amused by their grief, but by their remodelling Dick in memory into somebody entirely unlike what he actually was alive. When Anne 'suppressed a smile', Mrs Musgrove has just said that if Heaven had spared him he would by now have been 'just such another' as Captain Wentworth (64). Austen introduces Anne's capacity for amusement not tentatively, but blatantly.

Only one other person present is amused: Wentworth himself. For him too, the comic resides in the gulf between Dick in fact and Dick in memory; like Anne, he overcomes the momentary 'self-amusement' of his own clearer memory, to offer serious and respectful sympathy to the grieving, misremembering mother (67). Only Anne, because she knows him so well, perceives the outcropping of his satiric amusement. Her secret participation in his feeling is highly significant, establishing their likeness to each other, their potential sympathy. Instinctive sympathy between two exceptionally sensitive characters is a favourite device in the sentimental novel: but not sympathy in sardonic amusement. (Anne's anti-sentimental sharing of comedy, not pathos, extends to Wentworth's relations: though amused herself by the Crofts' style of driving, she later counts on them to share her amusement at the news of Louisa's engagement to Benwick: 92, 168.)

So amusement throws out the first filament of present connection between Anne and Frederick. It does so at a moment when the reader is still eager for clues to the character of this long-awaited male lead. Hearing how he 'could not deny himself the pleasure of taking the precious volume [the navy list this time, not the baronetage] into his own hands . . . and once more read aloud' the passage pertaining to himself (66), plants a suspicion that he might turn out to resemble Anne's father. His self-amusement about his own past actions is reassuring; Sir Walter could not encompass it. This hero's quizzical, superior amusement is momentarily legible, in 'a certain glance of his bright eye, and a curl of his handsome mouth' (67). His splendid masculine humour is wholly traditional for a hero; but Anne was amused first. For a heroine such amuse-ment is as *un*usual as a youthful infatuation for a heroine's mother.

This section of the book develops Anne's long-drawn-out distress as she sees more of Wentworth, loves him more, and becomes more certain that she has indeed lost him. But this is not its whole pur-pose. She is now less isolated, playing the role of extra or at least audience to the affairs of all the Musgroves, surrounded by people she has already begun to find comic. Her amusement at the Crofts' driving, while trivial in itself, is remarkable by its placing. She has only just suffered the blow of overhearing Wentworth's moral par-able which likens her to a damaged hazel-nut, dropping without coming to fruition, trodden under foot (88). Even the pain of this decisive rejection, she finds, can be lightened at least for a moment by affectionate amusement.

It is important that such amusement is a mark of affection and acceptance, not indignation or contempt. Anne 'suppressed a smile and listened kindly'; the last time her amusement is mentioned it comes with 'cheerful or forbearing feelings for every creature around her' (64, 245–6). Those who amuse her are good-hearted: the Musgroves and Crofts, all of them kind but in one way or another obtuse. (Her father and Elizabeth are, unlike Mary, no laughing matter.) At Lyme, Anne 'smiled more than once to herself' at Henrietta's artless self-interest on behalf of her fiancé's career; and she is variously amused by the changing attitudes of Henrietta and the other Musgroves to Lady Russell. It is immediately after this that Mr Elliot admires her restored bloom and her 'animation of eye' (103–4). Amusement must share with love the credit for improving her looks.

Anne is amused by Henrietta, though as a friend of Lady Russell's she could easily have been offended at the Musgrove view of Lady Russell. Anne is by now seeing the funny side not only of Henrietta or the Crofts but even of her own concerns. She is 'amused in spite of herself' at Admiral Croft's comments on her father's vanity (128); she 'could not but be amused' at finding herself laying down the moral law to Benwick while 'like many other great moralists and preachers' not following her own advice (101); she repeatedly finds something funny in tributes to her renewed beauty, even in her lover's U-turn on this subject (124, 143, 243). Having even smiled over her own unnecessary 'anxious feelings', she can look down 'to hide her smile' at the Admiral's manner of reporting Frederick's account of Louisa's engagement (128, 172).

Anne, that is to say, can include her own pangs of love, and her own lover's behaviour, among the foibles and contradictions which she reads as comedy, not tragedy or pathos. This is not a trait to win her everyone's admiration, but it re-emphasises her likeness to Frederick. He is capable of smiles and half-smiles and 'a momentary look of his own arch significance' (182, 176) as he recalls his involvement with Louisa. Their resemblance suggests two points: their compatibility as lovers, but also the non-gendered element of personality.

He even mock-heroicises his most vital learning experience: the lesson that he is not wholly self-made and self-reliant but also lucky. 'Like other great men under reverses . . . I must endeavour to subdue my mind to my fortune. I must learn to brook being happier than I deserve' (247). This echoes Anne's self-mockery when she finds herself acting 'like other great moralists'. As Anne perhaps thinks, 'I'm just like Johnson!' Frederick perhaps thinks, 'I'm just like Napoleon!' They are the novel's only two characters to laugh at themselves.

By sharing their amusement, the narrator merges with her heroine. When, for instance, Mrs Musgrove, in a 'domestic hurricane' of three families of small children, extols the benefits of a little 'quiet' home cheerfulness (134), Anne's amusement is implicit, contained in that of the narrator. Only once, late in *Persuasion*, does the heroine suddenly, without warning, become the butt of authorial satire.[11] It happens when Anne has realised Mr Elliot's serious designs on her, but tells herself that her love for Wentworth, even if not reciprocated, would prevent her ever accepting another.

> Prettier musings of high-wrought love and eternal constancy, could never have passed along the streets of Bath, than Anne was sporting with from Camden-place to Westgate-buildings. It was almost enough to spread purification and perfume all the way. (192)

Here amusement springs from awareness that noble feelings do not reform a squalid world; some readers are jolted by the impression that Anne's feelings are being mocked; but they are not. Though Austen provides less guidance than in the Dick Musgrove passage, it is clear that Anne's love is not in itself her butt, any more than was Mrs Musgrove's maternal love in itself. The target in each case is a failure of self-knowledge.

When Austen describes Anne's love, she uses simple assertion that gives no handle for ridicule. 'Anne saw nothing, thought nothing of the brilliancy of the room. Her happiness was from within. Her eyes were bright, and her cheeks glowed.' When she first guesses that Wentworth is jealous, 'For a moment the gratification was exquisite' (185, 191). When her feelings are not 'sported with', they are taken very seriously. 'An interval of meditation, serious and grateful, was the best corrective of every thing dangerous in such high-wrought felicity; and she went to her room, and grew steadfast and fearless in the thankfulness of her enjoyment' (245).

There again is the word 'high-wrought', elaborately worked. What Austen sees as fair game for amusement is apparently the nursing of feeling which Barbauld ascribes to women in their secrecy and silence, perhaps even the diversifying it with 'endless shades of sentiment' which she ascribes to women novelists. The context of Austen's mockery shows clearly that Anne is musing, not about love itself, but about hypothetical faithfulness unto death even if she should lose Frederick a second time: 'be the conclusion of the present suspense good or bad, her affection would be his for ever. Their union, she believed, could not divide her more from other men, than their final separation' (192). To predict the future and make vows or resolutions is certainly to 'nurse' sentiment; it is this which Austen finds risible.

Anne's mental vows of constancy separate her from her creator.

About Anne's first disappointment in love Austen wrote, 'No second attachment, the only thoroughly natural, happy, and sufficient cure, at her time of life, had been possible to the nice tone of her mind, the fastidiousness of her taste, in the small limits of the society around them' (28). That is to say: if Anne could have escaped her social restrictions, her female 'secrecy and silence', as Barbauld says, to 'mix at large in society' like a man, she would not have worn the willow all those years for Wentworth. (Austen continues neatly to evade any invidious comparison between the sexes. Anne's isolation from eligible men during those years has been no greater than his isolation from eligible women. This makes another, little-noted reason for Austen's choosing a naval hero for this plot.)

That sentence about second attachments is so unobtrusive that it needs some unpacking. The usual grammatical form for maxims or aphorisms or Truths Universally Acknowledged, like the one which opens *Pride and Prejudice*, is statement. That is the form used by Ovid when he writes, 'all love is vanquished by a succeeding love'.[12] Jane Austen, virtually paraphrasing Ovid here, conceals her Truth Seldom Acknowledged in an appositional phrase. Rejigging her syntax produces the statement (hedged about with certain qualifications): 'A second attachment is the only thoroughly natural, happy, and sufficient cure for lost love': a very odd aphorism to find embedded in a novel about fidelity, in which first love is magically restored.

The only second attachment actually displayed in *Persuasion* is that of Benwick to Louisa Musgrove, a comic one in several ways. It is a startling twist, even reversal, in the story-line; it is highly convenient for the couple who engage the reader more closely than this one does; it is produced merely by enforced proximity, that is, by happenstance. It involves Benwick not only in forswearing eternal fidelity to the dead, but also in hasty retreat from overtures to Anne. It involves Louisa in a transformation of personality which is attributed to her fall, but which looks nevertheless like satire on the way girls were expected smoothly to adapt themselves to the eventually chosen husband's requirements. In every way, this succeeding love which vanquishes earlier loves makes the couple concerned look like puppets of Fate or Chance.

Another second attachment is faintly shadowed in Mrs Smith's firm conviction that Anne will succumb to Mr Elliot, in Anne's real pleasure in his admiration, and above all in the narrator's ostentatious refusal to enquire how 'she might have felt, had there been no Captain Wentworth in the case' (192). Surely the point is being made that Anne, cheered and stimulated by mixing in society and having been forced on exertion, would now be ready for a new love if the old love were not available. (The capacity to love again suggests little consolation: this particular new love is clearly depicted as a snare she escapes.) Anne and Frederick, however, come close to being puppets of Fate or Chance like Benwick and Louisa.

What Austen provides is the real happy ending: love restored and longing satisfied, under the best possible conditions for rational happiness. Anne's amusement is last glimpsed, not in the final chapter but in the one before that, as 'sensibility and happiness', 'cheerful or forbearing feelings for every creature around her', carry her through her father's and sister's awful card-party. To feel 'amusement in understanding' people is clearly to feel superior (245–6).

Amusement is defensive, not called for on the heights of happiness. The narrator re-appropriates it for herself as she opens her last chapter with an aphorism which she cheerfully depreciates as bad morality: that two young people who are determined to marry will manage it no matter how their elders disapprove.[13] This is another shrewd stroke at the ideology of sentiment, which had wrung many a long story from the helpless suffering of correct young lovers in the face of parental disapprobation. In this novel Austen reshapes the creed of sensibility to embrace cheerfulness: 'sensibility *and* happiness'.

The essays in this book use various terms for the way that Anne defeats melancholy: even more important than distraction and activity, in my reading, is amusement, play of the mind. Anne comes to embody these things before she is granted happiness in love; they are beyond the reach of the heroine of sensibility, or even of Woman as Barbauld describes her. Austen's final sentence takes a parting shot at Barbauld. She calls the anxieties confronting Anne as a sailor's wife a tax 'for belonging to' the naval profession. All this, and a profession too! Anne in transcending her social and emotional confinement, and her creator in harnessing her humour and her flow of ideas, have done the things which Anna Barbauld suggests, perhaps reluctantly, that women cannot do.

Notes

1. E.g. Elizabeth Hamilton, *The Cottagers of Glenburnie*, 1808; Amelia Beauclerc, *Disorder and Order*, 1820.
2. Since *Persuasion* is unrevised, critics may be tempted to speculate, when facing a difficulty, that it would not have survived revision. Such thoughts may usefully encourage questioning, but cannot strengthen any particular interpretation.
3. Copy at UCLA; information from Johnson (1988, 160).
4. 'On the Origin and Progress of Novel-Writing,' 1. Her two predecessors in criticism of fiction, Clara Reeve in 1785 and John Moore in 1797, had both referred to Romance, not novels, in their titles. See Moore, 384.
5. 'Origin', 58–9. Her full list is Defoe, *Robinson Crusoe*, 1719; Henry Fielding, *Joseph Andrews*, 1742, and *Tom Jones*, 1748; Richardson, *Clarissa*, 1748–9, and *Grandison*, 1753; Francis Coventry, *Pompey the Little*, 1751; Charlotte Lennox, *The Female Quixote*, 1752; Johnson, *Rasselas*, 1759; John Hawkesworth, *Almoral and Hamet*, 1761; Frances Brooke, *Julia Mandeville*, 1763; Horace Walpole, *The Castle of Otranto*, 1765; Goldsmith, *The Vicar of Wakefield*, 1766; Smollett, *Humphrey Clinker*, 1771; Henry Mackenzie, *The Man of Feeling*, 1771, and *Julia de Roubigné*, 1777; Richard Graves, *The Spiritual Quixote*, 1773; Frances Burney, *Evelina*, 1778, and *Cecilia*, 1782; Clara Reeve, *The Old English Baron*, 1778; John Moore, *Zeluco*, 1786; Inchbald, *A Simple Story*, 1791, and *Nature and Art*, 1796; Ann Radcliffe, *The Romance of the Forest*, 1791, and *Udolpho*, 1794; Charlotte Smith, *The Old Manor House*, 1793; Robert Bage, *Hermsprong*, 1796; Edgeworth, *Belinda*, 1801, and *Modern Griselda*, 1805.
6. Claudia L. Johnson notes something of 'disturbing relevance to *Persuasion*' in Mr Bennet's cynical remark, 'a girl likes to be crossed in love a little now and then.... It is something to think of' (159).
7. I owe this point to Bruce Stovel.
8. It is of Anne's relationship with Wentworth that Gard writes, 'in her modest form we recognise, if anywhere in this novel, the "mentor" figure of whom literary scholars like to write' (198).
9. For what Fergus in her essay in this volume calls whining, Mary would doubtless find a word implying sentimental as well as social or bodily ills.
10. Some recoil. Mudrick writes, 'this savage caricature – without pretext itself – serves as a pretext for abusing Mrs Musgrove' (212).
11. Wolfe, among others, notes the author's separation from her character here (687ff.).
12. 'Successore novo vincitur omnis amor' (*Remedia Amoris*, line 462: translation from Loeb Library, p. 208).
13. Her erased notes for this idea are longer: 'Bad Morality again. A young Woman proved to have ... more discrimination of Character than her elder – to have seen in two Instances more clearly what a Man was.... But on the point of Morality, I confess myself almost in despair ...' (Chapman, 282, n. 23). To punish Louisa with death, however, would not have been bad morality.

2

'Staring in Astonishment': Portraits and Prints in *Persuasion*

Peter Sabor

If you had invested 24 shillings in one of the 2500 copies of Jane Austen's final, posthumous publication, issued in December 1817, your discerning taste would have been well rewarded. You would have acquired a first edition whose value would increase several thousandfold in less than two hundred years. And, for your more immediate pleasure, you would have been able to read two of Austen's six completed novels – *Northanger Abbey* and *Persuasion* – as well as Henry Austen's 'Biographical Notice'. This notice, often mocked by later critics for emphasising the strength of Austen's Christian faith at the expense of her importance as a novelist, is nonetheless invaluable in providing fresh, first-hand observations on many aspects of Austen's life and writings.

Several of these observations have been regarded by Austen's critics as merely conventional personal compliments, and some may well have been so: we cannot, for example, verify Henry's claim that his sister's 'carriage and deportment were quiet, yet graceful', that 'her complexion was of the finest texture', and that 'her voice was extremely sweet' (*Novels of Jane Austen*, V, 4). When, however, he states that 'she had not only an excellent taste for drawing, but, in her earlier days, evinced great power of hand in the management of the pencil' (V, 5) he introduces a subject of considerable importance to an understanding of her fiction: Jane Austen's interest in the visual arts. That Austen was a connoisseur of paintings as well as drawings is suggested by Henry's subsequent remark, 'She was a warm and judicious admirer of landscape, both in nature and on canvass' (V, 7), and confirmed by several of her letters. My object here is to consider the function of the visual arts in *Persuasion*. Before doing so, however, I should like to provide a context for my remarks by reflecting briefly on the other novels and on some of the letters – thus ignoring Austen's remark in *Persuasion* that 'no private correspondence could bear the eye of others' (204).

The significance of the topic is suggested by the last fictional sentence that Austen ever wrote, when she was forced by ill health in March 1817 to break off her work on *Sanditon*. The heroine, Charlotte Heywood, and her friend, Mrs Parker, have been ushered into the stately sitting-room of Lady Denham. Charlotte sees, centrally placed above the mantlepiece, a full-length portrait of Lady Denham's late husband, Sir Harry Denham; in another part of the room, crowded inconspicuously among a group of miniatures, is the portrait of a previously deceased husband, Mr Hollis. The passage, and the novel fragment, conclude with a witty narratorial observation:

> Poor Mr Hollis! – It was impossible not to feel him hardly used; to be obliged to stand back in his own House & see the best place by the fire constantly occupied by Sir H[arry] D[enham]. (*MW*, 427)

The episode plays an important part in *Sanditon*. Mr Parker has previously given Charlotte an account of the rivalry among the various claimants to Lady Denham's fortune, explaining that of the three competing camps, 'Mr Hollis' Kindred were the *least* in favour & Sir Harry Denham's the *most*' (*MW*, 376–7). Now the rivalry is physically embodied in the placings of Mr Hollis's miniature and Sir Harry's whole-length portrait, which clearly reveal Lady Denham's evaluation of the respective merits of her two late husbands. Austen has used pictures not merely for decorative purposes, but to reveal psychological nuances in her characters.

Few critics, however, have made much of this intriguing portrait scene. Park Honan, for example, regards it merely as 'a good joke, and her last in a novel' (391). And in general Austen's interest in and use of the visual arts remains a neglected subject, despite the vast and ever burgeoning secondary literature devoted to her writings. Several critics have written on the set-piece portrait scenes in two of her novels, *Pride and Prejudice* and *Emma*. But the prevailing view is that Austen, like Samuel Johnson, had little concern for the visual arts, which therefore played a negligible part in her fiction. Murray Roston, for example, who devotes a chapter to Austen in his recent book on literature and the visual arts in the eighteenth

century, mentions what he wrongly calls a 'rare reference to painting' in her letters, but has nothing to say on representations of
paintings in her novels (333). Lance Bertelsen, similarly, in a recent
article, declares at the outset that 'Austen's novels are not rich in
pictorial imagery, nor do the visual arts play an important part in
her fictional world' (350).

Despite this critical consensus, however, in each of Austen's
six completed novels, as well as in *Sanditon*, the visual arts play a
significant role. Austen depicts both amateur artists, characters
in the novels themselves, and imaginary professionals such as
those who painted Mr Hollis and Sir Harry Denham. Unlike Samuel
Richardson, who refers in *Clarissa* (509) to a portrait of the heroine
by Highmore and in *Sir Charles Grandison* (III, 279) to portraits of
the hero's parents by Kneller, Austen does not go so far as to create
links between her characters and specific artists; nor, unlike those
of many of her predecessors, were any of her novels illustrated
during her lifetime – although her juvenile 'History of England'
was illustrated in loving detail by her sister Cassandra.[1]

While Austen makes frequent use of the visual arts in her novels,
however, she eschews any detailed evocation of visual representations, and thus frees herself from the characteristic dilemma of
ekphrasis: the verbal evocation of visual representation. Theorists
such as James Heffernan and Murray Krieger have rightly noted
the tension that takes place when language and art are brought
together in an uneasy alliance through ekphrasis, with words being
called upon to carry out the function that only images can properly
perform. But when pictures appear in Austen's fiction, the focus is
on their effect on characters or on the characters' attitudes to the
pictures, rather than on the pictures themselves. Thus in the scene
from *Sanditon*, what matters is the use made of portraits by one
of the characters, Lady Denham, and the effect the portraits have
on others; no warfare between the verbal and visual takes place,
because the pictures as such are not described. This strategic withholding of pictorial detail, an approach to but withdrawal from
ekphrasis, characterises all of Austen's novels, in which she repeatedly uses pictures to throw light on her characters' psychology and
to reveal the dynamics of their relationships.

The earliest of her novels, *Northanger Abbey*, as well as the latest,
Sanditon, contains a prototype of such scenes. Catherine Morland,
unlike some other Austen heroines, is not an artist herself: as a
child 'her taste for drawing was not superior', although 'she did

what she could in that way, by drawing houses and trees, hens and chickens, all very much like one another' (*NA*, 14). Yet Catherine does have a capacity to appreciate art, and this capacity helps entrap her in the quasi-Gothic world of General Tilney's abbey. Before her arrival at the abbey, her imagination has been enflamed by Henry Tilney's inventive account of its Gothic trappings. Over the fireplace of her bedroom, he declares, she will behold 'the portrait of some handsome warrior, whose features will so incomprehensibly strike you, that you will not be able to withdraw your eyes from it' (158). Catherine's room, as it transpires, contains no such portrait – although it does contain other items adumbrated by Henry – but another picture plays an important part in her emotional entanglements at the abbey. Persuaded of General Tilney's cruelty to his late wife, Catherine asks her friend Eleanor Tilney whether he has her portrait in his room, while 'blushing at the consummate art of her own question'. Eleanor replies:

> 'No; – it was intended for the drawing-room; but my father was dissatisfied with the painting, and for some time it had no place. Soon after her death I obtained it for my own, and hung it in my bed-chamber – where I shall be happy to shew it you; – it is very like.' – Here was another proof. A portrait – very like – of a departed wife, not valued by the husband! – He must have been dreadfully cruel to her! (180–1)

When she is later shown the portrait in Eleanor's room, however, Catherine's expectations are disappointed. The subject is 'a very lovely woman', but Catherine

> had depended upon meeting with features, air, complexion that should be the very counterpart, the very image, if not of Henry's, of Eleanor's; – the only portraits of which she had been in the habit of thinking, bearing always an equal resemblance of mother and child. A face once taken was taken for generations. But here she was obliged to look and consider and study for a likeness. (191)

Catherine's being obliged to 'look and consider and study' epitomises the whole course of her experiences at the Abbey. Most of her assumptions there are found wanting; in this case her belief that mothers will resemble their daughters and sons is undermined.

Faces are not, as she had supposed, taken for generations; heredit-
ary and family ties, as well as portraiture itself, are less straight-
forward than this. As Marcia Pointon remarks in her recent study
of eighteenth-century portraiture, *Hanging the Head*, 'the portrait
has no unproblematic referent; it cannot be explained as a correlative to the text of a subject's life' (4). In this case, typically for
Austen, far from being a correlative the portrait fails to materialise.
The focus is on Catherine, contemplating what she will see and
then gazing at the portrait, but no attempt is made to represent the
portrait for the reader; far from resembling Henry or Eleanor, this
painting resembles no one at all.

Austen's own understanding of the gulf between image and text
is shown in a wonderful letter to her sister Cassandra of May 1813.
Here she writes of searching through art galleries, ostensibly in the
hope of finding a portrait resembling Elizabeth Bennet:

> Henry & I went to the Exhibition in Spring Gardens. It is not
> thought a good collection, but I was very well pleased – par-
> ticularly (pray tell Fanny) with a small portrait of Mrs. Bingley,
> excessively like her. I went in hopes of seeing one of her Sister,
> but there was no Mrs. Darcy; – perhaps however, I may find her
> in the Great Exhibition which we shall go to, if we have time; –
> I have no chance of her in the collection of Sir Joshua Reynolds's
> Paintings which is now shewing in Pall Mall, & which we are
> also to visit. – Mrs. Bingley's is exactly herself, size, shaped face,
> features & sweetness; there never was a greater likeness. She is
> dressed in a white gown, with green ornaments, which convinces
> me of what I had always supposed, that green was a favourite
> colour with her. I dare say Mrs. D. will be in Yellow. (*L*, 309–10)

At the end of the letter, Austen adds with mock chagrin:

> We have been both to the Exhibition & Sir J. Reynolds', – and I
> am disappointed, for there was nothing like Mrs. D. at either. I
> can only imagine that Mr. D. prizes any Picture of her too much
> to like it should be exposed to the public eye. – I can imagine
> he wd have that sort of feeling – that mixture of Love, Pride &
> Delicacy. – Setting aside this disappointment, I had great amuse-
> ment among the Pictures. (312)

The exhibition in Spring Gardens at which Austen found her portrait of Jane Bennet (styled with due decorum under her married

name of Mrs Bingley in the letter) was one held by the Society of Painters in Oil and Water Colours. It is intriguing to see Austen provide details about Jane's appearance, the 'shaped face, features & sweetness', and about her favourite colour, green, that supplement her depiction in the novel. Austen was well aware, of course, that no portrait could be 'excessively like' any of her fictional heroines, since none is described in painterly detail. In order to find a likeness she must first ascribe aspects of the figure in the painting to the character in the text. That Elizabeth's favourite colour is yellow is also new to the letter, as is the compelling description of Darcy's conjugal feelings combining 'Love, Pride & Delicacy'.

Austen's interest in the visual arts emerges clearly in her correspondence, although the relevant passages have been largely ignored by her critics: in part, perhaps, because they are omitted from the byzantine set of indexes to Chapman's edition. 'Painting' is a heading in his index of general topics, but it refers to the application of rouge on ladies' faces. Among Austen's various observations on the visual arts are comments on her own sketches, on the paintings, prints and drawings in her family's collection, and on the portraits she sees in visits to country houses.[2] In a letter to Cassandra of 1798, she writes intriguingly of her own 'designs', alas no longer extant, for her nephew George Austen Knight: 'Perhaps they would have suited him as well had they been less elaborately finished; but an artist cannot do anything slovenly' (30). The word 'artist' here is significantly ambiguous: while depicting herself humorously as an amateur of the arts, Austen is surely also pointing to the novels that were her vocation, and that are 'elaborately finished' indeed; so much so that the novels she was writing at this time, *Northanger Abbey* and *Sense and Sensibility*, were not to be published for many years. There is also an amusing ironic remark of 1813 on her own potential, as her fame increases, for becoming the subject of a portrait: 'I do not despair of having my picture in the Exhibition at last – all white & red, with my Head on one Side' (*L*, 368). There was, of course, no shortage of striking painterly prototypes for poses of this kind in works by Austen's contemporaries, such as George Romney, Henry Raeburn, John Hoppner and Thomas Lawrence, and although Austen was never to have her portrait taken, paintings by these artists have been used on the covers of recent editions of her novels, thus helping to form our mental images of her heroines.[3]

Of particular importance are two letters that Austen wrote late in her life. In September 1814, she recorded her responses to Benjamin West's immense history painting, *Christ Rejected* (Plates 1 and 2). Of this vast canvas, 17 feet high and 22 feet across, she declared:

> I have seen West's famous Painting, and prefer it to anything of the kind I ever saw before. I do not know that it *is* reckoned superior to his 'Healing in the Temple'. But it has gratified *me* much more, and indeed is the first representation of our Saviour which ever at all contented me. 'His Rejection by the Elders', is the subject. (*L*, 507)

The other West painting to which Austen refers is the somewhat smaller *Christ Healing the Sick* (Plate 3). In both cases, significantly, she takes no interest in the great assembly of Biblical characters, focusing her gaze instead on the single figure of Christ. Significant too is the phrase 'of the kind', which implicitly contrasts the genre of history painting, utterly alien to Austen's tastes and her fictional world, with that of the lowlier but to her much more valuable genre of portrait painting (see Bertelsen, 355, n. 15). This preference emerges clearly in the famous ironic contrast, made in a letter of 1816, between the 'strong, manly, spirited Sketches, full of Variety and Glow' of her nephew Edward and her own preferred medium: 'the little bit (two Inches wide) of Ivory on which I work with so fine a Brush, as produces little effect after much labour' (*L*, 468–9). As usual Austen is being precise: two inches across was a typical measurement for a Regency portrait miniature, the Lilliput to West's historical Brobdingnag. The first readers of *Persuasion* would have been familiar with Austen's memorable image, since it is quoted in the postscript to Henry Austen's 'Biographical Notice', although her brother had the temerity to attempt to improve her syntax: 'so fine a Brush', for example, becomes 'a brush so fine' (*V*, 8).

My subject is *Persuasion*, and space does not permit me to consider further Austen's use of the visual arts in her other novels. I must thus pass over *Sense and Sensibility*, in which Lucy Steele displays to Elinor her prized miniature of Edward Ferrars as an emblem of her exclusive rights to the subject, and in which Marianne reveals her sensibility in her heartfelt admiration of Elinor's artistic gifts. I must also neglect the elaborate portrait scene in *Emma*, in which the heroine conceives the plan of making Harriet Smith the subject of a whole-length portrait in water-colours, thereby raising Harriet's value and social standing and thus endearing her to Mr

Elton. I cannot consider the humble works of art adorning Fanny Price's room at Mansfield Park, which draw attention to her chronically subordinate position. And, most regrettably, I cannot dwell on Elizabeth's Bennet's tour of the picture gallery at Pemberley, where the sight of a portrait of Darcy 'with . . . a smile over the face' makes her think 'of his regard with a deeper sentiment of gratitude than it had ever raised before' (250–1).[4]

In *Persuasion*, as in several of her other novels, Austen includes a scene of a picture being analysed by one of the characters. Here it is a print observed in a printshop window by Admiral Croft. When Anne Elliot encounters the admiral gazing at the print, he discusses his responses to it (though not, typically, the print itself) in detail:

> 'Here I am, you see, staring at a picture. I can never get by this shop without stopping. But what a thing here is, by way of a boat. Do look at it. Did you ever see the like? What queer fellows your fine painters must be, to think that any body would venture their lives in such a shapeless old cockleshell as that. And yet, here are two gentlemen stuck up in it mightily at their ease, and looking about them at the rocks and mountains, as if they were not to be upset the next moment, which they certainly must be. I wonder where that boat was built! . . . I would not venture over a horsepond in it.' (169)

The scene forms part of Lorrie Clark's essay on *Persuasion* elsewhere in this volume. She states that the 'picture here subject to the Admiral's simultaneous admiration and ridicule clearly belongs to the "sublime" school of painting popular from 1750 to 1850, where the annihilation of boats and men at sea by mountainous waves and threatening rocks is a recurrent motif'. Since the ekphrasis of the admiral's commentary is so incomplete – we cannot be sure, for example, of the size of the boat or whether it is at sea or on a lake – Clark's interpretation is open to dispute, yet convincing.

The greatest English painter of the sublime is, of course, Turner, whose earliest paintings of shipwrecks and storms at sea predate *Persuasion* by some ten years. None of Turner's paintings features two gentlemen in imminent danger of shipwreck, yet 'mightily at their ease'. The admiral may, however, be interpreting in his own fashion a painting such as Turner's famous sea-piece *Shipwreck* of 1805 (Plate 4), from which prints made by the engraver Charles

Turner were issued in 1807 (see Wilton, 74). Intriguingly, the admiral's keen eye may have detected something at the heart of Turner's sublime, aptly described by W. J. T. Mitchell 'not just as the record of a vertiginous, disorienting experience, but as a representation of perceptual resistance to disorientation'. Mitchell notes Turner's 'amazing resistance to vertigo' and quotes a contemporary account of his sitting in a small boat in heavy waters, 'intently watching the sea, and not at all affected by the motion' (Mitchell, 1983, 140). This excursion took place in 1813, just two years before Austen began writing *Persuasion*; it is as though Austen's anonymous printmaker and Turner were responding to the sublime with similar equanimity.

Clark astutely describes the print in *Persuasion* as 'a concise and brilliant emblem of the entire world of Austen's novel . . . one of radical change which threatens to sweep all – including and especially its heroine – before it'. In her reading of the novel, the print, ignored by all previous critics, becomes central to Austen's design: a visual rendition of experiences such as the admiral's penchant for reckless carriage-drives that invariably result in his overturning himself and his wife; Louisa Musgrove's wilful but terrifying fall down the steps of the Cobb; and Anne Elliot's resolute stasis in the midst of all the frantic motion around her.

Another work of art plays an equally important part in *Persuasion*. In the penultimate chapter of the novel, one of two written by Austen to replace her original, unsatisfactory conclusion, Anne is again shown a picture. On this occasion it is 'a small miniature painting' of Captain Benwick, which Captain Harville has in his possession. It is to be presented to Benwick's fiancée, Louisa Musgrove, but, as Harville explains to Anne 'in a deep tone':

> 'it was not done for her. . . . He met with a clever young German artist at the Cape, and in compliance with a promise to my poor sister, sat to him, and was bringing it home for her. And I have now the charge of getting it properly set for another! . . .' And with a quivering lip he wound up the whole by adding, 'Poor Fanny! she would not have forgotten him so soon!' (232)

The account of Benwick's inconstancy that the miniature has inspired leads in turn to the famous debate about the respective constancy of men and women in love, a debate overheard by Wentworth, who now writes the letter that brings about his reunion with Anne. But the miniature does not merely facilitate the unfolding of the plot; it remains as a disturbing emblem of inconstancy. As Tony Tanner observes: 'the man changes in his affections; the portrait remains "constant." In this it is precisely a misrepresentation – an ideal image of the man which leaves all his emotional changeableness out' (240). It also serves to emphasise, in its solipsistic fashion, Benwick's narcissism, his being in love with love itself rather than with either Fanny or Louisa.[5] Like Edward Ferrars in *Sense and Sensibility*, Captain Benwick has had an image of himself made as a token of his devotion; both tokens, however, are used for purposes other than had originally been intended. To possess the image of one's beloved is not, as Lucy Steele had claimed, 'to be easy' (135). In both cases Austen shows her awareness of the disparity between visual images and the lives they purport to display.

Without this scene, the many previous references to Captain Benwick's devotion for Fanny Harville would lack a natural resolution. With hindsight, in the final version of the novel, these remarks take on a poignant irony. When we first hear of the couple, for example, we are told that 'Captain Wentworth believed it impossible for man to be more attached to woman than poor Benwick had been to Fanny Harville' (96–7); the portrait-scene illustrates graphically how wrong Wentworth can be. Wentworth has projected his own continuing devotion to Anne on to his friend's putative devotion for the memory of his beloved. Later, he expresses his astonishment to Anne when he hears of Benwick's engagement to Louisa:

'A man like him, in his situation! With a heart pierced, wounded, almost broken! Fanny Harville was a very superior creature; and his attachment to her was indeed attachment. A man does not recover from such a devotion of the heart to such a woman! – He ought not – he does not.' (183)

All of this, while true of Captain Wentworth and Anne Elliot, has little to do with Captain Benwick and Fanny Harville. In the portrait-scene inserted in the revised conclusion, Wentworth is made implicitly to acknowledge as much, when we see him writing to Benwick about the framing of the miniature, Captain Harville having made over this painful task to his friend.

Earlier in *Persuasion* Austen also uses portraits to elucidate the psychology of her characters, in this case the Musgrove family at

Uppercross. The Great House at Uppercross is notable for its 'air of confusion' (40). Mary Musgrove's sisters-in-law, Henrietta and Louisa, have introduced a grand-piano, a harp, flower-stands and small tables into a formal parlour, without regard for the incongruous effect that the clash of styles has created. The disorder is comparable to that created by the amateur theatricals at Mansfield Park, where Sir Thomas, on his return, finds a 'general air of confusion in the furniture', marked by 'the removal of the book-case from before the billiard room door' (*MP*, 182). In *Persuasion*, Austen uses the portraits of the Musgrove family hanging on the walls of Uppercross to dramatise the overthrow of the old order:

> Oh! could the originals of the portraits against the wainscot, could the gentlemen in brown velvet and the ladies in blue satin have seen what was going on, have been conscious of such an overthrow of all order and neatness! The portraits themselves seemed to be staring in astonishment. (40)

Like the description of the print of the storm at sea this approaches while never quite achieving ekphrasis. Details of the gentlemen's and ladies' clothing ('brown velvet' and 'blue satin') and their staring expressions enable the reader to envisage not so much the works of visual art that the verbal account has constructed as the models for those works, the 'originals of the portraits' rather than the portraits themselves.

It is interesting to compare Austen's depiction of the pictures at Uppercross with that of their counterparts at Kellynch-hall. All we hear of the latter comes from the scheming Mrs Clay, who in praising the Crofts as potential tenants assures Sir Walter that 'these valuable pictures of yours . . . if you chose to leave them, would be perfectly safe' (18). Later, Anne Elliot tells her sister Mary that she has been 'making a duplicate of the catalogue of my father's books and pictures' (38). Yet the 'valuable' pictures themselves are never described. Kellynch-hall, with the baronet's dressing room full of large looking-glasses, is a house of show, rather than substance. There are now two catalogues of Sir Walter's pictures, but no ekphrasis takes place and the pictures themselves are never made to appear. Kellynch is, as the admiral suggests, a house of mirrors: 'Such a number of looking-glasses! oh Lord! there was no getting away from oneself' (128).

The Kellynch-hall portraits are exceptional in their invisibility.

More typically in *Persuasion*, and in Austen's other novels, pictures
are used to create debates about their subjects. Thus in *Pride and
Prejudice*, Miss Bingley taunts Darcy about his interest in Elizabeth
by belittling her relations: 'Do let the portraits of your uncle and
aunt Philips be placed in the gallery at Pemberley. Put them next to
your great uncle the judge.' Continuing with her witticisms, she
advises Darcy: 'As for your Elizabeth's picture, you must not attempt to have it taken, for what painter could do justice to those
beautiful eyes?' (52–3). Miss Bingley has spoken more aptly than
she can know. In Austen's novels, pictures do not 'do justice' to
their models. What makes the pictures interesting is the extent to
which they are not purely representational, the way in which they
create debates about their subjects.

Austen's strategic withdrawal from ekphrasis, her evocation of
visual images with little specifically visual detail, forces readers to
take an active part in envisaging and interpreting the pictures in
her novels. A letter of 29 January 1813 contains a revealing comment on her own fictional technique, in a doggerel parody of Scott's
Marmion:

> I do not write for such dull elves
> As have not a great deal of ingenuity themselves. (298)

The pictures in her novels function in the same endlessly engaging
and provocative manner as the texts of which they are a part. They
are 'speaking pictures,' objects for textual interpretation rather than
ekphrastic creations, discussed within Austen's novels by her characters and designed to be discussed outside her fiction, with a great
deal of ingenuity, by her readers.

Notes

1. A facsimile edition of the *History*, with excellent colour reproductions
    of Cassandra's thirteen medallion portraits, has recently been pub-
    lished by the British Library, which possesses the original manuscript,
    part of Austen's 'Volume the Second'.
2. See *L*, 13–14, 30, 50, 101. These and other references are noted by
    Bertelsen, 352–6, who also speculates about the identity of the portrait
    which resembled Austen's conception of Jane Bennet. He proposes as

candidates miniatures by Jean François Marie Huët-Villiers, Charles John Robertson, James Stephanoff, and James Hewlett, but his 'inquiries have failed to turn up any of the above pictures' (359).

3. The only surviving likeness made of Austen during her lifetime is an unfinished miniature pencil and watercolour sketch by Cassandra, c. 1810, in the National Portrait Gallery, London. The Penguin edition of *Pride and Prejudice* and the Oxford World's Classics editions of *Mansfield Park* and *Persuasion* feature paintings by Raeburn; the World's Classics editions of *Northanger Abbey* and *Emma* have cover-portraits by Lawrence.

4. For a discussion of these scenes see Sabor, 'The Strategic Withdrawal from Ekphrasis'.

5. I owe this point to Lorrie Clark, letter to the author, 13 October 1993.

3

Transfiguring the Romantic Sublime in *Persuasion*

Lorrie Clark

[The sublime] not only persuades, but even throws an audience into transport. . . . In most cases it is wholly in our power, either to resist or yield to persuasion. But the *Sublime*, endued with strength irresistible, strikes home, and triumphs over every hearer.

Longinus, *On the Sublime*

Anne Elliot, the heroine of *Persuasion*, one day encounters Admiral Croft, the vigorous old retired sailor who is renting her father's estate, fixed in contemplation of a printshop window in Bath. 'Here I am, you see, staring at a picture,' he cheerily greets her:

'I can never get by this shop without stopping. But what a thing here is, by way of a boat. Do look at it. Did you ever see the like? What queer fellows your fine painters must be, to think that any body would venture their lives in such a shapeless old cockle-shell as that. And yet, here are two gentlemen stuck up in it mightily at their ease, and looking about them at the rocks and mountains, as if they were not to be upset the next moment, which they certainly must be. I wonder where that boat was built! . . . I would not venture over a horsepond in it. . . .

'Lord! what a boat it is!' taking a last look at the picture, as they began to be in motion. (169)

The picture here subject to the Admiral's simultaneous admiration and ridicule clearly belongs to the 'sublime' school of painting popular from 1750 to 1850, where the annihilation of boats and men at sea by mountainous waves and threatening rocks is a recurrent motif. It is also the central motif of *Persuasion*, which indeed can be understood as Austen's examination of and response to the fashionable romantic cult of the sublime.

Austen's ironic treatment of the equally fashionable cult of 'the picturesque' in *Sense and Sensibility* and *Northanger Abbey* has provided a locus for assessing her relationship to romanticism and its cult of sensibility. Yet despite general critical acknowledgement of the darker, more melancholy, even tragic 'romanticism' of *Persuasion*, it has not received critical attention in terms of the more profound aesthetic of the sublime it implicitly invites. The Admiral's picture is not a random representation but Austen's self-representation of the entire world of *Persuasion*, her way of telling us how to read her novel. Reading the picture accurately – as the Admiral, I shall argue, does not – is the key to reading *Persuasion* itself.

The picture represents not only the romantic sublime, but also Austen's critique of the sublime; further, it represents Austen's alternative to or refiguring of the sublime, in an extended pun or riddle she teases us to decipher just as the picture in the window repeatedly teases the Admiral on his walks. *Persuasion* is in fact thoroughly 'riddled' with the language of the sublime: with the rhetoric of 'persuasion' central to Longinus's treatise *On the Sublime*, so popular in the eighteenth century; with the sustained metaphor of the sea, according to Edmund Burke the very source of the sublime; with recurrent metaphors of 'hurricanes' and 'shipwrecks'; with the mingled 'pain and pleasure' central to Burke's aesthetic; with, above all, the unusually intense physicality and threat of death which aligns the sublime with tragedy. Finally, the novel's apparent celebration of Admiral Croft and Captain Wentworth as 'sublime' naval heroes of the Napoleonic wars (whose 'type' perhaps is the sublimely Byronic Lord Nelson) suggests what some critics refer to as the egotistical 'masculinist' bias which made the sublime so popular with male romantic poets (Mitchell, 1986).

Read as Austen's response to the sublime, *Persuasion* suggests, I shall argue, that Austen's central objection to romanticism is that it conventionalises, fictionalises, or aestheticises reality. More specifically, in the guise of celebrating 'nature', the romantic sublime instead renders nature and the threat of nature – *death* – 'unreal'. The sublime encounter with nature is a kind of 'pseudo-crisis', as Raimonda Modiano so aptly terms it, a playing with 'the *idea*' of death and self-annihilation in all the safety of an aesthetic distance without risk or consequence (235). *Persuasion*, by contrast, is above all about the very real *consequences* of taking risks, the risk-taking which culminates in the crisis of Louisa Musgrove's fall upon the Cobb at Lyme. In this respect it could be read, like Mary Shelley's

Frankenstein, as a critique of the irresponsibility and excesses of 'masculine' romantic idealism, a critique of sensibility and the romantic imagination made in the name of a 'conservative' or 'feminist' ideal of a corrective 'reason' (Mellor). But I shall suggest that Austen corrects the potentially tragic, idealist excesses of the romantic sublime in the name of a higher ideal of philosophic comedy. As Austen's final, most philosophic heroine, Anne Elliot does not so much refigure as 'trans-figure' the sublime; and in this respect she is indeed, as Nina Auerbach has suggested, the Prospero-like philosopher presiding over Jane Austen's *Tempest*.

Profoundly influenced by Longinus's 'rhetorical sublime', Edmund Burke's *Philosophical Enquiry into the Origin of Our Ideas of the Sublime and Beautiful* and Immanuel Kant's analysis of the sublime in his *Critique of Judgment* defined what became the central aesthetic of romanticism. As they described it, the experience of the sublime was essentially paradoxical: faced with the spectacle of natural disaster – a hurricane, an earthquake, an avalanche, a storm at sea – or simply with the spectacle of nature's magnificence, our powers of reason and judgement are temporarily overwhelmed and even annihilated by the awe-inspiring force and magnitude of the spectacle in front of us. What makes our experience of the sublime so intense is our fundamental fear of death or concern for 'self-preservation'. Yet this confrontation with the idea of death is only a momentary flood of fear or terror, eclipsed by the intense pleasure either of losing oneself in this rush of pure feeling (Burke) or of eventually reasserting one's powers of reasoning over this temporary self-annihilation (Kant). For Kant in particular, we feel finally triumphant over and superior to this spectacle of nature's might – for nature is after all only nature. We discover in ourselves, Kant says, 'a faculty of judging independently of and a superiority over nature, on which is based a kind of self-preservation entirely different from that which can be attacked and brought into danger by external nature. Thus humanity in our person remains unhumiliated' (396).

The dynamic of the sublime is thus very extreme, a kind of all-or-nothing: in the first moment of the sublime, when the self, reason and convention are annihilated or swept away by the superior power of nature and our 'fearful' sensations or feelings, our reason and conventions are exposed as mere fictions or illusions; the only reality is that of nature, the threat of death. But in the second moment of the sublime, when the powers of the self, reason, and convention reassert themselves, we declare ourselves free of nature in a state of supreme self-assertion, mastery, and total freedom.

We can do this, however, only because the threat of death is not *real*; and this is critical not only to our understanding of the sublime as a specifically *aesthetic* experience, but also to our understanding of why it might actually be a rather dangerous aesthetic experience. To enjoy the experience of the sublime, both Burke and Kant insist, one must not be in any *real* danger. Only a considerable distance – an aesthetic distance – from real disaster allows us to enjoy the spectacle of the sublime; it is the *idea* of danger – not actual danger itself – that is so thrilling. Those caught in the midst of hurricanes, volcanoes and shipwrecks rarely find this experience 'sublime'.

We can begin to see how *Persuasion* refigures the romantic sublime by returning to the Admiral's picture with which I began, for it is a concise and brilliant emblem of the entire world of Austen's novel. The world of the novel, like the sublime picture the Admiral both criticises and admires, is one of radical change which threatens to sweep all – including and especially its heroine – before it. This is why the sea – and the seashore at Lyme which is the scene of greatest violence in the novel – is so powerful a motif in *Persuasion*, a motif the more powerful because it is unprecedented in Austen's novels.

The novel's ostensible theme is that of constancy and inconstancy in the narrow sphere of romantic love: despite rejecting his offer of marriage eight years earlier, Anne Elliot has remained 'constant' to her former lover, Frederick Wentworth, as he has not apparently remained to her; and the novel explores the complex nature of constancy and inconstancy – of 'persuadability' – in love. But beyond this the novel explores the larger problem of constancy and inconstancy in a new, post-revolutionary world in which the old stabilities are rapidly dissolving, a world possibly on the verge of shipwreck on wider seas of radical change. It is not only Anne who clings precariously to her little boat, her constancy to an ideal object (the memory of Frederick Wentworth and the memory of her dead mother); all the characters cling to 'self-preservation', to their fragile boats of various kinds. Sir Walter Elliot, Anne's weak, vain father, tries to preserve 'appearances' – his handsome looks and the appearance of prosperity on the rapidly declining family estate of Kellynch; Anne's old schoolfriend Mrs Smith tries to preserve her independence despite losing her husband, her money and her health; the older generation of Musgroves tries to hold its own against the younger generation of Musgroves, who live 'in a state of alteration, perhaps of improvement,' next door (40). It is not the smaller loss of Frederick Wentworth but the larger loss of Lady Elliot (both losses before the narrative begins) that sets all the narrative events in motion, for it dislodges the entire family from the natural surroundings of Kellynch to the artificialities of Bath, and sends Anne in particular on a series of perambulations or displacements among the four locales of the novel: Kellynch, Uppercross, Lyme and Bath – a series of 'alterations' again threatening her self-preservation and autonomy.

Time and change have brought other losses: with the death or 'mortal change' of Anne's mother, Lady Elliot, the orderly, economical, 'gentlemanly' way of life at Kellynch threatens to disappear as well. Unable to economise and run his household, Sir Walter is forced to rent out the estate – to a brash and vigorous newcomer, Admiral Croft himself. Home from the Napoleonic wars, Croft is ready to settle down – but not without making significant 'alterations' to Kellynch. Indolent gentry such as Sir Walter find themselves rudely displaced by a new class of rising self-made naval men – of which Anne's former lover is also a member. Despite the apparent remoteness of politics to Austen's novel, such changes, as Austen surely understood, have profound political implications – for the loss of Kellynch and places like it displaces and disrupts England's steadiest, most principled class, the landed gentry, whose political principles are grounded in the stability of the land or nature. At the furthest edges of *Persuasion* may be the spectre of the English ship of state foundering on the seas of political change.

Admiral Croft is the new master of Kellynch, in his cheerful obtuseness an unhappy alteration, it might seem, from Anne's mother and all that she represented. But perhaps in this new world so turbulently riding the seas of change of the French Revolution and the Napoleonic Wars, he is its true master or spiritual heir, the only one who can preserve it from dissolution. For who can steer a better course than one who has several times sailed the world and fought successfully in war – and who has also, as Sir Walter is quick to observe, unlike most sailors (and unlike poor Anne) preserved his good looks against being weatherbeaten by the elements? Admiral Croft has the directness and vigour of the true man of action, the particularly masculine and masterful energy conspicuously absent from the other men in the novel. Sir Walter lives a life of vanity, gossip and languor, subject to 'womanish' complaints;

Charles Musgrove, Anne's brother-in-law, lives a slightly more masculine (one supposes) but no less indolent life devoted to hunting and sport; the sensitive Captain Benwick languishes with books by Byron and Sir Walter Scott; and the presumptive heir, Mr Elliot, is as fickle as the weather, 'too generally agreeable', as Anne finds, for 'various as were the tempers in her father's house, he pleased them all' (161). Only Frederick Wentworth, himself a naval captain with the advantages of youth, new-made wealth, and bachelorhood on his side, can rival Admiral Croft as the new master and preserver of Kellynch – and, possibly, of Anne.

Captain Wentworth and Admiral Croft are simply, in fact, 'sublime' – as indeed to varying degrees are all the naval men in the novel. Yet this sublimity is both their strength and limitation from Austen's point of view. Wentworth and Croft are masters of 'self-preservation,' again, the very essence of the sublime: both subject themselves to the vagaries of wind and weather and to the shifting fortunes of war only to triumph in masterful self-assertion, autonomy and freedom. They are the new, 'democratic' heroes of the sublime revolution – vigorous, self-made men who in opposition to the emasculated guardians of worn-out conventions and rigidities are in touch with nature and time and change. And it is clear that Austen does find them genuinely attractive, a real alternative to those who, like Sir Walter, live in an artificial world of pure convention, a world of mirrors or self-reflections entirely removed from nature. (Admiral Croft's first change upon his arrival at Kellynch is to remove Sir Walter's numerous mirrors.)

Yet the Admiral seems to ridicule the sublime when he stands so bemused before our picture in the printshop window in Bath, which surely suggests he cannot be himself sublime. This ridicule, however, is Austen's irony at the Admiral's expense – an irony directed doubly at the aesthetic of the sublime and at the Admiral, who in fact unwittingly embodies it. And this irony tells us why sublimity is not enough – why even the sublime Captain Wentworth has something to learn in the crisis on the Cobb at Lyme. Again, the real brilliance of Austen's use of the picture in this scene is that it images not only the sublime together with her criticism of it, but also her own alternative to the sublime, in a complex ironic layering of meaning.

The Admiral's response to the picture is most interesting. At first glance, he would seem to articulate Austen's own objections to the sublime. He objects that the picture aestheticises experience – that it presents a life-threatening situation as though it were not. An apparent realist and man of action, he cannot adopt the position of the spectator who feels terror and pity at the spectacle of imminent annihilation yet exaltation at the power of human resistance; he can only put himself in the boat, where one is in no position to enjoy the spectacle because real annihilation – death – is too close. The Admiral does not seem to have the aesthetic distance essential to enjoy the experience of the sublime. As he rightly sees, the painting transforms a tragic spectacle into a rather comical – or at least tragicomical – one, a richly dramatic irony that at once horrifies and amuses him. For what transfixes the Admiral here is the curious fact that the men *in* the situation are pictured as being also aesthetic *spectators of* it – as 'stuck up in it mightily at their ease, and looking about them at the rocks and mountains, as if they were not to be upset the next moment'. This is why he seems to ridicule the cult of the sublime from a perspective outside it.

Yet the attitude of the men in the boat is precisely the Admiral's own, as Austen makes ironically clear. For now that the Admiral is retired from the vicissitudes of war and of life at sea, he spends his time driving recklessly about the countryside in his equally precarious mode of sublime 'transport' – his 'cockleshell' of a carriage – overturning himself and his wife with such frequency that Captain Wentworth can casually ask, 'I wonder whereabouts they will upset to-day? Oh! it does happen very often, I assure you – but my sister makes nothing of it – she would as lieve be tossed out as not' (84). Like the men in the painting, the Admiral sits comically oblivious to the imminence of his own destruction, 'stuck up in it mightily at [his] ease . . . as if [he] were not to be upset the next moment'. No longer in peacetime the man of action, he is not an alternative to the sublime but its very embodiment. Away from the real dangers of nature he forgets that those dangers are real, and plays with his own destruction by *voluntarily* taking unnecessary risks. He loses sight of real danger, tragedy, and threat because he lives in a world of the sublime that treats 'risk' as an exciting adventure to be voluntarily sought out. This means, then, that on the one hand he lives in a world where no risks are real because they are always actively sought out or manufactured; and on the other hand, that he lives oblivious to the very real forces of destruction that may threaten him, oblivious precisely because he continually plays with his own self-annihilation and self-preservation in the cult of the sublime 'risk'.

In this respect the Admiral is simply living in the post-revolutionary, romantic world – a world where, Austen seems to say, the real threat of nature has been forgotten. And it is forgotten precisely because of the romantic cult of the sublime, which claims to get back to nature but instead fictionalises nature. Bored with the conventionality of their lives, the lack of real risk and excitement, *all* the characters in *Persuasion* actively seek out such excitement by taking, like the Admiral, unnecessary risks. Sir Walter rents out Kellynch rather than remain in it in reduced circumstances; Captain Wentworth flirts equally with Louisa Musgrove and her sister Henrietta, regardless of the consequences to them, to Anne, to Henrietta's fiancé, or to himself; Captain Benwick indulges his grief for his dead fiancée by prolonging it with seclusion and melancholy poetry; Mary Musgrove languishes in perpetual hypochondria on the sofa at home (again, a way of 'playing' with the idea of bodily illness and ultimately death); the Musgroves refuse to discipline their children, revelling in a perpetual 'domestic *hurricane*' (my emphasis, 134). All of these are risks with potentially dangerous consequences: by renting Kellynch Sir Walter greatly increases the risk of its alteration and precipitates its eventual loss at his own 'natural' death, placing it prematurely (and 'unnaturally') into other hands; Captain Wentworth finds himself nearly fatally trapped by Louisa Musgrove; Captain Benwick and Mary Musgrove risk the debilitating effects of prolonged grief and lethargy on the real state of their health. Most seriously, in the Musgrove family 'hurricane' one of the younger children actually suffers a bad fall that dislocates his collar-bone and injures his back (Chapter 7); and when Louisa Musgrove falls on the Cobb (prefigured by this earlier accident and equally – if indirectly – the consequence of parental permissiveness), she sustains a concussion that requires a lengthy convalescence.

All of these risks are voluntarily undertaken and enjoyed on the assumption that one will always be able to pull up short of disaster. But Louisa's fall changes all of this, at least for Wentworth if not for Louisa herself. 'Too precipitate by half a second' (109), her heedless plunge down the steep steps of the Cobb paralyses all who witness it with momentary 'horror' (again, the language of the sublime), for 'her eyes were closed, she breathed not, her face was like death' – and she is 'taken up lifeless' from the pavement (109).

Louisa is not of course dead; but this moment of astonishment and terror crystallises all of Austen's objections to the cult of the sublime. It is no accident that the scene is set at Lyme, whose beauties yet subliminal dangers are wonderfully evoked by Austen's description. In contrast to 'the cheerful village of Up Lyme' a few miles away, a melancholy air hangs over the town, for it is November, and all the tourists have gone. With its 'principal street almost hurrying into the water', Lyme visually evokes Burke's description of the sublime as that power which 'anticipates our reasonings, and hurries us on by an irresistible force' (57). Its 'old wonders and new improvements', and most of all, the 'green chasms between romantic rocks' which 'declare that many a generation must have passed away since the first partial falling of the cliff prepared the ground for such a state' (95–6) suggests the simultaneous destruction and creation characteristic of the sublime. Even the progressive descent – down 'the long hill into Lyme', down 'the still steeper street of the town itself' (95), 'down by the now deserted and melancholy looking rooms, and still descending . . . [to] the sea shore' (96) enacts the initial descending moment of the sublime – the descent reaching its bottom in Louisa's 'fall'. And her fall temporarily annihilates not only her own consciousness or powers of reasoning (hurting her 'head'), but also the rational powers of all her companions, stunned as they are by this intimation of death – the heart of the sublime experience. Yet the experience is too near to give them the requisite pleasure; only the workmen and boatmen near the Cobb, hearing about the accident, gather 'to enjoy the sight of a dead young lady, nay, two dead young ladies, for it proved twice as fine as the first report' (Henrietta, alas, has fainted; 111).

The more distanced workmen can take aesthetic pleasure in the 'sublime' spectacle of death. But only Anne of all the immediate observers retains her self-possession and rational powers; only Anne is capable of acting and swiftly taking command of the situation. Only Anne resists being swept away even temporarily in the 'irresistible persuasions' of the sublime moment, a moment on the verge of real and irrevocable disaster. Under her direction, a doctor is sent for, all are comforted as they variously require, and Louisa is transported, not indeed to the heights of sublimity, but to the safety of the Harvilles' house. And Anne's commanding composure is a revelation to Wentworth, revealing as it does the folly of his attraction to the heedless, impulsive Louisa, who insisted on being playfully 'jumped' by him down the steep steps of the Cobb. Louisa, who has enthusiastically declared that she 'would rather be overturned' (transported?) by Admiral Croft in his carriage 'than driven safely by anybody else' (85), is an inveterate taker of sublime risks; this time, her risk has had consequences.

Anne, by contrast, does not voluntarily take (or create) unnecessary risks, for she is well aware that life is risky enough. Louisa has entrusted herself to Wentworth, her partner in risk, as Anne did not under other circumstances eight years ago. And confident in his own sublime ability to take and yet master risks (as indeed he has always done successfully in the past), Wentworth yields to Louisa's entreaties to jump her down the steps, to give her (in hardly subliminally sexual terms) the 'sensation' so 'delightful to her' (109). Louisa's fall is not only her fault but also his own, a responsibility he feels, too late, with great anguish. How might not Anne have similarly been put at risk eight years before, had she entrusted herself to his protection? Embarked together on the risky seas of life, without the securities − financial and otherwise − to do so, what might the consequences for both have been?

Very possibly, the consequences endured by Anne's friend Mrs Smith, whose biography is surely meant to supply an object lesson in the fickleness of fortune. Mrs Smith has indeed weathered storms far beyond those suffered by any of the other characters, for in losing her husband and especially her health she has been thrown upon her inner resources to an unprecedented degree. 'Your peace will not be *shipwrecked* as mine has been', she remarks to Anne (196; my emphasis); yet she has remained cheerful, steady, and active, with a fortitude and 'elasticity of mind', Anne concludes, 'which was from Nature alone' (154).

Only Anne of all the characters displays a comparable independence of circumstances and elasticity of mind, as Wentworth sees on the Cobb at Lyme. More than this, Wentworth comes to realise his *dependence* on Anne instead of the masterful independence he had assumed. And this recognition of dependency for Wentworth involves in turn a recognition of his dependence on nature − that he is not independent of it as he has always assumed, always able to master or control the seas of time and change. Events are not always subject to one's control − particularly that final, most 'natural' event of all: death. The crisis on the Cobb explodes Wentworth's sublimely romantic and egotistical delusions of mastery over and independence from nature; he learns that he is not invincible.

But this revelation need not entail complete submission to, or dependence on, nature and the power of death, again as Anne's example illustrates. For Anne is at once fully aware of, yet nonetheless independent of, the forces of nature and time and change, in a way that allows her to function with unshakable equanimity. The crisis on the Cobb merely brings into the foreground the unobtrusive mastery that Anne has exercised throughout the novel, for the point of subjecting her to four different locales is precisely to demonstrate her independence from all of them. Anne has a distance from life that is not the distance of the sublime 'aesthete' – a distance and equanimity easily shattered by real threat or crisis – but the comic, ironic distance of the philosopher. Anne rationally 'knows' that in the midst of life we are in death. And because she lives with this knowledge rather than hiding from it, she is not easily 'horrified' or astonished. Anne knows philosophically the power of death or of nature to undermine the realm of reason and convention – to render horrifyingly unstable and contingent the conventions or precarious 'boats' by and within which we all must live. Yet she does not respond with either of the movements of the sublime: she does not conclude that reason and conventions are mere fictions to be abandoned in ecstatic fusion with nature, nor alternatively that one should try to deny the forces of nature and death by asserting the omnipotence of reason and convention. Her knowledge serves rather to acknowledge and strengthen the claims of both nature and convention. For she sees that if the sea of nature threatens our boats it also sustains them; and if those boats are precarious they are nonetheless what sustain us on and against the seas of nature, change and death. Their contingency renders them both sublimely 'horrifying' and ridiculously 'comic' and our situation both tragic and comic; but this vision is quite different from the inadvertent tragicomedy of Admiral Croft's picture of the sublime. Like the aesthetes of the sublime who spectate on their own imminent destruction, Austen's philosopher also sits contemplatively in her precarious mode of transport, her little boat, 'mightily at [her] ease, looking about [her] at the rocks and mountains, as if [she] were not to be upset the next moment, which [she] certainly must be'. But unlike the aesthetes of the sublime, who do not rationally 'know' or 'see' the imminence of death and who are thus rendered inadvertently tragicomic, her philosopher sits calmly in the full knowledge of death – in full rational awareness of the irony of her situation. She sees at once the real tragedy and comedy of life, the real tension between nature and convention, and from this tension derives a pleasurable feeling of independence, autonomy, and freedom akin to but transcending the delusion of 'self-preservation' and freedom characteristic of the sublime.

The world of tragedy, action, politics, and sexual passion – Lord Byron's 'dark blue seas' of the romantic sublime, which Captain Benwick points out to Anne on the seashore at Lyme (109) – is supposedly ignored in Jane Austen's novels. Yet Austen counters that romanticism itself has fictionalised this 'real' world in the cult of the sublime. Unlike the 'tragic' romantic poet, Anne Elliot, the comic philosopher, does not seek to rule or master life; she does not try to master or control nature and the power of death, which is a way of denying it. But neither does she submit to it in victimised passivity, as again the crisis on the Cobb makes clear. At the critical moment when nature threatens *prematurely* (or 'precipitately') to destroy rather than sustain human life, she intervenes and masterfully takes control. And when the crisis is over, she lets nature take its course again; as the entire narrative repeatedly illustrates, she always knows when to intervene in the course of events and when to yield to or be 'persuaded' by them. Anne is never transported by the persuasions – rhetorical and otherwise – of the sublime; but she is not inflexibly unpersuadable, either. Like Shakespeare's Edgar, she understands that in the world of time and inevitable change 'ripeness is all' – and this is the essence of tragedy, of philosophic comedy, and of Austen's transfiguration of the romantic sublime.

4

Gazing and Avoiding the Gaze

Douglas Murray

We all know the power of the human eye. We have all met some-one whose glance rouses fear – or at least incurs immobility – and most of us know those whom our own glances can disconcert. We all know how the fear of someone's distant gaze can alter behaviour.

Jane Austen would hardly have been surprised by the power of such real or imagined eyes, nor would she have been surprised by the late-twentieth-century scholarly interest in the gaze: that is, in recent investigations of the ways in which men and women see, are seen, and respond to being seen. It is the thesis of this essay that an understanding of contemporary theorists of the gaze can enrich our reading of Austen – and our admiration for her, since her fiction anticipates much recent writing on the gaze, in particular that of Laura Mulvey and Michel Foucault.

In articles concerning Hollywood film, Laura Mulvey discusses the gender-specific training and development of the gaze. She expands on Freud's observation (1953, 156–7) that gazes can some-times excite, sometimes divert, the libido and has studied the dis-tinct and diverse gazes which men and women are encouraged to direct toward each other in order to promote sexuality and matri-mony, society's primary mechanisms for self-perpetuation.[1] Thus, for Mulvey – and for Austen – the individual's gaze is partly the result of social acculturation beyond her or his control.

The second theorist whom Austen anticipates is Michel Foucault, who considers the effect on the individual of real or imagined gazes from outside. In *Discipline and Punish: The Birth of the Prison* (*Surveiller et Punir*, 1975), Foucault enumerates the increased mechanisms for surveillance which arose during the Enlightenment. He locates in Austen's era the institution of what he calls panopticism: unavoid-able, universal, ceaseless surveillance. His symbol or 'architectural figure' (200) for the age is Jeremy Bentham's panopticon (Figure 4.1),

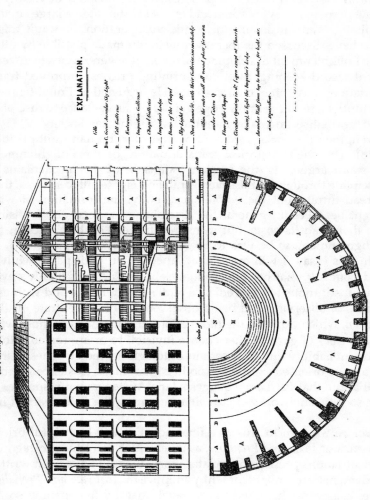

A General Idea of a PENITENTIARY PANOPTICON in an Improved, but as yet (Jan.y 23.d 1791.) Unfinished State.
See Postscript References to Plan, Elevation, & Section (being Plate referred to in no. V.)

EXPLANATION.

A. — Cells
B & C. — Several Area for Sky-Light
D. — Cell Galleries
E. — Entrance
F. — Inspection Galleries
G. — Chapel Galleries
H. — Inspector's Lodge
I. — Dome of the Chapel
K. — Sky-Lights to I.º
L. — Store Rooms &c. with their Galleries immediately within the outer wall all round: place for an annular Cistern Q.
M. — Floor of the Chapel
N. — Circular Opening in d.º (open except at Church time), to light the Inspector's Lodge
O. — Annular Well from top to bottom, for light, air, and separation.

4.1 'Penitentiary Panoption' (1791) from *The Works of Jeremy Bentham* (1843) a never-realised but much-discussed structure which allowed one central viewer in a school, prison, asylum, hospital or factory to view perpetually every room and every inhabitant in a large circular building – and to insure their efficient operation. Foucault might also have discussed the increased visibility made possible by other key Enlightenment developments: book reviewers, accurate government record-keeping, numerous printing presses, improved transportation, and better mail systems. He argues that Enlightenment institutions used the knowledge gained by surveillance to discipline and normalise, to make individuals 'useful' for society (211), to 'strengthen the social forces' (208), to order 'human multiplicities' (218). The chief 'historical transformation' of the Enlightenment, Foucault argues, is 'the gradual extension of the mechanisms of discipline throughout the seventeenth and eighteenth centuries, their spread throughout the whole social body, the formation of what might be called in general the disciplinary society' (209). Visibility, then, had its costs, but it insured full citizenship, since in the Enlightenment, to be was to be seen.

In this essay, I will argue that Jane Austen anticipated Mulvey and Foucault, that her novels analyse, first, society's highly developed institutions for surveillance and, second, men's and women's modes of observing and being observed. I will concentrate on *Persuasion*, which explores the motivations and methods of those who, in a society of gazes, either choose invisibility or are forced into it. Such invisibility entails a certain ontological precariousness, since in a gaze-oriented culture, visibility guarantees existence. Also, I will argue that *Persuasion* suggests Jane Austen's own responses to her society's networks of surveillance during the final years of her life.

Before we turn to Austen's final novel, it will be helpful briefly to consider *Pride and Prejudice*, a novel which introduces categories and situations present in the later work. It could have been written to demonstrate Enlightenment panopticism. In *Pride and Prejudice*, spies are everywhere and news travels fast. By the opening scene, everyone in the vicinity of Netherfield Hall knows much about Charles Bingley – his approximate income, his mode of transportation, etc. In the past, these first chapters have been read as misogynistic satire of female gossip, but it is difficult to maintain this interpretation. Mrs Bennet is the centre of a remarkably efficient and accurate network for the sharing of information: her 'solace was visiting and news' (5) – in other words, discovery and dissemination.

And, of course, the men are simultaneously conducting their own surveys: Charles Bingley takes Netherfield Hall so that he can hunt game birds *and* find a suitable marriage partner.

In a novel full of powerful information centres, the most knowledgeable and potentially the most powerful is Lady Catherine de Bourgh, whom I label the 'panoptic centre' of the novel. She gathers information first by noticing – in fact, the word 'notice' is often used to accompany her appearances – second, by asking questions – the interrogative is her favoured form of the sentence – and, last, through the use of the Rev. William Collins, whose career suggests the upper class's use of the lower orders as spies and manipulators. Her centre of intelligence is Rosings, which appropriately features numerous windows expensively glazed.

But if Lady Catherine is an information centre, we should not forget her defeat at the hand of the triumphant and independent gazer Elizabeth Bennet, who throughout the novel is symbolically associated with the eye. An attentive reader will find that, in Volume I, Austen mentions Elizabeth's eyes with almost predictable frequency, every ten pages or so. Elizabeth's abilities to attract more than a cursory gaze and to return others' gazes indicate her resistance and independence of mind amid powerful forces of conformity. It is this central core of resistance which allows Elizabeth to withstand the powerful gaze of Lady Catherine – or, as the cliché puts it, to look her in the eye.

If Elizabeth is a heroine of proud and independent gaze, other characters prefer not to see but to display; in other words, they demonstrate varying degrees of exhibitionism or, in a word coined by Freud, 'scopophilia' (157). I find this technical word particularly useful in describing the sad case of Jane Bennet. If Elizabeth is known for her bright eyes, Jane is correspondingly characterised by her smile. The frequent smile indicates several of Jane's characteristics, which I here arrange in ascending order of dire seriousness. First, the smile indicates her innate benevolence and optimism. Second, it indicates a desire to attract the attention of male gazers; thus, her smiles recall those of sparkling young persons in toothpaste commercials. Third, the smile indicates a suspicion of her real inequality in relationships, for she smiles in order to be noticed and approved. Fourth, the smile indicates that, while trying to show herself approved, she does not have leisure for insight: as Elizabeth tells her, 'You never *see* [italics mine] a fault in any body.... With *your* good sense, to be so honestly *blind* [italics mine] to the follies and nonsense of others!' (141). Fifth, the smile indicates a tendency to mask, even to herself, what she feels; such denial and repression results in Jane's lassitude and depression during the second volume of the novel.

If 'scopophilia' exists, so must 'scopophobia', though Freud left it to me to coin the term. There is perhaps slight scopophobia in Elizabeth: though generally an aggressive and fearless gazer, she occasionally needs to escape the panoptic. At Rosings, where she is perpetually inspected by Lady Catherine,

> Her favourite walk, and where she frequently went while the others were calling on Lady Catherine, was along the open grove which edged that side of the park, where there was a nice sheltered path, which no one seemed to value but herself, and where she felt beyond the reach of Lady Catherine's curiosity. (169)

Austen presents Elizabeth's trace of scopophobia as merely the healthy personality's desire for occasional solitude. The brevity of these scopophobic episodes confirms the consensus of readers that *Pride and Prejudice* is Austen's most optimistic novel, a work which celebrates without reservation the gaze of its heroine. For a more cautious work, in which invisibility becomes more habitual, inviting, and at times necessary, we turn to *Persuasion*.

In many ways, *Persuasion* recalls *Pride and Prejudice*. The figure in the later novel who corresponds to Lady Catherine and who, at least officially, commands the most power as viewer and viewed is Sir Walter Elliot, who simultaneously fills two roles: first, he is the cynosure, the subject of everyone's admiring gaze, including his own in his many mirrors; and second, he is the panoptic centre, inspecting and evaluating all around him.

Sir Walter gains considerable power and prestige by being in the public eye. As his estate agent Mr Shepherd tells him, 'consequence has its tax – I, John Shepherd, might conceal any family-matters that I chose . . . but Sir Walter Elliot has eyes upon him which it may be very difficult to elude' (17). Sir Walter gains and perpetuates his power by being seen, by ostentatiously bowing to the peasantry as he leaves Kellynch (36) and by religiously walking the streets of Bath every day, displaying his fine figure to as many passers-by as possible.

Sir Walter derives such prestige through this late-Enlightenment gaze system that he believes his presence magically confers social worth. He assumes that he sheds honour on Admiral Croft (32) or Mr Elliot (141) simply by allowing them to be seen in public with him. And he believes in the quickening power of his and his daughter Elizabeth's gaze; he believes that their 'regard' quickens the untitled into social life, raises them from social graves. He believes that those whom he does not notice – as he does not notice Captain Wentworth for much of the novel – simply have not been called into social existence. Close readers of *Persuasion* cannot forget Sir Walter and Elizabeth's visit to the Musgroves' lodgings near the end of the novel, when they hand out cards for their evening entertainment and simultaneously, as the Elliots must see it, 'look' ordinary people into social prominence (226). By this time, Sir Walter and Elizabeth are determined to resurrect Wentworth from the social grave to which they had once condemned him, and they perform their miracles with deliberate glances: the Captain 'was acknowledged again by' both father and daughter, then by 'Elizabeth more graciously than before' (226).[2]

If Sir Walter is the powerful gazer, he is also information central, the panoptic centre. He, like Mrs Bennet in *Pride and Prejudice*, has collected all the information he deems necessary about everyone worth knowing, partly through the baronetage, partly through newspapers, and partly through conversation or what is known as gossip: even though he has not seen Mr Elliot or the Viscountess Dalrymple for years, he carries about with him an accurate mental chronology of the important public events in their lives. And, like Lady Catherine de Bourgh, he sees himself as a surveyor of physical beauty, as fashion and beauty police, a self-appointed aesthetician and statistician. He reports that in Bath one meets one 'pretty' woman for every 'thirty, or five and thirty frights' (141). (Sir Walter reports that the proportion of pretty women is significantly lower in London, for at 'a shop in Bond-street, he had counted eighty-seven women go by, one after another, without there being a tolerable face among them' [141–2].) His typical query about friends and relatives is not about their health, morals, or mental state but rather about how they are looking (142).

It is no accident that Sir Walter gravitates toward Bath, for that city operates in the novel as a place of unavoidable surveillance. There Nash's characteristic architectural feature, the crescent, insured easy and perpetual visibility; everyone standing in the Royal Crescent can be seen by invisible viewers behind hundreds of windows. In a countryside of lanes and hedgerows, one can escape by walking, but characters in *Persuasion* are always seeing others from a distance, hailing them from up and down streets. Secrets are not safe at Bath, for networks of nurses – such as Mrs Smith's friend Nurse Rooke – spread information gleaned from sickbeds, and old school chums – such as Mrs Smith herself – provide character references and files of old correspondence. Surreptitious meetings are not possible; even though Mr Elliot and Mrs Clay rendezvous 'under the colonnade' for protection, they are visible from the Musgroves' crowded drawing-room (222). With such easy and frequent visibility, it is no accident that Lady Russell takes Anne Elliot to Bath when 'She wanted her to be more known' (15). And perhaps it is significant that Austen placed in Bath Anne's hated school, in the Enlightenment – as now – an institution of socialisation through surveillance.

Of course, though Sir Walter reminds us of the panoptic Lady Catherine, his power is more tenuous. Lady Catherine is indeed, in everyone's thoughts and eyes, a worthy and formidable opponent for the brave Elizabeth Bennet. Sir Walter is not so much an object of attention as he thinks. As Anne learns when she visits Uppercross, a community only three miles from Kellynch does not spend much time gazing at and envying an improvident baronet. Sir Walter's show to peasants has undoubtedly been staged, for Austen tells us that 'the afflicted tenantry and cottagers . . . might have had a hint to shew themselves' to the departing baronet (36), and no doubt not as many visitors to Bath observe him as he thinks. Finally, Austen ridicules the Elliots' notion that worth derives from their glances, for Frederick Wentworth's honour derives from meritorious service, verifiable in the Navy lists.

Austen also lessens Sir Walter's power by emphasising the detrimental effects within him of society's habitual gazes. Austen interests herself in Sir Walter's uncontrollable compulsion to be seen – in short, in his scopophilia. It is not only a sense of social obligation which compels him to parade through the streets of Bath; it is a psychological necessity. Sir Walter needs frequent reassurance that he is seen and admired. Hence his shameless fishing for compliments. To his daughters Elizabeth and Anne and to Mrs Clay, he describes walking through the streets of Bath 'arm in arm with Colonel Wallis (who was a fine military figure, though sandy-haired)' (142). Sir Walter announces 'that every woman's eye was upon him; every woman's eye was sure to be upon Colonel Wallis' (142). The Baronet's manipulation produces the desired effect of compliment and reassurance: 'His daughter and Mrs Clay united in hinting that Colonel Wallis's companion might have as good a figure as Colonel Wallis, and certainly was not sandy-haired' (142).

If no peasants, middle classes, or lesser gentry are available to present the tribute of admiration, Sir Walter must admire himself. Every reader recalls Sir Walter's great 'number of looking-glasses' (128) in the private chambers at Kellynch-hall; as Admiral Croft comments, 'Lord! there was no getting away from oneself' (128). Their number and unavoidable placement suggests that Sir Walter needs to be seen perpetually to be certain of his continued value and even existence. In contrast, a 'little shaving glass in one corner [of the room], and another great thing that I never go near' (128) suffices the less scopophilic Admiral.

Sir Walter's deep need to exhibit has been passed on to Mary Elliot Musgrove, who provides evidence of exhibitionism thwarted. Whenever she is left alone, when the gazes of others are not upon her, she languishes into inertia and incapacity, reviving again only when she has an audience. When the novel introduces her, we see her at one o'clock in the afternoon, at her most weak and lethargic, 'lying on the faded sofa,' as she says, never 'so ill in my life as I have been all this morning' (37). Austen soon makes clear the reason for her weakness: she has been denied the looks upon which she depends for psychic energy. She has 'not seen' her husband 'since seven o'clock' (37); she has banished her noisy children; she has 'not seen' anyone from the Great House (38); 'not one of them have been near me' with the exception of Mr Musgrove, 'who just stopped and spoke through the window' (38). The only cure is, predictably, someone's regard, in this case Anne's, under whose influence Mary 'could soon sit upright on the sofa', beautify 'a nosegay', eat 'cold meat', and 'propose a little walk' (39) to the Great House – an excursion to see and be seen. Such behaviour continues through the rest of the novel. On the long walk to the Hayters', Mary is 'very well satisfied so long as the others all stood about her' (86), but loses energy and sinks to the ground when she is 'quite out of sight and sound' (87) of the others, and she only regains full vigour when she joins her father and eldest sister in the panoptic centre of Bath.

Sir Walter and his ilk – compulsive and deluded – merit and receive considerable satire. But, significantly, Austen does not leave them disempowered. The Elliots *are* continuously talked of by the Mrs Smiths and Nurse Rookes of this world, and few refuse their invitations. Not being fully noticed by them – being treated as invisible and inaudible – has its costs, as Sir Walter's own daughter Anne illustrates.[3] Elizabeth Bennet, it will be recalled, occasionally sought solitude, but Anne's invisibility is more habitual, more worthy of the term scopophobia. Her imperceptibility is a well-established habit at Kellynch-hall, where she 'was nobody with either father or sister: her word had no weight; her convenience was always to give way; – she was only Anne' (5). Generally, Anne connives at her own invisibility, especially in the first half of the novel, in which phrases such as the following abound: 'Anne's object was, not to be in the way of any body' (84); or 'she had contrived to evade and escape' (123). Anne in particular hides from Wentworth. When they enter each other's presence after eight years' separation, her eye only 'half met' his (59), and she contrives to avoid him when he first spends an evening at Uppercross. This scene is usually read as a satire of Mary, who wheedles to attend the party at any cost (55–8), but we should not forget that Anne advertises – and perhaps exaggerates – 'a head-ache of her own, and some return of indisposition in little Charles' (77).

Austen provides tantalising hints that Anne had not always cultivated invisibility. In a poignant discussion of Anne's pianoforte-playing, Austen relates that 'never since the loss of her dear mother, [had she] known the happiness of being listened to, or encouraged by any just appreciation or real taste. In music she had been always used to feel alone in the world' (47). We imagine a child deprived of her best audience, now subject to the attention – or inattention – of her father, inhabitant of a world whose gospel is the baronetage, a volume in which Anne nearly disappears. In the entry for the Elliot family, Elizabeth merits some attention as the eldest child; a dead brother receives notice as the only son; Mary achieves regard as the final entrant in the list, and later as the only married child and progenitor of a new line of Musgroves. But as second daughter, Anne merits little consideration (3). Now, so accustomed are her companions to Anne's invisibility, that no one attends when she speaks. In Bath, her father and sister 'could not listen to her description of' Mr Elliot, about whom she had pertinent information (141). Even as she and the friendly Musgroves walk through the neighbourhood around Uppercross, no one responds to her query: ' "Is not this one of the ways to Winthrop?" But nobody heard, or, at least, nobody answered her' (85). Anne is thus forced to accommodate herself to a world whose gaze ignores and underestimates her. She remains hesitant, withdrawn, almost in disguise – in the words of Frederick Wentworth when he meets her again after eight years, 'so altered he should not have known [her] again' (60).

Anne, fortunately, has been able to make use of her invisibility. She has had time for 'a great deal of quiet observation' (34). Her invisibility insures that she can gather information, as in the scene, undoubtedly emblematic of many, when she sits unobserved 'under the hedge-row' (87) and overhears conversation between Frederick Wentworth and Louisa Musgrove. And it is also fortunate that *Persuasion* is a story of increasing visibility, a fairy-tale in which a forgotten princess gradually materialises. Anne becomes increasingly perceivable as the novel progresses. In Lyme, Anne catches Mr Elliot's roving regard 'by the animation of [her] eye' (104). Lady Russell fancies that Anne improves 'in plumpness' (124), and even her father 'thought her "less thin in her person, in her cheeks"' (145), as if a two-dimensional object, invisible from its sides, gains heft and thickness. But despite this happy conclusion, it is Anne's invisibility that generally haunts readers.

Many reasons, no doubt, compelled Austen to create her scopophobic heroine. If space permitted here, I would argue an autobiographical impetus – that Anne Elliot often recalls Jane Austen herself, whose Chawton years (1809–17) demonstrate considerable evidence of scopophobia. I would cite descriptions of Austen's reticence in company and the numerous accounts of her easy and frequent entrance into the world of children, a group not yet full participants in society's patterns of surveillance. I would describe Cassandra Austen's two surviving depictions of her sister, which convey the sitter's reticence and, perhaps, uncooperativeness with or even hostility towards the artist's endeavours. The novelist's response to the gazes of family and society – and, as she turned 40, her response to the more public gaze of editors, publishers, book reviewers and royalty – all this is the subject of another essay, but the evidence suggests that Jane Austen knew scopophobia from the inside.

Very early in Austen's career, she was able to imagine with enjoyment and humour a figure who can see all without himself being seen. In 'Jack and Alice', the second work in *Volume the First*, written in the late 1780s when Austen was in her early teens, appears Charles Adams, who 'was an amiable, accomplished and bewitching young Man; of so dazzling a Beauty that none but Eagles could look him in the Face' (*Catharine and Other Writings*, 11). Charles later appears at a masquerade in 'a Mask representing the Sun' (12). In general, levity reigns in 'Jack and Alice'. Yet a being who cannot be gazed upon but who, like the sun, can see everything, is frightening, like the supervisor in the centre of Bentham's panopticon. Here, by making a joke, Austen withstands the fright and demand inherent in being seen during the European Enlightenment. She could laugh at the panoptic gaze in her early teens, but she was, quite rightly, later to want to avoid it.

Foucault does not determine whether a member of a surveyed society ordinarily perceives the networks of surveillance surrounding her, and Laura Mulvey does not determine whether an individual gazer understands the origins and workings of his acculturated gazes. But Jane Austen's novels and biography suggest that she understood the gaze as well as we moderns. Her novels gaze relentlessly – and praise the eagle-eyed; as part of the Enlightenment project, they reveal to the light of day the deep recesses of human motivation. But – to mix metaphors – the light of Enlightenment always carried with it a weight, a burden, and Austen and her last heroine simultaneously needed – and found – places out of the sun. We can only praise Austen's success in simultaneously gazing and evading the gaze, for we still respect and discuss her fictional vision – but never capture the elusive gazer.[4]

Notes

1. Laura Mulvey's 'Visual Pleasure and Narrative Cinema' and 'After-thoughts on "Visual Pleasure and Narrative Cinema"', originally published in *Screen*, have been reprinted in *Feminism and Film Theory*, ed. Constance Penley, 57–79.
2. This expectation that persons of quality can 'look' social inferiors out of existence is shared by so 'wise' a character as Lady Russell. In Bath, she and Anne walk past Frederick Wentworth in Pulteney Street. Anne is 'perfectly conscious of Lady Russell's eyes being turned exactly in the direction for him' (179). But Lady Russell deliberately concentrates elsewhere: 'You will wonder', she says to Anne, 'what has been fixing my eye so long; but I was looking after some window-curtains, which Lady Alicia and Mrs Frankland were telling me of last night' (179). Lady Russell hopes she has willed Wentworth back into her – and into Anne's – past. More generally, the acculturated obliviousness of the genteel to lower orders explains why Austen's narrator and characters so infrequently mention servants.

3. Frequently in *Persuasion*, Austen substitutes inaudibility for invisibility, and Anne Elliot is often the silent – or at least unheard – heroine.
4. I wish to thank the National Endowment for the Humanities and the Belmont University Faculty Development Fund, whose financial assistance made this essay possible. Also, I wish to thank Margaret Anne Doody of Vanderbilt University and Richard Wendorf of the Houghton Library of Harvard University for advice and encouragement.

5

Shame or Espousal? *Emma* and the New Intersubjectivity of Anxiety in Austen

George Butte

PRELUDE

It did not surprise, but it grieved Anne to observe that Elizabeth would not know [Wentworth]. She saw that he saw Elizabeth, that Elizabeth saw him, that there was complete internal recognition on each side; she was convinced that he was ready to be acknowledged as an acquaintance, expecting it, and she had the pain of seeing her sister turn away with unalterable coldness. (*P*, 176)

And though there was no second glance to disturb her, though [Henry's] object seemed then to be only quietly agreeable, she could not get the better of her embarrassment, heightened as it was by the idea of his perceiving it. . . . (*MP*, 274)

Anne's experience of anxiety has something in common with Fanny's, with Emma's, Elinor's, with all of Austen's characters who are vulnerable to intelligent feeling. The common thread is the fundamentally intersubjective nature of the experiences; but the nature of that commonality is so fundamental that it has been difficult to identify. The shuttling movement of perceptions back and forth between characters seems so natural that we critics have not adequately explored the conventions of complex intersubjectivity in Austen. Anne and Fanny can lead us to understand the deeper construction of consciousnesses in Austen, beginning with a phenomenology of anxiety. Our two specific moments in *Persuasion* and *Mansfield Park* will serve to open up this complex matter, and then, after clarifying what I mean by intersubjectivity, I will approach the wonderful intricacies of *Emma*.

The first scene begins with observation, and in fact with observation of observation. Austen's favourite observers, who are often less privileged women, are finely tuned to the network of perceptions that surround them. Fixed as she is in Molland's bakery shop, where only limited movement is possible with the rain outside, and her authorised companions vying with Wentworth for her allegiance, Anne must use her keenest skills of navigation. Those skills allow her not only to watch others, nor simply to watch those whom the others watch. Anne as well maps a longer and more remarkable series of exchanged, blocked, anticipated, and denied acknowledgements. Within Anne's gaze, Wentworth and Elizabeth see each other, and they further recognise the sign in the other of being seen, and of being seen seeing. As if this maze of perceptions were not intricate enough, Austen turns the screw yet again: Anne is 'convinced' she tracks a specific negotiation. Wentworth offers the woman whom his courtship of Anne had offended a compromise fiction that he is an 'acquaintance', as he leans forward to be acknowledged, and Elizabeth rejects his offer, breaking the chain of gestures. In this scene Austen frames each perception with yet another gaze or gesture, each trumping, so to speak, the previous one.

Fanny's experience as observer in *Mansfield Park* has a similar density, when she becomes the victim of the gaze, in our second scene. When Henry looks at Fanny, he threatens her in a quite specific, extraordinary way: 'she saw his eye glancing for a moment at her necklace [his gift] – with a smile – she thought there was a smile – which made her blush and feel wretched' (274). The danger looms in the smile and the arrogance of anticipated possession it probably implies. But a greater danger lies in the residue of that look which Austen traces in a series of interior gestures. Fanny cannot regain her composure, because her embarrassment is extended in the mirror of Henry's eye, 'by the idea of his perceiving it'. Fanny's imagination brings to life for herself the series of perceptions of perceptions (Henry's, of hers of him). Fanny's image of her self is deeply implicated in Henry's first look at her, and also in his *second* look, which absorbs and acknowledges her response – her blush – to the first look. The mere 'idea' that Henry continues to observe her response to him paralyses Fanny, so that she is rescued only when Henry 'turned away to some one else', to concentrate on another human subject (274). The astonishing power of this scene lies in Austen's ability to suggest the sometimes frightening interiority and intimacy of the intersubjective.

The two exemplary scenes with which this essay began can help us approach anxiety in Austen from a new angle, to understand the form of these experiences in Austen's novels. The common element in these scenes is a particular representation not only of a state of mind, but also of states of minds in an ever-shifting series of gestures. The phenomenology of anxiety in Austen points toward an intersubjectivity of conflict and negotiation with the most profound implications, as my final reading of *Emma* will suggest.

SHAME OR ESPOUSAL?

It is time to step back a moment to clarify this approach to Austen, and set it in a wider context. A sea-change in the representation of consciousness in the English novel becomes visible in the work of Jane Austen. It is indeed a change so subtle and fundamental that it has been difficult to conceive and describe. One aspect of the change has received thoughtful and detailed attention in recent years, the move into the interior of the self. Critics as diverse as Erich Kahler, Dorrit Cohn, Elizabeth Ermarth and, more recently, Carol Rifelj have recounted the strategies which have allowed novels to turn 'inward', yet through conventions of what Cohn calls 'transparency' to scale scepticism's walls of solipsism separating self and other, especially by means of the newly powerful omniscient narrator, and to generate a sort of consensus about the world. The Other has still remained in some ways another country, especially when difference is filtered by gender, class or 'race'. Nonetheless, it has been possible to imagine the language and story that the Other constructs within, and to translate that experience as imagined for the privileged reader. Even monstrosity yields to this translation of the interior, when the novel takes us inside Victor Frankenstein's creation as he learns to read, or inside Dickens's Bradley Headstone as he relives the attempted murder of Wrayburn. What Tristram Shandy yearned for and yet feared, Momus's window on to the soul, appears at the end of his century, like a dream made real in the body of the novel.

It is a fundamentally different representation not only of consciousness, but also of consciousness*es*, of a newly framed intersubjectivity.

Jane Austen's novels are among the first in English to speak clearly in this new language within a language. What exactly does it mean to say that the representation of human consciousness had become intersubjective in a new way? A good place to begin is J. Hillis Miller's description of what he claimed was a new rendering of human experience in nineteenth-century novels:

> A characteristic personage in a Victorian novel could not say, 'I think, therefore I am,' but rather, if he could ever be imagined to express himself so abstractly, 'I am related to others, therefore I am,' or, ... 'I am conscious of myself as conscious of others.' ... A Victorian novel may most inclusively be defined as a structure of interpenetrating minds. (5)

Now, intersubjectivity does not seem to be a useful principle for understanding narrative if it deteriorates into the unremarkable notion that characters perceive themselves by way of others. Miller himself admits that intersubjectivity is the stuff of all fiction, and argues (only) that there is more of it in nineteenth-century novels, in a form altered by certain new forces, the sense of the disappearance of God and the omniscient narrator, to name the two most important. Miller is correct about changed historical and formal conditions; but not only the conditions have changed. The fundamental paradigm, the inner matrices and micro-organisations of intersubjectivity, have also shifted.

Representations and understandings of a simpler intersubjectivity are not new. The Russian critic Mikhail Bakhtin, for example, offers finely nuanced readings of the ways characters take the word of the Other, carrying the traces of the Other, and make use of that language themselves: the word is never virginal, for Bakhtin. All language is communal, is exchanged. The recent interest in the politics of the body traces in many forms how body or culture as text writes other bodies, in another kind of exchange of languages: Frances Burney describing the female body cannibalising itself at court to follow a demanding script (see Epstein, 30); Jane Eyre's conviction of her own monstrosity.

What is new in Jane Austen is the way her novels set groups of selves, of perceiving identities, into motion together in a new dance of subjects, of consciousness*es*. The energies of this dance build from tensions, as it were negotiations, among these consciousnesses who are present (partially) to each other, in body, gaze, and language, as self and Other. The results of this motion (and sometimes commotion) have been the subject of debate. Are these results primarily experiences of human shame, or do they offer a kind of espousal each of the other? Such at least is the argument between two twentieth-century French writers, Jean-Paul Sartre and Maurice Merleau-Ponty, who were students of the consequences of the intersubjective. Their quarrel can illuminate Jane Austen's achievement, as she measures in a new way the distance from shame to love and community.

If we define intersubjectivity as the web of partially interpenetrating consciousnesses that exists wherever perceiving subjects, that is, human beings, collect, then it is easy to see how this web can produce terror. The agent of terror is the gaze of the Other, according to Sartre, for whom the problem of the Other is shame, because shame is necessarily the result of being an object of the Look. 'The Other is not only the one whom I see, but the one *who sees me*. . . . He is the one for whom I am not subject but object . . .' (310). The Other excludes, endangers, and the tool of this threat is the Look, which makes one's fundamental, primary experience of the Other that of becoming-a-Thing: ' "Being-seen-by-the-Other" is the *truth* of "seeing-the-Other." . . . He is that object in the world which determines an internal flow of the universe, an internal hemorrhage . . .' (345). All of Sartre's images and examples of the Look express shame and fear, often in connection with blood and wounds. The Other always catches you off-guard. The Other is Emma watching Jane Fairfax across a crowded ballroom.

The Sartrean paradigm in a general sense has characterised the widespread discussion of the gaze in recent years, especially of the gaze as a male privilege, because Sartre opens up the dynamics of power in the gaze. Shame, aggression, defence before the attack of the Look – these are the givens of the Sartrean paradigm. Always, the gaze is a site of struggle between subjects, consciousnesses. Combat *is* a fundamental element of intersubjectivity in Jane Austen. A contest between gazes is exactly what occurs on the stairs from the beach at Lyme in *Persuasion*, for example, when Anne passes between Mr Elliot and Wentworth. Wentworth needs the shock of Elliot's 'earnest' and 'exceedingly' admiring look to see Anne again: 'Captain Wentworth looked round at her instantly in a way which shewed his noticing of [Elliot's admiration]' (104). In a sense Elliot challenges Wentworth to see Anne through his eyes. For Anne, who stands between the competing gazes of two admiring men, it is a subtle matter to decide if she gains or loses dignity and control as the object of their looks.

A very different notion of the intersubjective and the gaze appears in Merleau-Ponty. Although the gaze of the Other can be frightening in Merleau-Ponty, it can also be something quite different: a beginning of reciprocity, of espousal. For Merleau-Ponty, the process begins when a self perceives the gestures, either of body or word, of another consciousness; and it continues when the self can perceive in those gestures an awareness of her or his own gestures. Subsequently the self, upon revealing a consciousness of the other's response, perceives yet another responding gesture, so that out of this conversation of symbolic behaviours emerges a web woven of elements of mutually exchanged consciousnesses. Two friends stand before a landscape, and speak and gesture to each other; and within each there is 'a kind of demand that what I see be seen by him also', because what we see 'imposes itself . . . as real for every subject who is standing where I am'. And of the other, each says, 'I espouse his thought because this other, born in the midst of my phenomena, appropriates them' (*The Primacy of Perception*, 17–18). This web is too intricate to be only the product of private or mutual delusion.

The community of perceiving subjects is not, of course, anything like an exact fit. Merleau-Ponty writes, in the 'Introduction' to *Signs*, 'There is said to be a wall between us and others, but it is a wall we build together, each putting his stone in the niche left by the other' (19). We have seen in a few examples with what depth *Mansfield Park* and *Persuasion* render this wall, in exactly its paradoxical qualities as barrier and intimate connection, and we will see similar paradoxes in *Emma*. Nonetheless, shame is no longer the only result of the Other's gaze in this new circle of consciousnesses. Merleau-Ponty's most poignant description of that other result may be this sentence (the quotations are from the poet Valéry):

> I, who am irreducibly alien to all my roles, feel myself moved by my appearance in the gaze of others and that I in turn reflect an image of them that can affect them, so that there is woven between us an 'exchange,' a 'chiasm between two "destinies" . . .' in which there are never quite two of us and yet one is never alone. (*In Praise of Philosophy and Other Essays*, 82)

Phenomenology's project of understanding how human perception and the world are imbedded in each other provides a new and better way to understand Austen's study of how community emerges from subjects' mutual imbeddedness and how power works. This new paradigm performs two tasks: it expands the model of consciousness, beyond consciousness *of* consciousness, to the all-important third (and exponentially different) extension, to one's consciousness of the Other's awareness of the still previous trace of one's own gesture – and so on down the long corridor of the reflections in the mirrors facing each other – and it combines both language and body as gestures, as encodings, so that complex intersubjectivity includes imbeddedness, includes words *in* bodies, and bodies in words.

This paradigm of complex intersubjectivity offers a new range of coordinates in which to place the representation of experiencing in Austen. For example, the extremes of Fanny's experience in *Mansfield Park* point to the complexities of power, in her use of the look, and to her vulnerability before the gaze of others like Crawford who, so to speak, penetrate the fourth wall behind which she has hidden. Now we can see the depth of the paradoxes of power, in the network of ever-moving gestures in which Fanny's look takes its place and in which her fears multiply. Austen's narratives still represent blindness, stupidity, misunderstanding and the dawning of love. There is even an intersubjectivity of scattered, dismantled, decentred selves. But it is a different scattering now, an absence or disorientation against a different darkness. These will be deeper failures. Mrs Norris' self-absorption and Fanny's isolation as observer are drawn against new axes. One part of Austen's wisdom may be a new measuring, by means of complex intersubjectivity, of shame's barriers to espousal and of the degree to which they may be circumvented.

EMMA

In *Emma* the distance between shame and espousal of the other is especially great. Here, as in other Austen novels, bodies and gazes negotiate the tightly organised spaces of Austen's houses and gardens in wonderfully funny and sometimes brutally painful ways. The weight of the funniness and the suffering lies in Austen's representations of layered consciousnesses – a topic I can now discuss more adequately.

The presence, even pressure, of the Other and of others produces both anxiety and intimacy in *Emma*. In a sense, it is the intimacy of anxiety that a phenomenology of perception and misperception can grasp so usefully. In *Emma* that peculiar intimacy is a motive for many characters to screen, to block or subvert, the demand that what self and other see should impose itself as real for each. Austen's study of such screenings and subversions, however, is itself thoroughly intersubjective, especially in the terms in which Mr Knightley and Emma both recognise the dangers in a lowering of barriers between separate, possibly hostile, minds. During the Box Hill outing, Frank, wishing with Emma to spark some life into a dull, sullen group, announces that 'she desires to know what you are all thinking of'. Emma, who perceives at least some of the animosities and anxieties simmering in the afternoon heat, replies, 'laughing as carelessly as she could', 'Oh! no, no . . . it is the very last thing I would stand the brunt of just now.' She can imagine only one or two friends 'whose thoughts I might not be afraid of knowing' (369–70). Knowing what others really perceive one to be risks a responding honesty, and in the ensuing network of hostile responses, the fragile civility upon which Hartfield's world depends could be cracked beyond repair. Emma risks such a result in her carelessly direct reply to Miss Bates, about the difficulty for *her* of speaking only three dull things at a time. The ripples that spread out from Emma's remark, in Miss Bates's blush, in Mr Knightley's anger, in Emma's remorse, demonstrate the dangers of intersubjectivity.

The anguish of an intimate mutuality of perceptions is not only social. Merleau-Ponty speaks of the knowledge of the 'presence of oneself to oneself' which occurs only when one is threatened: 'for example, in the dread of death or of another's gaze upon me' (*Phenomenology of Perception*, 404). That dread, and a consequently defensive screening, consistently characterise many people in *Emma*. Their feelings of vulnerability seem to arise from specific social causes: one has something to hide, as Jane and Frank do, or one feels guilt and seeks solitude, as Emma does after the Box Hill reprimand from Mr Knightley, or characters feel a peculiarly Austenian social claustrophobia, as Emma does in the coach after Elton's proposal, or as Harriet does much of the time. But Jane Fairfax voices the broader yearning to escape the constant pressure of others' gazes when she speaks to Emma on fleeing the Donwell Abbey strawberry party: 'Oh! Miss Woodhouse, the comfort of being sometimes alone!' (363). The dread of not being alone is that the other's gaze must be returned, and that response will be observed in a manner which, yet again, one must observe and react to. One *must* see oneself being seen, and signal that one has performed this seeing with equanimity.

Austen understands well how intersubjective blocking occurs to avoid such a sequence of invasions of the vulnerable self. Frank proposes such an invasion (of Jane) to Emma, yet stands in front of Emma's gaze, denying the knowledge he has promised.

> 'Miss Fairfax has done her hair in so odd a way. . . . I must go and ask her whether it is an Irish fashion [Frank extends the fiction that Jane is in love with Dixon]. Shall I? – Yes, I will – I declare I will – and you shall see how she takes it; – whether she colours.'
>
> He was gone immediately; and Emma soon saw him standing before Miss Fairfax, and talking to her; but as to its effect on the young lady, as he had improvidently placed himself exactly between them, exactly in front of Miss Fairfax, she could absolutely distinguish nothing. (222)

This scene carefully and intricately reverses our paradigmatic process of intersubjective exchange. Rather than, in Merleau-Ponty's words, allowing the object one looks at to 'impose itself . . . as real for every subject who is standing where' the observer is, Frank stands precisely so as to disallow the observing other to be imposed upon. 'Impose' also raises fundamental questions of power: who or what imposes, under whose or what regime? Frank's position across the room between two gazes (Emma's and Jane's) explores the paradoxical nature of power here: he can both screen and expose, frustrate and protect, and do one and all for Jane and Emma simultaneously. Not only are gazes in this scene threatening and thus to be avoided, but they are part of a series of signals, of intended and expected exchanges. The intersubjective character of this scene's denial of observation is unmistakable. The blocked, deflected gaze within a complex human network of expectations is a brilliant example of the intersubjectivity of fragile, imperfect human intercourse in Austen.

Austen's intersubjective narrative also moves inside to shape Emma's experience of who she is. The drama of reciprocities occurs within the theatre of the inner consciousness, too, in Austen. This inward theatre of the intersubjective opens out in Emma's self-narrativising at the beginning of Volume II, Chapter 13, when Emma indulgently imagines Frank's return to court her, in every version of which she refuses him. But even Emma's pride enacts itself in intersubjective plots. Initially Emma's reverie of story-telling seems private and narcissistic, deaf to Merleau-Ponty's 'demand' of the other to be heard: '[S]he sat drawing or working, forming a thousand amusing schemes for the progress and close of their attachment, fancying interesting dialogues, and inventing elegant letters . . .' (264). But 'dialogues' and 'letters' suggest a fantasy of exchange. Then Emma, to play out the game of self-conceiving, takes another step, a step into layered intersubjectivity: 'Upon the whole, she was equally contented with her view of his feelings' (265). Wayne Booth emphasises Austen's control of narratorial distance in words like 'contented' which describe Emma's self-comforting (Booth, 257–8). But even in that distancing the new activity of characters' consciousnesses is remarkable. Emma's reveries need an idea of Frank's idea of her to be rewarding, and so she considers at some length the nature of his love for her. The golden thread in this scene, however, and the extraordinary new window in the European novel, is Emma's further effort not only to imagine Frank's feelings (however comically in error and self-servingly), but also to imagine Frank's imagination of *her* feelings.

'Not that I imagine he can think I have been encouraging him hitherto. No, if he had believed me at all to share his feelings, he would not have been so wretched. Could he have thought himself encouraged, his looks and language at parting would have been different.' (265)

Emma has an assumption of what it means to know the Other and to be known as she enacts her sense of self by means of imagined stories. Emma's implicated sense of self requires a series of subtle, mutual readings (*in*, one must remember, her mind's eye). That is, Emma imagines herself as the subject of Frank's meditation, as he is at the moment the subject of hers. Furthermore, each reading which she imagines, hers of Frank and Frank's of her, proceeds according to more or less canny notations of the other's behaviour, including both the physical and the verbal ('looks and language', says Emma). 'No, if he had believed me at all to share his feelings, he would not have been so wretched' represents Emma's interpretation of Frank's interpretation of her in his gestures *for* her.

Emma also sees herself as the mistress of perception who embodies her understanding in a behaviour *for* the other which she arranges so as to limit the degree to which the Other, Frank in this instance, can appropriate her consciousness. She is able, she believes, to control the extent of her and their mutual espousal: 'when he comes again, if his affection continue, I must be on my guard not to encourage it. . . . but I do not know that I expect [his affection] will [continue]' (265). The novel's wonderful irony, of course, lies in the final reversal of this fantasy, when the reader and Emma learn that she has been the 'object' of exactly such control of espousal. The larger significance, however, of this scene and of much of Emma's inner life in the novel, is that Emma's self-misunderstanding is framed in intersubjectively multiple appropriations. She misperceives Frank's gestures (dancing with her at the Coles', standing by her chair) and his words (all the repartee about Dixon and things Irish), misperceives his appropriation of her responses to him, and so, therefore, misunderstands herself. Emma's failure to know herself is a new kind of failure, the misappropriation of another's embodied perceptions of one's own perceptions. We discover in the new intersubjective fiction fresh depths of opacity.

But it would be unfair to Austen's comedy to suggest that fiction's new process of self-defining produces in Emma only a way to measure self-evasion or blindness. It also produces a complex measure of degrees of success at self-knowledge. Whatever one thinks of Emma's moral growth, and critics have differed widely on this subject, she manifestly changes to some degree, and demonstrably comes to perceive herself more exactly as imaged through others. Mr Knightley's anger in the Box Hill episode produces just such a demonstration of moral, epistemological, intersubjective illumination. Having delivered his lecture to Emma, Mr Knightley leaves, believing that Emma's pride has armed her against his criticism; and indeed it has made her angry with him. Emma's reaction demonstrates how much she has learned to gauge the connection between her self and the gestures of others by which she in part knows who she is:

He had misinterpreted the feelings which had kept her face averted, and her tongue motionless. They were combined only of anger against herself, mortification, and deep concern. She had not been able to speak; and, on entering the carriage, sunk back for a moment overcome – then reproaching herself for having taken no leave, making no acknowledgement, parting in apparent sullenness, she looked out with voice and hand eager to show a difference; but it was just too late. (375–6)

Emma's effort to respond to his gestures with her own gestures, of *both* 'voice and hand', is really her effort to espouse his behaviour, as it embodies his view of her.

There is an evasive undercurrent in Emma's effort, yes, that seeks Mr Knightley's approval, rather than the more painful knowledge of her errors. But her gesture is predominantly one of self-clarification, a process that must, in Austen's fiction, be structurally intersubjective. Emma fails now to acknowledge and be acknowledged by Mr Knightley, but she will not in Volume III, Chapter 13, when, courageously, she asks him to walk again around her garden. For Emma to understand better the intricate relations of her fantasies to her perceptions of the Other's perception and embodiment of her gestures (and so on, in the receding series of mirrorings) – for Emma to know herself more fully in this way is a morally and epistemologically difficult act, and a remarkable achievement.

For me the comic strain in Austenian intersubjectivity predominates, despite an emphasis upon the imperfection of discourse and disclosure. Emma and Mr Knightley and Frank and Jane do together place bricks in that wall, in the niche left by the other, not so that any of them achieves full presence to the other, but so that, in Merleau-Ponty's words, there is woven 'an "exchange," a "chiasm between two destinies" in which there are never quite two of us and yet one is never alone'.

Part II
What Speaks Aptly

6

'My sore-throats, you know, are always worse than anybody's': Mary Musgrove and Jane Austen's Art of Whining

Jan Fergus

Mary Musgrove is one of Jane Austen's best comic characters because there is so much of her in all of us, I think, though we may disguise it more decently than she does. What is wonderful about Mary is her relentless, endlessly inventive whining; you will see that by my taxonomy, she manages to emit both the most primitive and the most sophisticated sorts of whines. And what I love about Jane Austen's presentation of Mary is first that, though most of us hate nothing more than being in company with a relentless whiner, Austen manages to keep Mary's demanding misery and miserable demands comic. Even more, though, I admire Austen's ability to infuse so much meaning into this comic character, as I hope to suggest later.[1]

To begin with the comedy of Mary's whines, a rich subject. The first of two major functions of a whine is to communicate or vent unhappiness, and Mary does that often enough. But even her most open or primitive whines, such as her frequent laments at being left alone, I will argue, are usually imbedded in much more complex exchanges. They serve other functions, in other words, which can be loosely described as manipulative, for blaming involves an attempt to manipulate others' emotions. Consider the first words that Mary utters in the novel, also the first she says to Anne, who has come to help and cheer her at Uppercross. Mary almost immediately mentions that she has 'not seen a creature the whole morning', a fairly open whine. But what comes before it is even whinier: 'So, you are come at last! I began to think I should never see you.

I am so ill I can hardly speak. I have not seen a creature the whole morning!' (37). There is a crescendo of complaint here. No welcome, no 'thank you for coming, Anne', no 'it is a pleasure to see you'. Austen's art of representing Mary's whines involves turning even Mary's greeting to her sister into an accusation: 'So, you are come *at last!*' (emphasis added). Anne is immediately arraigned for not having come earlier.

This capacity to infuse blame into nearly every utterance is part of what distinguishes Mary's whining from the simpler whines of characters like Mrs Bennet, whose laments over the entail of Longbourn do not usually attack anyone but Mr Collins. Mary, by contrast, is always eager to get the knife in. Notice her technique in the next sentence, which continues to accuse Anne: 'I began to think I should never see you.' The knife comes in with 'never'. As all family members can witness, the word 'never', like 'always', is incendiary – 'You *never* take the garbage out so I *always* have to do it; you *always* get first pick, I *never* do.' 'Always' and 'never' raise the emotional temperature of any dialogue; they aggravate any accusation, as Mary senses very well. In this first scene with Anne, occupying just three pages in Chapman's edition (37–40), Mary uses 'never' five times and 'always' thrice, each time reproachfully: to say that she thought she would never see Anne, that her husband has never come back, that the Miss Musgroves never put themselves out of their way to see her, that she never wants them anyway, and that Anne has never asked her a word about 'our dinner at the Pooles yesterday' (39). She also asserts that she always makes the best account of her health, that you always know beforehand what dinner will be at the Pooles' (clearly a profound criticism of their menu), and that Mr Musgrove always sits forward, so Mary has to crowd into the back seat with Henrietta and Louisa – which unhappy arrangement she thinks might have caused her illness. 'Always' is so useful that it appears in my title whine – her sore throats are *always* worse than anybody's. But I'll have more to say about this wonderful sentence later.

We have now finally arrived at the third sentence of Mary's first speech to Anne, when she first directly mentions her illness. 'I am so ill I can hardly speak' – 'hardly' being also a fine adjunct to a whine, particularly here when she is speaking about hardly being able to speak. Then Mary comes to her favourite lament, 'I have not seen a creature the whole morning', one that is so central to her misery that she repeats it three more times in less than a page: 'I assure you, I have not seen a soul this whole long morning' and 'I have not seen one of them [the Musgroves] to-day', and 'though I told him [Mr Musgrove] how ill I was, not one of them have been near me' (37, 38). She even laments that Lady Russell did not come in to visit: 'I do not think she has been in this house three times this summer' (37). These repetitious wails of seeing no one, when she is finally seeing Anne, are not just contradictory, as when Mary says she is hardly able to speak: they typify the treatment of Anne by the rest of her family, Sir Walter and Elizabeth: Anne is 'nobody with either father or sister' (5).

In these four short sentences and the brief exchange with Anne that follows, Mary Musgrove covers the primitive and manipulative possibilities of whining with amazing efficiency. She vents her misery at being left alone with the repetitiveness characteristic of an inveterate whiner, and she openly and tacitly blames Anne and others for not paying attention to her. She adopts a striking variety of roles: when she speaks of always making the best of her health, she is the martyr; and when she refuses all comfort from Anne, she is Job, uniquely cursed with inadequate consolation that naturally she must reject. When Anne suggests that Mary has had her children with her, she retorts that their noise was unbearable and they did not mind her; when Anne predicts that the Miss Musgroves will visit soon, Mary does not want them because they 'talk and laugh a great deal too much for' her (38). And of course Mary makes no response whatsoever to Anne's concerns. When Anne excuses herself from coming earlier because she 'had so much to do', Mary's response is wonderfully narcissistic: 'Dear me! what can *you* possibly have to do?' (38). After Anne explains that she has been packing and taking leave and cataloguing and ordering the garden, Mary's entire response is ' "Oh! well;" – and after a moment's pause' comes the reproach about Anne never having asked about her dinner at the Pooles' (39).

The most striking examples of Mary's art of whining, however, are to be found in her letter to Anne at Bath; from it I have taken the splendid line that I have adopted for my title. In a letter, after all, Mary has more scope for whines – there need be no interruption, and there is none. Every sentence in the letter manages to be a lament and an accusation at once, that is, manages both the primitive venting and the more sophisticated blaming. In context, her sore throat appears as her first postscript, which some say contains the real message of every letter:

> I am sorry to say that I am very far from well; and Jemima has
> just told me that the butcher says there is a bad sore-throat very
> much about. I dare say I shall catch it; and my sore-throats, you
> know, are always worse than anybody's. (164)

There she is before us again, Job, uniquely, narcissistically cursed
with the worst sore throats in the universe, and she manages to
evoke all these past afflictions in one sentence. But it is particularly
inventive of her in the very same sentence to whine in the future
tense also – about a sore throat she has not yet got. The phrase 'you
know' is artful too: it manages to call upon Anne as a witness to her
suffering and at the same time to accuse her of insensitivity. Similarly, in the first sentence of the letter, as in her first words to Anne
at Uppercross, she is both accusing and aggrieved: 'I make no apology for my silence, because I know how little people think of letters
in such a place as Bath. You must be a great deal too happy to care
for Uppercross, which, as you well know, affords little to write
about' (162). Although she clearly owes Anne a letter, she offers no
conventional apologies for not writing.

Every sentence in the letter cries out for analysis and appreciation, but a few will illustrate some of the features of Austen's artful
representation of Mary's whines. After lamenting the dullness of
Uppercross, pointing out that *she* never had such long school holidays as the Musgrove children, and blaming Mrs Harville for parting with her own children for so long, Mary announces: 'What
dreadful weather we have had! It may not be felt in Bath, with your
nice pavements . . .' (163). It is amusing to remember how differently Austen herself treats a similar observation about bad weather
in her own letters: 'What dreadful Hot weather we have! – It keeps
one in a continual state of Inelegance' (*L*, 18). Back to Mary, who
wields the knife, as usual – *you* have nice pavements, *you* are happy
in Bath, better off than I am. Mary, we know, always fears that
everyone else is better off – that she herself is not getting her due.
On the hill above Winthrop, Mary enjoys herself until Louisa and
Captain Wentworth are out of sight; then she is sure that Louisa
has a better seat somewhere else and goes in search of it and of the
two people who might be having a good time without her. Mary
says later in the letter, in reference to Anne's making Mr Elliot's
acquaintance, that she wishes, 'I could be acquainted with him too;
but I have my usual luck, I am always [always, again] out of the
way when any thing desirable is going on; always the last of my

family to be noticed' (163). In lines like these, Mary almost anticipates Eeyore in *Winnie-the-Pooh*, who also has the attitude that others are out to get him, and who also turns every statement into an
accusation. For instance, when Pooh offers to find Eeyore's tail, his
response is 'You're a real friend, . . . Not like some' (47).[2] Unlike
Mary, Eeyore usually blames Others, not whomever he is addressing, but like her he has an abiding sense of ill-usage: he points out
that everyone is eating, 'All except me . . . As Usual' (121).

To return to what really irks Mary about the bad weather at
Uppercross: the lanes are wet and she has 'not had a creature call
on me since the second week in January, except Charles Hayter,
who has been calling much oftener than was welcome' (163). We
must admire the way that Mary gets two of her habitual whines in
here, one about not having enough company, and the other about
having Henrietta's choice of a husband be 'disagreeable and incon-
venient to the *principal* part of her family, and . . . giving bad connections to those who have not been used to them' (76). Finally,
having whined openly and tacitly about not being in Bath, Mary
angles openly for an invitation: 'What an immense time Mrs Clay
has been staying with Elizabeth! Does she never mean to go away?'
(163). Mary is troubled here by no consideration about a possible
'bad connection' between her father and Mrs Clay; she continues,
'But perhaps if she were to leave the room vacant we might not
be invited. Let me know what you think of this' (163). And having
blamed Mrs Harville for leaving her own children at Uppercross
for weeks, Mary adds, 'I do not expect my children to be asked, you
know. I can leave them at the Great House very well, for a month
or six weeks' (163). Then a few whines at the Navy – Admiral and
Mrs Croft have been guilty of 'gross inattention' as neighbours –
and Mary is Anne's affectionately, followed by her postscript on
sore throats and then her retraction regarding the Crofts, who
have after all offered to convey anything Mary wishes to Bath, in 'a
very kind, friendly note indeed, addressed to me, just as it ought'
(163, 164). And this letter proceeds to inform Anne of Benwick's
engagement to Louisa.[3]

What is interesting about Mary as a whiner is that she has so
complete a sense of both deprivation and entitlement: she continually fears being ill-used, thinks she is, whines about it, thinks herself ill over it – as when in the first scene with Anne she blames
her alleged illness on having to sit backward in the Musgroves'
carriage the night before. She feels entitled to sit in the best seat,

of course. I have passed comparatively lightly over Mary's hypochondria, but it is worth mentioning how it differs from that of Mr Woodhouse or Isabella Knightley, for instance. They focus on their health rather than whine about it. Admittedly, their focus is manipulative, particularly in Mr Woodhouse's case. He is completely absorbed in the activity of holding on to his habits, including his habits of ill-health; his great fear is of any change that might threaten those habits (as Miss Taylor's marriage does), and his fears often work to get others to do what he wants. But he also is capable of worrying over others whose habits differ from his; he is capable of pitying others, not just of self-pity, albeit in his case it is not always easy to distinguish the two. 'Poor Miss Taylor' is a way of saying 'poor me', after all.

Mary, however, never gets beyond self-pity. Remember her 'What can *you* possibly have to do?' to Anne. There is in fact no whiner in Austen's novels to compare with Mary. Mrs Norris isn't a whiner, not even when she has 'much exertion and many sacrifices to glance at in the form of hurried walks and sudden removals from her own fire-side' (*MP*, 188), for she is not whining but having much 'to insinuate in her own praise' to Sir Thomas. Mrs Norris is in fact a boaster, like Mrs Elton, whom one can hear droning on, but not whining. Mrs Price in Portsmouth is a talented whiner, especially about her servant Rebecca, but we actually hear her voice very seldom. Mrs Allen of *Northanger Abbey* might at first seem to be a candidate, with her repeated wishes that she knew someone in Bath so that Catherine might have a partner. But in fact, these remarks are delivered 'with perfect serenity' (22), so that although they have the repetitiousness of whines, they haven't the proper tone – the characteristic moan. The only real and frequent whiner, again, apart from Mary, is Mrs Bennet, but her laments over the entail of Longbourn do in fact register a serious grievance, and her concern over the fate of her daughters when their father dies compares favourably with Mr Bennet's indifference. Her methods are vulgar, but at least she tries.

Mary Musgrove's character was created for *Persuasion*, I think, because the novel is to some extent about ways that people cope with the sense of ill-usage as well as with loss and grief.[4] The phrase 'ill used' with or without the hyphen appears eight times in *Persuasion*, according to the De Rose and McGuire *Concordance*, more than half the times that it appears in all Austen's works. *Pride and Prejudice* uses it twice, *Mansfield Park* once, and the minor works

(*Lady Susan, The Watsons,* and *Sanditon*) four times – and that's it.[5] Though half of the eight instances of ill-usage in *Persuasion* refer to Mary's sense of it, as we might expect, the other four occasions suggest how pervasive the notion is in the novel. We are told that Elizabeth Elliot 'felt herself ill-used and unfortunate' by having to retrench their expenditure, 'as did her father' (10); that Captain Wentworth '[felt] himself ill-used' by Anne's breaking their engagement (28); and that Anne hopes that Captain Wentworth's letter to the Admiral announcing Louisa's engagement 'does not breathe the spirit of an ill-used man,' and then hopes that Wentworth's 'manner of writing' does not convey that 'he thinks himself ill-used by his friend' (172, 173). Interestingly, the Admiral assures her in response to her first query that 'there is not an oath or a murmur from beginning to end. . . . No, no; Frederick is not a man to whine and complain; he has too much spirit for that' (172). The Admiral's use of the word 'whine' represents Austen's sole use of this word in any form in all her novels. 'To whine' was gendered female by Samuel Johnson in his famous *Dictionary* as 'To lament in low murmurs; to make a plaintive noise; to moan meanly and effeminately.' In her single use of the word, Austen inverts Johnson and makes whining male, using it in reference to male behaviour; though the Admiral doesn't say that Captain Wentworth whines, the phrase 'a man to whine and complain' intimates very clearly that other men do.[6]

In a novel that juxtaposes Anne's lasting grief at losing Captain Wentworth with the more malleable and fanciful grieving of Captain Benwick for Fanny Harville or Mrs Musgrove for her son Richard, we are inclined to expect that a sense of ill-usage, too, will ordinarily prove false. Certainly Elizabeth and Sir Walter have no right to feel ill-used by the amount of his debts; Captain Wentworth feels not ill-used but profoundly relieved by Benwick's engagement to Louisa; and Wentworth is not fully entitled to feel ill-used by Anne's breaking their engagement, as he himself recognises at the end, telling Anne that 'I shut my eyes, and would not understand you, or do you justice' (247). But what about Mary's thinking herself ill-used? The narrator produces the first two instances, telling us first that, 'inheriting a considerable share of the Elliot self-importance, [she] was very prone to add to every other distress that of fancying herself neglected and ill-used' (37). Later, the narrator informs us that, during the walk back from Winthrop, 'Mary began to complain of' Charles's dropping her arm to cut nettles, 'and lament her being ill-used, according to custom, in being on the hedge side, while Anne was never incommoded on the other' (90). The other two instances are filtered through Anne's consciousness. At Lyme, Anne recognises that Mary 'would have felt quite ill-used by Anne's having actually run against' Mr Elliot 'in the passage' (107), and later at the White Hart, Anne has to find Mary's keys and sort her trinkets, while 'trying to convince her that she was not ill used by any body; which Mary, well amused as she generally was in her station at a window overlooking the entrance to the pump-room, could not but have her moments of imagining' (221).

What I want to consider is whether Mary's sense of ill-usage is to be dismissed as completely as Sir Walter's and Elizabeth's. That is, is there any legitimacy at all in Mary's inveterate whines? In short, why is Mary a whiner – a person who expresses continual frustration, who makes it known that she never gets enough? Isn't she partly right, after all? Her four initial whines to Anne about being left alone convey to us that people try to avoid her as much as they possibly can: her husband goes out, Mr Musgrove passes by without coming in and either doesn't tell his daughters that Mary feels ill, or does tell them, which induces them to stay away, and Lady Russell doesn't come in. Mary is of course largely responsible for these desertions, none of them absolute – the Musgroves see each other daily in any case – but what makes her act so as to provoke avoidance?

Mary was evidently a neglected child. Elizabeth was her father's favourite, and we can infer that Anne was her mother's as she is now Lady Russell's. Even if Lady Elliot conscientiously attempted to give each daughter equal love and attention, as presumably she did, Mary was youngest when she died, just 8 or 9; Anne was about 13 and Elizabeth about 15. Mary is less attractive than either of her sisters, and less secure. She feels competitive with her sisters – witness her fear that Captain Wentworth might be made a baronet at the end. Even in her marriage she was a second choice, and perhaps knows it, as certainly the Musgroves do: Louisa tells Captain Wentworth that Charles asked Anne to marry him before asking Mary. Anne was 'about two-and-twenty' (28) when Charles proposed to her, which makes Mary, according to the Baronetage, either 17 or 18, perhaps away at school, perhaps not. She married Charles shortly after she turned 19. It is hard to avoid inferring that Charles married her on the rebound from Anne. She may have sought him; we are told that he is 'really a very affectionate brother' (110), so that he would be likely to respond to affection. Curiously, their wedding day was 16 December 1810 – Jane Austen's thirty-fifth birthday! (I've always wondered what private joke Austen was enjoying by using that date. A friend has speculated that perhaps she was congratulating herself on having reached thirty-five without marrying, and I think she is probably right.)[7]

I have been arguing that whining is a form of communication – either for self-expression, venting one's own emotions, or for power, to manipulate others' emotions and behaviour. But it is of course also a way to protest against the way one's life is ordered, as Mrs Bennet does. Mary's attempts to assert her class – to precede her mother-in-law out of local dining rooms, to boast about the Elliot consequence – is certainly self-aggrandising, but it also reflects insecurity and unhappiness, as all Mary's whines do. Does the novel ask us to view her suffering as wholly illegitimate?

Claudia L. Johnson's book on Mary Wollstonecraft, Ann Radcliffe, Frances Burney and Jane Austen, *Equivocal Beings*, points out that the legitimacy of suffering was a gendered issue in the 1790s.[8] The gendering of suffering, the question of who suffers longer over loss, men or women, is certainly at issue in the famous conversation between Anne and Captain Harville. Johnson's compelling analyses of *The Mysteries of Udolpho* and *Camilla* argue that only men in those novels seem to have the right to suffer and lament; women are constantly enjoined and exhorted to repress and deny their suffering. In *Persuasion*, Anne Elliot clearly suffers from burying her unhappiness; she has had no outlet at all for her pain at losing Wentworth – she and Lady Russell never discuss Anne's engagement or regrets. As a result, Anne is evidently depressed at the start of the novel, a state reflected in her 'early loss of bloom and spirits' (28). That is, Anne suffers in her body and in her emotional life; in my view, Anne comes out of her depression by being forced by her visit to Mary into the pain of seeing Wentworth again, which paradoxically makes her come alive, recovering her youth and sexuality as she enjoys the temporary admiration of Captain Benwick and Mr Elliot at Lyme.

Austen has, then, set up the most profound contrast between Anne and her sister Mary in their ways of expressing female suffering: Mary whines, venting her unhappiness, and Anne suppresses hers. Austen also sets up a profound contrast in the way characters respond to the sisters: Mary alienates people by whining, sometimes succeeding in driving them away; Anne is liked by the

Musgroves for her self-effacement and willingness to interest herself in them. That is, Mary is punished for her mode of expressing unhappiness; Anne is rewarded for hers.

It is not possible to dismiss this contrast by saying that of course Anne is the heroine, 'almost too good' for Austen herself (*L*, 487), and Mary is comic, so that their unhappiness must be treated antithetically. Captain Benwick's unhappiness, for example, is treated quite differently from theirs, and much more tenderly. Admittedly, he is *openly* mourning a lost love, unlike Anne, whose suffering is concealed. As a result, his behaviour can be favourably interpreted in conventional romantic terms, as the Musgroves do at first. His 'story' ensures first that the 'sympathy and good-will excited towards Captain Benwick was very great' (97). Then once the Musgroves meet him, 'He had a pleasing face and a melancholy air, just as he ought to have, and drew back from conversation' (97). By comparison, a parallel female sufferer, Anne's friend Mrs Smith, who is mourning her husband, in addition to having lost health and affluence, is praised for not expressing her suffering. She is not even given full credit for stoicism, for Anne reflects 'that this was not a case of fortitude or of resignation only. . . . here was that elasticity of mind, that disposition to be comforted, that power of turning readily from evil to good, and of finding employment which carried her out of herself, which was from Nature alone' (154).

Benwick's is the first unhappiness that people treat at all sympathetically in *Persuasion*, for Mrs Musgrove's mourning of Richard is indulged, not sympathised with. The introduction of Benwick's unhappiness is followed by Louisa's accident, when male emotional responses are again treated more tenderly than female ones. Anne remains in control of herself, Henrietta faints, Mary screams and becomes hysterical; by contrast, Wentworth suffers at first in an 'agony of silence', then asks for help 'in a tone of despair' (109, 110). Similarly, Charles Musgrove, 'really a very affectionate brother, hung over Louisa with sobs of grief' (110). The expression of male suffering is legitimate; female suffering apparently less so.[9] Even the victim, Louisa, is implicitly blamed in Anne's thoughts for the 'very resolute character' that contributed to the accident (116).

Austen always gives us more than we expect in her comedy. Although we may think we have encountered simple comedy in a character like Mary, a mere whiner, we always have something more, something deeper and more complex. Mary's character, I would suggest, following Claudia L. Johnson, forms part of a deliberate attempt by Austen to interrogate the way the expression of suffering seems to be admirable or legitimate in men, excessive or comical or otherwise illegitimate in women. Nonetheless, because whines are so irritating, because Mary doesn't really appear to be ill, because the underlying reasons for her unhappiness are implied rather than stated, and because nothing nasty that she says or does really hurts Anne (which would make us take her more seriously), Mary's unhappy whines remain richly comical, despite the suggestions on Austen's part of a cultural critique of the conditions that make us laugh at Mary, not sympathise.

Notes

1. I would like to thank Ruth Portner, as usual, for help in developing ideas for this essay, and for her patience in listening to blocks of text over the telephone; and I am grateful to Isobel Grundy for several helpful comments. I am also grateful to Virginia Hjelmaa for first calling my attention to the richness of Mary's character.
2. The perennial appeal of whining – in comedy – is suggested by this text.
3. Mary's summary is worth noting: 'And this is the end, you see, of Captain Benwick's being supposed to be an admirer of yours. How Charles could take such a thing into his head was always incomprehensible to me. I hope he will be more agreeable now' (165). That Charles should notice admiration of Anne seems particularly disagreeable to Mary, a possible sign that she is aware of his former admiration of Anne.
4. See Elaine Showalter's essay in this volume.
5. The instances from the other works are as follows: in *Pride and Prejudice*, Mrs Bennet wants to 'require Jane to confess that if [Bingley] did not come back, she should think herself very ill used' (129), and she reports to Mrs Gardiner, 'They had all been very ill-used' since her last visit, in that two marriages for her daughters had come to nothing (139). In *Mansfield Park*, Fanny feels that Mr Rushworth 'had been very ill-used' by the failure of Maria and Henry Crawford, and later Julia, to wait for him to fetch the key (101). Catherine Vernon reports that Lady Susan says of Reginald, 'His disposition you know is warm, & he came to expostulate with me, his compassion all alive for this ill-used Girl [Frederica Vernon], this Heroine in distress!' (*MW*, 290). Margaret Watson, fearing that she might have to share her bedroom with her sister Emma, is 'rather mortified to find she was not ill used' in *The Watsons* (*MW*, 351). In *Sanditon*, Charlotte Heywood imagines briefly that Clara Brereton 'seemed placed with her [Lady Denham]

on purpose to be ill-used' (391), and feels later that Clara and Sir Edward Denham are 'really ill-used' in being seen by her to meet clandestinely (427). I have not included instances of 'ill usage', though there are some.

6. Admittedly, Johnson is probably, like the Admiral, thinking of a male's whining when he writes of mean and effeminate moaning: that is, he is referring to a lover's complaint for the loss or coldness of his mistress, a very common use for the term 'whining'. Still, what seems to Johnson to be 'mean' about whining is that it is like something women do; even if he is thinking of male lovers in his definition, he genders their behaviour as female or effeminate.

7. A suggestion made by Virginia Hjelmaa.

8. I am very grateful to Claudia L. Johnson for permitting me to see a good deal of this book in manuscript and for allowing me to refer to her argument here: *Equivocal Beings: Politics, Gender, and Sentimentality in the 1790s, A Study of Wollstonecraft, Radcliffe, Burney, and Austen*, published in 1995 by the University of Chicago Press.

9. We need not believe, of course, that Charles and Captain Wentworth actually suffer more than, say, Henrietta does.

7

Talking about Talk in
Pride and Prejudice

Juliet McMaster

When Mr Collins's first letter is read aloud at the Bennet breakfast-table, we are privileged to hear a whole family's response to a stranger's prose style. Elizabeth doubts he can be 'sensible', Mr Bennet hopes he isn't, Mary is impressed, Mrs Bennet is 'softened by his manner of expressing himself', Kitty and Lydia have no attention for any man who doesn't wear a scarlet coat (*PP*, 62–4). The critical faculties, in one way or another, are awake and alert in all of them.

A similar process of attention to and assessment of other people's language is going on throughout *Pride and Prejudice*. In case we as readers missed a nuance or an implication, there is usually a character within the novel to alert us, accurately or otherwise, to the significance of what the other characters say and how well they say it.

The characters in Jane Austen's novels, at least the intelligent and discriminating ones, bring an almost professional expertise to their conversations with each other: speaking aptly (to recall Charlotte Brontë's phrase) is indeed their business. Because social intercourse is their main occupation, and speech their primary means of carrying it on, it concerns them nearly to be skilful and effective in it.[1] Their own speech (or other people's) becomes itself a subject of their talk; and their skill in discourse has a great deal to do with their success or failure in their lives. Language is sometimes so all-absorbing for the characters that it becomes almost a mode of existence in itself, and one in competition with what we usually call reality.

There are many eager talkers in *Pride and Prejudice*. They talk aggressively, and for talking's own sake: such are Mrs Bennet, Mr Collins, Lady Catherine; Wickham is a glib and self-interested talker. Even Mary Bennet, in her pathetically ineffectual way, longs 'to say something sensible, but knew not how' (7). The characters are self-conscious about their own use of language, and alertly critical of each other's. It is not only we as readers who are busily listening to and assessing the characters; the characters themselves make it their business to analyse and judge each other's oral and written performance in language.

Let's listen to some of these critics.

When Elizabeth detects Darcy listening to her talk with other people, she immediately assumes his stance as critic, and challenges him, 'Did not you think, Mr Darcy, that I expressed myself uncommonly well just now, when I was teazing Colonel Forster to give us a ball at Meryton?' (24). Instead of retiring in confusion, Darcy rises to the occasion, and shows himself able to talk pointedly about talking. In another context, Mr Bingley's careless and hasty style of letter-writing becomes the subject of alert criticism by the company assembled at Netherfield. 'My ideas flow so rapidly that I have not time to express them', he admits humbly. Darcy proceeds to classify Bingley's 'appearance of humility' as 'an indirect boast'; and with a sort of stately playfulness he elaborates in general terms, 'The power of doing any thing with quickness is always much prized by the possessor, and often without any attention to the imperfection of the performance' (48–9). He sounds rather like that ironic narrator, who is able to deliver the 'truth universally acknowledged' with smiling solemnity (3). This ability to discuss other people's language, and to use language himself with wit and measured deliberation, is one thing that marks Darcy out from the beginning as a man of intelligence, and a fit mate for Elizabeth.

Mr Collins piques himself on his critical powers, and brings them to bear on his own verbal practices. He exerts his creative powers in thinking up 'little delicate compliments which are always acceptable to ladies', and even develops an aesthetic for 'the talent of flattering with delicacy' (67–8). Even Mrs Bennet can deliver critical precepts with the confidence of a professional. She declares Sir William Lucas to be 'so much the man of fashion! . . . He has always something to say to every body. – *That* is my idea of good breeding' – with pointed reference to Darcy's proud taciturnity (44).

Skill in expression *matters*, and not merely the content of what is said. Darcy's first proposal, we know, would have been refused in any case, because Elizabeth has her reasons (however misguided) for disliking him; but the *style* of his proposal is a major factor in Elizabeth's reception of it. 'The mode of your declaration', she tells him hotly, has determined the angry mode of her rejection (192). And when her other reasons for refusing him are all done away with, the mode, the form of the expression, must still be changed if Darcy is to win her.

As in the other novels, in *Pride and Prejudice* speech is action. The great set-piece battle between Elizabeth and Lady Catherine is as exciting a piece of heroism and adventure as a blow-by-blow description of a duel in chivalric romance. Elizabeth plays St George to Lady Catherine's dragon;[2] and her magic weapon is her nimble dexterity in language in the face of Lady Catherine's massive weight of authority.

> 'Miss Bennet, do you know who I am? [rumbles Lady Catherine]. I have not been accustomed to such language as this. I am almost the nearest relation he has in the world, and am entitled to know all his dearest concerns.'
> 'But you are not entitled to know *mine*' [Elizabeth neatly parries]. (354)

So proceeds the whole exchange: Lady Catherine always using more words, heavier words, longer sentences, cumbrous claims to power, and Elizabeth as consistently dodging blows, eluding charges, and delivering her neat thrusts with the sharp lance of her wit. The battles that count in Jane Austen are verbal ones.

It matters *what* you say, *how much* you say, and *how well* you say it; and also what you *leave unsaid*. 'Frankness', like 'firmness' in *Persuasion*, is a trait which, 'like all other qualities of the mind, . . . should have its proportions and limits' (*P*, 116), and its merits are debated accordingly. We are inclined to admire Elizabeth's brave forthrightness; but when Lady Catherine boasts, 'My character has ever been celebrated for its sincerity and frankness' (353), the quality loses some of its charm. Elizabeth apologises to Darcy for her *'frankness'* in her angry refusal; but Darcy persists in admiring her propensity to speak 'frankly and openly' (367), even though he has reason to regret his own frankness in his first proposal. So the proper degree of frankness is debated to and fro, and the issue of how much of the truth should be articulated, and how much left unsaid, gets full coverage.

Reticence, or a certain niggardliness of speech, is also a failing – or a virtue – that is problematised and explored. The issue is important enough to affect the structural scheme of the novel, for to a large extent [Elizabeth's suitors are aligned and compared on the basis of their speech habits.] Mr Collins talks too much, Mr Darcy too little. Mr Collins's vocation is [praise,] and he never misses an occasion for 'testifying his respect' (101); Darcy is inclined [to find fault.] Of Bingley and Darcy we hear, 'The manner in which they spoke of the Meryton assembly was sufficiently characteristic. Bingley had never met with pleasanter people or prettier girls in his life; . . . Darcy, on the contrary, had seen a collection of people in whom there was little beauty and no fashion' (16). If we add Wickham to Elizabeth's list of potential husbands, the contrasts are just as pointed. [Wickham is a facile and plausible talker:] on a first meeting with Elizabeth he gives her, she says, a 'history of himself', with 'names, facts, every thing mentioned without ceremony' (86); while Darcy is constantly giving [offence by his taciturnity.]

Of course it is also the case that Wickham lies, while Darcy tells the truth; and I will return soon to the varying relation of characters' words to reality – a relation which is an essential constituent of their identity. But for a moment I want to talk about a characteristic of the characters' verbal practice that is particular to *Pride and Prejudice.* [In this novel language as used by several of the characters almost constitutes a realm of its own, a free-floating entity that has severed its expected connections with fact and the material base.]

Language has many uses, but we like to think that [its basic function in society is to communicate reality.] We hope for a recognizable relation between words and their referents, between the signifier and the thing signified. In an ideal performance of this function, if such a condition were possible, language itself, or at least our consciousness of it, would disappear: it would be like a clear pane of glass through which the reality beyond is clearly visible. Needless to say, language as several of the characters use it in *Pride and Prejudice* is very far from being this pellucid medium of communication. More often it becomes opaque, a screen more or less decorated, inserted between the viewer and the reality that is ostensibly being communicated. For several of the characters in this 'highly verbal culture' (as Tony Tanner calls the world of *Pride and Prejudice* [15]), [language is an end in itself, almost a separate realm of existence.] In some contexts we see speech almost shouldering reality out of the way.

Here's a little instance to suggest what I mean. Miss Bingley, as usual trying to impress Darcy, objects to the proposed ball at Netherfield, and suggests,

'It would surely be much more rational if conversation instead of dancing made the order of the day.'
'Much more rational, my dear Caroline, I dare say [responds her brother], but it would not be near so much like a ball.' (55–6)

'Conversation' may be a fine and proper thing, but it is not dancing, and can't be made to replace it. And yet speech, in many contexts in this novel, often aspires to displace other forms of reality. For Mr Collins, particularly, language will do instead of the real thing. He has a Walter-Shandean propensity to locate reality in the word rather than its referent. He cares not a whit if there is any truth behind the elegant compliments he invents: they are merely a form of words, verbal flourishes for their own sake. Not only is he a compulsive talker and writer, but he has a strong (if misguided) sense of the different modes of verbal structures and of their conventions, and he performs each – the compliment, the apology, the letter of condolence – as though it were an exercise in rhetoric. Hence his speeches and letters function as unconscious parodies of whatever mode he is operating in. His promised letter of thanks after staying at Longbourn is so consciously and premeditatedly a performance[3] that a 'Collins', as the Oxford Dictionary informs us, is the name for a thank-you letter. When it comes to a more demanding genre, the proposal of marriage, he shows a developed sense of form and precedent: 'He set about it in a very orderly manner, with all the observances which he supposed a regular part of the business' (104). His speech constantly draws attention to its status as language, becoming as it were its own subject: Here are some of the phrases he pads it with: 'the purport of my discourse . . . it will be advisable for me to state . . . I ought to have mentioned earlier . . . allow me, by the way, to observe . . . thus much for . . . nothing remains for me but to assure you . . . on that head, therefore, I shall be uniformly silent.' In this highly self-referential rhetorical exercise of a proposal of marriage, he proceeds according to a mental checklist, punctually enumerating his 'reasons for marrying . . . first . . . secondly . . . and thirdly', dealing with the financial arrangements, and congratulating himself on arriving at the end of the list: 'And now nothing remains for me but to assure you in the most animated language of the violence of my affection' (105–6). The affection is about as violent as the language is animated. We know, of course, that the violence of his affection is a

purely verbal entity, and refers to no actual emotion. Moreover, he
serenely assumes that other people also use language in the same
way, as a sort of decorative padding. Elizabeth's spirited and emphatic refusal must be 'merely words of course' (108).

Merely words of course. This is a phrase I'll be returning to.
There is no comma, for the 'words of course' come as a unit, suggesting that the words carry on as of their own momentum. Collins
sees no reality beyond Elizabeth's verbal refusal. For him it is simply part of that separate world of words where he is quite used to
residing, a world where words may be ornamental and pleasurable,
but where they have been divested of most of their obligation of
expressing meaning.

Though Mr Collins is the character who most obviously separ-
ates words from their referents, he is not the only one. Mrs Bennet,
another compulsive talker, similarly produces language as a kind
of emotional noise, the tone of which may be expressive, but the
statements merely unfounded and self-cancelling. Characteristically
she contradicts herself. Angry with Elizabeth for refusing Mr Collins,
she scolds, 'I told you in the library, you know, that I should never
speak to you again, and you will find me as good as my word'
(113). She keeps asserting what she simultaneously denies, saying
and unsaying; full of sound and fury, signifying nothing.

Mr Bennet is very different from his wife in level of intelligence
and powers of articulation; but not so different as we might expect
in commitment to reality or to seeing things, in Arnold's phrase, 'as
in themselves they really are': in these respects he is defective as
she is, though not as much so. Having been once severely disappointed by life, Mr Bennet has retreated from it. Just as he retires
from his family and visitors to the secluded safety of his library, so
he withdraws from full human engagement to some cerebral com-
partment of the mind where he can reconstruct the personnel of his
family and his society as mere figures of fiction that prance about
for his amusement. He saves himself from being exasperated by his
wife at the price of reducing her from human being to mere figment;
and so with the other troublesome figures in his life, his silly daughters and importunate sons-in-law. They are most important to him
as they entertain him: they become in effect only characters in a
book which he may choose to close at any time. When he jokes
about Jane as 'crossed in love', and suggests to Elizabeth that
Wickham 'would jilt you creditably' (137–8), it is hard not to accuse
him of a withering aestheticism.

Though Mr Bennet is not a good role-model for fathers, he is an excellent one for readers. Because he has opted out of life, treating it as a mere performance, he has become a critic and a connoisseur; he appreciates the surrounding people as 'characters', mere verbal constructs, and he teaches *us* how to appreciate them too. Mr Collins would not be the delightful character that he becomes for us, but for our learning from Mr Bennet how to distance ourselves and so to savour his 'follies and nonsense'. After all, *we* don't have to experience his treading on our toes on the dance floor, as Elizabeth does, or sharing our house and bed, as Charlotte does. We can shut Mr Collins up merely by closing the book; and so can Mr Bennet by retreating to his library. Mr Bennet, in fact, stands on the boundary between two worlds: he ably mediates, as critic and commentator, between us the readers and Jane Austen's created world, and he does much to make us savour and appreciate characters distanced, fictionalised, and artistically complete. But he can do so only because of his tendency to reduce his wife, his daughters, and their chosen partners to mere fictional entities, mere bundles of words in a script. That's fine in a reader; not so fine in a husband or a father.

Other characters use language to attain different kinds of power over reality. Wickham simply lies, giving a false version of reality for his own gain – a verbal activity familiar enough. He is skilful at this, using his good looks and plausible manner to reinforce false claims, and deploying his verbal powers, as Lady Susan does in another of Jane Austen's works, 'to make Black appear White' (*MW*, 251). But to an attentive ear his claims, like Mrs Bennet's, also announce themselves as false. 'Till I can forget [Mr Darcy's] father, I can never expose *him*,' he declares, while in the very act of doing what he says he never will do (80).

Lady Catherine uses language – or at least aspires to do so – as a determinant of reality. As a dictator she strives for a causal relation between her edicts and the shape of the world. We are told that 'Man proposes, God disposes'; but Lady Catherine does a fair amount of disposing too. 'Let me be rightly understood', she says (354), in the same third-person imperative voice in which God said 'Let there be light' (and there was light). Among her tenantry, we hear, 'whenever any of the cottagers were disposed to be quarrelsome, discontented or too poor, [Lady Catherine] sallied forth into the village to settle their differences, silence their complaints, and scold them into harmony and plenty' (169). At the end of a dinner party at Rosings, her guests 'gathered round the fire to hear Lady

Catherine determine what weather they were to have on the mor-
row' (166).

In this world in which so many characters make a separate world
of language, and seek, in some senses, to displace the real world
with it, where do Elizabeth and Darcy stand? Are they too engaged
in separating words from their referents, and dwelling in a verbal
realm which tends to displace the reality it is supposed to express?

When Mr Collins assumes that Elizabeth, instead of actually refusing him, is employing 'merely words of course,' she insists, in
understandable exasperation, that she is 'a rational creature speaking the truth from her heart' (109). This sounds hopeful; and indeed
her wonderfully direct and forthright language often, as in this
scene, cuts through the verbal clutter to some valuable and essential
truth.

In a society so formal, with rules of decorum so strict that social
intercourse must inevitably be conducted in elaborate flourishes
and at some distance, Elizabeth nevertheless manages to establish
a kind of meeting of minds and a direct intimacy seldom attainable
even in our relaxed and casual times. At Netherfield, for instance,
where she is staying as an uninvited outsider, she is able to discuss
Bingley's character traits with him in such a way as to engage and
delight him. 'I understand you perfectly', she claims playfully (42).
Such analysis, like a horoscope or a psychiatrist's assessment, is
irresistible, even if its accuracy is questionable. As a recognised
'studier of character', Elizabeth immediately gains a kind of licence
in direct and personal commentary that gives her, as it were, advanced placement in intimacy. She can pass the screen of polite
verbal ceremonies, and achieve a remarkably free and direct communication with others about themselves. Here the words do their
full work, and more, in direct and frank representation. Elizabeth
and Bingley have already established the close and personal relation that will be formalised later, when he becomes her brother-in-
law. Presently we see the same process at work with Darcy.

During Elizabeth's stay at Netherfield we witness Miss Bingley's
strenuous attempt to establish intimacy with Darcy. She butters
him up in manifold ways, conducting a running battery on his
attention. She attempts banter, and extracts from him what she
calls a 'shocking' witticism. 'How shall we punish him for such
a speech?' she appeals to Elizabeth. Attempting banter, she dis-
ingenuously asks Elizabeth for advice on how to 'punish' Darcy for
a witticism:

'Nothing so easy, if you have but the inclination,' said Elizabeth. 'We can all plague and punish one another. Teaze him – laugh at him. – Intimate as you are, you must know how it is to be done.'
'But upon my honour I do *not*. I do assure you that my intimacy has not yet taught me *that*. Teaze calmness of temper and presence of mind! . . .'
'Mr. Darcy is not to be laughed at!' cried Elizabeth. 'That is an uncommon advantage, and uncommon I hope it will continue, for it would be a great loss to *me* to have many such acquaintance. I dearly love a laugh.' (57)

Poor Miss Bingley! In trying to recommend herself by empty flattery, she has actually turned the spotlight on her rival's more piquant and probing criticism. The talk turns first on Elizabeth's almost professional delight in 'follies and nonsense, whims and inconsistencies' (57), and then on Darcy's pride, and whether it is under good regulation. Presently she and Darcy are diagnosing each other's particular 'natural defect', and succeeding in using language as a fine instrument with which to explore each other's minds and characters. Miss Bingley's long-established intimacy becomes as nothing in comparison with the considered self-revelation and probing criticism of one another that Elizabeth and Darcy can achieve on the spot, with language refreshingly precise and direct.

But although Elizabeth is able to cut through empty forms to achieve and provoke a remarkable degree of personal expressiveness and discovery, she is her father's daughter too; and not all her verbal sallies would pass a test requiring a direct relation between language and reality. If she acquires a quasi-professional status as 'studier of character', still in the major cases of Darcy and Wickham we know she makes egregious errors. Wickham is simply a skilful deceiver, and she is fooled in spite of herself. But in the case of her judgement of Darcy there is an element of wilful misreading that smacks of her father's propensity to reduce human beings to mere literary figments of themselves. 'I meant to be uncommonly clever in taking so decided a dislike to him, without any reason [she admits later]. It is such a spur to one's genius, such an opening for wit to have a dislike of that kind' (225–6). Like her father, she has used a human being merely as an occasion to say something witty.

Language is a mode that Elizabeth is good at, and takes delight in for its own sake. But she uses it for many other purposes than merely to speak the truth from her heart, or merely to represent reality. Even in the scene with Collins, when we delight in her direct and lucid expression as a contrast to his verbiage, the accuracy of her description of herself is ironically called into question. 'I am not one of those young ladies [she insists] . . . who are so daring as to risk their happiness on the chance of being asked a second time' (107); but of course in the case of Darcy's proposal she does just that.

Language is both more and less than a means for a rational creature to speak the truth from her heart. For Elizabeth it is a medium for play and wit as much as for direct communication; at its best, it is an art form, an enlargement of consciousness, and a means of discovery. But she too, like Collins and her father, sometimes constructs a separate world out of language, and one that bears little relation to her actual world. She employs language very ably and very self-consciously, being critically alert about other people's style in language and awake to her own verbal operations. She too is a parodist – a more conscious one than Collins – of modes of speech, and she has a developed sense of the rules and conventions that belong to each. Like Henry Tilney, another expert on language, she parodies ballroom conversation:

'It is *your* turn to say something now, Mr. Darcy. – *I* talked about the dance, and *you* ought to make some kind of remark on the size of the room, or the number of couples.'

He smiled, and assured her that whatever she wished him to say should be said.

'Very well. – That reply will do for the present. – Perhaps by and bye I may observe that private balls are much pleasanter than public ones. – But *now* we may be silent.' (91)

To project a piece of colourless small-talk into the future, to announce you will say this boring thing 'by and bye', is to turn the small-talk into witty conversation. And whatever we think of the way such people as Collins make talk the subject of talking, we are inclined to be charmed, as Darcy is, when Elizabeth does it. For of course, our readiness to enjoy such a separate verbal world has a great deal to do with the quality of the product. Elizabeth uses language creatively, and she is apt to stray from the strict path of truth in the process – as in her 'prejudice' against Darcy, so prominent in plot and theme, which as we have seen is a largely verbal matter.

Elizabeth in her language is charming but unreliable; and Darcy steadily keeps track of her deviations from fact. 'I have had the pleasure of your acquaintance long enough to know, that you find great enjoyment in occasionally professing opinions which in fact are not your own', he tells her at Rosings (174). And he early diagnoses her particular defect as a propensity 'wilfully to misunderstand' people (58) – not bad, as an assessment of Elizabeth's prejudice against himself.

In his own verbal practice, Darcy refuses to separate the verbal from the real: he is the character whose language most nearly expresses the truth. His letter is a prolonged and careful attempt at the exact expression of things as they are. He tries, at least, to be cool and objective, though he realises later that 'it was written in a dreadful bitterness of spirit' (368). His rather literal and visibly principled language stands as a contrast and foil to Elizabeth's playful inventiveness. 'Disguise of every sort is my abhorrence', he announces (192). But there is moderation in all things; and on the occasion of his first proposal Darcy serves up all together too strong a dose of truth. His problem through much of the novel was his taciturnity, his saying too little. Now all at once he says a good deal too much.

But just as Darcy has been a perceptive commentator on Elizabeth's sayings, Elizabeth provides a brilliant and finely nuanced commentary on Darcy's. At the piano at Rosings, she has playfully recounted to Colonel Fitzwilliam Darcy's unsocial behaviour at the Meryton assembly. They are talking about talking again.

'I certainly have not the talent which some people possess,' said Darcy, 'of conversing easily with those I have never seen before. I cannot catch their tone of conversation, or appear interested in their concerns, as I often see done.'

Elizabeth, with a fine artist's instinct, moves into an appropriate analogy:

'My fingers,' said Elizabeth, 'do not move over this instrument in the masterly manner which I see so many women's do. They have not the same force or rapidity, and do not produce the same expression. But then I have always supposed it to be my own fault – because I would not take the trouble of practising. It is not that I do not believe *my* fingers as capable as any other woman's of superior execution.' (175)

Here is the point at which Elizabeth has most to teach Darcy, if he would only listen; and her language, with her finely introduced metaphor, and her courteous shift from his failings to her own, has just the right tone to convey a shortcoming and suggest its remedy, without giving offence. Gracious verbal exchange in society, she graciously lets him know, is not a trick or an innate capability (like being double-jointed, say), but a developed *skill*, like playing the piano, to be learned by constant application and practice. If only Darcy had paid attention at this point, he would have saved himself from some agony and vexation of spirit a few days later, when he proposes. But his response indicates a degree of deafness, with a touch of snobbery thrown in – the snobbery of the privileged amateur who looks down on the mere professional.

'You are perfectly right [he responds]. You have employed your time much better. No one admitted to the privilege of hearing you [play], can think any thing wanting. We neither of us perform to strangers.' (176)

Darcy should have listened![4] He has made the mistake of assuming Elizabeth is merely at linguistic play again. He fails to hear the undercurrent of seriousness in her witty analogy – and just when it most concerns him to pay attention.

Darcy has no small-talk; but when he needs to express himself he acts under strong compulsion, and the truth bursts from him into words as though by an almost physical necessity: 'In vain have I struggled. It will not do. My feelings will not be repressed. You must allow me to tell you how ardently I admire and love you' (189). So far so good. But once he has burst through the barrier of his habitual reticence, he does not know where to stop. He must keep pronouncing unpalatable truths, until, 'roused to resentment by his subsequent language, [Elizabeth] lost all compassion in anger' (189). Her playful instruction at the piano having been neglected, she now lashes out against his unseasonable explicitness with her rare but effective anger. He paid insufficient attention to the theory of gracious verbal exchange she had offered him. Now when his defective practice is laid bare, he is likely to remember the lesson all his life. 'Had you behaved in a more gentleman-like manner' is a phrase he can still quote, verbatim, months later. By then, instead of dwelling on 'the inferiority of [her] connections' (192), he can say – and mean – 'Much as I respect [your family], I believe, I thought only of *you*' (366). She has taught him to extend his communication, and to mend his language. And through him she has learned to regard truth as well as style in her pronouncements.

To sum up, then. Elizabeth and Darcy are placed among a set of characters who use and abuse language in vivid ways, making it the vehicle not only of pointed criticism and conscientious communication, but of false claims, self-contradiction, empty aspiration, pompous declaration and (as Elizabeth would put it) 'follies and nonsense' (57). In this highly formal and formidably verbal culture, language often becomes inflated, and in the mouths of Mr Collins and others it tends to displace reality rather than to express it. Elizabeth is subject to this kind of hubris, but at the same time, by her creative and liberated use of language, on her lips it becomes an instrument to discover and extend truth and enlarge consciousness. Tony Tanner has summarised *Pride and Prejudice* as 'a novel in which the most important events are the fact that a man changes his manners and a young woman changes her mind' (Introduction, 7). These changes are not accidental: each effects the change in the other, and through their powers in language. Darcy, by the integrity of his word and deed, acts as a corrective to Elizabeth's linguistic excesses at the same time that he delights in them and learns from them. He is the 'chapter of sense' that Jane Austen said the novel needed (*L*, 299). Elizabeth, by her precept and her reproof, makes him change his manners along with his verbal practices. She, bless her, acts as her author's assistant in providing the 'light, bright, and sparkling'.

Notes

1. I have elaborated on these claims in 'The Secret Languages of *Emma*'.
2. Here and elsewhere in this paper I use some material (with permission of the editor) from my paper, 'Talking about Talking', in the collection edited by Marcia McClintock Folsom, pp. 167–73.
3. Howard S. Babb focuses on 'performance' as 'the word that lies at the heart of the novel's meaning'. Tony Tanner, in his introduction

to *Pride and Prejudice* and in his book, also focuses on 'performance' in exploring the characters' propensities in verbal representations.

4. In his otherwise sensitive and revealing commentary on this passage, Babb overlooks Darcy's failure to profit by the advice Elizabeth is giving him at this point (140–1). Babb's reading is avowedly an apologetic for Darcy, intended to exonerate him from the hostile readings of other critics (114).

8

Words 'Half-Dethroned': Jane Austen's Art of the Unspoken

Inger Sigrun Thomsen

It has become commonplace to attribute to Jane Austen a conservative attitude towards words, reminiscent of her much-admired mentor, Dr Johnson, who, after all, spent much of his time stabilising, standardising, protecting the English language by writing and revising his famous dictionary. Mary Lascelles, for example, emphasises Austen's passion for 'proper words in proper places' (87); Jean Hagstrum, her 'rational and categorizing mind' (268); and C. S. Lewis, the 'hardness – at least the firmness – of Jane Austen's thought.' Lewis continues:

> The great abstract nouns of the classical English moralists are unblushingly and uncompromisingly used [by Austen]. . . . These are the concepts by which Jane Austen grasps the world. . . . All is hard, clear, definable; by some modern standards, even naïvely so. (28)

Following Lewis's lead, many of the most insightful Austen scholars have focused on Austen's use of these 'key words' (cf. Phillips, 13), abstract nouns that provide a stable key to unlock her irony and reveal the truth about the characters in her novels. Norman Page, too, comments on the Augustan 'firmness and certainty' with which she uses the same abstract nouns 'as labels which correspond to realities that can be detected by observation and reflection' (84–5). In other words, the idea is that once one really has clearly defined what Austen means by words such as 'propriety', 'delicacy', 'amiability', 'constancy', and 'candour', one can proceed to understand how each character uses these words and to illuminate important moral themes. Although it is certain that there *is*

such a group of important words – primarily the names of virtues
– it remains to be seen whether the words are quite as 'hard, clear,
definable' as most of these critics claim.

I will argue that by understanding the precise form of her distrust of words and its relation to the Cult of Sensibility's moral
aesthetic, we can see that Austen not only profoundly distrusted
words, but that she actually sought to instil a similar distrust in
her readers. Let us begin by looking at the critical attitude towards language that tends to emerge from Austen's letters and
minor fiction. In her letters, Austen shows herself keenly aware of
small imprecisions in logic. For example, she corrects herself mid-
sentence in one letter: 'I called yesterday morning (ought it not in
strict propriety to be termed yester-morning?)' (*L*, 142). But Austen's
acumen is not limited to pedantic corrections of the redundancies
in the English language. She is keenly aware of *ridiculous* language,
especially in people who use language to affect airs of fashion. One
example occurs when she warns an aspiring novelist (her niece
Anna) against what Austen calls 'novel slang':

> Devereux Forester's being ruined by his Vanity is extremely good;
> but I wish you would not let him plunge into a 'vortex of Dissi-
> pation'. I do not object to the Thing, but I cannot bear the expres-
> sion; – it is such thorough novel slang – and so old, that I dare
> say Adam met with it in the first novel he opened. (*L*, 404)

It is, of course, only a hop, skip and a jump from keen and aptly-
worded criticism to parody. And in Sir Edward Denham of *Sanditon*,
who has read 'more sentimental novels than agreed with him', we
see 'novel slang' embodied. When Charlotte asks him to describe
the sort of novel he likes, he responds lavishly (and incoherently):

> 'Most willingly, Fair Questioner. – The Novels which I approve
> are such as display Human Nature with Grandeur – such as shew
> her in the Sublimities of intense Feeling – such as exhibit the
> progress of strong Passion from the first Germ of incipient Sus-
> ceptibility to the utmost energies of Reason half-dethroned, –
> where we see the strong spark of Woman's Captivations elicit
> such Fire in the Soul of Man as leads him . . . to hazard all, dare
> all, acheive all, to obtain her. . . . They hold forth the most splen-
> did Portraitures of high Conceptions, Unbounded Views, illimit-
> able Ardour, indomptible Decision . . . our Hearts are Paralized.'
> (*MW*, 403–4)

The moralist in Jane Austen does not allow her to present such parodies of 'Reason half-dethroned' unbalanced by other, corrective examples. The heroines who are most likely to overindulge in a love of clever words at the expense of sense have partners in the novels who correct and challenge their speech: Elizabeth has Darcy, Marianne has Elinor, Catherine has Henry Tilney, and Emma has Mr Knightley. Each functions as a frame to control the excesses of the (linguistically as well as otherwise) immature counterpart. Austen often illuminates the moral flaws of her characters through their indiscriminate or imprecise word choice – an imprecision recognisable to the careful ears of future husbands such as Henry Tilney and Mr Knightley as well as to the discriminating reader. Austen's use of 'imprecise' speech is not merely to parody fools; she shows that a great range of speakers of varying mental capacities all fall prey to mis-speaking and mis-conceiving.[1]

In order to get a sense of how the interrelation between linguistic and moral discrimination fits into Austen's *oeuvre*, let us step back a moment and take a quick survey of the six major novels. Although various critics have tried to divide them up into categories, the groupings have traditionally not been as varied as the justifications for the groupings. Marilyn Butler in *Jane Austen and the War of Ideas* describes the main division among the novels as between 'the Heroine who is Right' and 'the Heroine who is Wrong' (166): referring to Elinor of *Sense and Sensibility*, Fanny of *Mansfield Park*, and Anne of *Persuasion* on the one hand, and Catherine of *Northanger Abbey*, Elizabeth of *Pride and Prejudice*, and Emma on the other. This division of the novels is important, but there may be complementary ways of describing it. Another way to categorise the difference is between external and internal obstacles to the heroines' enlightenment: the Heroines who are Right face external obstacles and the Heroines who are Wrong face internal ones. Susan Morgan uses other terms to describe the same division: in the 'novels of crisis' the heroines face mortification and humiliation in order to grow, and in the 'novels of passage' the heroines do not need humiliation and crisis in order to grow.

It so happens that the linguistic atmosphere of the six novels also breaks down neatly into the same two categories; for surely the atmospheres of *Sense and Sensibility*, *Mansfield Park*, and *Persuasion* are much darker and quieter than the lighter and more verbal *Northanger Abbey*, *Pride and Prejudice*, and *Emma*. If we combine this with Butler's scheme, we see that the Heroines who are Right are also Quiet, and the Heroines who are Wrong are Loquacious. Why is it that precisely in the three novels where the heroines are both right and quiet, talk is so terribly *treacherous*, and the heroes are generally silent; whereas, in the novels where the heroines are wrong, the battles are verbal, the heroines love to speak, and those who speak best emerge triumphant? In fact, it is worth noticing that the heroines who speak 'best' of all (Emma and Elizabeth) are those who have most to learn. Could there be some connection between a heroine's ability (and willingness) to speak and the location of the obstacles she encounters? Could it be that it is her own fondness for and quickness with speech that eventually limits her morally and intellectually? If so, then Austen appears to agree with the Cult of Sensibility's general argument that words (like other 'artificial' by-products of cold, disengaged reason) hamper emotional development.

I would suggest, then, that we can recast this division among the novels as the division between Knowing and Speaking. Elinor, Fanny and Anne are united by the fact that they initially *know* but do not (or cannot) *speak*, while Catherine, Elizabeth, and Emma initially *speak* but do not *know*. This would seem to imply an inherent tension in Austen between speaking and knowing, between words and knowledge. Extremely voluble and garrulous characters in Jane Austen's novels are seldom, if ever, the ones who feel most deeply. To some degree then, as we have seen, Austen believes in the tension between words and emotions, as well as between words and knowledge.

In *Mansfield Park*, we detect a similar tension between speaking and feeling. James Thompson counts twenty-four specific passages in this novel in which the narrator tells us of feelings that are 'indescribable', 'unspeakable', or 'indefinable' (Thompson, 85). Of Fanny, we learn that we are not to interpret silence as lack of feeling – quite the contrary: 'Had she ever given way to bursts of delight, it must have been then, for she was delighted, but her happiness was of a quiet, deep, heart-swelling sort; and though never a great talker, she was always more inclined to silence when feeling most strongly' (369). And it is only in Henry Crawford's rare moment of silence that we detect his capacity to feel: '[Fanny's] heart was softened for a while towards him – because he really seemed to feel. – Quite unlike his usual self, he scarcely said any thing' (365).[2] This tension between words and feeling is, as I have said, not merely limited to the quieter half of the novels. In *Emma*, when Mr Knightley is about to propose to Emma, not only do we hear that Emma 'could really say nothing', but Mr Knightley also says: 'I cannot make speeches, Emma. . . . If I loved you less, I might be able to talk about it more' (430). Even Elizabeth Bennet 'was too much embarrassed to say a word' at the crucial moment and finally 'force[s] herself to speak' (*PP*, 366).

Some abuses of language may give us a clue to why Austen views it as particularly dangerous – especially to knowledge and feeling. Let us consider for a moment Mr Collins from *Pride and Prejudice* and Mr and Mrs John Dashwood from *Sense and Sensibility*. As Juliet McMaster points out in the preceding essay, Mr Collins' lasting fascination with polite forms of address (notably the apology and the thank-you) is particularly vicious in that it allows him to substitute form or expression for substance. Who needs virtue if you have mastered the forms of virtuous rhetoric? This is one prevalent danger of words in general: they give the speaker the sensation of having actually accomplished what he has, in fact, only named.[3] (All the world becomes a performative utterance.) This is another moral danger in too much attachment to Tristram's 'tall, opake words' (Sterne, 148). A much more pernicious example of the same linguistic temptation is exemplified by the John Dashwoods in the opening chapters of *Sense and Sensibility*, where in successive stages, they convince themselves through the manipulation of their father's words on his death-bed, and with profuse self-congratulation, that they really have satisfied their promise to do 'everything in [their] power to make [his surviving family] comfortable' (5).

Austen was aware from a very early age of the way words can be manipulated and made to supplant reality. It is not only the Mr Collinses of the world who speak much of virtue yet possess very little. Nor is it only the artful Lady Susans whose 'happy command of Language' can make 'Black appear White' (*MW*, 251). She shows even in her earliest writings that she is aware of the dangers involved in speaking of or in naming virtues. A look at Chapter One of 'Jack and Alice' (written in her early teens) will help us see how she does this:

> Miss Simpson was pleasing in her person, in her Manners & in her Disposition; an unbounded ambition was her only fault. Her second sister Sukey was Envious, Spitefull & Malicious. Her person was short, fat & disagreeable. Cecilia (the youngest) was perfectly handsome but too affected to be pleasing.

In Lady Williams every virtue met. She was a widow with a handsome Jointure & the remains of a very handsome face. Tho' Benevolent & Candid, she was Generous & sincere; Tho' Pious & Good, she was Religious & amiable, & Tho' Elegant & Agreable, she was Polished & Entertaining.

The Johnsons were a family of Love, & though a little addicted to the Bottle & the Dice, had many good Qualities. (*MW*, 12–13)

What does it *mean* to say that Lady Williams was Generous tho' Benevolent, Sincere tho' Candid, Religious tho' Pious, Amiable tho' Good, Polished tho' Elegant, and Entertaining tho' Agreable? Austen is playing with pairs of words, names of virtues, often taken as synonymous (generous and benevolent, sincere and candid, religious and pious, etc.), and is grammatically ('tho") distinguishing between them; however, the result is ludicrously nonsensical and pokes fun at attempts to distinguish between these words. I am not implying that Austen thinks it is impossible to come to understand the differences between such words, but instead that this passage displays a young girl's scepticism about most people's attempts to *define* virtue. It shows an extremely precocious understanding of the association between precise definition and vanity. The general difficulty of using words to speak about virtue – that is, the tendency for words to obscure and replace the virtues themselves – has its locus in human nature; it is not the occasional problem of fools.

On the other hand, we have also seen that Austen uses *imprecision* of speech as a way of characterising moral weakness, immaturity, and lack of discrimination. Mrs Dashwood's conflation of love and esteem will serve as an example:

'It is enough,' said she; 'to say that he is unlike Fanny is enough. It implies everything amiable. I love him already.'

'I think you will like him . . . when you know more of him.'

'Like him!' replied her mother with a smile. 'I can feel no sentiment of approbation inferior to love.'

'You may esteem him.'

'I have never yet known what it was to separate esteem and love.' (*SS*, 16)

Mrs Dashwood's inability to discriminate between the meanings of these words – and indeed her *pride* at her inability – displays her inability to make moral distinctions as well. To misspeak, in these instances, is to misconceive. However, it does not mean that the difficult process of refining meaning, defining virtue, of limiting misconception, ever ends.

It is in this connection that Stuart Tave analyses the following passage from *Persuasion*: 'It was agitation, pain, pleasure, *a something between* delight and misery' (*P*, 175; my emphasis):

> The ambiguities of 'a something between' can be, in Jane Austen, treacherous ground, Mary Crawford's or Emma Woodhouse's evasion of responsible definition; Anne never seeks those moments of ambiguity and never avoids them, but bears them all as she must and until they can be brought to clarity. (Tave, 276)

'A something between' is neither to be relished nor to be feared, as Tave suggests; however, in this instance, true to the tenets of Sensibility, the sheer indefinability of the sentiment only *adds* to its poignancy. In the same way, we sense the deepest emotion in Elizabeth Bennet at the very times when her feelings escape definition: 'Her feelings . . . were scarcely to be *defined*' or 'could not be exactly *defined*' (*PP*, 204, 266, my emphasis). Correspondingly, it is Mary Bennet's empty pedantic assurance in her ability to define 'vanity' and 'pride,' which in another context displays moral weakness. It is truly 'treacherous' to relish obscurity for its own sake, as Emma is wont, on occasion, to do; however, an equally, if not even more pervasive danger, is confidence in the *ability* to define – or rather to bring the process of definition to a close.[4]

Such a thought was hardly original to Jane Austen. Not only did the general moral aesthetic of Sensibility attack the uses of language which claim to achieve complete order and to communicate methodically and rationally, so also did several prominent philosophers, such as Burke, Hume, and Smith.[5]

> I have no great opinion of a definition, the celebrated remedy for the cure of this disorder. For when we define, we seem in danger of circumscribing nature within the bounds of our own notions, which we often take up by hazard, or embrace on trust, or form out of a limited and partial consideration of the object before us, instead of extending our ideas to take in all that nature comprehends, according to her manner of combining. (Burke, 12)

'To define', as Tristram Shandy says, 'is to distrust' (Sterne, 162); it is also to indulge in a false sense of power or authority.

Austen's art is an art that teaches the value of discrimination rather than definition: 'the awareness of fine distinctions, or the importance of seeing beyond rules and formulas' (Cox, 79–80). Unlike Samuel Richardson, who collected all the important 'maxims' uttered by his heroines and published them in 'one volume small enough to fit the pockets of all such as "were desirous of repeatedly inculcating [them] on their own minds, and the minds of others"' (Brissenden, 100), Austen had a different sense of education, as well as less faith in conduct books and clear, crisp, 'portable' rules. Her purpose was perhaps closer to that of John Locke, who wrote: 'I shall imagine I have done some Service to Truth, Peace, and Learning, if, by any enlargement on this Subject [Words], I can make Men reflect on their own Use of Language' (438).

In her novels, then, Austen develops a technique to attack the unthinking reliance upon words and instil in the reader a healthy distrust of words by showing the difficulty of *naming* virtues. Austen shows throughout her life that she is deeply interested in the relation between the name of a virtue and the virtue itself. No reader can emerge from her novels without sensing the importance of words like 'propriety', 'delicacy', 'amiability' and 'constancy' in her idiolect – that is, the 'key words'. However, she consistently shows 'false' examples as well as 'true' examples of each virtue within her novels, thereby encouraging the reader to interpret *beyond* the words. These treacherous words come not only from the mouths of foolish characters, but often from the 'unreliable' narrator, making distinction between them very difficult:

> We must never trust the narrator in Jane Austen's novels, no matter how Johnsonian her moral commentaries may sound, for . . . [she] fragments her narrative point of view precisely because the central consciousness behind her novels is one which sees reality as multifaceted. (Nardin, 9)

This has a dramatic effect upon the education of the reader of her novels. Since readers cannot take away any pat expression to define (and remember) these terms, they must use their perceptive abilities constantly to recognise and define the virtue *anew* in differing circumstances. It is a technique which Aristotle used for very similar purposes in the *Nicomachean Ethics*.

Nameless virtues encourage this nimble ethical manoeuvring by avoiding the false sense of security that a nominalisation, or a fixed form, gives. The task of the reader is not completed, for example, when the reader has identified 'propriety' or 'delicacy' as a virtue or a 'key word': the point is that the task *never* ends. Words, like virtue itself, need to be defined anew in every context. Austen often juxtaposes two abstract nouns for a similar effect: the most obvious example of this is her use of double nouns in the titles *Sense and Sensibility* and *Pride and Prejudice*. The reader must work alongside the characters to find a mean, a form of virtue that is appropriate to the context. The world she creates is, as Ann Molan writes, 'not reducible to terms of simple alternatives, especially simple moral alternatives'; readers cannot 'fix on or derive any "system" of values' (150–5). Thus, Austen constructs her novels to train readers to rethink names, words, and categories.

Rather than simultaneously using conservative word-choice and adventurous syntax, Austen's use of words is far more profound and involved. To those who, like Norman Page (187), wonder why Austen engaged in 'burlesque and mockery' in her letters and juvenilia and in a Johnsonian pursuit of precise and stable definition in her novels, the answer is, in a way, quite simple: she did not. Austen's burlesque was not limited to her letters and juvenilia: it appears in many of her novels (certainly in her earliest, *Northanger Abbey*, as well as in her last, *Sanditon*), and her 'Johnsonian' pursuit of clear definition also never ends. And that is precisely the point. Her earlier burlesque and mockery of abuses of language are less subtle but not different in substance from her later, gentle provocations to attempt (and fail) at definition: What really distinguishes Sense from Sensibility? Is Candour a virtue or a vice? When is Propriety beneficial and when is it destructive? Austen uses the complexity of these three questions to shape the central themes of *Sense and Sensibility*, *Pride and Prejudice*, and *Mansfield Park*, respectively.

Austen's answer to the tension between words and virtue is not silence, but rather a 'rhetoric of silence' – a language which allows for public meaning and order, but leaves gaps for private unspoken meanings as well. Throughout the Sensibility movement, perhaps stemming from the thought of Shaftesbury, there was the lingering question of whether any text could be simultaneously private and public (Marshall, 19, 60). In Jane Austen's hands these issues take a slightly different turn. Her characters, as Juliet McMaster observes, 'conduct apparently rational conversations with each other on subjects of general interest, while simultaneously their *hearts* are deeply engaged [on another subject]': for example, in *Sense and Sensibility*, when Edward arrives at Barton Cottage and Elinor believes him to be married to Lucy Steele, 'we can gather enough of the agonized state of her feelings by hearing merely that "she sat down again and talked of the weather"' (McMaster, 'Surface,' 40). This apparent understatement is another form of the narrator's rhetoric of silence, for it is really not simply understatement, but rather the attempt to sustain, simultaneously, *two discourses*, a public and a private.[6] The two are not entirely separate, however: they meet in the rare moments of true intimacy. The gap between private thought and public language, or between sentiment and self-representation, can cause both isolation and solipsism, but it is also that which allows the central opportunity for moral agency in the novels, the freedom to construe meaning. 'How were his sentiments to be read?' asks Anne Elliot (*P*, 60), and so must the reader in every novel.

Austen draws attention not only to the abuse of words by foolish and vicious characters but also to the limitations of language itself. This does not lead (as it might in another author) to relativism or despair. In Austen's fictional world, the difficulties of naming, the difficulties of judging, and the difficulties of communicating provide no excuse for not observing well, judging correctly, and trying to communicate clearly. To put this in other terms, Austen finds a positive function for Locke's dark gap between sign and meaning. She finds in this gap a way to ensure the survival of meaning itself – like Aristotle, she realises that the slipperiness or even absence of the name of a virtue does not mean it does not exist; in fact, it can be an important way of keeping it vital.

To study Austen's art of the unspoken is one way of disentangling two dominant and competing interpretations of Austen: the 'light' and the 'dark'. Austen's ambivalent attitude towards language reveals her to be neither strictly 'Johnsonian' in her faith in the possibility of precision, nor to be despondent about the possibility of meaningful communication and community.[7] The dark side of Austen is important to perceive, but that is not where Austen herself ends. For Austen, there are some cruel facts about language and human nature: that there are great gaps between things and the words we use to refer to them, between the way each of us may use the same words, and between what we name and what we know; however, these cruel facts ultimately serve a positive, social force. Not only do these gaps pose *verbal* challenges, they pose intellectual and moral challenges as well. These are gaps for the moral imagination to fill. They are the gaps which can only be filled through what John Mullan calls the 'social pursuit of meaning' – that is, through conversation. We can see, therefore, that the search for the *mot juste* is neither trivial, nor purely artistic: it lies at the very heart of Austen's ethics of conversation.

Notes

1. Two excellent examples of this technique are the 'nice' sequence in *Northanger Abbey*, 107–8, and the 'amiable' passage in *Emma*, 148–9. Emma's fault is the inverse of Catherine's; for where Catherine is too *un*discriminating, Emma is, in a sense, too much so: she cleverly arranges alibis, exceptions, elaborate plans to outdo and undo her common sense.
2. Cf. the passage where Emma goes to apologise to Miss Bates – the fact that there is no direct apology disappoints some readers; however, within the themes of the novel, it is more convincing to witness Emma's rare silence than it would be to hear her words.
3. Diderot and Voltaire use the 'noble savage' theme to achieve the same effect – to show that those who can name virtue are actually less likely to possess it.
4. For Socrates, philosophy is synonymous with the attempt to define, to answer the ever-elusive question 'what is x?', whether the x be 'justice' or 'virtue' or 'piety'. Definition is, for Plato, another way of formulating the philosopher's endless quest; it is endless because to succeed in the sense of finding, through words, one final definition is to cease to be mortal.
5. Cf. Hume, *An Enquiry Concerning the Principles of Morals*, 99, and Smith, *Theory of Moral Sentiments*, 312.
6. The following passage exemplifies another form of the separation of the two realms:

> 'But I thought it was right, Elinor,' said Marianne, 'to be guided wholly by the opinion of other people. I thought our judgments were given us merely to be subservient to those of our neighbours. This has always been your doctrine, I am sure.'
> 'No, Marianne, never. My doctrine has never aimed at the subjection of the understanding. All I have ever attempted to influence has been the behaviour. You must not confound my meaning.'
> (*SS*, 93–4)

7. 'Jane Austen was herself aware of the double vision in her art, of the fact as an ironist she would often ridicule aspects of institutions or values, to which as a moralist she gave her basic approval. But she did not find these two modes of viewing the world difficult to reconcile' (Nardin, 2).

Part III
What Moves Flexibly

1. Benjamin West: *Christ Rejected by the Jews* (1814). Reproduction courtesy of the Pennsylvania Academy of Fine Arts, Philadelphia. Gift of Mrs Sarah Harrison (the Joseph Harrison Jr, Collection).

2. 'The first representation of our Saviour which ever at all contented me' (Austen, letter of 2 September 1814). Detail from Benjamin West's *Christ Rejected by the Jews*.

3. Benjamin West: *Christ Healing the Sick* (1810). The painting hangs in the Gallery Pavilion at Pennsylvania Hospital in Philadelphia.

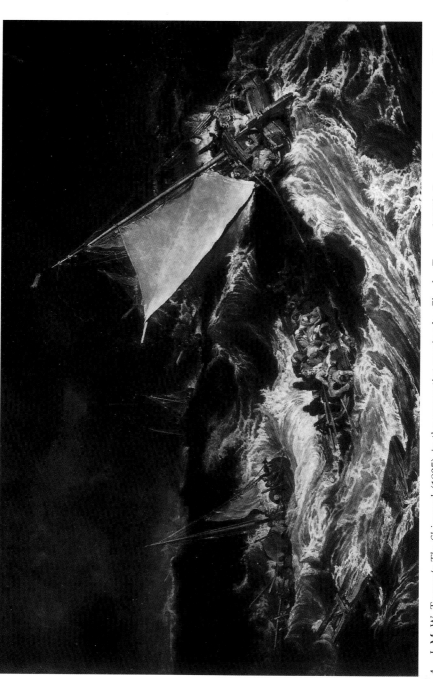

4. J. M. W. Turner's *The Shipwreck* (1805), in the mezzotint version by Charles Turner (1807). Reproduction courtesy of the

9

Prudential Lovers and Lost Heirs: *Persuasion* and the Presence of Scott

Jane Millgate

If one asks what Walter Scott and Jane Austen had to say to each other, the question fortunately does not have to be treated as entirely metaphorical – a matter of silent dialogue between the novels of the two authors – for both Austen and Scott are on record with comments about each other of a direct and explicit kind. Peter Sabor has catalogued for us the surviving references to Scott in Austen's correspondence and novels, starting his account with the famous September 1814 remark to her niece Anna about the rumoured authorship of *Waverley*:

> Walter Scott has no business to write novels, especially good ones. – It is not fair. – He has Fame and Profit enough as a Poet, and should not be taking the bread out of other people's mouths. – I do not like him, & do not mean to like Waverley if I can help it – but fear I must. (*L*, 404)

Sabor then crisply summarises the other direct allusions to Scott in Austen's works:

> In previous letters she had mentioned *The Lay of the Last Minstrel* (1805), parodied two lines from *Marmion* (1808), and compared her small family gatherings ironically with those in *The Lady of the Lake* (1810). Later she took notice of Scott's poem *The Field of Waterloo* (1815), his travel book *Paul's Letters to his Kinsfolk* (1816), and his novel *The Antiquary* (1816). . . . In Austen's novels, too, there are several allusions to Scott's poetry. Marianne Dashwood admires it; Fanny Price quotes from *The Lay of the Last Minstrel*; Captain Benwick is 'intimately acquainted' with all of Scott's

109

poems, which Anne Elliot also enjoys; and Sir Edward Denham quotes from both *Marmion* and *The Lady of the Lake*. (Sabor, 1991, 88)

The first thing that strikes one about this list is the preponderance of references to Scott's poetry over references to his fiction. It would be disingenuous to argue that Scott's choice of anonymity for his novels, as opposed to the prominence with which he proclaimed his authorship of the poems, was a significant factor in the paucity of Austen references to Scott the novelist – since Austen, like many other people, clearly regarded the identity of the Author of *Waverley* as an open secret. On the other hand, it probably was a factor that Scott had been world-famous as a poet for almost a decade prior to the appearance of *Waverley* in 1814, whereas he had published only three more fiction titles by the time of Austen's death in 1817. The suspicion nevertheless remains that Austen's relative silence about Scott's fiction may to some extent derive from that resistance to the incursions of a rival artistic power expressed in mock-serious form in her avowed determination not to like *Waverley* if she could help it.

Another significant feature of the list is the frequency with which Austen invokes Scott – even Scott the poet – for parodic or ironic purposes. And while the appearance of Fanny Price and Anne Elliot among the cast of his admirers is on the face of it reassuring – given the presence of such suspect enthusiasts as Marianne Dashwood and Captain Benwick – Fanny's and Anne's actual references to Scott turn out to constitute less than unambiguous endorsements. Fanny's quotations from *The Lay of the Last Minstrel* (Canto 2, stanzas 10, 12) during the Sotherton chapel visit, her regret at the absence of banners 'blown by the night wind of Heaven' or of signs that a 'Scottish monarch sleeps below' (*MP*, 86), belong to that bookishly romantic aspect of her sensibility that Edmund is quick to undercut with his reminder of the family chapel's recent date and private purposes. The novel's second direct allusion to the *Lay* is self-deflating, in that it involves the comic incongruity of a comparison between the powerful and somewhat sinister figure of Scott's Lady of Branksome Hall (*Lay*, I, 20) and a Fanny merely 'sore-footed and fatigued' (*MP*, 281) at the end of her first ball. And if one turns to *Persuasion*, one registers that Anne Elliot, while delighted to discover that Captain Benwick shares her admiration for Scott's poems, quickly cautions her new friend against reading 'only poetry', apparently considering some kind of health warning to be in order, at least for imbibers of Benwick's sentimentally suscepti- ble constitution. She is eager to prescribe for him a corrective and therapeutic course of 'such works of our best moralists, such collec- tions of the finest letters, such memoirs of characters of worth and suffering . . . calculated to rouse and purify the mind by the highest precepts, and the strongest examples of moral and religious endurances' (*P*, 100–1).

The evidence in respect of Austen's public response to Scott might thus be summarised as pointing to a somewhat quizzical admira- tion for the poetry combined with a tantalising reticence about the novels. If one looks, however, for less overt evidence of her aware- ness of Scott, matters become slightly more complex.

In pursuing that part of the Austen–Scott dialogue that occurs at the level of subtext rather than direct allusion, I want to focus on *Persuasion* and begin by considering the question of which Scott novels Austen is likely to have read by the time she finished writ- ing that novel in August 1816. It seems safe to assume that she read Scott's first novel, *Waverley*, fairly soon after her reference to it in the letter to Anna of 28 September 1814, and a letter to her nephew J. Edward Austen of 16 December 1816 (*L*, 468) shows that she certainly read Scott's third novel, *The Antiquary*, probably not long after it came out in May 1816. In these circumstances it seems to me likely that she also read the second novel, *Guy Mannering*, pub- lished in March 1815.

It is customary to consider Scott's first three novels within the overall context of his amazingly successful eighteen-year career as a writer of fiction, and thus to take advantage of that long perspec- tive which allows us to see *Waverley*, *Guy Mannering*, and *The An- tiquary* as merely the vanguard of an extended sequence. To look back in this way over Scott's entire production is to be overwhelmed by the persistently historical nature of the later novels, that long series of works dealing not only with events in seventeenth- and eighteenth-century Scotland but also with periods as remote as the early Middle Ages and with locations as distant as the Palestine of the Crusaders. For us the crucial achievement of the Author of *Waverley* is the creation of the historical novel as it was to be prac- tised throughout the remainder of the nineteenth century and on into the twentieth.

But in 1816 a contemporary such as Austen who had read only the first three novels would have seen matters somewhat differently.

It is true that the first novel, *Waverley*, was enacted against the backdrop of a major historical event, the 1745 Jacobite rising, but the next two, *Guy Mannering* and *The Antiquary*, involved no such public action and treated of the comparatively recent past. *The Antiquary* was set a mere fifteen or so years before its publication date, and while English readers would inevitably have been struck by its overall concentration on Scottish manners, its conventional young hero and heroine could well have appeared in a novel set almost anywhere in the British Isles. Readers in 1816 contemplating *Waverley* and its two successors as a group would have had no real reason to challenge his description of the three works as 'a series of fictitious narratives, intended to illustrate the manners of Scotland at three different periods', *Waverley* presenting 'the age of our fathers', *Guy Mannering* 'our own youth', and *The Antiquary* 'the last ten years of the eighteenth century' (*Antiquary*, I, [v]).

In stressing Scott's own emphasis on the portrayal of Scottish manners in relatively recent times and the absence from this ostensibly valedictory advertisement of any reference to public history, I do not wish to challenge the argument so persuasively presented in Ina Ferris's recent book *The Achievement of Literary Authority* – that the most striking feature of *Waverley* as perceived by contemporary critics was its incorporation of the masculine world of public history into a novelistic discourse that had come to seem, in the early years of the nineteenth century, a largely female domain. Given, however, the absence of major public historical material from Scott's second and third novels, I would argue that in 1816 a reader without the prophetic vision to imagine the sequence of historical texts with which Scott was about to storm the novel-reading public – *The Black Dwarf*, *Old Mortality*, *Rob Roy*, *The Heart of Midlothian*, *The Bride of Lammermoor*, and *A Legend of Montrose*, to mention only the titles of the next three years – that such a reader could have been forgiven for viewing the ostensibly completed career of the Author of *Waverley* as shaped by an increasing concern with Scottish manners and a correspondingly reduced concern with world-historical events.

Austen was in any case never tempted to imitate Scott's direct engagement with public history, though it could, I think, be argued that *Persuasion* does at least glance in an historical direction through its allusions to those naval engagements of the recent past by which Wentworth has made his fortune and its hints of possible future conflicts in which his life may be endangered. One might even risk a similar if more hesitant claim in respect of the specifically regional aspects of the Scott model. Though even the most ardent collector of examples of regional fiction might balk at claiming *Persuasion* as a representative of the 'Somerset novel', it does seem to me that Austen as consummate professional could indeed have registered the opportunities afforded by the 'local colour' aspects of Scott's depiction of Scottish manners across a wide range of social groups. And while not proposing to herself any portrayal of the farm labourers of Somerset to place beside Scott's depiction of the smugglers and gypsies of Galloway or the fisher-folk of Fife, she might well have picked up on his detailed depiction of the style of living of middle-class figures such as the lawyer Pleydell in *Guy Mannering* or the antiquary Oldbuck in the succeeding novel.

It is of the 'manners' dimension in Scott's first three novels that I am reminded when I encounter Austen's depiction in *Persuasion* of the home of the elder Musgroves with its 'old-fashioned square parlour, with a small carpet and shining floor, to which the present daughters of the house were gradually giving the proper air of confusion by a grand piano forte and a harp, flower-stands and little tables placed in every direction' (40). Austen does not of course attempt to match the specificity of Scott's account of Oldbuck's study, from which I quote a few selected details:

> It was a lofty room of middling size, obscurely lighted by high narrow latticed windows. One end was entirely occupied by book-shelves, greatly too limited in space for the number of volumes placed upon them, which were, therefore, drawn up in ranks of two and three files deep, while numberless others littered the floor and the tables, amid a chaos of maps, engravings, scraps of parchment, bundles of papers, pieces of old armour, swords, dirks, helmets, and Highland targets. Behind Mr Oldbuck's seat, (which was an ancient leathern-covered easy-chair, worn smooth by constant use,) was a huge oaken cabinet, decorated at each corner with Dutch cherubs, having their little duck-wings displayed, and great jolter-headed visages placed between them. . . . The rest of the room was pannelled, or wainscotted, with black oak, against which hung two or three portraits in armour, being characters in Scottish history, favourites of Mr Oldbuck, and as many in tie-wigs and laced coats, staring representatives of his own ancestors. (*Antiquary*, I, 51–2)

But while Austen may not attempt such density of visual texture she does seem to have registered Scott's sharp-eyed appreciation of domestic detail conceived of in temporal as well as in visual and social terms, deliberately placing the life of the present-day Musgroves within a context which is certainly generational if not explicitly historical:

> Oh! could the originals of the portraits against the wainscot, could the gentlemen in brown velvet and the ladies in blue satin have seen what was going on, have been conscious of such an overthrow of all order and neatness! The portraits themselves seemed to be staring in astonishment. (40)

Despite the temptation of the verbal parallels, I do not wish to labour the point here or to argue at all insistently for direct influences – Austen may well not have read *The Antiquary* at the point when she composed this passage, though indeed there is in both *Waverley* and *Guy Mannering* material that might equally have served her as precedent. I do suggest, however, that the presentation of the Musgrove family from a historico-sociological perspective, concerned with the diachronic as well as with the synchronic understanding of manners, can be fruitfully linked to the example of Scott. What seems to me to distinguish *Persuasion* from its predecessors in the Austen canon is precisely its heightened sensitivity to the temporal dimension of the lives of its characters, registered not only in the personal terms of the impact of time's passage on the 'bloom' of the heroine, but also in the larger terms of generational change.

What I have thus far been arguing for in this essay is the presence in Austen's work of a responsive awareness of the narrative strategies made familiar to the Regency audience by the enormously successful trio of novels with which Scott opened his career. At this point, however, it may be appropriate to take more fully into account Scott's side of their partly explicit, largely implicit, literary dialogue. For if Austen could not ignore the aggressive invasion of the territory of the novel by the famous poet, Scott for his part was acutely conscious that the territory had previously been dominated by Austen and other women novelists.

Scott, of course, repeatedly and enthusiastically expressed his admiration for Austen's novels, above all in that remarkable review of *Emma* in which, as Peter Sabor puts it, he 'takes the much belittled genre of the novel more seriously than could have been expected in 1816, and . . . looks more closely and incisively at *Emma* than any other essay was to do for several decades' (Sabor, 1991, 91). Scott's comments in the review chime with the scattered remarks in his journal and letters and with the extempore comments recorded in the Lockhart *Memoirs*, emphasising above all Austen's talents as a realist, her 'wonderful' ability to describe 'the involvements, and feelings, and characters of ordinary life' (Lockhart, 6, 264).[1] And he especially praises her portraiture of life in the middling ranks of society, comparing her technique to that of 'the Flemish school of painting' (*Emma* review, 197).

It may seem inexcusably circular to suggest that the very feature of *The Antiquary* I earlier singled out as likely to have caught Austen's attention – that realistic presentation of the surface texture of Oldbuck's world viewed as a product of historical development as well as of immediate social circumstance – might itself be attributed, at least in part, to the effect of Austen's example on Scott. But we are dealing here with the reciprocal awareness of contemporaries, the sensitivity of one artist to the practice of another, and it works in both directions. For Sabor the *Emma* review is notable for its expression of the contrasts between the two, between the 'cornfields and cottages and meadows' seen as constituting Austen's novelistic territory and 'the rugged sublimities of a mountain landscape' (200) associated with Scott. But I would want to lay rather more emphasis on affinities than contrasts, on the degree to which Scott's presentation of Fairport in *The Antiquary* – the novel on which he was beginning work at the very moment he was writing the review – can be associated with the admiration expressed in that review for Austen's skill at 'copying from nature' (193). *The Antiquary*'s Austen-like focus on two or three families of middling rank in the neighbourhood of a small town is, to be sure, accompanied by the gothic excesses of the aristocratic Glenallen subplot, but that subplot is carefully segregated from the main narrative as the stuff of tale and legend rather than of present action, and the central focus throughout is on the lives of the ordinary inhabitants of Fairport, presented with an insistent attention to realistic detail.

A sharper – indeed, almost poignant – sense of Austen's impact on Scott can perhaps be derived from the extended peroration on Austen's handling of her love-plots with which the *Emma* review concludes. It is a passage that has attracted relatively little critical comment, perhaps because it has rather the look of a generalising flourish designed to afford the reviewer a graceful exit from his essay. The ground for it, however, has been carefully prepared earlier in the review by the plot-summaries of the three Austen novels specifically discussed: *Sense and Sensibility*, *Pride and Prejudice* and *Emma*. In each case Scott stresses the prudential aspects of the resolution of the love-plot. Elinor is described as 'a young lady of prudence and regulated feelings' who has the initial misfortune to attach herself 'to a man of an excellent heart and limited talents, who happens unfortunately to be fettered by a rash and ill-assorted engagement' (194), a situation that is only resolved when the 'marriage of the unworthy rival at length relieves her own lover from his imprudent engagement' (194). Marianne is described as 'turned wise by precept, example, and experience' and as belatedly transferring 'her affection to a very respectable and somewhat too serious admirer, who had nourished an unsuccessful passion through the three volumes' (194). In recounting the story of *Pride and Prejudice* Scott chooses, somewhat mischievously, to report at face-value Elizabeth Bennet's own perhaps tongue-in-cheek explanation of her change of heart:

> [She] does not perceive that she has done a foolish thing until she accidentally visits a very handsome seat and grounds belonging to her admirer. They chance to meet exactly as her prudence had begun to subdue her prejudice. (194)

In *Emma* we are told that 'at Highbury Cupid walks decorously, and with good discretion, bearing his torch under a lanthorn, instead of flourishing it around to set the house on fire', enabling the story to conclude with Emma's marriage to Mr Knightley, 'the sturdy, advice-giving bachelor', the two having discovered 'that they had been in love with each other all along' (196).

Having summarised the Austen plots in this disenchanted – not to say slanted – fashion, Scott concludes the review with a celebration of the attractions of quite a different kind of love-plot – the plot of early passion and potentially imprudent desire. In life, Scott concedes, 'there are few instances of first attachment being brought to a happy conclusion', for we live 'in a state of society so highly advanced as to render early marriages among the better class, acts, generally speaking, of imprudence.' But it strikes him nevertheless as an act of treachery when 'that once powerful divinity, Cupid' is deserted 'even in his own kingdom of romance, by the authors who were formerly his devoted priests':

Who is it, that in his youth has felt a virtuous attachment, however romantic or however unfortunate, but can trace back to its influence much that his character may possess of what is honourable, dignified, and disinterested? If he recollects hours wasted in unavailing hope, or saddened by doubt and disappointment; he may also dwell on many which have been snatched from folly or libertinism, and dedicated to studies which might render him worthy of the object of his affection, or pave the way perhaps to that distinction necessary to raise him to an equality with her. Even the habitual indulgence of feelings totally unconnected with ourself and our own immediate interest, softens, graces, and amends the human mind; and after the pain of disappointment is past, those who survive (and by good fortune those are the greater number) are neither less wise nor less worthy members of society for having felt, for a time, the influence of a passion which has been well qualified as the 'tenderest, noblest and best.' (200–1)

That this is a surprisingly personal passage to find in the pages of the *Quarterly Review* is, I think, obvious enough, but it is also specifically – if codedly – autobiographical, and that perhaps needs to be spelled out a little for those unfamiliar with the details of Scott's life.[2] Scott is the least confessional of writers, shying away instinctively from self-analysis and preferring always to approach self-understanding by generating a story rather than undertaking an exploration of conscious or subconscious motivation. The one sore place in his personal history that consistently arouses the kind of present pain that requires if not analytic then narrative alleviation is the loss of his first great love, Williamina Belsches, only child of Sir John Belsches of Fettercairn and his aristocratic wife. In this courtship, the penniless young lawyer had deployed all his professional and literary hopes and ambitions in a vain attempt to counter the more substantial attractions of his rival, the son of the wealthy banker Sir William Forbes of Pitsligo.[3] What happens in the *Emma* review is that the encounter with Austen's more prudential lovers for some reason triggers in Scott not only the memory of his loss, but the need to celebrate more generally the energies and aspirations generated by the lover's pursuit of the beloved, even when that pursuit proves ultimately vain.

Why should his response have been so strong – possibly even to the extent of feeding into the immediately subsequent composition of *The Antiquary* as a compensatory fiction generated by the same memory of personal anguish? I suggest that *The Antiquary* and the conclusion of the *Emma* review were both direct challenges, the one professional and novelistic, the other personal and rhetorical, to Austen's perceived desertion of the cause of romance and of the socially redemptive power of love in favour of the stonier if solider paths of prudence and good sense.

Persuasion, in progress when the *Emma* review appeared, and finally revised some four months later, has its own contribution to make to the dialogue with Scott. Its structure has, after all, faint though discernible affinities with the two-generational pattern employed by Scott in *Guy Mannering* and in a modified way in *The Antiquary*. The eight-year gap between the first and second phases of the Wentworth–Anne courtship is, to be sure, much less dramatic than the shift from the first appearance of the youthful Guy Mannering at Ellangowan to his return twenty years later, a widowed colonel with a brilliant public career and a host of private mistakes behind him. But *Persuasion* and *Mannering* are both centrally concerned with coming to terms with past events, and in *The Antiquary* the middle-aged antiquary, Jonathan Oldbuck, a self-appointed expert in interpreting historical relics, must reengage with his own personal history, with the experience of loss that has affected his entire subsequent life. The tribute to the memory of loss is further intensified in *The Antiquary* by a mutually reinforcing linkage between the gentle sadness of the Oldbuck material and the darker and more violent passions of Lord Glenallen's dynastic tragedy.

In *Guy Mannering* and *The Antiquary*, the double focus on both the aspiration story of the youthful lovers and the reconciliation story of the older figures – both implying the possibility of wider social redemption for the entire community – generates a powerful narrative structure that allows the plot of consequences, with its transcendence of regret, and the wish-fulfilment plot of the traditional love story to co-exist in the same textual space without one being erased by the other. In *Persuasion*, on the other hand, the focus remains resolutely single and one-generational. The triumph of love, its transcendence of the sadness and loss resulting from past mistakes, is achieved by a single hero–heroine pair and affects only themselves. It seems almost a direct result of this generational restriction that the healing power of the love-plot is confined to the personal dimension, having none of that extended romance valency for the community as a whole that characterises Scott's early novels. The impact of this restriction can be felt most powerfully in *Persuasion*'s handling of the father–daughter relationship, a central motif throughout Scott's fiction and especially prominent in his first three novels.

For Scott daughters have a saving power that enables them to protect their difficult, improvident or foolish fathers, and the happiness of the daughter is never achieved at the price of leaving the father behind. The marriage of Rose Bradwardine and Edward Waverley is accompanied by the rescue of the outlawed Baron of Bradwardine from his hunted-badger cave and his restoration to his ancestral estate and full legal authority. *Guy Mannering* presents two versions of the father–daughter relationship, on the one hand the recurrent Scott motif of Lucy Bertram's faithful and protective service to her ruined father, and on the other the witty but always affectionate sparring between Mannering and his daughter Julia. The lively Julia has interesting antecedents, on which I might just comment in passing. She clearly owes something both to Shakespearian heroines of the Beatrice or Rosalind type and to the sparkling female protagonists of Restoration comedy, but given Scott's admiration for his women novelist contemporaries, it seems arguable that he is here attempting to match his female rivals on their own ground of social comedy. The dialogues between Julia and her father certainly do not equal those of Elizabeth and Mr Bennet, but they are powerfully imagined and engagingly articulated.

It is, however, in *The Antiquary* that Scott raises the father–daughter relationship to almost emblematic status in what was to become one of his most famous scenes, the occasion of innumerable paintings and much admiring commentary throughout the century that followed the novel's publication. I refer to the cliff-rescue episode in which Isabella Wardour and her proud and foolish father are saved from death by drowning through the combined efforts of the hero Lovel and the old beggar Edie Ochiltree. This early episode not only prefigures Lovel's ultimate rescue of Sir Arthur from financial ruin, but also captures in essence Isabella's entire relationship with her father – at once devotedly filial in its sedulous maintenance of conventional deference and quasi-maternal in the kind and degree of the protection and comfort continuously provided. Sir Arthur, that 'baronet of ancient descent' and 'embarrassed fortune' (I, 97), lamentably combining financial incompetence, delusions of family grandeur, and gullibility in the face of charlatanry, has to be repeatedly rescued in the course of the novel, but there is never any doubt that the ultimate resolution of the many plot-strands will include his restoration to his estate with dignity and authority intact.

Anne Elliot is certainly a match for Isabella Wardour in both self-abnegation and determination to protect parental dignity. But where *The Antiquary* presents a father and daughter literally clinging to each other in loving, mutual support at a moment of violent physical danger, *Persuasion* never brings Anne and her father remotely within touching distance. Austen's baronet remains blindly impervious to the virtues of his second daughter and cut off from her healing power. He belongs in the icy, mirror-enclosed world he shares with his eldest daughter, and Austen sternly turns her back on any attempt to integrate him into the future Anne and Wentworth will share.

In thus parting company on the question of love's socially redemptive power, Austen and Scott inevitably take very different and indeed directly opposite paths in respect of their central plots. On the one hand *Guy Mannering* and *The Antiquary* enact a process by which the communal past is redeemed and continuity maintained between one generation and the next. In these texts Scott deploys a particular narrative pattern, involving the rediscovery of a lost heir, as a way of linking past with future and articulating the restoration of the community through the romance ending of the marriage of hero and heroine. His narratives turn on legitimacy and inheritance and the future management of that inheritance so as to benefit the ancestral community. In *Persuasion*, on quite the other hand, Austen alludes to this type of plot only to execute a deliberately ironic rejection of almost everything that it entails.

That she means the readers of *Persuasion* to take the point of this rejection I have little doubt.[4] Austen counts upon her audience's familiarity with the lost-heir plot and involves her two male protagonists in what might be called variations on a theme by Scott. William Walter Elliot, the rightful heir of Kellynch, far from being unknown and untraced, is merely estranged and unworthy. And when he enters upon the scene his identity is quickly established and does not require to be proved. In a deliberate parody of the validation ritual that crowns the lost-heir plot Austen has the family-obsessed Mary engage in a breathless recitation of all the physical details proclaiming Mr Elliot's credentials that were *not* in fact observed:

What a pity that we should not have been introduced to each other! – Do you think he had the Elliot countenance? I hardly looked at him, I was looking at the horses; but I think he had something of the Elliot countenance. I wonder the arms did not strike me! Oh! – the great-coat was hanging over the pannel, and hid the arms; so it did, otherwise, I am sure, I should have observed them, and the livery too; if the servant had not been in mourning, one should have known him by the livery. (106)

Lady Russell's fantasy version of Anne's future would have marriage to the rightful heir follow rapidly on his reappearance, to be succeeded in due course by the restoration of the family fortunes and the reestablishment of those social bonds that should ideally prevail between good landowner and grateful community. In such a narrative the rightful heir, though not requiring to be 'discovered' as in the classic lost-heir plot, could at least fulfil something of the traditional pattern by proving to be worthy despite earlier appearances to the contrary, and the final outcome would be Anne's taking of her rightful place as Lady Elliot and mistress of Kellynch. But Lady Russell is doomed to disappointment. What occurs in *Persuasion* is a fuller exposure of the fundamental worthlessness of the official heir and his ultimate entrapment by the artful woman whose schemes to possess the Kellynch estate he has been seeking to outwit.

Readers familiar with the lost-heir plot might see in Wentworth the possibility of a different kind of variation on the familiar theme. He has many of the qualifications of the Scott romantic hero of ostensibly obscure origins – sharing with Bertram in *Guy Mannering* and Lovel in *The Antiquary* a record for military courage and a taste for literature – and were he and Anne somehow to be brought into possession of Kellynch the combination of private happiness and social healing of the Scott endings might perhaps be achieved. But Austen's narrative sternly precludes such possibilities. There is nothing mysterious about Wentworth's origins; he is 'quite unconnected' (23) to the Wentworths of the noble Strafford family, and his connections are instead a solidly middle-class curate brother and an energetic and unconventional sister. What is more, the inheritor position in the story is emphatically *not* vacant. The official heir may be defeated in the competition for the hand of the heroine, but his claims to the estate are never in doubt.

Inheritance, which possesses in the plots of Scott's early novels a redemptive power linking older and younger generations, remains in *Persuasion* simply an arid legal procedure. Where the fathers in Scott's plots are granted forgiveness for past errors and the chance to participate in the renewal process at least as witnesses if not as prime movers, the father in *Persuasion* remains excluded from the glow associated with the heroine's marriage. Unenlightened and unredeemed, Sir Walter stays trapped inside his past mistakes. There is no place for him in a Kellynch future that belongs to his nephew and Mrs Clay, and there is no possibility of preempting, or even postponing, that future by some act of grace permitting his restoration, at least for an interlude, to the ancestral home.[5]

Wentworth and Anne have neither the power nor the desire to effect paternal restoration. And Austen, as we have seen, is at pains to make her readers aware that Wentworth is categorically not an inheritor. Far from having to do with any of the continuities articulated through the passing on of land and title from one generation to the next, Wentworth is the hero as self-made man. Instead of returning the heroine to her ancestral home he will carry her off into a wider world where family takes on an entirely different meaning in a society whose values are professional and comradely rather than aristocratic and communal. The inheritors of land in this novel remain meanwhile solipsistically estranged from their own rightful community, and it is only one of the many ironies that play around the conclusion of the tale that the unspeakable Mary is allowed the consolation of an insight whose true significance completely escapes her limited powers of perception: 'Anne had no Uppercross-hall before her, no landed estate, no headship of a family' (250).[6]

Notes

1. The catalogue of Scott's library indicates the presence of first editions of *Emma* and *Northanger Abbey* and *Persuasion* (Cochrane, 332). It is clear from Scott's discussion of *Sense and Sensibility* and *Pride and Prejudice* in the *Emma* review that he had also read and admired those two works, but there is no evidence he was acquainted with *Mansfield Park*.
2. I would argue that the masculine pronouns in this passage are deliberate rather than conventional, expressive of its grounding in direct personal experience.

3. Scott's own account, jotted down in his journal in December 1825 as he faced financial ruin, captures the essence of the Williamina affair as well as the pain it was still capable of arousing after almost thirty years:

    > What a life mine has been. Half educated, almost wholly neglected or left to myself – stuffing my head with most nonsensical trash and undervalued in society for a time by most of my companions – getting forward and held a bold and clever fellow, contrary to the opinion of all who thought me a mere dreamer – Broken-hearted for two years – My heart handsomely pieced again – but the crack will remain till my dying day – (*Journal*, 42–3)

4. Austen includes a joke at the expense of the lost-heir convention in the opening chapter of *Northanger Abbey*, where Catherine, in her role of potential heroine, labours under the disadvantage of a neighbourhood that boasts 'not one family among their acquaintance who had reared and supported a boy accidentally found at their door – not one young man whose origin was unknown' (*NA*, 16).

5. Austen's disenchantment with the fitness of the traditional gentry for continuing rule has been much discussed; see, for example, Butler, 108. More recently Daniel Cottom has contested Alistair Duckworth's claim that 'the estate is a saving structure of great permanence' in Austen's thought, seeing it merely as 'a traditional reality' that is 'in danger of usurpation' (96). All this contrasts sharply with Alexander Welsh's account of the attitude to landed property in Scott's fiction: 'The proper hero and heroine are not individual persons but representatives of civil society: Scott carefully protects them from too close an association with "personal" property and heartily endows them with real estate' (117).

6. The novels that immediately succeeded *The Antiquary* show Scott himself undergoing a progressive loss of faith in the power of the lost-heir fable. Either the act of personal exorcism attempted in *The Antiquary* failed of its intended effect, or his conservative faith in the transformative power of inheritance and improvement wavered under the fracturing pressures emerging in the postwar Britain of 1816. Rather than abandon the lost-heir motif, however, he inverts or subverts its once simple and hopeful outlines so as to produce darker and darker effects – the tragic climax of *The Bride of Lammermoor* or the grotesque transformation that brings back the lost heir in *The Heart of Midlothian* only to reveal him as a parricide fit only for permanent exile among savages.

10

The Slow Process of
Persuasion

Judith Terry

I never liked *Persuasion* much as a girl; *Pride and Prejudice* I read
from cover to cover many times over, but it was years before I grew
fond of *Persuasion*. I had not given this much thought until, speaking quite casually with a friend, I discovered that our experience of
the two novels had been identical; in fact, we agreed – so far as one
wants to make such distinctions – that *Persuasion* was now our
favourite among the novels. Since I was aware, from talking to
other Janeites, that ours was not an unusual experience, I grew
interested in why it should be so, why *Pride and Prejudice* would
inspire such instant affection, when *Persuasion* did not. Thus my
focus is on us as readers, why *Persuasion* might be, as David Daiches
has said, 'the novel which in the end the experienced reader of Jane
Austen puts at the head of the list' (quoted by Bradbury, 1976, 214).

Many readers will instantly admit that one has to be 'mature' to
appreciate *Persuasion*, but they usually mean a maturity of outlook
required to appreciate Anne the person; I am going to argue that
the maturity required is much more closely related to our capacity
as readers, interpreting and responding to the text. Some compari-
sons with *Pride and Prejudice* are helpful, since, although not everyone may put *Persuasion* at the head of the list, it is certain that *Pride
and Prejudice* is a very general and early favourite (witness how
frequently it turns up as a movie or school text). The contrasting
responses to these novels are in large measure due, I believe, to significant differences in Austen's narrative technique and the demands
that that makes upon the reader.

The superficial similarity between all Austen novels can be a
hindrance here. It is part of their attraction, of course – what makes
them so marvellous for the kind of games we love to play, like
who's your favourite heroine and why (a game not entirely absent
from this argument). But consider a young reader opening *Persuasion*

with some expectations born of reading *Pride and Prejudice*. She finds herself in the same world of family, village and quiet country life, with a heroine whose drama revolves around the securing of a husband. The similarities in story, however, camouflage major differences in technique. Where *Pride and Prejudice* is straight-forward, *Persuasion* is subtle and unexpected, so much so that for us as young or first-time readers, there is likely to be a great disparity between what we *think* we are reading, and what we actually experience during reading, a disparity which strongly affects our emotional response to the novel, and especially to the heroine.

Both *Persuasion* and *Pride and Prejudice* begin by introducing us to parents, the Bennets through dialogue, Sir Walter Elliot through description. But the heroine enters the narrative very differently in each case. When Mrs Bennet is dilating upon the chance of marrying off one of her daughters to Bingley, Mr Bennet says, 'I must throw in a good word for *my little Lizzy*' (my italics). The statement demonstrates his unashamed favouritism, which is immediately confirmed in Mrs Bennet's reply: 'Lizzy is not a bit better than the others; and I am sure she is not half so handsome as Jane, nor half so good humoured as Lydia. But you are always giving *her* the preference' (4).

This is the first time the Bennet daughters are named in the text, and the order exactly parallels their order of importance to the story: first Lizzy, then Jane, then Lydia. Kitty and Mary – comparatively unimportant – remain nameless at this point. Lizzy is further marked for us because she has been singled out by her father, whom we have already learnt through their conversation to be the sensible parent. Jane has already flagged Lizzy for us as heroine.

By contrast, Anne enters covertly. Her name is mentioned first merely as an entry in Debrett, in birth order, sandwiched between her sisters, either of whom might equally well be heroine. It is not until the third page that the narrative focuses upon her, and then only for a mere half page before shifting back to Elizabeth, for four pages. That half-page description is scant, and provides nothing of Anne speaking or doing – nothing of her in action, that is. The authoritative voice of the narrator tells us that she has 'elegance of mind and sweetness of character' (5), but although these flattering terms alert us to her central importance, they are quite without vivid associations. Anne is still pale and shadowy; it is the technicolour images of Sir Walter and Elizabeth which are foregrounded.

This state of affairs continues for a remarkably long time, in some quite curious and deliberate ways. In the second chapter, for instance, Lady Russell has been asked to suggest ways in which the Elliots may retrench, and does 'what nobody else thought of doing, she consulted Anne' (12). Austen gives us something of this scene, but not what we might expect. This would be a good moment, surely, to show us Anne in the flesh, as it were, to hear her speak with wisdom and common sense about the retrenchments. What we get instead is an odd, almost truncated excerpt, in which Anne's views are condensed into four lines, and presented very indirectly, while Lady Russell speaks in her own voice at five times greater length:

> Every emendation of Anne's had been on the side of honesty against importance. She wanted more vigorous measures, a more complete reformation, a quicker release from debt, a much higher tone of indifference for every thing but justice and equity.
> 'If we can persuade your father to all this,' said Lady Russell, looking over her paper, 'much may be done. If he will adopt these regulations, in seven years he will be clear; and I hope we may be able to convince him and Elizabeth, that Kellynch-hall has a respectability in itself, which cannot be affected by these reductions; and that the true dignity of Sir Walter Elliot will be very far from lessened, in the eyes of sensible people, by his acting like a man of principle.' (12)

By comparison with Lady Russell (and this is only half of what she says), Anne is inaudible. Indeed, we hear many other voices, and are given a much fuller sense of their personalities before Anne's own voice is heard at all. Elizabeth Elliot, Mr Shepherd, Mrs Clay, as well as Lady Russell, all have more space in the text than Anne, and speak in their own voices. The text privileges them over her. It is as if, instead of being the protagonist, she were a minor character.

We recognise easily enough on a first reading how Anne is excluded by her family and their friends, but I suggest we are much less likely to notice how she is also squeezed out of the text, how the text itself seems calculated to make everyone else seem – not *better* – but more interesting.

Things do not improve greatly when Anne does speak for the first time, during the discussion of a tenant for Kellynch-hall. After Mr Shepherd's toadying comments – 'Your interest, Sir Walter, is in pretty safe hands. Depend upon me for taking care that no tenant has more than his just rights. I venture to hint, that Sir Walter Elliot cannot be half so jealous for his own, as John Shepherd will be for him' – Anne intervenes, to say:

'The navy, I think, who have done so much for us, have at least an equal claim with any other set of men, for all the comforts and all the privileges which any home can give. Sailors work hard enough for their comforts, we must all allow.' (19)

Her remark has no apparent connexion with what is being said. Indeed, it obviously stops the conversation dead in its tracks. You can hear the silence through Mr Shepherd and Mrs Clay's attempt to cover it:

'Very true, very true. What Miss Anne says, is very true,' was Mr. Shepherd's rejoinder, and 'Oh! certainly,' was his daughter's. (19)

Everyone is nonplussed.

The important point here is that that 'everyone' includes the reader. A first-time reader knows nothing as yet about Frederick Wentworth. Where *is* Anne coming from? We don't know, any more than Mr Shepherd and Mrs Clay. Under instructions from the narrator, as it were, we are ready and willing to be sympathetic to Anne, but there's really nothing to be sympathetic about: what she says is merely baffling. It can *only* be in retrospect that we realise why Anne would pick up on a remark about the navy dropped by Mr Shepherd a whole page earlier. Later, in Chapter 4, the Anne/Wentworth story is told and it contains the explanation, but another seven pages have elapsed, and in any case what Anne said seemed so general, almost irrelevant, that we probably did not mark it as needing explanation.

Nothing else in that scene counteracts that first impression of Anne's ineffectualness. She speaks twice more, but each time only to perform a secretary-like function, which is accepted but unacknowledged, slipping the others information about Admiral Croft (21), and then about the name of Wentworth (23).

The presentation of Lizzy Bennet is much more straightforward. She speaks much sooner than Anne (page 6 compared with page 19), and, although she does not say much, she is the first character to speak other than her parents. Mr Bennet is teasing his wife by withholding the information that he has called upon Mr Bingley:

Observing his second daughter employed in trimming a hat, he suddenly addressed her with,

'I hope Mr. Bingley will like it Lizzy.'

'We are not in a way to know *what* Mr. Bingley likes,' said her mother resentfully, 'since we are not to visit.'

'But you forget, mama,' said Elizabeth, 'that we shall meet him at the assemblies, and that Mrs. Long has promised to introduce him.'

'I do not believe Mrs. Long will do any such thing. She has two nieces of her own. She is a selfish, hypocritical woman, and I have no opinion of her.' (6)

The reader recognises that Lizzy speaks judiciously and is listened to, that she is trying to mediate between her parents, whose destructive sparring we have already witnessed. Her words demonstrate that she is loving and kind and sensible. By contrast, in Anne's first words there is nothing we can admire or respond to.

Surveys have been conducted, as Menakhem Perry points out, which show that as readers we are enormously influenced by what we read first, that 'information and attitudes presented at an early stage of the text tend to encourage the reader to interpret everything in their light', that we are 'prone to preserve such meanings and attitudes for as long as possible' (quoted by Rimmon-Kenan, 120). Common reading habits are worth taking into account also. How long elapses between readings of a novel? It is often quite some time – years perhaps – before we pick up a novel again, especially, of course, if we have mixed feelings about it, as I am suggesting may be the case with *Persuasion*. How well do we have to know and remember the text if we are to resist and revise an initial, unfavourable impression of Anne? I suspect that the idea that she is a bit of a nonentity takes very deep root.

That is also why I think it can be misleading to think of *Persuasion* as a Cinderella story. Certain features of the story do certainly correspond quite neatly: the two 'ugly sisters', etc. But there is a crucial difference: the *narrative* in Cinderella always works in opposition to the *story*, privileging the heroine even when the story doesn't. As a brief illustration, here is the opening of the best-known version:

Once upon a time a man and woman married. They had both been married before. By his first wife the husband had a sweet and gentle daughter. But the second wife was quite the most

unpleasant and stuck-up creature in the country, and what was worse, she had two daughters exactly like herself.
The new marriage had no sooner taken place than the step-mother showed her spiteful nature. Her stepdaughter was such a happy child that it made her own two daughters seem more horrid. So she gave her all the housework to do: the washing-up, sweeping the steps, dusting, making beds . . . everything. She sent her to sleep up in a dark little attic, on a lumpy old mattress, while her own two daughters' rooms had beautiful polished floors, and beautiful soft beds, and beautiful tall mirrors they could see themselves in from puffed-up head to puffed-up toe. The poor girl suffered all this as best she could. (Fowles, 5)

This makes it clear that, although in the *story* Cinderella is relegated to the cinder-corner by her stepmother and sisters, in the *narrative*, and thus to us as readers, she is centre-stage, in the spotlight. This is conventional narrative strategy, and it operates in Austen's presentation of Lizzy Bennet.

But not in the presentation of Anne Elliot. Instead of the narrative playing in opposition to the story, much of the time Austen reverses the technique and makes the narrative mimic the story. Anne has not merely a lowly status in the story; she has also a lowly status in the narrative. I suggest that the time it takes to learn to love Anne is directly related to that unusual circumstance.

The presentation of Wentworth actually contributes to our ambivalence towards Anne. We are a quarter of the way through the text before he appears, are rarely privy to his thoughts, and naturally think of ourselves as more distant from him than from Anne. But he is preceded by good report, and when he enters the narrative it is with dash and a drumroll: the hero cannot be mistaken – unlike the heroine. All the girls love him, all the men respect and admire him, Anne still adores him. Wentworth is lucky, plucky, bright, glowing, kind, sensible, right-thinking (except about Anne). In other words, unlike Anne, he instantly commands our affection and sympathy. Bearing that in mind, consider the initial description of his feelings towards her:

He had not forgiven Anne Elliot. She had used him ill; deserted and disappointed him; and worse, she had shewn a feebleness of character in doing so, which his own decided, confident temper could not endure. She had given him up to oblige others. It had been the effect of over-persuasion. It had been weakness and timidity.

He had been most warmly attached to her, and had never seen a woman since whom he thought her equal; but, except from some natural sensation of curiosity, he had no desire of meeting her again. Her power with him was gone for ever.

It was now his object to marry.... He had a heart... for any pleasing young woman who came in his way, excepting Anne Elliot. This was his only secret exception....

...and Anne Elliot was not out of his thoughts, when he... described the woman he should wish to meet with. 'A strong mind, with sweetness of manner,' made the first and the last of the description. (61–2)

This is very endearing – a wonderful piece of tangled logic, especially in this slightly abridged form – and so exactly the way in which other people contradict themselves completely within the space of ten minutes. Moreover, we acknowledge that Wentworth has suffered, as well as Anne, from the broken engagement, which was, indeed, although not Anne's fault, certainly her doing. If we are already lukewarm towards Anne, as I have maintained, when Wentworth charges Anne here with feebleness, weakness and timidity, it authorises us to acknowledge, perhaps even justify, what we may have been trying to suppress: our irritation with Anne for being so stupid as to listen to that old bat Lady Russell instead of the urgings of her own true love. So what we do as readers outside the text is not unlike what Wentworth does within it: misread Anne. That unacknowledged conflict within him is ours also.

An earlier point in the text, the often-noted shift into Anne's consciousness, seems the obvious place for the reader's perceptions of Anne to shift also. Indeed, the final sentence of Chapter 3 is a real page-turner, promising dramatic revelations and a new intimacy with the heroine:

Anne, who had been a most attentive listener to the whole, left the room, to seek the comfort of cool air for her flushed cheeks; and as she walked along a favourite grove, said, with a gentle sigh, 'a few months more, and *he*, perhaps, may be walking here.' (25)

But in the event, the promise is only minimally fulfilled: Anne's earlier affair with Wentworth is revealed, but condensed in such a way as to rob it of much of its drama, and Anne herself is still presented to us largely through her reactions to others, in that spinster-aunt role to which she has been consigned by the people around her. Her words and actions are still downplayed by the author; her speech still frequently summarised. When she determines to alert Elizabeth to Mrs Clay's designs on their father, Austen says merely: 'She spoke, and seemed only to offend' (34). The voice we hear is Elizabeth's, angrily repudiating Anne's suggestion for the better part of a page (35). Anne makes only a single direct remark: 'There is hardly any personal defect . . . which an agreeable manner might not gradually reconcile one to' (35) – two lines versus twenty-seven. Yet it is not that Anne did not speak. But the good sense of what she said, the tactful way in which she approached a difficult topic, her courage in raising it at all with that formidable sister, we must invent for ourselves.

This 'compression' of Anne's words and actions is especially noteworthy on the occasion of little Charles Musgrove's bad fall:

> His collar-bone was found to be dislocated, and such injury received in the back, as roused the most alarming ideas. It was an afternoon of distress, and Anne had every thing to do at once – the apothecary to send for – the father to have pursued and informed – the mother to support and keep from hysterics – the servants to control – the youngest child to banish, and the poor suffering one to attend and soothe; – besides sending, as soon as she recollected it, proper notice to the other house. . . . (53)

The length of a scene is usually understood by the reader, quite naturally, as an indicator of its importance. When it is expanded, related in detail, we take more notice, inevitably. Summary like this we expect to be reserved for lesser events. Thus, although the facts about little Charles's accident are presented, since they occupy only twenty-eight lines, we are actually encouraged to pass over this account of Anne in action – pass it off, indeed, much as the people in Anne's world do – not oblivious to her excellence, but simply taking it for granted.

The only part of this event to be elaborated is Mary Musgrove's about-face when, having been in hysterics one day as a result of the child's fall, the next day she argues herself into leaving him because she does not want to miss the fun at the Great House. During this scene Anne speaks, but it is Mary's scene, not Anne's (as the former scene was Elizabeth's). The word-count matters here. Although the analogy is slightly faulty, it helps to think of a play: can you imagine a play in which six other characters have more lines than the heroine?

It is enlightening to compare the narration of little Charles's broken collarbone with that much more celebrated scene, Louisa Musgrove falling off the Cobb wall. Here we have an exactly (almost oddly) parallel event: a serious accident when all lose their heads but Anne. (I compress this scene, but the point to remember is how fully Austen elaborates it.) Anne is the only one of all those present who remains calm and in control. Her suggestions are brief and to the point, full, as the narrator points out, of 'strength and zeal, and thought' (111). Both Charles Musgrove and Wentworth seem 'to look to her for directions' – which indeed, at this moment of crisis, she provides.

I maintain that a first-time (probably second- and even third-time reader) has to wait until this point (nearly halfway through the novel) before being presented with a scene which proves, as it were, what stern stuff Anne is made of. This delay is unrelated to the nature of what happens – Louisa's bump on the head is, after all, no more serious than little Charles Musgrove's dislocated collarbone – but arises from Austen's decision to compress the earlier event and expand the later (the proportion being about three-quarters of a page to six).

Moreover, the scene at the Cobb follows more than one hundred pages of Anne being overlooked, not just by those in her world, but by us. As a result it may well take a while – certainly more than one reading – to perceive all its implications: that what we are seeing is not merely elegance of mind and sweetness of character, but also leadership and competence of a high degree. Anne asserts herself very quietly. She uses the imperative only once. Immediately after the event, in response to Wentworth's desperate plea 'Is there no one to help me?', she orders, 'Go to him, go to him, . . . for heaven's sake go to him. . . . Rub her hands, rub her temples; here are salts, – take them, take them.' After this what she says is less peremptory. The advice 'A surgeon!' is framed as an exclamation, and the next instructions as questions: 'Captain Benwick, would not it be better for Captain Benwick?' (110), and 'Had not she better be carried to the inn? Yes, I am sure, carry her gently to the inn' (111). This is Anne taking charge while still remaining within the boundaries of female discourse – which means that she is trying hard not to *sound* as though she's taking charge. That in itself may deflect us in early readings from recognising how impressive she is.

I am not for one minute advocating that Austen should have done any of this differently. On the contrary, once we have reached this point at, let's say, the third reading, it becomes clear that downplaying the heroine achieves something that a more usual narrative technique could not: once we have recognised our own misreading, light dawns: we might well say how clever (how *unlike* the fairy tale). Our inclination to misjudge Anne, almost deliberately fostered, it seems, by the text, means that our subsequent change of heart is all the greater. Believing, as I do, that when a reader engages with a text, it is as if the characters were real, I find our mistake imposes a kind of moral charge. We feel it incumbent upon us to make up for the error. And reading the novel again, in that spirit of apology, almost produces a different book. Recognising that Austen is deliberately allowing Anne's voice to be submerged, as it is in Anne's 'real' life, we start looking for her more carefully, and suddenly find she was there all the time.

As a result, re-reading makes us much more alert, on the one hand to the true horror of Anne's absolute isolation within her family and society, and on the other to the efforts she makes to retain her identity, and, when opportunity offers, to take steps towards freedom and independence.

So, for instance, though we probably recognised the significance of the 'only Anne' phrase on first reading, now other phrases and statements attract our attention: 'she had hardly any body to love' (26); 'in music she had been always used to feel alone in the world' (47); her envy of the Musgrove sisters' 'good-humoured mutual affection, of which she had known so little herself with either of her sisters' (41). Indeed, when, much later, we hear that 'Anne had gone unhappy to school, grieving for the loss of a mother whom she had dearly loved, feeling her separation from home, and suffering as a girl of fourteen, of strong sensibility and not high spirits, must suffer at such a time' (152), we may well, in new-found sympathy, wonder whether even the highest spirits could have survived the conditions of Anne's home life. We more fully enter into her dread of going to Bath, for 'who would be glad to see her when she arrived?' (135). She names that visit, indeed, 'an imprisonment' (137).

These are direct, unequivocal statements, but they are brief, scattered, and – in a state of ambivalence towards Anne – all too easy to ignore. But once we start connecting and assembling them, we recognise a nightmarish emotional undertow, a claustrophobia, a psychological incarceration of quite horrible dimension. Anne is condemned to a daily existence among those with such different attitudes and interests that she can only function as a sounding-board for their problems. The frequent omission of her actual words becomes, in that light, an underlining of her isolation and power-lessness, indicated more directly in statements such as 'How was Anne to set all these matters to rights? She could do little more than listen patiently' (46); and 'Anne longed for the power of represent-ing to them all what they were about' (82). Even the smallest op-portunities for self-expression are denied her.

The most striking example of this concerns her relationship with Wentworth. The 'only three of her own friends in the secret of the past' display 'perfect indifference and apparent unconsciousness . . . which seemed almost to deny any recollection of it' (30) when the Crofts' tenancy of Kellynch makes it likely that Anne will see him again. There is no one at all in whom she may confide a par-ticle of her joy, misery and perturbation – a cruelty emphasised by the fact that between her and Lady Russell 'the subject was never alluded to' (29). Anne is denied a voice in a peculiarly painful way.

Having recognised all this, when we return once more to those first words Anne speaks, that apparently irrelevant remark about the Navy, we read it entirely differently: it is not baffling at all, but Anne's secret, small pleasure in speaking some words which refer, however obliquely, to the man she loves. They are an expression of love and an indication of fortitude; they are balm to her heart.

Those few lines are the perfect example of why the narrative technique of *Persuasion* demands more active participation and ef-fort from the reader than that of *Pride and Prejudice*. Successive read-ings expand and deepen our understanding of *Pride and Prejudice*, but they take us further in the direction we were headed from the beginning. By contrast, re-reading *Persuasion* makes us radically revise our emotional response to the heroine and to the events of the story. Our 'delayed reaction' may not be unlike Anne and Wentworth's eight-and-a-half years, after which we were 'more exquisitely happy, perhaps' in our re-reading 'than when it had been first projected' (240). The delight in Anne's small triumphs during the second half of the novel increases in proportion to our understanding of the trials she has endured. There are high spirits and imminent laughter when she feels 'all over courage' (180) about

speaking to Wentworth, or in the spread of 'purification and per-
fume all the way' from Camden-place to Westgate-buildings (192).
She has not only survived the ordeal but also retained a capacity for
joy. Re-reading *Persuasion* does not just increase one's pleasure;
it involves – to a greater extent than any other Austen novel – a re-
assessment and self-questioning. It is a slow but infinitely rewarding
process, in the course of which Anne undoubtedly persuades us.

11

The Austens and the Elliots: A Consumer's Guide to *Persuasion*

Edward Copeland

Taste and class feed off each other.

Stephen Bayley, *Taste* (1991)

The usual state of consumer life in Jane Austen's novels imagines two separate acts of consumption: on the one hand, the low life of money exchange in the market, and, on the other, the elegant life of genteel consumption in the home. The first act of consumption belongs to Austen's fools and villains – Robert Ferrars, the John Dashwoods, Lucy Steele, Lydia Bennet, Harriet Smith, among the many. The second act, when the purchased objects are decently at home, belongs to the world of Austen's heroes and heroines, to Elinor Dashwood, Mr Darcy, Henry Tilney, Mr Knightley, and so on. This is the usual run of things in the Austen novel until *Persuasion*, where, in contrast, everyone shops. Instead of silencing the voice of the market or ridiculing its claims for attention, Austen brings the two acts of consumption into a single mutually revealing relationship.

In *Persuasion*, the marketplace and the home-place suddenly have something to say to one another. Take the snobbish Mary Musgrove at Uppercross Cottage, for example, with her expensive furniture, 'gradually growing shabby, under the influence of four summers and two children' (37); or her shameless, debt-ridden father's gratuitous mirrors at Kellynch: 'Such a number of looking-glasses! oh Lord! there was no getting away from oneself' (128); or Elizabeth Elliot's rented finery in Bath, at which the heroine 'must sigh, and smile, and wonder too' (138); or the empty-headed Musgrove girls at the Uppercross Great House with their confusion of a 'grand piano forte and a harp, flower-stands and little tables placed in every direction' (40). An extended list of unfortunate purchases. But what is 'wise' in *Persuasion*'s consumer world? What objects come stamped with the author's seal of approval? What camel can pass through that needle's eye?

The surviving accounts of Ring Brothers of Basingstoke, a home-furnishings emporium where the Austens shopped regularly in the 1790s may have the answer.[1] Ring Brothers sold mainly furniture, but also yard goods, carpets, wallpaper, lace, tape, tacks, nails, and an abundance of small household hardware, like stove blacking, sash cords for windows, Venetian blinds, lumber, glue, paint, and the like. The firm built furniture to order (including coffins), rented furniture if needed, and even received used furniture from regular customers to be credited to their accounts. It sent men out to hang wallpaper and lay carpets, sempstresses to make curtains and fit out beds, and carpenters to make household repairs as well as to do on-the-spot built-ins. Rather like the better-known firm of Gillows in Lancashire, Ring Brothers of Basingstoke served a similar genteel trade in Hampshire.[2]

Austen's father, in addition to his regular household purchases at Rings, in 1794 bought two special made-to-order matching beds, now lost, for Jane and Cassandra, and, probably also at Rings, Jane's handsome little writing desk, now in the possession of Joan Austen-Leigh.[3] In 1792, Austen's eldest brother James furnished his entire house from Rings, from soup-bowls and nutmeg-graters, to chairs, sofa, clock, carpets, beds, linens and chamber-pots.

Ring Brothers served, for the most part, a genteel local clientele, including a good mix of reverends, some naval men, the occasional army family, the Hampshire landed gentry, an aristocrat or so, and for two unusual seasons, the Prince Regent himself (in the unsteady spelling of Rings' clerks, the 'Prince of Whales'), who was renting a house at nearby Kempshott Park. In fact, a sizeable number of Rings' customers find mention in Austen's letters, either as social acquaintances or as objects of local gossip, among the closest being the Lefroys (Austen's niece Anna married a Lefroy), the Harwoods of Deane, the Chutes of the Vyne, the Bigg-Withers of Manydown Park (the family of the unsuccessful Harris who proposed marriage to the author, was accepted one day and refused the next), and the outrageous Charles Powlett, later the Reverend Powlett, who threat-ened to kiss Jane Austen, didn't do it, but gained local fame any-way as a notorious spendthrift. At the lower end of Rings' clientele, there are a few marginal and distinctly non-genteel aspirers to the right consumer signs: several ambitious Basingstoke attorneys, at least two surgeons (including Mr Lyford, Austen's own), a brewer, a tanner, a horse-cloth manufacturer, a schoolmaster, a schoolmistress, and a number of farmers. At Rings a full pocketbook could buy gentility, or the markers of it, regardless of rank.[4]

In *Persuasion*, however, relations between the ranks suggest a distinctly edgy state of social competition. The great dollops of contempt thrown around in that novel are astonishing. The pool of sneerers spreads from Sir Walter on down, with even minor characters in the novel harbouring the sentiment: Nurse Rooke reveals a gloating contempt for her patients, and Mrs Clay, a hearty contempt for everyone. But what can a typical list from the Ring Brothers' ledgers that consists of '5 Led Weights, Tassells, 2 brass hooks, and 2 Large thick Crankey flock mattrasses' tell us about social competition in *Persuasion*? Taken as antiquarian oddities, not much; but the consumer patterns revealed in ten years' running accounts of acquisitive customers – parsons, esquires, aristocrats and a few risers from the hoi polloi – throw the consumer context of *Persuasion* into recognisable terms of pounds, shillings and pence.

If we place the Austen family at the centre of the Ring Brothers' consumer universe, looking on one side of the Austens to their social betters and on the other side to those customers situated below the salt, the furniture store's ledgers show, surprisingly, that everybody, high, middle, and low, bought more or less the same goods. Rings' customers came to buy genteelly, to pay the asking price, and to take their trophies home in triumph. The only obvious difference between high folk and low folk in their consumption of luxuries lies in the obvious fact that more gilt sconces and oval tea trays go home with Lord Rivers than go home with Mr Austen. Rich people simply buy more of these things than people with smaller incomes, though the goods themselves remain pretty much the same. There are those subtle differences – moot questions for the gentle-minded of course – that always reward examination, the distinction between *walnut* fireplace bellows or *mahogany* fireplace bellows, for example, but even these are no more than variations on the same theme of gentility.

The consequence to fiction is that all the old literary measures of sumptuary excess get thrown out of the smoothly functioning sash windows of Ring Brothers' emporium. Visions of outrageous indulgence and indescribable consumer pleasures simply do not obtain in the Austen world, at least not in Hampshire and not at Ring

Brothers. 'Remember the country and the age in which we live', says the hero of another Jane Austen novel as he stands in the doorway of his late mother's comfortably furnished bedroom: 'Remember that we are English, that we are Christians' (*NA*, 197). The world of extravagant display on the Brighton Pavilion model is simply not the world that Jane Austen has any interest in pursuing. Susan Ferrier, a contemporary novelist, does supply a bedroom in her novel *Marriage* (1818) fitted up in 'the most boundless extravagance, the most refined luxury . . . rather suited for the pleasures of an Eastern sultana or Grecian courtesan than for the domestic comfort of a British matron' (201) and Austen herself makes a nodding gesture towards such shopping melodrama in Mr Elliot's disreputable London career: 'nothing to wish for on the side of avarice or indulgence' (206); but even this remark comes from Anne's friend Mrs Smith, who has an axe to grind with Mr Elliot. The expression for Austen is at best a tired euphemism. 'Consult your own understanding, your own sense of the probable,' says Henry Tilney, 'your own observation of what is passing around you' (*NA*, 197).

So if we start with the two tent-beds bought by Mr Austen for his daughters at Ring Brothers and compare their cost with two tent-beds purchased at Rings by the wealthy Sir Henry Paulet St John Mildmay, also known as 'Sir Harry' in the ledgers, we begin to pry open *Persuasion*'s system of consumer expense (Figure 11.1).

The practice at Rings was to make beds to the specifications of the customer. Mr Austen ordered '2 Tent Bedsteads on Casters turnd. posts Colr^d, Maho-Nobs.'[5] He paid £2. 8s. 0d. for the bedsteads themselves, that is, £1. 4s. 0d. each. That was the smallest expense of the project. The largest costs came with the required 'furniture' – that is, the 42 yards of Cotton blue and white check, the 69 yards of blue and white diamond lace, and in addition the $15\frac{3}{4}$ yards of bed ticking for two bolsters at about £1. 19s. 4d., 76*ee* of mixed Feathers (goose and hen) for £6. 6s. 8d., and much more in thread, labour, new blankets, and so on. The total came to £21.11s. 0d. for the two beds. (If we multiply the Austenian pound by a factor of 100, we get a comparative notion of a late-eighteenth-century consumer expense in 1993 US dollars; multiplying by a factor of 70 would similarly approximate the expense in current English pounds.)[6]

Sir Harry Mildmay also bought two tent-beds at Rings, the equivalent in size to Mr Austen's, but with mahogany posts, rails and knobs instead of the cheaper 'color^d' posts with mahogany knobs

11.1 Field bed (or 'tent-bed')

chosen by Mr Austen, and paid £3. 12s. 0d. for both beds, or
£1. 16s. 0d. each, 12 shillings more per bed than Mr Austen paid for
his.[7] As for the essential and costly extras, Sir Harry ordered bolsters
with 'best goose feathers' instead of 'mixed feathers', 'white fustian
down pillows' instead of 'broad stripe ticking', and much more
expensive kinds of yardage, lace and tape, for the 'furniture', with
bed curtains and valances of white dimity at 2s. 6d. a yard rather
than the cheaper Austenian blue and white cotton check at 2s. a yard,
and white calico lining – the Austens left theirs unlined – at 18d. a
yard, all of which came to a total additional outlay of £25. 16s. 10d.,
including the labour. As a result, Sir Harry's two tent-beds cost him
about £31. 8s. 2d., as opposed to Mr Austen's £21. 1s. 0d., that is,
a swingeing one-third more than Mr Austen paid for his. Jane's and
Cassandra's beds, however, *looked* very much like the Mildmay beds,
as was certainly intended, but Mr Austen, by deliberately cutting
costs on the more or less invisible parts of the package, got genteel
beds for his daughters and stayed within his limited parson's budget
as well. No small victory.

Beneath the Austens in social rank, Miss Mainwarring, 'At the School', presumably a schoolmistress, shows the same pattern of genteel display and canny spending as Mr Austen, though on a scale reflecting her smaller pocketbook. In 1791, she bought a tent-bed from Rings for £1. 5s. 0d., a bargain since her price included the labour of erecting the bed and Mr Austen's did not, but, in fact, she actually got her bed for much less than Mr Austen because she ordered no expensive 'bed furniture' at all and no other extras either, probably having adequate bolsters, pillows, mattresses, bed curtains, blankets and 'furnishings' on hand at the school. Nevertheless, all these variously priced tent-beds – the aristocratic Sir Harry's, the clergyman Austen's, and the hard-working Miss Mainwarring's – left the premises of Ring Brothers of Basingstoke flying the same flags of genteel allegiance.

This is the spending pattern so highly praised in Austen's depiction of the Harville family in *Persuasion*, who, in somewhat straitened circumstances themselves, make the best of their situation. Anne is at first dismayed at the smallness of the Harvilles' quarters in Lyme Regis, then all admiration at seeing

> the ingenious contrivances and nice arrangements of Captain Harville, to turn the actual space to the best possible account, to supply the deficiencies of lodging-house furniture, and defend the windows and doors against the winter storms to be expected. (98)

The good Mrs Harville may well deserve to live with more fashionable furniture for the goodness of her heart alone, but it must be noted that according to her rank and breeding, 'a degree less polished than her husband' (97), there is nothing to affront her or the reader's sense of her fate in these arrangements. Captain Harville, of course, belongs more firmly than his wife to the genteel ranks of society by virtue of his officer's rank in the navy, and he demonstrates his right to station by displaying in the home 'some few articles of a rare species of wood, excellently worked up' brought back from foreign parts (98). Such a notable consumer triumph brings the entire Harville establishment safely within the pale of genteel consumerism so admired by the heroine and her author.

Targeted consumer display: that is the name of the game, both at Ring Brothers and in Austen's *Persuasion*. In the Rings' accounts, tent-beds and goose-down pillows, gilt sconces and ebony mirrors,

Wilton carpets and Pembroke tables, all mark the genteel territory of the Austens and their neighbours by their presence in the home. Rare woods, too, like those brought back by *Persuasion's* Captain Harville, play a significant role. The more mahogany in a customer's Ring Brothers' account, the better, and the sharper the spirit of competitive spending. But the most significant consumer marker by far in *Persuasion* and in the Ring Brothers' ledgers is, quite literally, the bottom line: the graduated amount of credit allowed by the Rings to their variously genteel customers and by Austen in *Persuasion* to her variously genteel characters.

The ledgers at Ring Brothers show a customer's running balance at the top of each page, the customer's balance as it is 'brought on' from page to page of the firm's folios. At regular intervals determined by the rank and income of the customer, the 'brought on' balance gets settled and crossed out. An analogy might be our Visa card's personal credit line. Rings' clergymen customers, the Austens, the Lefroys, and many others, seldom carry 'brought ons' of much more than £20 or £30 before they clear them, and usually pay them long before they reach such heights. Lesser folk, like Farmer Wingate, Farmer Pern, or Farmer Wise, clear their 'brought ons' before they mount to more than £10. In contrast, the landed gentry and aristocratic customers, like Sir Harry Mildmay or Lord Rivers, when they don't pay their bills immediately (which they most often do), show credit lines or regular 'brought ons' of between £40 and £60, though sometimes they extend them to £300 and more. Sir Harry's two tent-beds, for example, are included in a Ring Brothers' 'brought on' of £289. 5s. 4d.[8]

Lady Russell's familiar words on debt bear repeating: 'The person who has contracted debts must pay them; and though a great deal is due to the feelings of the gentleman, and the head of a house, like your father, there is still more due to the character of an honest man' (12). In Austen's *Persuasion*, the industrious and economical Captain Harville is far more respectable than the debt-hounded Sir Walter Elliot, as Anne ruefully concedes.

Ring Brothers' account books contain two stories that illustrate the point. An instructive tale, a living version of 'The Grasshopper and the Ant', lies in the lists of saucepans and spoons, mahogany oval tea-trays and best parlour bellows:

> Once there were two young men, both of them beginning clergymen, who ran up accounts at Ring Brothers of Basingstoke far

beyond the normal 'brought ons' expected of men in their modest line of life. These two young men, one named James Austen, the eldest brother of the famous author, and the other named Charles Powlett, the man who threatened to kiss her, met very different fates. Ring Brothers stopped Charles Powlett in mid-shopping spree by cancelling his credit, whereas James Austen was allowed to spend double the amount. The Ring brothers had sound reasons for what they did.

In 1792, James Austen married Anne Mathew, the daughter of General Edward Mathew, on an anticipated income of about £300 a year: £200 a year from his clergyman's income, and £100 additional to be contributed by Anne's wealthy father. A comparison in Austen's novels would be the more generous living of £400 a year that James Morland is promised in *Northanger Abbey*, a living unacceptable to that lively shopper, Isabella Thorpe. To begin his marriage in genteel style, James Austen ran up an astonishing debt of £200. 15s. 0d. at Ring Brothers, and this in the space of little more than five months.[9] But James, the prudent Ant of the Ring Brothers' account books, had appeared at the establishment with the equivalent of a gift certificate amounting to £200, presumably the wedding gift of Anne's wealthy father (there are no known candidates for such generosity from the Austen side).

Four years later, in 1796, Charles Powlett, the giddy Grasshopper of the tale, married Anne Temple, the daughter of the Rev. William Johnstone Temple, Vicar of St Gluvias, Cornwall.[10] Though Powlett had aristocratic connections as the grandson (in the illegitimate line) of the third Duke of Bolton, he was a clergyman nonetheless and sentenced like James Austen to life on a clergyman's small-to-moderate living.[11] In contrast to James Austen, Charles Powlett arrived at Ring Brothers with only the good news of his marriage and the fame of his glittering family connections to gain him credit.[12] The miracle is that these went as far as they did.

Like James Austen, Powlett commenced marriage on a great wave of genteel shopping and was more than halfway to equalling Austen's magnificent debt of £200. 15s. 0d. at Rings when the Ring brothers stopped his credit. Charles Powlett's tragedy, however, was not simply the lack of a guarantor for his debts. Powlett had spent time at Hackwood Park, the sixth Duke of Bolton's estate, in the company of aristocrats, even the Prince Regent himself, and had acquired consumer tastes far beyond his clergyman's income.[13]

Midway through his spending extravaganza at Ring Brothers it must have become increasingly apparent to the Rings that young Charles Powlett was not spending in the accepted pattern of the firm's clergymen customers at all, including the recently flush James Austen, but in a strange and unfamiliar pattern, reckless and even dangerous. The crucial difference between James Austen's accounts at Rings and Charles Powlett's is not in the furniture that the two men bought – they bought much the same things – but in their patterns of expense. James Austen was firmly entrenched in the prudent habits of the professional class from which he came, whereas Charles Powlett swung wildly between the sober economic principles of Austen's class, the one he had to live in, and his pretensions to aristocracy, packaged conveniently but unhappily for him in consumer temptations.

James Austen, for example, began his account at Ring Brothers on 6 March 1792 with a great fortissimo of clergyman elegance:

A neat 2ft. 10 Inch Maho-Pembroke table on
casters, fine wood, wth Drawer .... £ 1 18 0.
An Ovel Maho-Card Table & Lined Green Cloth .... £ 2 2 0.
2 Mahogany Convenient stools .... £ 1 11 0.
3 Ovel Dress Glasses [at 19s. 6d., 10s., and
10s. 6d.] .... £ 2 0 0.
Neat Sconce Glass . . . Carv'd & Gilt frame .... £ 2 2 0.
A 4 ft Wainscot Dining Table .... £ 1 11 6.
Cherry tree Claw Table .... £ 0 8 0.
Maho-Dress Table with Drawer................................. £ 0 13 6.
2 Beds, with Maho-Posts on casters........................... £ 4 4 0.
115 y^{ds} of Dimity at 2/5 for 2 bed furn^{ts} .... £13 17 11.
3 Mahogany Bason stands with D^{rs} .... £ 1 19 0.
Set Circular End Light Mahogany Dining Tables
with strap Hinges and Brass fastenings...................... £ 5 7 6.
A 4 Post Bedst, Casters, posts round, Rod & Rails ... £ 1 18 6.[14]

And that's about it for James Austen and conspicuous consumption. Except for the expensive order of dimity for the two beds and the sizable outlay for the 'Set Circular Light Mahogany Dining Tables with strap Hinges and Brass fastenings' (a kind of eighteenth-century extension table),[15] there are no really grand expenditures. The great remainder of the day's purchases are dutiful, behind-the-scenes household items: kitchen bellows, '2 Pair old Iron Candlesticks', a pudding bowl, a hand dish, one large pail and a smaller one, some scrub brushes, a few pieces of deal (pine) furniture, and such things, all of which ran up the bill to a considerable 'brought on', however, of £83. 10s. 7d. A few weeks later, no doubt after consultation with his wife-to-be, he was back for more household necessities, and increased his 'brought on' to £124. 12s. 3d., again with very few items of genteel display on the list: a 'Mahogany Dumb waiter on Casters' (£2. 2s. 0d.), '2 Neat mahogany face screens on Clawes' (£1. 1s. 0d.), and a 'Mahogany Side Board Table, with Celleret Drawers Lined with led Posts' (£7. 17s. 0d.), an expensive, showy addition to the dining room. The rest, for the most part, were such things as flat irons, a twenty-gallon tub, a deal ironing-board, a nutmeg-grater, and other backstairs necessities. Tellingly, in mid-list he decided against an expensive eight-day clock with a walnut case and cancelled the order (£4. 0s. 0d.).

The following two visits to Ring Brothers were equally dutiful in their ordering, enlivened with only the small luxuries of Rings' 'Best Urn Top^d Shovel Tongs & Poker' (£0. 8s. 6d.) and some 'fine Strip^d Cotton for the drawing Room' at 2s. 11d. a yard (£2. 6s. 8d). But on his last two visits, the prudent James Austen sprang for the two ritual objects of genteel display that he had been saving back to buy all the time: first, that clock that he had wanted earlier, but now, with the rewards of delayed gratification, in a more expensive 'arch head' model at £5. 15s. 6d., with a walnut case at £1. 11s. 6d. (total: £7. 7s. 0d.); and, second, a fine new 'sopha', which, with all the extras of covers, pads, pillows and so forth, amounted to 'Sopha Comp^l Charg^d £7-0-0'. Together, with delivery and installation, these two final, topping-it-off markers of genteel station demanded an extravagant, but carefully budgeted, outlay of £14. 14s. 6d.

James Austen's grand total appears in the Ring Brothers' ledger boldly rendered with unusual calligraphic splendour for the Rings' sober clerks – '£200-15-0' – exactly as if the clerk had reached across the counter with a kind word and a congratulatory handshake: 'A fine job of shopping, Mr Austen. Well done, indeed, Sir!'

Charles Powlett, it must be granted, did try to spend like a clergyman. His earliest experiences at Ring Brothers in 1793 show a bill promptly paid at the usual clergyman's final 'brought on' of around £30.[16] He contented himself with a few pieces of deal furniture, a pair of modestly priced 'Parlour Bellows' at 3s. 6d., and a shovel and tongs for 3s. 9d., along with considerable amounts of lumber, bed cord, pulleys, nails, some bell cranks: a list that is absolutely indistinguishable from the Austens', the Lefroys', or any other of Rings' typical clergymen customers. Subsequent shopping trips continued to show the expected clergyman's pattern of careful spending: a 'Pair Painted Chest Drawers' (£1. 11s. 6d.) and an 'Old [used] Maho-Dining Table' (£1. 18s. 0d.) as the most expensive additions to his household furniture.

In short, Charles Powlett began his disastrous shopping expedition of 1796 with a clean slate. Like James Austen, he commenced marriage with a spirited assertion of genteel prosperity, a little extravagant perhaps, but appropriately so considering the occasion, and not enough to cause the Ring brothers any immediate concern. In fact the list looks much like James Austen's list, with perhaps some subtle warning signals on the horizon, though probably visible only with hindsight.

Mahogany wardrobe ... 4 Shelves 4 Drawers .... £7 0 0.
Pair Sollid Mahogany Chest Drawers .... £3 15 0.
Neat Mahogany Butlers Tray 2 f^t 2^{in}, 1 f^t 10 Inches
Wide, Sides 4 Inches .... £0 10 6.
Japan^d Cole Hodd Gild Edg^d .... £0 6 6.
2f^t 6 In Mahogany Pembroke Table with Drawer
[Figure 11.2] .... £1 11 6.
23 In Ovel Mahogany Tea Tray with Plated
handles .... £0 11 6.[17]

Powlett's order, as we see, is suspiciously scanty in the small, day-to-day household items so typical of a clergyman's order list, although it could be argued that Powlett had already stocked his home with such necessaries. Nevertheless, in subsequent visits to Rings, Powlett's orders became even less clergyman-like and more extravagant in items of conspicuous consumption. A brief selection from his final orders illustrates the alarming pattern that begins to emerge:

Mahogany Book Case Bedstead [including
the 'furniture', the bolster, pillow, ticking,
cords, pulley, lace, binding, etc. .... Total: £18 17 7.]
Neat Mahogany Night Stool with one Drawer
at top with White stone pan to D° .... £ 2 4 9.
A Neat Leather Back Gammon Table Boxes
and Men 14 Inches .... £ 1 10 0.

Pembroke Tables and Tea Trays

11.2   Pembroke tables and tea trays

12   Neat Plain Ivory handle Dub Top Knifes,
12 3-prong forks, 12 Desert D° and D°,
1 Carving D°, and D°, and sharpe[ner] .... £ 3 8 6.
A Neat Mahogany Night Table Commod,
Handles & Brass Lock Comp[l] .... £ 2 16 0.
Tent Bedstead on Casters, 2 Maho-Posts &
4 nobs, Dome Top 5ft w[d], 6 ft high [with all
the 'furniture' and extras of mattresses,
pillows, etc. .... Total: £23 9 5.]
Maho-Night Table with folding Tops and
Cupboards Comp[l] with W[t] Stone pan to D° .... £ 2 15 3.
A neat Mahogany Biddit [bidet], White Stone
pan to D° .... £ 2 5 0.[18]

At this point, the Rings said, 'No More.' They submitted a bill
to Powlett for immediate payment totalling £128. 6s. 7d. Even without the surprising 'Biddit' (none of Rings' customers, aristocratic
or otherwise, had ever ordered such a thing), or the extravagant

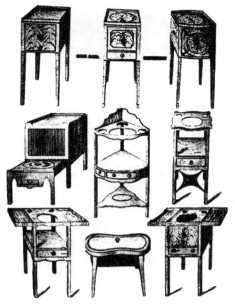

Pot Cupboards, Night Table, Basin Stands, and Bidet

11.3   Pot cupboards, night table, basin stands, bidet

backgammon table, the pattern of Powlett's spending had departed so emphatically from the prudent clergyman's pattern of James Austen that this could not go unnoticed. A Japanned, gilt-edged 'cole hodd' might seem a little extravagant – James Austen had cancelled his order in favour of a cheaper model – but two bedsteads that exceed £18 and £23 *each*? This would give pause to Sir Harry Mildmay himself. And whoever heard of a 'Bookcase Bedstead'? And what about that *dome*-topped tent-bed? Who did young Powlett think he was, the Prince Regent?

As for all those elegant mahogany night stools, night tables, and 'biddits,' these were beyond James Austen's wildest fantasy (Figs 11.3 and 11.4). Austen did celebrate his marriage, it must be admitted, with two mahogany 'Convenient stools', at £1. 11s. 0d., the pair, the same as the 'Convenient stools' preferred by Mr Demazy of Hertford Bridge, and Thomas Colthard, Esq., of Farleigh, and Mr Seagram, Surgeon – a sensible purchase certified by a good range of Rings' customers.[19] But this was a far less expensive assertion of gentility than Charles Powlett's extravagant array of mahogany furnitures

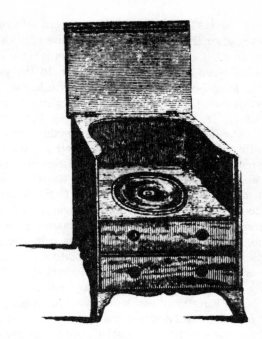

11.4   Night table ('convenient stool')

'with Stone pan'. Any needs beyond the capacity of James's two elegant, but supremely standard, mahogany pieces could be met at the Austen house by the two 'White Stone Chamber Pots' that James had ordered for eight pence each.

Moreover, it is not at all possible to tell with any certainty which one of the several beds that James Austen ordered from Rings was to be the grand matrimonial couch, since James, like his father, cut corners by buying some of the bed furniture 'old' and by supplying most of the bolsters, pillows, and mattresses himself. No 'Book Case Bedstead' or 'Dome Top' beds for the Austens. In fact, Charles Powlett's 'Book Case Bedstead', with all its expensive trappings, was repossessed by Ring Brothers almost as soon as they stopped credit, with eight shillings, and sixpence added to the bill for the Powletts' three months' use of it. As a sad little coda to the tale of the giddy Grasshopper, Charles Powlett's final, monstrous bill went unpaid for five years, until 1801, when it was recorded in the Ring Brothers' ledger as paid to the estate of the deceased John Ring.[20]

Jane Austen's strikingly sharp-edged references to Charles Powlett and his bride – she was a partner in this concern – in her letters of 1798, two years after their marriage, reveal the seriousness of the principles involved. Gossip about the Powletts was already rife: 'Charles Powlett gave a dance on Thursday, to the great disturbance of all his neighbours, of course, who, you know, take a most lively interest in the state of his finances, and live in hopes of his being soon ruined' (*L*, 36). Two weeks later the Powletts made the news again: 'his wife is discovered to be everything that the Neighbourhood could wish her, silly & cross as well as extravagant' (39). In 1801, Austen dined with the couple and reports: 'Mrs Powlett was at once expensively & nakedly dress'd; we have had the satisfaction of estimating her Lace & her Muslin' (105). Austen's interest in the Powletts, always in reference to their overspending, expresses the unyielding facts of economic life for cash-dependent professional people. News of financial disaster is not idle gossip. For Austen's rank, the Powletts represent a positive danger.

Persuasion is in this sense an expanded version of the Austens' own spending patterns. But then, so are Jane Austen's other novels. The records of the Ring Brothers' store reinforce the argument that none of her novels is truly about the gentry or about the aristocracy, but about the survival of Austen's own professional rank. It is true that Mr Darcy, Sir Thomas Bertram, and Mr Knightley sport credentials from the gentry and even the aristocracy, but these privileged characters are also among Austen's firmest advocates for the prudent, tempered, middling-way spending patterns of her own family.

Persuasion, however, does have the distinction in Austen's novels of celebrating the professional ranks frankly and openly, of placing them above the aristocracy and the gentry as responsible economists, but such celebration is no more than a secondary issue in the novel. *Persuasion* is first of all a Cautionary Tale, one directed specifically to Austen's own social rank. As with the Powletts in real life, spendthrifts in *Persuasion* find no mercy from the author, and for the same reason. Such a reading puts the consumer melodrama of Mrs Smith's sad story into the same cautionary frame as the rest of the novel. As Austen perceives it, and as the Ring Brothers' accounts make clear, the real dangers to the professional ranks come from within. For that reason, the major issues of *Persuasion* find expression in the metaphor of credit and the domestic budget.

Can an individual by the measure of his or her income afford the growing balance in Rings' ledgers? Sir Walter Elliot fails the test.

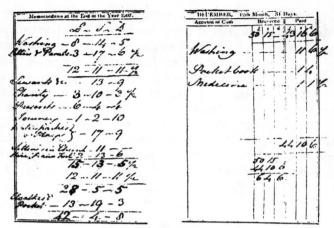

Pages from Jane Austen's Pocket Book

11.5   Pages from Jane Austen's pocket-book

He cannot pay his bills, and that reason alone, for Austen, makes him, like the Charles Powletts, thoroughly contemptible. Charles and Mary Musgrove also have consumer aspirations too grand for their purse and, as a result, they share too in the author's contempt. The Musgrove girls may face a dubious future as well, if, as the prospective wives of professional men, their expensive additions to the Great House parlour are an early warning sign of trouble to come. In contrast, the good economists of *Persuasion*, Anne, Lady Russell and Mrs Croft, receive unqualified praise for their sound arithmetic and strict principles of prompt payment.

Jane Austen joins the company of these worthy women as a list-maker and good economist herself. Her pocket-book entry, 'Memorandums at the End of the Year 1807' (Figure 11.5), shows a carefully budgeted list of household and personal expenses: washing, letters and parcels, gifts to servants, presents for family and friends, travel expenses, entertainment, the hire of a piano forte, clothes, pocket expenses, and medicine.[21] For a woman from the genteel professional ranks, there could be no more typical assertion of her social responsibility than Austen's careful, moderate list.

Even so, Jane Austen is no enemy to consumer luxuries. In *Emma*, the Coles get their new dining-room and that's fine: they can afford it (207). In the same novel, Mr Perry denies his wife a carriage because, as Mr Weston observes, he can't afford it, at least not *yet*

(345). But in *Emma*, credit is not the issue; in *Persuasion*, it is the central issue, just as it is at Ring Brothers – calculated to the last consumer penny. In the light of all the unmet longings and abortive shopping in Austen's last novel, *Emma's* Mr Knightley seems in retrospect more than a little naïve when he announces grandly to Mrs Elton that 'the simplicity of gentlemen and ladies' is best observed in their own dining rooms, 'with their servants and furniture' around them (355). One can picture such a show of genteel 'simplicity' now, the happy party seated for mutual gratification, no doubt about it, at a 'Set [of] Circular End, Light Mahogany Dining Tables, with strap Hinges and Brass fastenings, Compl^t. . . . £5-7-6'.

Notes

1. I am indebted to Deirdre Le Faye, who cites the Ring Brothers' records (262), for encouraging me to examine them. The records of the firm are housed at Winchester in the Hampshire Records Office 8M62/14 and 8M62/15. The Rings are listed among 'the principal inhabitants' of Basingstoke in *The Universal Directory of Trade, Commerce and Manufacture* (London, 1791).
2. See Amanda Vickery's essay, 'Women and the World of Goods: A Lancashire Consumer and Her Possessions, 1751–81'.
3. Mr Austen ordered the beds on 20 January 1794. A writing desk was purchased on 5 December 1794: 'a Small Mahogany Writing Desk with 1 Long Drawer and Glass Ink Stand, Compleat . . . £0-12-0'. Le Faye, *Jane Austen: A Family Record*, suggests that it may have been intended as a gift for Austen's nineteenth birthday (83).
4. I follow David Spring's essay, 'Interpreters of Jane Austen's Social World: Literary Critics and Historians', in my understanding of the consumer practices of Austen's social rank, the 'pseudo-gentry' (non-landowning professionals). These people, writes Spring, 'devoted their lives to acquiring the trappings of gentry status for themselves and especially their children' (60).
5. 'Revd. Mr Austin [sic] Senr. Steventon', 20 January 1794.
6. Edward Copeland, 'The Economic Realities of Jane Austen's Day'.
7. These orders were placed 10 January 1793. The sums I have given for Mildmay are closely approximate, with some slack in determining exactly which lace, tape, and tacks, etc., went with each of the four beds in this large order.
8. Such large lines of credit are unusual. Mildmay is the Rings' customer who most frequently carried such a large 'brought on'. Lord Rivers had one when there was a large project, but that is rare. When lesser folk run up very large bills, the accounts sometimes indicate

that previous arrangements had been made. See accounts for John Byron, Esq., 25 January 1787, where a bill has mounted to £310, and the ledger records, 'Rec^d as behind', for a £100 payment on the debt. Interest could also be arranged, as it was for Byron.

9. For more on James's marriage to Anne Mathew, see Le Faye, 67.
10. *Jane Austen's Letters*, ed. R. W. Chapman, 2nd edn (Oxford: Oxford University Press, 1979), 'Indexes II: Other Persons'.
11. Like Jane Austen's father, Charles Powlett resorted to taking in students to supplement his income. See Deborah Kaplan, *Jane Austen among Women*, 80.
12. The furniture from Rings was sent to Hackwood Farm, part of the Hackwood Park estate of the sixth Duke of Bolton. Deborah Kaplan (letter to the author, 23 September 1993) says that in August 1797 the Powletts moved from Hackwood Farm to Winslade. Winslade is less than ten miles from Steventon, where presumably the Powletts were living when Jane Austen reported gossip of them in 1798.
13. For more information about the debt-plagued Powlett marriage, see Kaplan, 18–19.
14. James Austen's series of wedding purchases at Ring Brothers runs from 6 March to 5 September 1792. This selection is taken from his list of purchases for 6 March. The 'brought on' came to £83. 10s. 7d.
15. Ralph Edwards notes a bill for Sir Edward Knatchbull, 1769, from Chippendale, for '2 Mahogany round ends to Join his Dining Tables, with 2 pair of strap Hinges, Hooks and Eyes, etc. £5'; this was the most recent development in extendable dining tables until 1800, when Richard Gillows patented a new device for extending tables (540–1).
16. 2 February to 7 March 1793.
17. The selection of goods is taken from Powlett's first visits to Rings, 18 and 21 March 1796.
18. These selections come from lists of orders placed by Powlett from 29 March to 23 May. Repossession of some pieces of furniture began on 8–9 July 1796.
19. These customers were regular buyers of targeted elegance. Their 'convenient stools', all at approximately 15s. 6d. each (not including the 2s. 'stone pan'), were purchased on the following dates: Demazy, 20 June 1791; Colthard, 20 April 1793; Seagram, 20–3 September 1794.
20. A prominent citizen, having served Basingstoke as mayor and alderman, John Ring was 'buried 7th May, 1796, aged 65' (Baignent and Millard, 447).
21. The list, in the Pierpont Morgan Library, is reproduced in 'The Jane Austen Society: Report for the Year 1980,' in *Collected Reports of the Jane Austen Society, 1976–1985*, 147. I am indebted to Jan Fergus for reminding me of this list.

12

Jane Austen's Real Business: The Novel, Literature and Cultural Capital

Gary Kelly

Jane Austen's place in literature seems secure, and has long seemed so. Her novels are universally ranked with what the English writer Fay Weldon calls 'Literature with a capital L,' or books connected to 'the very essence of civilization' (9). Yet the apparent stability and continuity of Austen's literary standing conceal a history of contradiction and conflict. For, whatever else it might be, literature is a form of cultural capital, its meaning and value formed in an economy that is socially and historically particular, and subject to change. Material capital, including property, possessions and investments, underpins the status and power of its possessors, or what might be called social capital. But such status and power are legitimised and reproduced by cultural capital, including certain kinds of knowledge, skills, tastes, language and manners. These are hierarchically differentiated and unequally distributed according to social differences, especially of class (Bourdieu, 1984). Thus the differential distribution of material capital creates and is reproduced by differential distribution of cultural capital (Bourdieu, 1990, 124–5). As John Guillory argues, since Jane Austen's time, literature with a capital 'L' has become a major form of such cultural capital (Guillory, xi). Austen contributed to that process by transforming the hitherto sub-literary form of the novel into Literature as cultural capital for her time. This was her 'business' in several senses: her occupation, task, province, profession, agenda, concern and – not least – her line of commerce.

In her time, 'literature' was primarily 'the body of writing that constitutes learning or knowledge' (Williams). It was a form of cultural capital derived from Renaissance humanism and long shared by the upper and middle classes. It was a way to accumulate moral and intellectual capital, or the intellectual discipline, methods, and information useful in the professions and public life. It was a way to acquire linguistic capital, or knowledge of kinds of language useful in influential society, the professions and public affairs. But it was also a form of symbolic capital, displayed in order to establish membership in a particular social group. This group included both 'Society', or the upper classes and those who served, associated with, and aspired to join them, and the 'political nation', or those with direct or mediated influence on affairs of state. The men of the Austen family, who were in the professions, depended on literature in this sense for their livelihoods, their social standing and their advancement. To what extent women needed literature in this sense was a matter for ongoing debate, a debate to which Jane Austen contributed through her novels.

The primary sense of 'literature' today is 'written verbal art of high moral and intellectual value'. In Austen's day this was a secondary and emergent sense, but it was gaining ground because of complex social and cultural changes, in which the Austens participated. At that time literature as verbal art was mainly a form of symbolic capital, usually called 'polite literature' or *'belles-lettres'*, terms borrowed from the French in the early eighteenth century. But it was ambiguous symbolic capital. On one hand it was considered a sign and a cause of the 'progress' of 'civil society', or the transformation of feudalism into a 'modern' social, cultural and economic order. On the other hand it was considered a sign and a cause of 'modern' decadence and corruption, characteristic of societies under court government and aristocratic hegemony, such as France. Nevertheless, in the eighteenth century many middle-class Britons took up the *belles-lettres* as symbolic capital. For the aristocracy and gentry had long practised conspicuous consumption to manifest their accumulated material and cultural capital. These patterns of consumption stimulated the eighteenth-century commercial revolution, which depended on a 'fashion system' that marketed to the middle classes cheaper versions of the goods and services consumed by the dominant upper classes (McKendrick). The *belles-lettres* conveyed information about all aspects of the fashion system, from how to dress to how to feel, from how to converse to how to court a mate. The *belles-lettres* were also objects of fashionable consumption, from pamphlets of verse to tomes of 'polite learning', from magazines to 'modern novels'. Knowledge of the *belles-lettres*, including both vernacular 'classics' and 'books of the day', became important symbolic capital, opening access to 'Society' and the 'political nation'.

Jane Austen knew this well. In the late 1780s she probably contributed a satire to her brothers' Oxford magazine *The Loiterer* (Honan, 57–61), directed at forms of the *belles-lettres* that the Austens considered to serve a decadent and corrupt social and political order. The *belles-lettres* also come into play in Austen's novels, placing character, as in Robert Martin's range of reading, in *Emma* (29); illustrating values, as in Anne Elliott's advice to Captain Benwick in *Persuasion* (100-1) to avoid Romantic poets such as Byron and Scott; or defining relationships, as in the use of Kotzebue's *Lovers' Vows* in *Mansfield Park*. But unlike many other novelists, Austen uses such allusions sparsely, avoids being either showily learned or ostentatiously up-to-date, and stays within a decorously feminine range of reading. In this way she indicates a critical attitude to the *belles-lettres* as cultural capital.

Literature as cultural capital did not necessarily coincide with literature as material capital, however. By Austen's day, a well-appointed and well-stocked library was indispensable to the gentleman, be he a modest squire like Mr Bennet or a great landowner like Mr Darcy. But books were expensive, with a typical three-volume novel, for example, costing the equivalent of two weeks' wages for a labourer. Literature, especially 'fashionable' literature, was made affordable through commercial circulating libraries, often furnished to resemble the gentleman's private library (Varma). Jane Austen patronised such libraries, and they are a feature of genteel life in her novels (*Sense and Sensibility*, appendix: 'Reading and Writing'). Small reading societies also circulated and discussed 'books of the day', thereby reinforcing local networks of social, political, or economic interest, within a nationwide community of identity and interest. Jane Austen belonged to such a Book Society at Chawton, claiming that it set the intellectual and cultural standard for the county (*L*, 294). Meanwhile, ownership of books was becoming easier through reprinting in cheap formats of texts with continuing readership or in the public domain. Publishers marketed such books by appealing to the middle classes' desire for cultural capital – claiming the patronage of a leader of taste and fashion (Cooke's reprints), presenting texts in 'elegant' format 'embellished' with illustrations by 'leading artists', engaging a recognised cultural authority such as Samuel Johnson or Anna Laetitia Barbauld as editor, or issuing texts in series of 'classics' or 'standard' works.

Thus literature circulated as cultural capital of different kinds. Most 'books of the day' were part of the fashion system, their value as cultural capital depended on their novelty, they were consumed in quantity, and they were considered ephemeral, to be rented rather than purchased as material capital. 'Classics' were considered moral and intellectual capital, accumulated by rereading or studying 'standard' texts rather than engaging in restless diversity. Classics served as symbolic capital by providing a common, secularised ground of diversity-in-unity for the socially dominant classes and their immediate associates (Kermode, 139–41). Therefore they could be acquired as a permanent investment. Austen's novels were first published for the circulating-library trade, and only made available as reprints some years after her death. Yet it was the reprint edition that first made their claim to be classics, and enabled them to become so. In fact, both 'books of the day' and 'classics' were forms of commercialised consumption.

This was most obvious in the form of *belles-lettres* practised by Jane Austen. Novels were thought to comprise the largest proportion of literary consumption, yet most were considered subliterary (Taylor), condescendingly referred to as 'fashionable novels', 'modern novels' – 'modern' signifying 'not classic' – and 'the trash of the circulating libraries'. Most were considered deficient in 'useful' or 'solid' information and in artistry. They were the last form of *belles-lettres* to be honoured by reprinting as 'classics'. Novels were even considered dangerous. They were supposed to arouse desire for 'Society', leading to disgust with 'real life', or the middle-class station of most novel-readers. Since such desire could not be satisfied in reality, it was thought to create an appetite for more novels, similar to dram-drinking and over-eating. Novels were supposed to stimulate imagination at the expense of reason and to cause neglect of 'solid' and 'useful' reading, thereby obstructing accumulation of moral and intellectual capital needed in middle-class life. Novels were supposed to inspire imitation of fashionable life and vices, leading to expenditure of time better invested in self-improvement, and of money better invested in material capital.

Yet novels also provided readers with information of great interest, related directly to their material interests. Most novels portrayed the manners, tastes, and power relations of the classes to which many novel readers aspired. Most novels also portrayed models for gentrified middle-class social conduct, subjective experience, class relations, and negotiation with upper-class ideology and conduct. Thus most novels formalise, in their structure and themes, the middle classes' increasing ambivalence about their relationship of emulation, in the sense of both rivalry and imitation, with the dominant classes. On the other hand, novels were also thought to be produced *en masse*, according to mere formula, and to be consumed promiscuously. Consequently, their popularity was thought to represent and reinforce the culture of the 'vulgar', or lowest elements of the new 'reading public'. This was an unknown and therefore frightening cultural force, resulting from displacement of a literary system that was ordered, hierarchical, and patronage-directed by one that was unpredictable, unpoliceable, and market-driven. Thus the tension between culture and commodity, art and commerce, had social and political implications that compromised the novel's status as cultural capital. It continues to do so for some kinds of fiction, such as the 'Regency romance' which is, ironically, a development from Austen's own novels.

For Jane Austen made it her business to transform the situation of the novel, paradoxically by exploiting it. She understood her business well. The Austens were avid, unashamed, and self-consciously discriminating novel-readers. Jane Austen began her writing career as a critic of the 'novel of the day', burlesquing its moral exaggeration, intellectual thinness, and artistic crudity. She began writing serious fiction in the 1790s, when Elizabeth Inchbald, Robert Bage, William Godwin, Mary Wollstonecraft, and others were reclaiming the novel from service to what they saw as a decadent upper-class culture that helped cause revolution in France and social conflict in Britain (Butler, 1975). They designed their novels to criticise both the established order and the literature that served it. To achieve greater rhetorical force for this project, and to make their novels into moral and intellectual capital, they aimed for more intellectual content, formal coherence, and fidelity to common experience than they found in 'novels of the day', or even many 'classic' novels. In these ways, they aimed to re-educate the reading public for participation in a 'political nation' transformed in the image and interests of the middle classes, led by 'progressive' forces such as themselves.

Many people, including the Austens, were alarmed by this project, however, fearing that it would unleash forces it could not control, as in France. This was the scenario presented in Edmund Burke's

Reflections on the Revolution in France (1790), which attacks 'men of letters' in France and their counterparts in Britain for fomenting revolution to serve their own ends. This argument exploited both familiar criticism of hack-writers for pandering to the 'vulgar' and increased anxiety about the nature and power of the new 'reading public'. Writers such as William Gifford and Hannah More then included women writers in condemnations of literature as a commodity that aroused social dissatisfaction, leading to political revolution. Advocates of reform countered that the 'rise of the reading public' and participation of women and plebeians in literature showed the 'spread of truth' and 'enlightenment', heralding a revolution that would be non-violent because based on the 'diffusion of literature' as works of information, instruction and taste. By the mid-1790s, when Austen took up serious novel-writing, advocates of reform were in retreat, a change signalled by the appearance of novels attacking them, their ideas and their fiction (C. Johnson). Austen knew the most important of these, including burlesques such as Elizabeth Hamilton's *Memoirs of Modern Philosophers* (1800), serious critiques such as Jane West's *A Tale of the Times* (1799), and apparently apolitical novels such as Frances Burney's *Camilla* (1796), which omitted overt discussion of politics, thereby suggesting that politics should be irrelevant to central concerns of the novel-reading classes. The latter was the kind of novel Austen chose to write.

In the mid-1790s she began and completed novels later published as *Sense and Sensibility* and *Pride and Prejudice*. Though more or less transformed between composition and publication, they can be related to the novelistic side of the revolution debate. They attack snobbish and self-serving clergy, upper-class arrogance, middle-class vulgarity, and female ignorance and coquetry – topics found in reformist novels before the revolution and in pro-revolutionary novels of the 1790s. Austen's novels also illustrate a constructive interchange of gentry and middle-class virtues, the necessity for women to have cultivated minds and yet the dangers of female intellectual presumption, the association of the culture of Sensibility with transgression of various kinds, the importance of social understanding and tolerance, and the stabilising force of a social hierarchy led by a coalition of enlightened gentry and professionals. These topics could be found in moderately reformist pre-revolutionary and post-revolutionary novels (Kelly, Chapter 3). Though Austen did try to sell the early version of *Pride and Prejudice* in 1797, neither it nor the early version of *Sense and Sensibility* was published until well after the revolutionary decade, perhaps because of widespread criticism of women writers for contributing to social, cultural, and political disorder merely by publishing at all.

When she did publish, circumstances were more favourable. In the revolutionary aftermath, literature was reconstructed to shed negative associations of the revolution debate and to serve a renewed coalition of upper and upper-middle classes. This would be done by bringing together art and instruction, hitherto seen as the respective cultural capital of the coalition's different partners. Increased emphasis on artistry would shed literature's associations with the dangerous utility of literature as political intervention, then called 'philosophy' (Simpson), in a new literary-philosophical discourse later called Romanticism. Other movements, such as Utilitarianism, Evangelicalism and science, remained hostile to both literature and philosophy because of their different associations with upper-class genteel culture and revolutionary conflict. All of these movements, however, re-emphasised the centrality of the domestic sphere to the social, cultural, and political life of nation and empire. This emphasis reinforced restriction of women to their supposedly 'traditional' roles in household management, early education, construction of home as a preparation for and refuge from the conflicted public sphere, and local social improvement and mediation. Most women writers settled for depicting and promoting these roles, in appropriate genres, from conduct-books to narrative poems, from popularised scholarship to didactic fiction. Partly because of their association with women's sphere, however, these genres or women's work in them continued to be excluded from literature as art of serious moral and intellectual purpose.

Austen first sold her work to a publisher in 1803, and though it was not published until after her death, Northanger Abbey clearly addresses this post-revolutionary situation. For example, many writers used various devices to shed the novel's associations with the fashion system, transgressive conduct and politics, popular formulas, excessive 'sensibility', artifice and fantasy, and intellectual shallowness. These devices include self-exculpatory prefaces (Maria Edgeworth, Belinda, 1801), use of alternative generic terms such as 'A Tale' (Jane West, A Tale of the Times, 1799), condemnations of the 'mere novel' by narrators or fictional characters, ostentatious use of settings and characters from 'common life' (Elizabeth LeNoir, Village Anecdotes, 1804), insistence on 'realism' and probability (Maria Edgeworth, Popular Tales, 1804), and inclusion of material from respected discourses such as poetry or history (Ann Radcliffe, *The Italian*, 1797; Elizabeth Hamilton, *Life of Agrippina*, 1804). *Northanger Abbey* participates in this post-revolutionary negotiation between the novel and literature, but in its own way.

It eschews many anti-novel devices used by others, and draws attention to the fact, and it contains (Volume 1, Chapter 5) the best-known brief defence in English of the novel as Literature. But it, too, deals with serious social issues by exposing the plight of middle-class women in a society dominated by courtly patriarchy, and it, too, criticises novelistic excesses and their social counterparts. These include social emulation (the Thorpes), excessive sensibility (Isabella), gullible reading (discussion of 'horrid novels'), the supposed pre-dominance of women among novel readers (Catherine and Henry's discussion of reading), and the exposure of 'Gothic' or *ancien régime* culture in contemporary society (Catherine's imaginings about General Tilney). Yet, as novel readers then would know, General Tilney's attempt to manipulate others for his own and his family's profit was widely condemned as a general characteristic of the *ancien régime*, leading to the violent reaction of revolution.

More important, *Northanger Abbey* reconstructs the novel as liter-ature with a capital 'L', as cultural capital for its time. Austen repre-sents, through management of form and style, a crucial relationship between reading literature – even novels – and reading the world, or 'life'. Thus Charlotte Brontë was right to say that Austen's 'busi-ness' is 'delineating the surface of the lives of genteel English people', their modes of perception and judgement, social interaction, and manners, or 'what sees keenly, speaks aptly, moves flexibly'. For in Austen's real and fictional worlds such seeing, speaking, and moving are important forms of cultural capital, evidence of one's member-ship in 'Society'. But they are also outward signs of the inward merit that should, and in the comic world of her novels does, profit both their possessors and those who can read such signs right. Austen aims to reclaim the novel as cultural capital for the revolu-tionary aftermath by offering lessons in 'what sees keenly, speaks aptly, moves flexibly', connected to lessons in right reading.

Accordingly, her novels represent protagonists reading their immediate social world in order to negotiate a successful accom-modation with it. In this world, as in that of Austen's readers, success is measured in terms of an ideology and culture being forged in the coalition of gentry and upper-middle class. Thus *Sense and Sens-ibility* presents two different readers, erring in different ways, but ultimately converging in true reading and the almost hackneyed happy ending for both. *Pride and Prejudice* presents another pair of grounds for misreading, and another pair of sisters, complicated by a misreading and misread hero. *Mansfield Park* recasts the problem of reading differently. Educated by her cousin Edmund, Fanny is able to read others correctly, but like those around her she does not read herself correctly, undervaluing herself until she is appreciated by the fashionably well-read Henry Crawford, and in rejecting him is judged by her relations to overvalue herself. In time, however, her merit is manifested to others in ethical correctness based on her ability to read others right, especially in crises. The heroine of *Emma* is a poor reader of people, books and herself, and acts on her misreadings, thereby hurting others and almost destroying her own prospect of happiness. Fortunately, she marries a man capable of re-educating her. In *Persuasion* Austen returns to the well-read and right-reading heroine misread by others, but now shows how the relationship between reading, ethical action, and reward may be affected through time.

Novelistic representation of the relationship between reading books and reading the world can be traced from Renaissance romance and anti-romance through seventeenth-century courtly novellas, early eighteenth-century anti-court novels, the 'female quixote' tradition, and novels of sensibility, to novels by many of Austen's contemporaries (Butler, 1975). Motivating this tradition is the experience of social difference and subordination of many novel-readers, for whom security and success depended on correct reading of a world dominated by the social 'other'. The protagonist of such novels is often female, but these were read as much by men as women, fictional characters are figures more than representations, and middle-class readers of both sexes could read themselves into a female protagonist perilously engaged with a dimly understood system of patronage and paternalism. Furthermore, reading was of particular value to the professional middle class to which the Austens and most novel-readers belonged. Professional men required reading of specialised kinds in order to earn a living, and both professional men and their wives and daughters required socially and culturally informed kinds of reading in order to get on in life. Novelistic representation of the problematics of reading was of compelling interest to them because it represented their material interests in real life – the interest to be derived from accumulated cultural capital of several kinds. Austen is very particular about such material interests, including estates, jointures, legacies, entails, marriages, 'establishments', preferments, postings, and so on (Moers, 101–19). Austen goes beyond representation of reading, however, to engage the reader in a process parallel to that engaging the fictional protagonist (Handley, 122–30). She does so, provocatively, by putting in play elements of the novel as the 'trash of the circulating libraries', or waste of cultural capital. Many of Austen's contemporaries, especially Romantic writers, attempted to avoid that waste by being manifestly 'original', rejecting both the repetitive formulas and the restless novelty of much 'literature of the day', demonstrating their professionalism, their transcendence of both amateur belletrism and vulgar hack-work, both the pseudo-genteel and the crassly commercial. But Austen adopts instead an indirect and more covert kind of originality, an acceptably feminine and genteel professionalism. For example, she first identified herself on a title page as 'A Lady', and she makes her work look old-fashioned in several ways. Her titles and formal elements are somewhat more typical of the 1780s than the 1810s. When many novel-writers were disclaiming the genre while practising it, Austen defiantly subtitles each of her works 'A Novel'. She uses hackneyed devices of plot, setting, incident, characterisation, dialogue, description and narration similar to those of the 'trash of the circulating libraries', but she tests her reader to recognise her original use of them. Among these devices are the trustworthy narrator, the infallible or the educable protagonist, the apparently unsuitable or suitable suitor, the female rival, the siblings with different yet similar characters and destinies, ineffectual parental authority, the ruinous transgression or lapse of conduct, the damaging relationship or association, the correlation of social status and correct judgement and taste, counter-productive scheming, and the apparently imminent unhappy ending.

Austen reformulates these devices in several ways, thereby establishing her originality as a critical mastery of the formal and thematic repertory of the 'trash of the circulating libraries'. For the most part she reformulates such devices by toning them down in contrast to what readers might expect from reading other novels. This is the basis of her celebrated 'naturalness', 'realism' and 'fidelity to common life', but she is less interested in 'reality' than in chastening her readers' acquired taste for the excesses of 'fashionable novels'. She achieves this effect by tempting her readers to interpret characters, incidents, or emerging plot lines as instances of devices found in the 'trash of the circulating libraries'. She strengthens that temptation by a fairly new method of fictional narration, the omnis- cient but not all-disclosing narrator combined with 'free indirect discourse', or representation of the inward thoughts and feelings of the protagonist (Page, 123–36). This technique reinforces the read- er's tendency to identify with the story's protagonist. The protago- nist may turn out to be right about some readings and wrong about others, like Catherine Morland; or right about important things but generally disregarded by others, like Elinor Dashwood, Fanny Price, and Anne Elliott; or wrong about important things but educable, like Marianne Dashwood, Elizabeth Bennet, and Emma Woodhouse. In each case, the narrator's collusion with the reader's wish to iden- tify with the protagonist tempts the reader into judgements that are then revealed to be wrong. The narrator's ironic distance from the protagonist is unlikely to moderate this temptation, for the irony is intermittent, and easy for the naive or uncritical reader to overlook.

Revelation of the protagonist's misreading forces on the reader recognition that he or she, too, has been a careless, inattentive, or prejudiced reader – in short, fallibly human, and, like the protago- nist, needing both instruction and grace. The shock of re-cognition, or revised understanding, is meant to produce improved reading in life, literature and the novel. Such re-cognition implies redefining the novel, or novels such as Austen's, as a form of cultural capital from which it was usually excluded – literature as 'solid' and 'use- ful' reading. Such redefinition also claims Austen's novels as cul- tural capital of a further kind – art, or literature with a capital 'L'. For recognition of misreading arouses desire to reread with know- ledge of how to read right. Such rereading should then produce recognition of the hitherto overlooked presence of irony, often praised by critics and readers as the essence of Austen's art, in a sense common in Austen's time and culture, combining 'wile or trick' with 'skill in objects of taste'. Having recognised the managed misreading, the reader can, in rereading, recognise the skilfulness of the management. This progress parallels that from ignorance and supposition to knowledge and certainty, a progress undergone by Austen's protagonists.

The ability to recognise and appreciate irony and art had long been considered a test of intellectual discrimination, a form of cul- tural capital based in social and economic class. For it was assumed that such discrimination could only be acquired by those with the leisure and motive to do so – principally the upper and upper middle class. A long line of critics and readers has valued Austen's novels precisely as a test of readers' powers of intellectual and artistic discrimination. Austen made her novels rereadable for this reason, to create a readership united in possession of a certain kind of cultural capital, in a particular economy of knowledge and taste, regulated by a system of interrelated and hierarchical social and cultural difference. Self-recognition as an insider, of having joined this economy, is reaffirmed by rereading. But such rereading is unlike that involved in either the compulsive consumption of formulaic 'trash of the circulating libraries' or the utilitarian study of 'solid' and 'useful' books. A book reread for its art is a 'classic', and marketing of reprints helped such vernacular classics to replace the ancient classics as the cultural capital of a particular social formation. Nevertheless, the rereading enforced by Austen's novels was and is a form of training in the kind of analytical thought, especially as applied to written texts, from schoolbooks to holy scripture to legal documents, necessary in the professions, and especially the 'learned professions'. In Austen's day feminists such as Mary Wollstonecraft had argued that such training was just as necessary to middle-class women if they were to participate in civil society on the domestic front. By representing and calling into being educable female readers, Austen supports Wollstonecraft. Yet it is significant that many of Austen's most committed rereaders have been men in the learned professions.

By transforming the novel into Literature, Austen helped create Literature as a complex form of cultural capital, having intellectual and moral usefulness and symbolic and social value. Literature still has this complex meaning and use in the accumulation and reproduction of material capital. Significantly, Austen, with her banker brother as her literary agent, was reluctant to give up her copyright, or material interest in the reprinting of her novels. For the transformation of the novel into Literature, and Literature into cultural capital of a particular kind, was associated with the rising social status of the author, the professionalisation of authorship, and the constitution of Literature as intellectual property, through changes in copyright (Rose). Thus Austen's interest in her novels as material assets accords with the fact that, in purposely making them rereadable, she was claiming for them, and for the novel generally, a place in Literature as it was being reformed and redefined in the revolutionary aftermath.

She had immediate and lasting, though qualified and paradoxical success. Her novels did well on first publication, but did not stand out much from the 'trash of the circulating libraries', except with a few readers and reviewers. But they were successful enough to bring her a tidy amount of capital, which she prudently invested in government stock, to yield continuing interest (Honan, 393). The novels were also accepted as a form of cultural capital that would yield continuing interest, in the sense of being rereadable. Many people of social or cultural distinction are recorded as rereading them regularly, including Walter Scott, William Macready, Alfred Tennyson, Matthew Arnold, and Queen Elizabeth II. Critics also declared that the novels would 'bear reading and rereading', thus fulfilling 'the real purpose of literature' (G. H. Lewes in Southam, 1968, 125). Yet in the decades that followed, claims for Austen's novels as Literature often contradicted each other, as Literature was defined from conflicting ideological, cultural, social, and political positions (Southam, 1968 and 1987). The novels were praised for naturalness, realism and artistic control that appealed to the discriminating few, thereby implying resistance to the sensationalism in Romantic writing, associated with mere popularity and hence with cultural, social and political disorder. The same qualities were treated as limitations by those with an investment in a different, Romantic construction of Literature.

Such varying responses coincided with the gendering of Literature according to the nineteenth-century domestic ideology of 'separate spheres' for men and women. Some praised Austen's delicacy, artistry, and refinement as appropriately 'feminine', while others condemned these traits as signs that her work lacked 'masculine' energy and 'power', the highest form of art. Appreciations of Austen's novels were also linked to social and political issues. Many saw the novels as representations of a gentrified middle-class rural life outside time, a refuge from urban industrial society and its conflicts. Similarly, the novels were seen as essentially 'English', part of Literature as the repository and reproducer of the 'national' identity and destiny (Court, Chapter 4). Consequently, Austen's novels came to be widely used in schools and universities, as Literature became increasingly important in national public education, with the social mission of ideological reproduction, social mediation, and distribution of cultural capital (Doyle). On the other hand, there were many who insisted that the novels were above criticism, thereby protecting a genteel amateur culture of rereading from the increasing professionalisation of criticism and study.

The republication of the novels interacted with their varying acceptance as Literature (Gilson, 1982). They first acquired public status as 'classics' in 1833 thanks to their inclusion in Bentley's 'Standard Novels' – 'standard' having the force of 'classic'. This series was, however, a commercial venture, like earlier ones, marketing cultural capital to middle-class readers willing to invest in its material form. By the turn of the century Austen's novels were available in school editions, and by the 1920s they were ensconced in the educational curriculum in Britain and the United States. In 1923 the novels received the honour of a critical edition; by the 1930s they had been issued in the major series of literature for the general reader (Everyman's Library, World's Classics, Modern Library, Penguin Books), and after the Second World War they appeared in various editions for students in rapidly expanding higher education. Meanwhile, they continued to be reprinted in both cheap editions for the popular market and elegant illustrated editions for the middle-class collector-reader.

Austen's novels retain their status as Literature and cultural capital, despite recent academic challenges to the literary canon. But this status continues to be problematic. Much of Austen's readership now is in schools and universities, where reading is compulsory, as study. Recent attacks on Literature as either élitist or a frill raise questions as to Austen's continuing importance in education, and Literature's continuing value as cultural capital. Austen does continue to be a 'popular classic', as evidenced by local chapters and national organisations of Jane Austen Societies, frequented mostly by non-academic readers. Ironically, a subgenre of popular fiction, the 'Regency romance', was created in the 1920s from the novels of Austen and her contemporaries. In one of these, Georgette Heyer's *Regency Buck*, knowledge of Austen's *Pride and Prejudice* is even used to indicate the heroine's possession of appropriate cultural capital. This form of 'popular romance' continues to be prominent in commercialised fiction mainly written and read by women. Some critics defend such novels as a distinct form of cultural capital, while others attack them as subliterary and even dangerous. In much the same way did Austen's contemporaries regard the 'trash of the circulating libraries' that she made it her business – as woman, artist, builder of a dominant social coalition, and a money-earning professional – to turn into Literature. In doing so, she founded not so much a business as an industry, to which this essay, of course, belongs.

13

Private and Public in *Persuasion*

Julia Prewitt Brown

The subject of this essay is very broad: what may be called the new historical experience of privacy in Austen's world. Austen's last novel, *Persuasion*, will be the focus, and I shall divide my discussion into three areas of concern: moral, philosophical and biographical.

In the biographical area, I am interested in the relation between Austen's personal or private life and her public ambition as an artist. In moral terms, my focus will be on the way private and public experience is judged in *Persuasion*. And in philosophical terms, attention will centre on the terms *nearness* and *distance*, philosophical and aesthetic categories that are very present in *Persuasion*. Now *private* and *public* are not synonymous with *nearness* and *distance*. The relation between the moral and biographical meanings of private and public and the philosophical meanings of nearness and distance is of course very complicated. All I want to point out here is that there is a homologous relation among these three categories; they seem to correspond in position, value, or structure. The relation between Austen's personal life and her art, between private and public in *Persuasion*, and between nearness and distance in *Persuasion* are all paradoxical relations; they represent polarities that define one another.

A good place to begin is with the word *private*. This word is often used in descriptions of Jane Austen's world in a way that constitutes a major misconception. It has often been said in criticism of the novels, for example, that they are too narrow in their exclusive attention to the private marriage-decisions of a single class; this complaint is found in traditional and feminist critics alike. Even when it is not used as criticism, it is taken for granted. Yet this use of the word private is based on a later conception of social organisation, with its separation of the public and private domains. The word private is itself applied anachronistically to her world. What is its opposite? Is it perhaps public? Yet for much of the nineteenth century, the public authority of the state was only in the process of extending its territory to include all that it would encompass in this century. For most people living in Austen's society, it could be argued that all of life was private, because it was centred on the private estate. Of course there is a sense in which at least for the man, this could mean that all of life was public. In *Emma* Mr Knightley speaks of his responsibilities as a magistrate in the same breath as his deliberations about the plan of a drain.

Perhaps we should define the opposite of *private* and *social* or *communal* and then see if we can locate this *non-social, non-communal* presence in Austen's novels, especially within the institution that she places at the centre of society: marriage. Austen permits us to overhear so-called 'private' conversations between husband and wife in several novels, and there we notice that even when alone, Mr and Mrs Bennet address one another as 'Mrs Bennet' and 'Mr Bennet', suggesting a social and formal dimension within the 'private' experience of marriage that has all but disappeared today. At the same time, the fact that Austen makes us privy to such conversation points to one of her greatest overriding themes: the growing privatisation of marriage. In Austen's earlier novels, marriage is linked to the general functioning of society and to the land; in her last, it is separated from the land and from stable community. In *Persuasion* particularly we see the origins of modern marriage, with its intense focus on the private 'relationship' that a secular society imposes and its anticipation of the egalitarian marriage of companionship, represented by Admiral and Mrs Croft. This shift from marriage as a public, social institution to a private relationship is apparent in all the novels and is attended by Austen's ever-increasing attention to what we might perhaps fuzzily call the 'private self', most particularly in her rendering of the heroine's inner life.

Austen understood privacy in its deepest historical and etymological sense to be a *social* concept. The experience of privacy arose simultaneously with the emergence of a public domain. It is a social concept, probably going back to the Romans; the word itself comes from the Latin *privatus*, meaning simply *not in public life* – that is, not a positive state in itself but merely the state of not being public. Privacy cannot be articulated alone; it implies a public world from which we withdraw, retreat, or from which we may be excluded, but a public world with which we are in relation in spite of and because of the fact we are severed from it. The adjective *privatus* comes from the verb *privare*, which has two antithetical meanings: first, to deprive of, and second, to free from. The etymology suggests that to be private is to be in a state of both freedom and deprivation.

The contradictory character of private experience makes itself felt in earlier novels, but in *Persuasion* gains a new clarity and complexity. Take, for example, the remarkable passage at the end of the novel which envisions the reunited Anne and Wentworth together outside on a street at Bath: their 'spirits dancing in private rapture', Austen writes, at the prospect of being left alone by Charles Musgrove, they seek a secluded place, a 'quiet and retired gravel-walk' where they can speak intimately.

> And there, as they slowly paced the gradual ascent, heedless of every group around them, seeing neither sauntering politicians, bustling house-keepers, flirting girls, nor nursery-maids and children, they could indulge in those retrospections and acknowledgements, and especially in those explanations of what had directly preceded the present moment, which were so poignant and so ceaseless in interest. (240–1)

This passage may be unique in Austen. I can think of no other passage in earlier works in which she places an image of private, intimate reunion of hero and heroine in what is so clearly a public, democratic milieu, on the busy street of a town with its 'sauntering politicians' and its Dickensian vision of a lively, anonymous population.

The closing image of the novel repeats this dichotomous, private–public image:

> His profession was all that could ever make her friends wish that tenderness less; the dread of a future war all that could dim her sunshine. She gloried in being a sailor's wife, but she must pay the tax of quick alarm for belonging to that profession which is, if possible, more distinguished for its domestic virtues than in its national importance. (252)

By means of the reference to Navy life and the possibility of another war, the lovers are placed in relation to English history, specifically to what Austen knew would occur about six months after the story closes: the Battle of Waterloo. This image of the sustaining private love of two people, of atomistic personal life, understood in terms of its polar opposite, large-scale political history and war, brings to mind the close of Arnold's famous poem, 'Dover Beach', in which a private relationship is placed in a world-historical perspective, defined and justified by it. In both instances, private life is realised only by means of public, historical consciousness; that is, we feel private and near only when we are conscious of a public history and a distant perspective. Or, to word it more exactly given Austen's lines: we feel private and near only when we are conscious of being unconscious of what is public and distant. (In the passage quoted above, Austen emphasises what the lovers do not see and hear, rather than what they do.) In both Arnold and Austen, to be private is to be in a state of both freedom and deprivation, to be free *from* public life yet deprived *of* it.

The moral implications of the new historical experience of privacy in *Persuasion* further confirm this antithesis. The traditional question posed by ethics – how to live one's life – is given no clear answer in the novel. To the moral questions related to privacy (such as, How private, solitary, or introspective should I allow myself to be? Is the more extroverted life superior to the more introverted one?), no answer is suggested. Instead of a clear ideological or partisan position on these questions, we find a finely wrought, absolutely irresolvable set of contradictions. At every point at which the novel suggests that privacy is bad, for example, it also suggests that privacy is good. The private 'seclusion of Kellynch' (135) and solitude within an unsympathetic family have led Anne to be too passive and self-pitying, unwilling and unable to make spring come, as the farmer she gazes at during the walk to the Hayters' farm is doing as he tills the field. At the same time, the private and secluded character of Anne's life has led to the cultivation of inwardness, and it is precisely this inwardness that makes her the heroine, that makes her morally superior to the other characters. With all the criticism of Anne's estrangement then, she is surrounded by people who are seen as shallow and coarse precisely because they cannot be alone, because they have no inner life. Her sister Mary cannot be alone for more than a half hour without whining, and Mrs Musgrove is ridiculed partly because she cannot be alone with her grief. The two houses at Uppercross get together continually, as Anne notices, because neither can bear solitude. The shallowness of social intercourse at Uppercross fully acknowledged, Anne nonetheless 'admired again the sort of necessity . . . of every thing being to be done together' (83). There are as many moments in the novel in which we *cannot* 'admire the necessity of every thing being to be done together' and are in fact invited to sneer at it, as there are moments in which we can. (Austen would have been aware of the Latinate meaning of the verb *to admire* – to wonder at – which adds an appropriately negative nuance.) We are continually invited to deplore Anne's estrangement, yet feel contempt for all the characters in the novel who would lack the moral strength to sustain it. In other words, no Aristotelian ethical mean is put forth as a solution – in the way that a mean is repeatedly suggested in relation to all sorts of ethical questions raised in *Pride and Prejudice*, from mercenary vs. prudent marriages to how responsive one should be to the request of a friend. Instead, unsatisfactory ethical choices are represented – a damned-if-you-do, damned-if-you-don't perspective. The separation of private and public has brought about two unsatisfactory states of being.

The ethically undecidable rendering of solitary life in *Persuasion* is perfectly embodied not only in the character of the heroine but also in that of Benwick, whom Anne encounters as a mirror-reflection of her own strengths and weaknesses. Later Wentworth praises Benwick in the highest terms for his character and intelligence: Louisa Musgrove is 'very aimiable,' he admits, 'but Benwick is something more. He is a clever man, a reading man . . .' (182). Yet we know from an earlier scene that, like that of Anne, Benwick's reading has made him introspective to the point of neurotic. To say, as Anne does to him, that he should read less of some authors and more of others is no answer – i.e., does not achieve an Aristotelian balance – because Austen suggests that Benwick's reading has made him what he is, just as Anne's inwardness – her liability and her strength – has made her what she is. Her friends 'could . . . wish that tenderness less' (252), as Austen writes at the close of the novel, but all they can do is wish. In other words, while characters in *Persuasion* often behave as if there *are* moral choices to be made, the narrator is showing us there are none.

There are many more examples of this 'solutionlessness', as it were, like the medieval debate at the end of the novel between Anne and Captain Harville on the relative constancy of women and men. This is one thing that distinguishes *Persuasion* from earlier novels. For example, in *Pride and Prejudice*, the traditional values represented by Pemberley and Darcy and the new, democratic values represented by Elizabeth are synthesised in their marriage and in

their life at Pemberley, where they receive the Gardiners, representatives of the new business class. Both Darcy and Elizabeth consciously admit to mistakes in their point of view; they educate one
another. All of this has of course been written about at length in
Austen criticism. What is remarkable is how thoroughly Austen
abandons such syntheses in her last novel. The heroine won't even
admit that she was wrong in taking Lady Russell's advice. In the
private–public polarity in the novel (Wentworth has a public life;
she has only a private one) no compromise is made. She was right,
she says, to give way to her passivity, her emotional vulnerability
to her dead mother's friend – to all the things associated with the
secluded, private, withdrawn life at Kellynch. Whereas at the end
of *Pride and Prejudice*, an ideal vision of community is offered in the
vision of life at Pemberley, where traditional English values are
revitalised by new ones, the community controlling the end of *Persuasion*, ironically, is a military institution, a 'community' to be sure,
as institutional communities are, but limited by the fact of its institutional and military purpose and character. Only 'the dread of a
future war' (252), we are told, can disturb the idyllic domestic life
enjoyed by those in this community in times of peace, a qualifica-
tion that Austen's readers must have taken seriously, given the
moment in history at which Austen chooses to end the story.

Persuasion is like *Pride and Prejudice* in having a marriage that
brings together the lower aristocracy or high gentry and the rising
middle class. But the hero and heroine don't change one another –
no real inward revitalisation has taken place. And at the end of the
novel they are heading, not for an estate or a secure place in the
social structure, but for war. The classical balance of *Pride and Prejudice* gives way in *Persuasion* to a world of determined paradox, in
which private and public, inner and outer, peace and war, the self
and history are at something of a deadlock.

Written at a time of increasing separation of private and public,
the novel records all the social and psychological dangers that come
with this separation: both for England and for the individual. The
passage quoted earlier which envisions a public population of 'sauntering politicians, bustling house-keepers, and flirting girls' is almost Pickwickian; it resembles the cheerful vision of social life in
the early chapters of *Pickwick Papers*, published eighteen years after
Persuasion. This *seems* a safe world, yet like *Pickwick Papers*, it really
is not. The novel is full of curious and rather dark prophecies. The
Musgroves lose a son in the war, have a daughter who cracks her

head, and a grandson who breaks his collarbone. Why is it that this most traditional English family – whose Englishness is alluded to more than once – is so accident-prone?

I would like to use Louisa Musgrove's accident as a jumping-off point for the second area of concern: philosophical and aesthetic. The power of this remarkable scene has a lot to do with the fact that in it Austen overcomes the opposition of nearness and distance, showing them to be intertwined, categories that belong to one another. In terms of psychological and moral themes, the way to put this is to say that it is only within the most expansive landscape that Anne and Wentworth finally make close contact.

When her characters arrive at Lyme, Austen emphasises vista: 'its high grounds and extensive sweeps of country, . . . its sweet retired bay, backed by dark cliffs . . .' (95). Words like *chasm, rock,* and *cliff* place the characters in a grand and distant frame. The accident itself occurs next to the ocean on a sunny and windy day. Earth, sky, water and wind provide a vast context for the first moment of real intimacy between Anne and Captain Wentworth. The accident, which catapults every person present into a state of vertigo or disorientation, strips Wentworth of his defences, and only under these conditions does he turn to Anne, as she knows, when he cries out, 'Is there no one to help me?' (110). Our attention is finally on the lovers in this scene, not the accident or Louisa. Their mutual sense of distance is as great as the sense of nearness at the moment of crisis. 'Is there no one to help me?' he cries, as though alone in the world, yet the cry itself, the loss of his defences, binds him to Anne.

The accident itself is also rendered in antithetical images of high and low, up and down, perfectly summed up in the antithetical image of the 'steep flight' of stairs. A great deal more could be said about the temporal and spatial genius of this scene: for example, it is a symbolic reenactment and reversal of the mistake that was made eight years before the novel opens, when Anne was not precipitate *enough* in falling into Wentworth's arms. Fittingly, the lovers come back together in the same critical atmosphere in which they parted. But I would like to turn instead to the latter half of the novel, in which Austen's equation of *nearness* and *distance* intensifies.

In *Persuasion*, what is nearest is paradoxically most remote. From the first appearance of Anne, the ordinary linear conception of time is shown to have little to do with her sense of what is near. 'Alas! with all her reasonings, she found, that to retentive feelings eight years may be little more than nothing' (60). Measurable distance in either time or space is not what is important. To give an everyday example of this philosophical problem, as one critic suggests: when we speak on the telephone, the telephone speaker that we hold to our ear is far more remote than the distant party to whom we speak. Such objects come to seem strange in their very familiarity if we meditate on them. Although they are literally present in our world and always near, they are also always absent and far. Presence, or what seems present or near to us, is what is being meditated. In Anne's case, Wentworth is present when he is absent ('to retentive feelings, eight years' are as nothing) and absent when he is present: dining in his company Anne can think, 'Once so much to each other! Now nothing!' (63). Anne puzzles over the fact that 'Now they were as strangers' (64). She observes him: 'When he talked, she heard the same voice, and discerned the same mind.' Yet he is nonetheless absent, a stranger. (Physically, you could say that he is like the telephone receiver.) Anne can 'find' Wentworth in this scene only through memory: 'she heard the same voice' and his conversation with Louisa Musgrove 'reminded Anne of the early days', Austen writes, in which she had had similar conversations with him (64). It comes as no surprise that Virginia Woolf tied this novel to those of Proust.

The interplay of near and far, past and present is constant in *Persuasion*, and especially concentrated in the latter half of the novel. Seeing Captain Wentworth walk down the street, Anne starts: 'For a few minutes she saw nothing before her. It was all confusion' (175). The surprise of seeing him is 'blinding' to her. Later, in the concert scene as Anne senses their impending reunion, 'Anne saw nothing, thought nothing of the brilliancy of the room' (185). And finally, in the reunion scene itself, 'Anne heard nothing distinctly; it was only a buzz of words in her ear, her mind was in confusion' (231). The cognitive order of Anne's visual, aural world is effaced in these scenes in which the distinction between inner and outer, past and present, near and far is virtually erased. The word 'nothing' is used repeatedly. Anne's experience of Wentworth is a blank: both a nothing and an everything. Presence, in other words, is what is here but also what is out there.

What Austen shows here is that we are never simply 'here', but by virtue of our ranging concern, we are first of all 'there'. We come to a 'here' only from afar. Thus, we exist as individuals in a field of concerns, in which near and far are at every moment potentially intertwined.

Jane Austen was dying when she was writing *Persuasion*. The telescoping of experience, the compressing inward of distant objects, may belong to such a time. Similar and far more explicit interplay of near and far, past and present, up and down, going and coming, expanding and contracting takes place in Tolstoy's study of the mind of a dying person, 'The Death of Ivan Ilyitch'.

Of Jane Austen's life we know very little; she was very private, and her works were published anonymously, 'By A Lady'. Very possibly, Austen's gender and social class played a role in the decision to publish anonymously, as has been argued. But we should not rule out the possibility this was something Austen herself may have actively chosen. Not all women writers published anonymously. Perhaps Austen wanted privacy. We know that she withdrew from an introduction to Mme de Staël, and it used to be thought that she did so because she objected to Mme de Staël's moral reputation. But in his excellent biography, Park Honan gives evidence that it is very likely that Austen withdrew from other literary introductions as well: she was probably in Bath when Fanny Burney and Maria Edgeworth were there but withdrew from these introductions. To speculation as to why Austen never married, the most convincing answer, since we know that she had more than one proposal, is that she chose not to in order to devote herself to her art. All of Austen's drive for public attention was located in the ambition to see her works in print. She evidently had no desire for personal attention. But her interest in how people read her work is proven by the fact that she carefully saved the most offhand comments upon the novels from friends and acquaintances.

Austen needed privacy to write, because privacy provides the condition for solitude. She probably had to lay claim to privacy for this reason in the way a male writer would not have had to. A man would have been given the time to write, because he would have been given the time to work. In this sense, Austen's privacy was her career. The further she withdrew from the public, the closer she came to fame. The more personal and restricted her life, the wider its sphere. In other words, the paradox I have pointed to earlier in Austen's conception of private and public, nearness and distance, is at work in her own life. Austen's privacy is intimately bound up with her public ambition – the two must be seen together.

I should like to conclude with a few speculations concerning the larger implications of what I have suggested here as they relate to the current state of Austen criticism. Private and public are historical categories, whereas *nearness* and *distance* are metaphysical and ultimately perhaps theological ones. For example, it has often been remarked that archaic societies do not experience the distinction between 'public' and 'private,' but *nearness* and *distance* are categories of thought that can be recognised in their art and ritual. These categories predate the separation of the private and public domains; ideas of nearness and distance, for example, are very strong in the New Testament, particularly in the Gospels. It is my sense that the source of these paradoxes in Austen is Biblical, as it is in Tolstoy's story mentioned earlier. That Austen was a seriously religious person is suggested by various kinds of evidence – her sister's commentary and the prayers she wrote are two examples. I am not suggesting any sort of church-going, institutional Christianity. We are familiar with her unrelenting satire of the English church in almost every one of her novels, and with her well-known sympathetic comment about the more primitive Christians known as Evangelicals. Austen's Christianity, which may have had more in common with that of the late Tolstoy than with that of (for example) Dickens, has received almost no attention. There is only one book on the subject, Gene Koppel's excellent book, *The Religious Dimension of Jane Austen's Novels,* and that book received very little attention because its interests fly in the face of the overriding neo-positivist orientation of current criticism.

What I have suggested here – in arguing a homologous relation between historical categories and metaphysical ones – is that the historical and the metaphysical, as dimensions of human existence, need not exclude one another, and may in fact be studied together.

Part IV
What Throbs Fast and Full

14

Retrenchments

Elaine Showalter

Persuasion begins with a problem of cash flow that is all too familiarly modern. At Kellynch-hall, the 'method, moderation, and economy' (9) of Lady Elliot is gone, and through vanity and carelessness, Sir Walter Elliot has grown 'dreadfully in debt' (9). Despite its substance, the property is unequal to his 'apprehension of the state required in its possessor' (9), and as his tradespeople and his agent become more pressing, Sir Walter plaintively appeals to his eldest daughter Elizabeth for advice: 'Can we retrench? does it occur to you that there is any one article in which we can retrench?' (9). In 'the first ardour of female alarm' (9), Elizabeth applies herself to the question, and comes up with 'two branches of economy' (9): 'to cut off some unnecessary charities' (9), 'to refrain from new-furnishing the drawing-room' (9–10), and to take no yearly present to her sister Anne. Indeed, both Sir Walter and Elizabeth react to debt by feeling themselves 'ill-used and unfortunate' (10); they are totally stumped by the need to cut their expenses without 'compromising their dignity' (10), 'relinquishing their comforts' (10), or losing 'any indulgence of taste or pride' (10). But in the end Sir Walter and his agent decide that rather than change his lifestyle in any substantial way, he should quit Kellynch-hall and settle in Bath, where 'he might . . . be important at comparatively little expense' (14).

This aristocratic scenario of retrenchment has a familiar ring in the nineties, as we have become accustomed to talk of cutbacks and reductions, elegant economy and downward mobility. Shall we stiff the United Fund, pass up the new rug, downsize the Christmas list? Only a week ago, in fact, I had a telephone call from a persistent reporter on the *Boston Herald*, who wanted to know what I thought of the proposition that the conspicuous consumption of the eighties had given way to the more politically correct consumption of the nineties. Instead of buying BMWs, she wanted to know, weren't people now just buying Land Rovers? As someone who drives a ten-year-old Toyota I found it hard to come up with a

181

reply. But for some years in the universities, in government, and in private life, there has certainly been a feeling that retrenchment is in the air. In his novel *Cuts* (1987), the British novelist and literary critic Malcolm Bradbury puts it this way about England in the summer of 1986:

> Every morning, when you opened the morning newspaper . . . 'cut' was the most common noun, 'cut' was the most regular verb. They were incising heavy industry, they were slicing steel, they were . . . axing the arts, slimming the sciences, . . . reducing public expenditure, . . . eliminating over-production and unnecessary jobs. . . . They were chopping at the schools, hewing away at the universities, scissoring at the health service, . . . slashing out at superfluity, excising rampant excess. . . . So it was . . . a time . . . for doing away with far too much of this and a wasteful excess of that. It was a time for getting rid of the old soft illusions, and replacing them with the new hard illusions. . . . And everyone was growing leaner and cleaner, keener and meaner, for after all in a time of cuts it is better to be tough than tender, much more hardware than software. (2–3)

'All this', Bradbury notes, 'was helped by the useful ambiguity of the handy word "cut"' (3), which could mean anything from a surgical incision to a social rejection. In 1817, the word 'retrenchment' had a similarly handy and ambiguous range. It primarily referred to pruning, trimming, excising, curtailing, limiting and cutting down expenditure, a usage that entered the English language in the seventeenth century. But it also had a number of additional usages, from being a synonym for physical cutting-off, as in this quotation from 1654, 'if I should deprive her of the Crown without the retrenchment of her head', to referring to deleting, editing, or eliminating passages of a text, as in the introductory epistle to Sir Walter Scott's *The Abbot* (1820), a few years after *Persuasion*, where he admits 'that my retrenchments have been numerous, and leave gaps in the story' (xiv).

'Retrenchment' is so useful and versatile a metaphor for the themes of *Persuasion* and so significant a problem for its cast of characters that it might well have served as the title of the book. *Persuasion* opens with the necessity for economic retrenchment, and with an account of the various recipes for reduction put forth by some of its leading characters. More importantly, retrenchment is also a metaphor for psychological withdrawal and recovery, for the ways that the various characters, and especially Anne Elliot, deal with loss and personal defeat. If the proper sort of financial retrenchment can renew one's fortunes, then the proper kind of emotional retrenchment can enrich one's spirit.

How a person chooses to retrench in *Persuasion* becomes a test of both values and maturity. Indeed, as John Wiltshire astutely explains in *Jane Austen and the Body*, this is a novel about trauma and 'the art of losing' (Wiltshire, 196). 'Every character in *Persuasion*', Laura Mooneyham comments, 'has suffered loss or adversity' in at least one of five areas: property, status, connections, health and love. As we move through the novel, the ways that Austen's characters respond to their losses become a cross-section 'of how the human personality copes with adversity, disappointment and lost opportunities' (Mooneyham, 147, 146). To be a good loser, one who knows how to retreat and retrench, is eventually to be a victor in Austen's terms; and in looking at the ways that her characters retrench, Austen displays her 'intense interest in the resources of the human spirit in the face of affliction' (Wiltshire, 166).

The least introspective of the characters in *Persuasion* are Sir Walter and Elizabeth Elliot, who quickly absolve themselves of any blame or responsibility for their debts and project the problem on to others with elaborate conditions for its solution. When they consult Lady Russell for advice on retrenchment, she too has difficulty reaching a decision, because she is divided between her sense of integrity and her solicitude for the position of the family. In her view, the 'scheme of retrenchment' (12) must be carried out 'with the least possible pain' (12), over a period of seven years of economy. This combination of realism and a lingering classbound blindness makes Lady Russell an ineffectual presence at best, and a destructive one at worst, as in the romance of Anne and Frederick Wentworth.

But Anne Elliot is not content with these half-way measures and opts for a 'severe degree of self-denial' (13): 'She wanted more vigorous measures, a more complete reformation, a quicker release from debt, a much higher tone of indifference for every thing but justice and equity' (12). Anne's recommendations for financial retrenchment are similar to her psychological programme for recovering from the wreck of her romance with Wentworth: 'vigorous measures' (12) and 'severe self-denial' (13). More than one critic has suggested that in the first volume, Anne is 'attempting to live the life of the

Christian stoic', as depicted in Johnson's essays, trying 'to argue herself into a state of emotional aloofness from outer hazards' (Wiltshire, 175, 176).

Thus Anne refuses to brood on her unhappiness; she will not make a display of her feelings, go into a decline, or become a recluse. For years she has not spoken of Wentworth with Lady Russell, much less reproached her for bad advice. Instead she tries to achieve contentment through self-mastery, determining to 'harden her nerves' (30), to 'teach herself to be insensible' (52), and to combat depression through long walks and good works. She makes an effort to avoid painful situations; when the Crofts visit Kellynch, for example, she takes care to 'keep out of the way till all was over' (32). When the Elliots go to Bath, she is saved by her sister Mary, who needs help at Uppercross Cottage. 'To be claimed as a good, though in an improper style, is at least better than being rejected as no good at all; and Anne, glad to be thought of some use, glad to have any thing marked out as a duty, . . . readily agreed to stay' (33). There is even a sense in which she gets some pleasure from her routine, from 'the influence so sweet and so sad of the autumnal months in the country' (33), so symbolic of her life. But in general Anne chooses the least conspicuous, least self-dramatising course of action.

For modern readers, especially women readers steeped in self-help literature about learned optimism, co-dependency, recovery from the loss of a love, and women who love too much, like nineteenth-century readers looking to fiction for such advice, *Persuasion*, as the Victorian novelist Margaret Oliphant wrote in 1882, is 'the least amusing of Miss Austen's books, but perhaps the most interesting' (Southam, 1976, 141). Austen anticipates contemporary studies of sex differences in depression which suggest that there are two basic ways of responding to bad news and depressive symptoms, the *ruminative* and the *distracting*, and that these are loosely correlated with sex. According to psychologist Susan Nolen-Hoeksema,

> People who engage in ruminative responses to depressed mood [such as self-criticism, isolating oneself to dwell on the feelings, writing a diary, and repeatedly telling others how bad one feels] will experience amplification and prolonging of the mood, whereas people who engage in distracting responses . . . [like blaming the problem on others or external events beyond one's control, engaging in a physical activity, working on something that takes

concentration, or spending time with friends] will experience relief. (161)

In a variety of studies, women appeared more likely to be ruminators, men to be distractors.[1] In large part, ruminating or distracting are learned cultural behaviours or acquired sexual responses. 'Being active and controlling one's moods are part of the masculine stereotype; being inactive and emotional are part of the feminine stereotype.' But in some modern religious communities, where 'self-centeredness in any form is considered a sin', there are lower general levels of reported depression and no sex difference in how they are handled (Nolen-Hoeksema, 171, 174). In extreme forms, the masculine response of distracting may be maladaptive; Sir Walter distracts himself splendidly by denying the problem, and one popular distracting response is through alcoholism. But to avoid depression in daily life generally, modern psychologists advise, it is better to be a distractor than a ruminator.

Yet in Austen's world, as now, it is difficult for women to distract themselves and easy for them to ruminate. In her famous speech to Captain Harville, Anne cogently analyses the circumstances that make women depressed beings, when all the circumstances of their cloistered lives conspire to keep them from diversion: 'We live at home, quiet, confined, and our feelings prey upon us. You are forced on exertion. You have always a profession, pursuits, business of some sort or other, to take you back into the world immediately, and continual occupation and change soon weaken impressions' (232).

It is impressive to see how hard Anne works to find continual occupation, and how ingenious she becomes in distracting herself. Before leaving Kellynch, for example, she makes a full routine of makework and minutiae: writing out 'a duplicate of the catalogue' of her father's books and pictures; consulting with the gardener about the plants, arranging and packing all her own 'little concerns' (38), and visiting almost every house in the parish 'as a sort of take-leave' (39). All these activities, a Peterson's or Murphy's Law of the empty life, 'took up a great deal of time' (39), and killing time is part of Anne's strategy of retrenchment. Art cannot fill the gap left by love; although she is a good musician, without 'fond parents to sit by and fancy themselves delighted' (47), her musical gifts are not supported and are only a social resource and escape at parties. It is perhaps around the subject of music that Austen makes her strongest statement about the radical nature of Anne's retrenchment and the isolation in which she must find her way: 'she had never, since the age of fourteen, never since the loss of her dear mother, known the happiness of being listened to, or encouraged by any just appreciation or real taste' (47).

Yet Anne's motherless state becomes less a source of self-pity than a spur to finding surrogate parents and mothering herself. In sharp contrast, her sister Elizabeth suffers acutely from 'the sameness and the elegance, the prosperity and the nothingness, of her scene of life . . . a long, uneventful residence in one country circle' (9). Her hypochondriacal sister Mary, who fills her empty hours with imaginary illnesses that demand attention, is a whining ruminator, whose imagined illnesses are only transparent self-delusion. Only Anne, as Nina Auerbach has noted, 'is provided with a significant and autonomous inner world, which is strong enough to pull her from the incessant conflicts around her' (45).

Yet at the beginning of the novel, Anne seems worst off of the three motherless sisters, and her stern advice about retrenchment reflects her own tough-minded experience in handling depression, for if the Elliots are facing seven years of retrenchment on an economic level, she has endured seven years of retrenchment on an emotional level. Her wrecked romance with Frederick Wentworth has left her without hope, for 'she had to encounter all the additional pain of opinions, on his side, totally unconvinced and unbending, and of his feeling himself ill-used by so forced a relinquishment' (28). Her every 'enjoyment of youth' (28) has been clouded, and 'an early loss of bloom and spirits' (28) has been the 'lasting effect' (28).

There is present in these circumstances, as Elizabeth Bowen wrote, 'everything that could have made a warped creature. Do we not all know women with poisoned temperaments, in whom some grievance or disappointment seems to fester like an embedded thorn?' In contemporary society, Bowen observed in 1957, 'with a hundred careers open, it is or should be easier to forget – but Anne, condemned to the idleness of her time and class, has not an interest or an ambition to distract her. Endlessly, if she so willed, she could fret and brood. But no: she shows an unbroken though gentle spirit and, with that, a calm which does not fail' (Southam, 1976, 166–7). It is the spirit she shows in adversity that makes Anne Elliot so great a heroine, despite the fact, noted by W. D. Howells, 'never was there a heroine so little self-assertive, so far from forth-putting' (Southam, 1976, 144).

Indeed Anne is *so* good that Austen has set herself a difficult task in making her sympathetic. 'She is almost too good for me', Austen herself famously confessed in a letter to her niece (*L*, 487). The Cinderella theme, as D. W. Harding has explained, 'is inevitably difficult to handle. For one thing the fantasy of being mysteriously superior to one's parentage is rather common . . . and commonly unjustified. And the crushed dejection (masking resentment) of the self-cast Cinderellas of real life always provokes a sneaking sympathy for the ugly sisters' (Southam, 1976, 194). Austen has to proceed by enforcing the reality of Anne's depression in the first half of the novel, and securing an interest in Anne without caricaturing her oppressors or making Elizabeth and Mary the underdogs.

Most important, Austen makes clear that Anne's labour of self-mastery is not wholly the result of injustice. As D. W. Harding observes, rather than being a victim, or 'a passive sufferer of entirely unmerited wrongs', Anne 'has brought her chief misfortune on herself through a mistaken decision' (Southam, 1976, 195). Thus, 'we start . . . with a much more mature Cinderella, more seriously tragic herself in having thrown away her own happiness, more complex in her relation to the loved mother, who not only made the same sort of mistake herself but now, brought back to life in Lady Russell, shares the heroine's responsibility for her disaster' (Southam, 1976, 195).

Since Anne is not a passive victim, she must do more in the novel than simply ward off depression. Unlike her father and sister, who evade confronting responsibility for their dilemma, Anne must right the balance by taking active steps to heal the breach with Wentworth. She must find ways to speak with him in private, and must risk showing him how she feels about constancy, even though her assertiveness in these matters, and Austen's view of it, seem to violate the precepts of eighteenth-century feminine conduct.

Much of Anne's progress through stoic retrenchment to assertive strength comes from her study of the behaviour, both positive and negative, of others around her, and indeed one of the main ways she keeps herself busy is to observe them with the novelist's ironic detachment. The visit to Uppercross, in addition to giving her busywork to fill the hours, also teaches Anne another useful lesson of retrenchment: 'the art of knowing our own nothingness beyond our own circle' (42). Lesson two here is observation and adaptation: 'With the prospect of spending at least two months at Uppercross, it was highly incumbent on her to clothe her imagination, her memory, and all her ideas in as much of Uppercross as possible' (43).

Among the bad examples at Uppercross is Mrs Musgrove. Austen's famously brutal remarks about Mrs Musgrove's 'large fat sighings' (68) over the death of 'a son, whom alive nobody had cared for' (68) have shocked many generations of critics. D. A. Miller, for example, scolds Austen for her satire of 'the semantically unco-operative body', 'the semiotic outrage' of a 'fat-phobic culture' expressed by an 'anerotic and anorectic' narrator who 'will never cease invigilating over what she puts into her mouth' (60–4). And yet for Anne, 'fat sighings' (68) are incompatible with genuine grief, which demands some sign of retrenchment in the body. If Anne herself has lost her bloom, or as her father more bluntly states, grown 'haggard' (6), from the loss of a love, then Mrs Musgrove's 'comfortable substantial size' (68) should be somewhat reduced by the loss of a son. In contrast to Anne, Mrs Musgrove is a ruminator, someone who chews her cud and her grief. Her public display risks seeming showy and sentimental. Indeed, notes Mary Lascelles, 'one might almost take *Persuasion* for a satire on the frailty of human sorrow and the support it seeks from delusion' (Southam, 1976, 157).

Similarly, Captain Benwick's romantic intensification of his sorrow through tremulous recitations of 'the various lines which imaged a broken heart, or a mind destroyed by wretchedness' (100), strikes Anne as a dangerous form of rumination. She recommends 'a larger allowance of prose in his daily study; and on being requested to particularize, mentioned such works of our best moralists, such collections of the finest letters, such memoirs of characters of worth and suffering, . . . calculated to rouse and fortify the mind by the highest precepts, and the strongest examples of moral and religious endurances' (101). Although Anne fears that 'like many other great moralists and preachers, she had been eloquent on a point in which her own conduct would ill bear examination' (101), we feel that the reading-list she prescribes for Benwick is the one she uses often herself.

Louisa Musgrove, Anne's imagined rival for the affections of Wentworth, also plays an important role in Anne's study of others, especially in her accident at Lyme. With regard to the fall, John Wiltshire makes the brilliant suggestion that it should be seen from a Freudian perspective as 'an instance of the psychopathology of everyday life' (187). According to Freud, 'falling, stumbling and slipping need not always be interpreted as purely accidental mis-carriages of motor actions. The double meanings that language attaches to these expressions are enough to indicate the kind of phantasies involved, which can be represented by such losses of bodily equilibrium' (174–5). If Louisa cannot discipline her body to conceal the fantasies of her mind, Anne never allows herself to slip.

Persuasion is also unusually rich in women who are strong poten-tial role-models. But the most inspiring model is Mrs Smith, whose astonishing resilience, self-reliance, and ability to develop new net-works and skills leads Anne to meditate on the capacity for survival:

> Her accommodations were limited to a noisy parlour, and a dark bed-room behind, with no possibility of moving from one to the other without assistance, which there was only one servant in the house to afford, and she never quitted the house but to be con-veyed into the warm bath. – Yet, in spite of all this, Anne had reason to believe that she had moments only of languor and depression, to hours of occupation and enjoyment. How could it be? – She watched – observed – reflected – and finally deter-mined that this was not a case of fortitude or of resignation only. – A submissive spirit might be patient, a strong understanding would supply resolution, but here was something more; here was that elasticity of mind, that disposition to be comforted, that power of turning readily from evil to good, and of finding employment which carried her out of herself, which was from Nature alone. It was the choicest gift of Heaven. (154)

In the terms of current psychology, this 'gift of Heaven' (154) of optimism can be learned, and whether or not Anne has received it from heaven, she masters it on her own. Yet even for such an adept student, optimism is never perfectly mastered. As Anne discovers when she is consciously trying to 'be feeling less' (60), the eight years of her separation from Wentworth, although almost a third of her life, 'may be little more than nothing' (60) to a person with 'retentive feelings' (60). She still finds that 'her eyes would some-times fill with tears' (71), even though she conceals them by hiding at the piano, and playing 'mechanically' (72). When Wentworth rescues her from young Walter, she is 'speechless' (80) with 'dis-ordered feelings' (80), in 'a confusion of varying, but very painful agitation' (80). 'She was ashamed of herself, quite ashamed of being so nervous, so overcome by such a trifle; but so it was; and it required a long application of solitude and reflection to recover her' (81). She cannot resist 'repeating to herself some few of the thousand poetical descriptions extant of autumn' (84), with images 'of the declining year, with declining happiness, and the images of youth and hope, and spring, all gone together' (85). She cannot help trying to overhear snatches of conversation when Captain Wentworth is talking to the Musgrove girls. She cannot conceal her joy when she begins to realise that he still loves her.

But this emotional retentiveness, in addition to endearing her to the reader, only enriches her emotional development. In the second part of the novel it is Anne's initiative with Wentworth that leads to their reconciliation. Through years of disciplined self-control, Anne reaches a maturity which enables her to speak out. But in this respect, the process of retrenchment brings its final rewards. The first romance of Anne and Captain Wentworth, Austen suggests, was superficial and circumstantial, 'for he had nothing to do, and she had hardly any body to love' (26). But Anne's seven years of retrenchment, of having love cut off, of reducing emotional expenses, makes her a stronger, more self-sufficient woman. As Margaret Oliphant pointed out, 'Anne Elliot would have lived and made herself a worthy life anyhow, even if Captain Wentworth had not been faithful' (Southam, 1976, 141). But her manner of handling their 'division and estrangement' (240) has also deepened her ability to make a free and loving choice. They will be in their reunion, Austen tells us, 'more tender, more tried, more fixed in a knowledge of each other's character, truth, and attachment; more equal to act, more justified in acting' (240–1).

One of the most moving ways they are made equal, partners to go shares in all things, like the Crofts, is that by the end of the novel Wentworth too has accepted responsibility for their loss and has shouldered half the responsibility for the years of separation. Originally he scorns her maidenly doubts about their marriage as 'feebleness' (61) and weakness. Wentworth is convinced that what he seeks in a wife is firmness. But he too comes to understand that 'Anne's submission to Lady Russell was neither a symptom of weakness, nor cold-hearted prudence', but a well-intended mistake for which she has paid in suffering and fortitude (Butler, 176). Moreover he sees that he has been more of an enemy to their union than Lady Russell, for pride has prevented him from renewing his proposal to Anne many years since.

'This is a recollection [he tells her,] which ought to make me forgive every one sooner than myself. . . . It is a sort of pain, too, which is new to me. I have been used to the gratification of believing myself to earn every blessing that I enjoyed. I have valued myself on honourable toils and just rewards. Like other great men under reverses, I must endeavour to subdue my mind to my fortune. I must learn to brook being happier than I deserve.' (247)

In this final paradoxical understanding of retrenchment, not only Wentworth but also her family and her readers must finally come to 'do [Anne] justice' (247).

The movement between retrenchment and advancement is one of the reasons that *Persuasion* has had such a mixed response from readers and critics. 'This is at once', wrote Reginald Farrer in 1917, 'the warmest and the coldest of Jane Austen's works, the softest and the hardest. It is inspired, on the one hand, by a quite new note of glacial contempt for the characters she doesn't like, and, on the other, by an intensified tenderness for those she does.' Though it 'moves very quietly, without sobs or screams, in drawing-rooms and country lanes,' Farrer concludes, 'it is yet among the most emotional novels in our literature' (Southam, 1976, 148–9).

As Austen's contemporary critics, perhaps leaner, keener, and meaner in this age of cutbacks than is entirely compatible with pleasure, we must also subdue our minds to our fortunes, and learn to brook in *Persuasion* being happier than we deserve.

Note

1. See, for example, Martin S. Seligman: 'when trouble strikes, women think and men act. When a woman gets fired from her job, she tries to figure out why; she broods, and she relives the events over and over. A man, upon getting fired, acts: He gets drunk, beats someone up, or otherwise distracts himself from thinking about it. He may even go right out and look for another job, without bothering to think through what went wrong. If depression is a disorder of thinking, pessimism and rumination stoke it' (Seligman, 85–6).

15

'The Sentient Target of Death': Jane Austen's Prayers

Bruce Stovel

Jane Austen's prayers have a place in her writings that resembles that of many of her own heroines within their fictional worlds. Apparently of little interest, they have been generally ignored. These three short prayers survive in undated manuscripts inscribed 'Prayers Composed by my ever dear Sister Jane'; the prayers themselves indicate that one member of the Austen family is reading to the assembled household at night before all retire to bed. Like Elinor Dashwood or Fanny Price or Anne Elliot, the prayers have, in general, not been attended to: biographies and critical studies tend to ignore the prayers (with some striking exceptions, to be mentioned later in this essay). Yet, like those heroines, the prayers have a good deal to say for themselves if one does listen – in this case, a good deal about Jane Austen's life and about the novels. They tell us that Jane Austen was a devout Christian and suggest that the novels are more suffused with religious feeling than we might have thought. Charlotte Brontë's famous disparagement of Jane Austen was written in 1850, and so without the benefit of any biographical knowledge: it is at least possible that if Brontë had known of Jane Austen's prayers she might not have considered the novelist 'a complete and most sensible lady, but a very incomplete and rather insensible (*not senseless*) woman', one who cannot represent the final truths known by 'the sentient target of death' (Southam, 1968, 128).

The manuscripts of Jane Austen's prayers, like the prayers they contain, have been overlooked. No accurate scholarly edition of these prayers has yet appeared, and, as we shall see, it is uncertain who actually copied out the prayers. B. C. Southam, justifiably, does not discuss the manuscripts in his authoritative *Jane Austen's Literary Manuscripts*. A clear account of the not-very-clear textual situation may thus be a helpful starting-point.

Jane Austen's sister Cassandra left the manuscripts at her death in 1845 to Cassandra Esten Austen, the eldest daughter of their brother Charles, and two of his grand-daughters sold them, along with other Austen papers and memorabilia, at Sotheby's in 1927 (Le Faye, 244), for a price of £175 (Gilson, 1986, 13). They were subsequently acquired by the California book-collector William Matson Roth, who produced a limited edition (of 300 copies) of the prayers in 1940. Roth's text of the prayers is a little strange: it is all in capital letters, and the punctuation is frequently modernised. When Chapman included the prayers in the *Minor Works* of 1954, the sixth and final volume of his Oxford Illustrated Jane Austen edition, he relegated them to the volume's final pages and reproduced Roth's text (though reversing his typography, using lower-case throughout). Even the 1993 edition of *Catharine and Other Writings*, edited by Margaret Doody and Douglas Murray, bases its text, not on the manuscripts, but on a 'typed transcription made by William Matson Roth' (283).

Roth donated the manuscripts in 1957 to Mills College in Oakland, California; they now reside in the Heller Rare Book Room of the F. W. Olin Library at Mills College. The prayers are found on two sheets of paper of quarto size, each folded into two leaves (or four octavo pages). The inscription 'Prayers Composed by my ever dear Sister Jane' appears on the outside of the folded quarto sheet on which the first prayer, with the heading 'Evening Prayer', is written. The sheet has a watermark dated 1818. The handwriting of this first prayer is said by Chapman to be 'probably – almost certainly? – Cassandra's' (*MW*, 453). The inscription appears to be in a different hand (and under the inscription is pencilled lightly the name 'Charles Austen'). The second and third prayers appear, without title or number, on the second sheet of manuscript, which lacks a watermark. The second prayer appears on pages one and two of the four octavo pages, and the third on pages three and four.

A fascinating question emerges here: down to the second-last line of 'page three' of the second sheet (that is, for the first half of the third prayer), one finds what seems to be the same hand as on the first sheet. However, beginning with the last line of that octavo page and on the next occurs a much neater, if still flowing, hand –

writing that seems fairly clearly to be that of Jane Austen herself. R. A. Austen-Leigh, co-author of *Jane Austen, Her Life and Letters* and editor of *Austen Papers, 1704–1856*, was 'quite sure' that it was Jane Austen's handwriting (Roth, Introduction, 2). Chapman, however, considered the handwriting 'doubtful' (Chapman, 1926, 27). If this second sheet does contain Jane Austen's handwriting, it would obviously have to pre-date both her death in July 1817 and the sheet containing the first prayer. Chapman's headnote in the *Minor Works* volume compounds the confusion. He says the second MS sheet 'is partly in a hand which I think may be Henry Austen's, partly in a hand which has been thought by experts to be JA's own' (*MW*, 453). The switch from first-person ascription to passive summary underlines the implied doubt.

And yet the confusion is more apparent than actual. What does it matter who copied out the prayers if we continue to believe – and there is no reason not to – their inscribed title, 'Prayers Composed by my ever dear sister Jane'? It seems clear that Jane Austen composed the prayers, and that they were copied out, at two different times, by a combination of the Austen brothers and sisters. The manuscripts of Jane Austen's prayers were a family production.

This is fitting, because Jane Austen's prayers are communal in nature. Though one person is reading, they are the prayers of the family, not a person, and the third prayer concludes with the petition, 'may we by the Assistance of thy Holy Spirit so conduct ourselves on Earth as to secure an Eternity of Happiness with each other in thy Heavenly Kingdom'.[1] All three prayers end with those present joining voices to recite the Lord's Prayer; the third prayer thus goes on from the words 'Heavenly Kingdom' to conclude, 'Grant this most merciful Father, for the sake of our Blessed Saviour in whose Holy Name & Words we further address Thee. Our Father &c.'

Furthermore, Jane Austen's prayers, like the *Book of Common Prayer*, which they echo in many ways and at many points, speak in a shared voice of a generic predicament (unlike the very personal *Prayers and Meditations* of her mentor Samuel Johnson). The predicament is that outlined in the Prayer Book, the Thirty-Nine Articles, and indeed in the Bible itself: men and women need God's grace and guidance, since human nature is inherently sinful and yet proud, and so prone to self-deception and discontent. A long quotation from Jane Austen's first prayer demonstrates that, as Henry Austen said, 'her opinions accorded strictly with those of our Established Church' (*NA*, 8):

> Look with Mercy on the Sins we have this day committed, & in Mercy make us feel them deeply, that our Repentence [*sic*] may be sincere, and our Resolutions stedfast of endeavouring against the commission of such in future. – Teach us to understand the sinfulness of our own Hearts, and bring to our knowledge every fault of Temper and every evil Habit in which we have indulged to the discomfort of our fellow-creatures, and the danger of our own Souls. – May we now, and on each return of night, consider how the past day has been spent by us, and what have been our prevailing Thoughts, Words and Actions during it, and how far we can acquit ourselves of Evil. Have we thought irreverently of Thee, have we disobeyed thy Commandments, have we neglected any known Duty, or willingly given pain to any human Being? – Incline us to ask our Hearts these questions Oh! God, and save us from deceiving ourselves by Pride or Vanity.
>
> Give us a thankful sense of the Blessings in which we live, of the many comforts of our Lot: that we may not deserve to lose them by Discontent or Indifference.[2]

As this passage suggests, the difficulty and yet the necessity of self-knowledge is the principal theme in Jane Austen's prayers. A parallel theme is the struggle for Christ-like forbearance and charity (the 'candour' that Jane Bennet exemplifies and Elizabeth acquires in *Pride and Prejudice*). A paragraph from Jane Austen's third prayer is quite explicit:

> Give us grace to endeavour after a truly Christian Spirit to seek to attain that temper of Forbearance & Patience, of which our Blessed Saviour has set us the highest Example and which, while it prepares us for the spiritual happiness of the life to come, will secure to us the best enjoyment of what this World can give. Incline us Oh God! to think humbly of ourselves, to be severe only in the examination of our own conduct, to consider our fellow-creatures with kindness, & to judge of all they say and do with that Charity which we would desire from them ourselves.[3]

Note that in the prayers morality and religion coincide. In the first passage, the same acts endanger our souls and cause discomfort to fellow creatures, while thinking irreverently of God and disobeying his commandments are equated with neglecting known duties and causing pain to other human beings; in the second passage, spiritual happiness in the life to come and the best enjoyment of this world are gained by the same means.

Given her orthodox beliefs, it is not surprising that Jane Austen's letters reveal her Augustan (and Augustinian) scorn for the new, evangelising, subjective forms of Christianity: 'We do not much like Mr. Cooper's new Sermons; they are fuller of Regeneration and Conversion than ever – with the addition of his Zeal in the cause of the Bible Society' (*L*, 467). On the other hand, she admired the tough-minded sermons preached by Thomas Sherlock, Bishop of London, to an audience of lawyers at the Temple Church: 'I am very fond of Sherlock's Sermons, prefer them to almost any' (*L*, 406).

Quite apart from the orthodox beliefs they express, Jane Austen's prayers employ the diction and rhythms of the *Book of Common Prayer*, as Margaret Doody has observed (Doody, 347; Austen, *Catharine and Other Writings*, 371–2). Indeed, it would be surprising if they did not: she would have heard and said the Prayer-Book prayers at least once a week throughout her life. Besides, those prayers were regarded as models: Johnson told Boswell, 'I know of no good prayers but those in the *Book of Common Prayer*' (Boswell, 1292). Jane Austen's prayers are particularly close to the Collects in the *Book of Common Prayer*. Compare, for instance, Jane Austen's prayer for charity, cited above, with the Collect for the Sunday before Lent:

> O Lord, who hast taught us that all our doings without charity are nothing worth, send thy Holy Ghost, and pour into our hearts that most excellent gift of Charity, the very bond of peace and of all virtues, without which whosoever liveth is counted dead before thee. Grant this for thine own son Jesus Christ's sake.[4]

Significantly, Jane Austen's petition for self-knowledge (represented in the long excerpt from Prayer I quoted above) does not have such a direct origin in the Prayer Book Collects. Two Collects, however, will serve to suggest its general derivation from the beliefs, stance, and language of the *Book of Common Prayer*:

> Almighty and everlasting God, who art always more ready to hear than we to pray, and art wont to give us more than either

we desire, or deserve; Pour down upon us the abundance of thy mercy; forgiving us those things whereof our conscience is afraid, and giving us those good things which we are not worthy to ask, but through the merits and mediation of Jesus Christ, thy Son, our Lord. *Amen.* (Collect for the twelfth Sunday after Trinity)

O God, who knowest us to be set in the midst of so many and great dangers, that by reason of the frailty of our nature we cannot always stand upright; Grant to us such strength and protection, as may support us in all dangers, and carry us through all temptations; through Jesus Christ our Lord. *Amen.* (Collect for the fourth Sunday after the Epiphany)

The Collect, defined in Johnson's *Dictionary* of 1755 as 'A short comprehensive prayer, used at the Sacrament', is the form most frequently used in the *Book of Common Prayer*, and is 'so called because it collects and gathers together the supplications of the multitude, speaking them all with one voice; and because it is a collection and sum of the Epistle and Gospel for the Day' (according to a seventeenth-century dictionary cited in the *OED*). In form, the Collect consists of five parts: Salutation, Ascription, Petition, Reason for Petition, and Conclusion (Tillotson, 1116). These five parts can be seen clearly in the three Collects cited above. In the first quoted, for instance (the prayer for charity), the Ascription begins with the word 'who', the Petition with 'send', the Reason for Petition with 'without', and the Conclusion with 'Grant'.

The same form can be found in each of Jane Austen's prayers. The long passage from the first prayer beginning with 'Look with Mercy' occurs in the second and third paragraphs of the prayer and begins the Petition, after a first paragraph devoted to Salutation and Ascription; similarly, the paragraph beginning 'Give us grace' is the second paragraph of the third prayer and begins the Petition after an opening paragraph of Salutation and Ascription.

The beliefs, language, and form of the Prayer-Book prayers were, of course, found in many other books of prayers that Jane Austen knew, including Johnson's *Prayers and Meditations*, published in 1785 and cited frequently and at length in Boswell's *Life*, which Jane Austen seems to have known by heart.[5] Another intermediate model for Jane Austen's prayers is one of the 20 surviving books that she owned, *A companion to the altar: shewing the nature & necessity of a sacramental preparation in order to our worthy receiving the Holy Communion, to which are added Prayers and Meditations.* Apparently written by William Vickers and published in 1793, 'this book of devotions always used by Jane Austen', to quote her great-niece Florence Austen, is inscribed with her signature and the date 1794 (Gilson, 1982, 445). It is a guide for those about to be confirmed in the Church of England; Jane Austen's copy was probably presented to her at the time of her own confirmation – she was 18 in 1794 (Tucker, 203–4). The prayers appended to the book, as its author points out, paraphrase the Collects in the *Book of Common Prayer*, just as they in turn paraphrase the Scriptures (Preface, ii).

One interesting difference between Jane Austen's prayers and those of the Prayer Book lies in their language: Jane Austen's is scrupulously conceptual and non-figurative. The Prayer Book, a monument of Renaissance sensibility, is much more 'poetic': for instance, 'pour into our hearts that most excellent gift of Charity, the very bond of peace, and of all virtues' (in the Collect for the Sunday before Lent) is much more concrete and metaphorical than the equivalent phrasing in Jane Austen's third prayer, and the same can be said of phrases such as 'we cannot always stand upright' in the Collects cited above. Jane Austen concurs with Samuel Johnson in this respect: Johnson notoriously disapproved of Milton's use of 'trifling fictions' to convey 'the most awful and sacred truths' (Johnson, 699), and he tells Boswell roundly, 'I do not approve of figurative expressions in addressing the Supreme Being; and I never use them' (Boswell, 1293).

In general, then, Jane Austen's prayers are meant to be read as the work of the common, generic believer, not the idiosyncratic individual – the first-person plural rather than the first-person singular. Like the Prayer Book, her prayers are not conceived of as literature, though they may have superadded literary interest or value. A passage from *Mansfield Park* dramatises the point neatly. Henry Crawford is addressing Edmund, but also trying to impress Fanny with his knowledge of religion:

Our liturgy [Henry says] has beauties, which not even a careless, slovenly style of reading can destroy; but it also has redundancies and repetitions, which require good reading not to be felt. For myself, at least, I must confess being not always so attentive as I ought to be – (here was a glance at Fanny) that nineteen times out of twenty I am thinking how such a prayer ought to be read, and longing to have it to read myself – Did you speak? (*MP*, 340)

The contrast between 'I' and 'our' as attitudes to prayer could hardly be sharper, as Fanny's evident, but unarticulated, gesture of dissent suggests.

Jane Austen's prayers tell us a good deal about her life. At the same time, they raise some very puzzling questions – which is no doubt why her biographers have by and large left them alone.

The most important thing they tell us is also the most obvious: that Jane Austen had a deep and sincere religious faith. Her prayers provide the most telling, if far from the only, evidence of this piety. Proof exists also in her one serious poem, on the death of her friend Mrs Lefroy (*MW*, 440–2); the comments she made about religious books (for instance, in addition to her disapproval of Dr Cooper's sermons and her praise of Bishop Sherlock's, her pleasure in Thomas Gisborne's Evangelical conduct-book, *An Enquiry into the Duties of the Female Sex* [*L*, 169]); the passages of religious consolation in her letters (e.g. *L*, 19, 144, 219–20); and her attitude of pious submission in the letters written shortly before her death (*L*, 493–8). And, of course, her grandfather, her father, and two of her brothers were clergymen, as were many others in the family circle, including Cassandra Austen's fiancé Thomas Fowle, who died of yellow fever before they could marry. As Jan Fergus observes in her recent biography, 'For Austen, religion was an essential part of her daily life' (36).

Jane Austen's prayers also point to the effect that the *Book of Common Prayer* must have had upon her style. Her prayers display the syntactical control and balance, the diction, and the speech-rhythms that characterise both the *Book of Common Prayer* and Jane Austen's own prose when she is writing formally. Doody summarises the case for such an influence:

The Book of Common Prayer is, to speak profanely, a good influence on style. Its sentiments are emphatic without crudity, and its cadences have the grace of strength rather than of decoration. It is also a language meant to be spoken aloud. . . . It is here, I believe, that we must look for the origins of Austen's balanced and coordinated sentences rather than to the later and more partial influence of Johnson. (347–8)

Jane Austen's prayers also pose some difficult biographical questions. Did the Austen family hold evening prayers at home? What is the date at which the prayers were composed? Why do only three short prayers by Jane Austen survive? The answers to these questions must be tentative and incomplete (which is why they have not been treated by her biographers); still, a certain amount can be said.

It *does* seem likely that the Austen family observed evening prayers at home: both Gisborne and *A companion to the altar* recommend it, and in *Mansfield Park* Fanny Price says of morning and evening prayers at Sotherton, 'A whole family assembling regularly for the purpose of prayer, is fine' (86). Jane Austen's letters do not allude specifically to evening prayers, but a letter to Cassandra of 1808 refers to evening devotions (which would include prayers) as a matter of course: 'In the evening we had the Psalms and Lessons, and a sermon at home' (227).

As for their date of composition, surmise is the best we can do: the prayers themselves contain no hint of their date. It seems quite possible that Jane Austen would have composed the prayers only after the death of her father, an active and devout clergyman, in 1805. Deirdre Le Faye states, without further explanation, 'These prayers are undated, but seem to be products of Jane Austen's later life' (274). Certainly, the three novels that Jane Austen composed during the final years of her life at Chawton (*Mansfield Park, Emma, Persuasion*) have a much more overtly religious dimension than the first three, drafted during the 1790s, and Marilyn Butler has made a strong case for viewing the later novels as reflections of 'the wartime religious reform movement spearheaded by the Evangelicals . . . a national mood of self-assessment and regeneration' (Butler, 1986, 207).

Surmise, again, must suffice as to why only three short prayers by Jane Austen survive. It is possible, but I suspect unlikely, that Jane Austen wrote further prayers that do not survive. Jane Austen's three prayers were probably meant to supplement others that the family would normally use at evening prayers – prayers from the Prayer Book, or from other books of devotion, or indeed prayers composed by other family members, and especially Jane Austen's clergyman father and brothers.

These concrete questions, however, pale beside the overwhelming question raised by Jane Austen's prayers: that of consistency. They seem so different from her letters – chatty and observant, gossipy and often malicious – and from her novels – so worldly in tone, so seemingly silent on spiritual matters. And just as with the specific biographical questions, this question has been generally avoided: it is no easy matter to reconcile the Jane Austen revealed in her prayers with the catty letter-writer and the shrewd comic novelist. Park Honan, in his *Jane Austen: Her Life*, does face the issue and even offers a view of the novels as Jane Austen's resolution of an inner conflict:

> There is no greater contrast in Jane Austen's writings than that between her sharp, comically malicious letters and the Christian prayers she composed. . . . The effort of reconciling her faith with her fury was enough to try her, and as happy as she was in green country at Chawton she was to make amends in part through her fictional comedies in which no living being is attacked, but life itself is recreated and appraised for every reader. (255; cf. 124)

One way of tackling this issue is to simplify it. The real problem lies in the apparent discrepancy between the prayers and the novels. The letters are mainly of interest because they are written by Jane Austen the novelist; furthermore, the letters are much more mixed in tone than the most acid (and memorable) excerpts from them suggest – it would not be hard to produce a set of excerpts that would make them seem entirely pious and proper. None of us is, or would like to be, everywhere and always the same. And in any case Jane Austen's letters survive only in part and have the intimate indirectness of writing not meant to be read outside the family circle. What Jane Austen says in her letters can hardly be held against her. The novels, however, are a very different matter.

The contrast between Jane Austen's prayers and her novels brings us back to Charlotte Brontë's insistence on Jane Austen's limitations. Several critics have asserted (and many others have assumed), with Brontë, that the novels are without religious reference or dimension:

> Jane Austen the novelist did not believe in God. . . . She did not arrange, control, or interpret her deepest experience in the light of [her piety]. (Lerner, 23)

Jane Austen draws the curtain between her Sunday thoughts, whatever they were, and her creative imagination. Her heroines face their moral difficulties and solve their moral problems without recourse to religious faith or theological doctrines. (Ryle, 117)

Of course, there is another view, one that sees Jane Austen as less schizophrenic and the novels as less simply secular. A. C. Bradley put it succinctly in his essay of 1911: 'Her inmost mind lay in her religion – a religion powerful in her life and not difficult to trace in her novels, but quiet, untheoretical, and rarely openly expressed' (29). This is the view of the novels taken in the first essay to be devoted to Jane Austen's *oeuvre*, Richard Whately's review-essay on *Northanger Abbey* and *Persuasion* in the *Quarterly Review* in 1821:

> Miss Austin [*sic*] has the merit (in our judgment most essential) of being evidently a Christian writer: a merit which is much enhanced, both on the score of good taste, and of practical utility, by her religion not being at all obtrusive. . . . The subject is rather alluded to, and that incidentally, than studiously brought forward and dwelt upon. . . .
> The moral lessons also of this lady's novels, though clearly and impressively conveyed, are not offensively put forward, but spring incidentally from the circumstances of the story; they are not forced upon the reader, but he is left to collect them (though without any difficulty) for himself; her's is that unpretending kind of instruction which is furnished by real life. (Southam, 1968, 95)

Whately's conception of the interdependence of fiction, morality and religion is, I believe, shared by Jane Austen herself. Two incompetent readers from her fiction, Catherine Morland of *Northanger Abbey* and Sir Edward Denham of *Sandition*, illustrate the point. Catherine as a girl has a natural tendency to read without thinking: 'provided that nothing like useful knowledge could be gained from them, provided they were all story and no reflection, she had never any objection to books at all' (15); Sir Edward is much worse, since he perversely misinterprets Richardson's *Clarissa*: 'ill-luck . . . made him derive only false Principles from Lessons of Morality, & incentives to Vice from the History of it's Overthrow' (*MW*, 405).

Jane Austen's prayers confirm this view of Jane Austen as a 'Christian writer'. Both Bradley and Whately wrote without knowledge of the prayers. Several recent critics of the novels develop roughly the same conception of the novelist, and four of these refer briefly to her prayers: Stuart Tave's *Some Words of Jane Austen* (see 112–13); Marilyn Butler's *Jane Austen and the War of Ideas* (see 189, 192, 196); Gene Koppel's *The Religious Dimensions of Jane Austen's Novels* (see 7–8); and Jan Fergus's *Jane Austen: A Literary Life* (see 36).

Nevertheless, as I hope to have shown, the relationship between Jane Austen's prayers and her novels deserves fuller treatment than it has yet received; I would like to conclude this discussion of the prayers by outlining three ways in which they might illuminate the novels.

The first way is the most obvious: the beliefs and terms of the prayers inform the novels. One quick way of demonstrating this is to cite from Marianne's speech of contrition in *Sense and Sensibility*:

I wonder at my recovery, – wonder that the very eagerness of my desire to live, to have time for atonement to my God, and to you all, did not kill me at once. . . . Whenever I looked toward the past, I saw some duty neglected, or some failing indulged. (303)

Note that this speech assumes that religious and moral duties coincide ('to my God, and to you all') – the same assumption that we saw earlier in both Jane Austen's prayers and Whately's account of her novels. By far the most striking aspect of the prayers is their insistence on self-knowledge (an insistence based, as we have seen, on a belief in original sin), and of course Jane Austen's novels, particularly the two best of them, *Pride and Prejudice* and *Emma*, are dramas of self-discovery. The prayers also stress 'candour' (or charity of judgement). The passage from Prayer III cited above shows that Jane Austen considered that it is natural 'to think meanly of all the rest of the world, to *wish* at least to think meanly of their sense and worth compared with my own', to use Darcy's words from the concluding pages of *Pride and Prejudice* (369). That is, one can think meanly ('severely' is the word in the prayer) of others and well of oneself, like Emma Woodhouse and Elizabeth Bennet when they are still unreformed, or apply the golden rule and reverse that natural tendency – thereby becoming able to think well of others and severely of oneself (like Miss Bates, or Jane Bennet, or the reformed heroines). Similarly, a conflict between gratitude and discontent is central in both the prayers and the fiction.

These ideas suggest a second way in which Jane Austen's prayers may throw light on her novels. The prayers do, as I have argued, speak for a community of believers, rather than as the voice of a particular individual; nevertheless, they do reveal a distinctive emphasis. The central petition of all three prayers is for self-knowledge, with an explicitness that has no model in the *Book of Common Prayer*; similarly, in her third prayer Jane Austen seeks charity *of judgement* (whereas the Prayer Book speaks of charity in 'all our doings'). The prayers, thus, must reveal to us the sins to which Jane Austen felt she was most inclined. We can then see the novels as having at their heart the painful struggles that dominated Jane Austen's own inner life: the struggles for self-knowledge, charity of mind, gratitude, and the other virtues of the prayers. This conception of the novels' basis in Jane Austen's experience is very old-fashioned – but it may none the less be true, and it is at least a less lurid formulation than Park Honan's suggestion (cited above) that in her novels Jane Austen 'makes amends' for her spiritual lapses.

Honan does, however, link the prayers to Jane Austen's choice of comedy, which she calls 'my own style . . . and my own way' (*L*, 453), and this connection is a third and final way in which the prayers illuminate the novels. In the prayers, as in Christianity as a whole, life is a Divine Comedy: it is good, just, harmonious, and all will turn out well in the end – unless 'we . . . , by our own neglect, throw away the Salvation Thou hast given us' (Prayer I). And so it is in the novels: for every Emma there is a Mr Knightley, for every Elizabeth a Mr Darcy, for every Anne a Captain Wentworth (and vice versa). Furthermore, good and bad actions, as in Dante's *Divine Comedy*, are not only part of a moral cause-and-effect sequence, so that the good end happily; these actions also bring into being spiritual states which are themselves fitting rewards or punishments. The final and exact reward for Emma (or punishment for Mrs Elton) is simply to go on being what she has chosen to become. Similarly, nothing could in the end be more harmonious than the disharmony Lucy Steele has achieved at the end of *Sense and Sensibility*:

[Robert and Lucy Ferrars] settled in town, received very liberal assistance from Mrs. Ferrars, were on the best terms imaginable with the Dashwoods; and setting aside the jealousies and ill will continually subsisting between Fanny and Lucy, in which their husbands of course took a part, as well as the frequent domestic disagreements between Robert and Lucy themselves, nothing could exceed the harmony in which they all lived together. (377)

Jane Austen's prayers, then, reveal a good deal about both her life and her novels. They show that in her own life she was concerned for the state of her soul, and with an intense awareness that gives the lie to Charlotte Brontë's claim that Austen was ignorant of 'the sentient target of death'. To be fair, Brontë knew of Austen only what she gathered from reading two novels, *Pride and Prejudice* and *Emma* (Southam, 1968, 126–7). And yet Jane Austen's novels themselves, as her prayers suggest, contain much more than Brontë found there: 'ladies and gentlemen in their elegant but confined houses' (Southam, 1968, 126). Austen's novels *do* tell the stories of ladies and gentlemen; they *are* set in elegant houses. They also, however, present a moral and spiritual terrain that stretches far beyond those dwellings.

Notes

1. Quotations from Jane Austen's prayers are from the manuscripts at Mills College and are cited by permission of the librarians there.
2. Douglas Murray has suggested, in a letter to me, that the dashes may indicate pauses for the insertion of voiced petitions particular to any given day or of silent petitions.
3. The last sentence here is especially important as a summary of Jane Austen's moral thinking; interestingly, it is in the middle of this sentence that Jane Austen herself (or someone whose hand resembles hers) begins to write out the prayer.
4. The *Book of Common Prayer* was standardised in 1662; quotations here are from the Oxford: Clarendon Press edition of 1803.
5. She alludes to Boswell's *Life* at least six times in the *Letters* (*L*, 32, 33, 49, 181, 363, 368); she paraphrases Boswell's final tribute to Johnson at the end of her poem 'To the Memory of Mrs. Lefroy' (cf. *Life*, 1394–5, and *MW*, 442); and Jane Austen's image of 'my dear Dr Johnson' (*L*, 181) was no doubt derived largely from Boswell's presentation of Johnson – just as Jane Austen uses the phrase, as Chapman points out in his note on the letter, in the course of agreeing with an opinion in a letter from Johnson to Boswell cited by the latter in his *Life* (563).

16

The Dower House at Kellynch: A Somerset Romance

Margaret Drabble

It is not always easy to distinguish attachment to person from attachment to property. I know it is widely held that Elizabeth was joking when she declared that she fell in love with Darcy when first she saw Pemberley. I used to think so myself. Now I am not so sure. Let me tell you my story, and you may make your own judgement. I have yet to make mine.

They call it the Dower House, but really it is nothing of the sort. It once fulfilled the function of a Dower House, some time in the last century, the period at which the facade looking down over the pleasure gardens had been refurbished. One of the always more or less unfortunate Lady Elliots (or had it been a Lady Bridgewater?) was said to have been secluded there, and the improvements had been made for her benefit. The terrace with its Gothic alcoves, the urns and the sun dial, the rounded finials on the roof had been added at this time, but it was no more a dower house than nearby Uppercross Cottage was a cottage. Both were renovated farm houses. Uppercross Cottage, incidentally, is now known as The Elms, after the unfortunate whim of an early-twentieth-century owner who decided the word cottage was inappropriate for so substantial a residence. The elms are all dead, of Dutch elm disease, but the name remains. It is a happy house and well maintained. It belongs to an architect from Taunton. His children and grandchildren play table tennis on the verandah in the summer evenings.

The Dower House is neither happy nor well maintained. But it is beautiful.

I fell in love with it at first sight. I was taken there by my friend Rose, with whom I was staying at her farm on Exmoor. I did not know Somerset well, and we had spent a pleasant few days, walking, swimming in the icy river Barle, looking at churches and country houses. Rose was working on the illustrations for a book of European pond and river plants, and we collected specimens. On the whole we kept our own company, talking over our own affairs – I was still giddy with relief at having not long left my cad of a husband, she was involved with a philandering philosopher – but one evening she arranged for us to go over to Kellynch for dinner.

As we left the chalky uplands and descended into the red deeps, driving through increasingly narrow, high-banked purple-flowering lanes of foxglove and rosebay, Rose told me its history. Ever since some early Elliot had been obliged to let the Hall, at the beginning of the last century, the property had been hedged with difficulties. There had been a scandalous liaison round the time of Waterloo, which had scattered illegitimate children through the county, followed by a marriage which had promised well, the bride being a Bridgewater and wealthy. But it had ended in long-drawn-out disaster. The Bridgewaters figured well in Debrett's but not in other organs of record. They were, not to beat about the bush, said Rose, barmy. The duties and dignities of a resident landowner had appealed neither to Elliots nor to Bridgewaters. But they had hung on there, as the estate fell to pieces. During the Second World War Kellynch Hall had been requisitioned as an Officers' Training Centre and it had never recovered. It was now a Field Study Centre. She herself occasionally taught a course on botanical drawing there.

Yes, she said, slowing to avoid a pheasant, accelerating to overtake a tractor, there had been dramas. There had been suicides and incarcerations. The men drank and the women wept. The cold blood of the Elliots had mingled disastrously with the black blood of the Bridgewaters. One bride had thrown herself from an upper storey of Kellynch Hall on her wedding night: she had been caught in the arms of the great magnolia tree and had lingered on, an invalid. A daughter had taken her brother's shotgun and blown out her brains on Dunkery Beacon. A son had drowned himself in the pond. When the pond was drained, in the 1920s, said Rose, it was found to contain a deposit of bottles of claret both empty and full: old Squire William, the one who had sold off Parsonage Farm and the woods beyond Barton, had been in the habit of wandering down there of an evening, sometimes drunk, sometimes in a frenzy of remorse. In either state he had thrown bottles. The tench had thrived on them: never had such vast fish been seen. There was one stuffed on show in the Hall.

With such legends she entertained me as we drove westward. The present owner of the estate, Bill Elliot, with whom we were to dine, was now in his late thirties. His father, Thomas Elliot, had been a military man and had fought in the desert with Montgomery of Alamein, but the peace had disagreed with him and he had come home to drink himself to death, dying of cirrhosis of the liver in his sixties. Bill had inherited a property that was mortgaged, entailed, and ill-starred. Oppressed by this legacy, he had made a brief stay of execution by hiring the house, parkland, and pleasure gardens to a film company for a costume movie. This venture had turned out well, for his dowerless sister Henrietta had insisted on appearing as an extra in the hunting sequence, had taken a nasty fall, and had been wooed on her sickbed in Taunton Hospital by one of the film's more portly and substantial stars, who had married her. Did I know Binkie? Maybe I had seen him as a bishop in the latest Trollope series? He was really rather good.

But one cannot live off one windfall. And so Kellynch Hall had been let to the Field Study Centre on a 99-Year Maintaining and Repairing Lease. The Elliots had washed their hands of it. Bill was now camping out in the Dower House. I would like him, she hoped.

I wondered. As I struggled with the heavy metal latch of a broken-down five-barred gate – for it seemed we were to drive down a cart track to Kellynch – I struggled also with my feelings about the English land and its owners. I come, though I trust you cannot detect this, from the lower middle classes, to whom property is important – but by property we mean the freehold of a suburban house with a garden where you can hang out the washing, not farms and tenancies and arable acres. The Elliots of old would not have acknowledged the existence of my category of person. To them we did not signify. And now it was they who hung on by a thread. Kellynch Lodge, which had once belonged to the Russells, was owned by an absentee Canadian newspaper proprietor, and the Vicarage by a designer of computer software. Trade and the middle classes had triumphed.

Even Rose, who had done her best to declassify herself, sometimes annoyed me. She worked for her living, after a somewhat haphazard manner, but she carried with her the assumptions of a gentlewoman. She assumed I knew things I did not know, people I did not know. She lives in a world which I know largely through literature. I am the second-hand person, the ventriloquist. She is the real thing.

I relatched the gate with difficulty, got back into the car, and we edged carefully down what I now realised was not a cart track but an avenue of oaks leading towards Kellynch Hall. This had been the grand approach, and the trees, though some were stag-crested, were grand still: but they had returned so much to nature that the formality of their planting, ordained by some Elliot four centuries ago, was not at once apparent. They had been reabsorbed into the landscape, as had the great sweet chestnuts of the park boundary. Soft lumps of honey fungus sprouted from the old wood. The gold of a field of barley rose to our right. There was a hint of autumn fulness in the August air.

We descended, past the Big House, down the curved drive, through what had been the stable courtyard, to the Dower House. The melancholy deepened and tears stood in my eyes. I had never seen anywhere so beautiful in my life. Pink peeling walls, grey-yellow lichen-encrusted stone, single white roses, white doves. It had reached the moment before decay that is perfection.

Bill Elliot, too, was in his own way perfect. Decay had hardly touched him, though perhaps his hair was very slightly receding. He was extremely good looking – the Elliots are famed for their good looks. He was of no more than middle height, with the blue eyes, fair tanned skin, fine blonde hair, regular features and open yet quizzical look of the beleaguered late-twentieth-century English country gentleman. He was wearing a pair of moss-stained trousers rolled up to the knee and a limp blue shirt lacking most of its buttons. He put himself out to charm me, and I was charmed. I felt that it was a privilege to meet him. It was fortunate for me that he was not my type, I told myself.

It was a memorable evening. Bill's estranged wife Penny, who now lived with a trout farmer at Winthrop, had come over to join us. She had not brought the trout farmer. There was one other couple, a doctor who worked in Bristol and her husband, an ornamental blacksmith. Bill did the cooking, on an old-fashioned temperamental solid-fuel kitchen range which I was to get to know all too well. He made us a risotto, with a mixture of field mushrooms and slices of a sulphurous yellow growth called Chicken of the Woods. He said he would show me where it grew. It was delicious. We ate Somerset cheese, and salad, and blackberries and cream.

The Dower House was derelict. Patterned curtains hung tattered and drooping from bare rails, broken-springed chairs sprouted feathers, and feathers drifted under the kitchen door from a vast woodshed full of nesting doves. The wiring dated from between the wars. I had not seen such bakelite plugs, such furred and twisted flex, since my childhood.

We talked of the difficulties of the landed gentry as we sat around the scarred paint-stained seventeenth-century kitchen table. What should one do? Turn the stately homes into venues for pop concerts, into miniature zoos, into hotels? The Big House at Uppercross was now an expensive retirement home. The National Trust would not accept properties as gifts unless they were heavily endowed. I knew of these problems, but I had never met anyone who faced them in person. I had never felt much sympathy with them. But there was something touching about Bill Elliot, rinsing out a glass and drying it on a tea towel covered with garish pictures advertising Lyme Regis and its dinosaurs.

I said I had never been to Lyme. We wandered back into the drawing-room with our coffee, and Bill showed us his grandfather's battered dusty cabinet of treasures. There were little drawers of fossils and minerals, all labelled, and drawers full of pinioned butterflies and moths, and dried leaves from the rare trees in the pleasure gardens. Bill said he preferred the minerals. He had added specimens of his own, some of them collected at Lyme. He loved Lyme. He said I should go there one day.

At Bill's suggestion, we took a turn in the gardens. It was hardly dark, but Bill courteously took my arm as we stumbled through the undergrowth. There were nettles waist high, overgrown rhododendrons, Himalayan balsam, wild garlic. It was a wilderness. The mild air was heavy, rank, lush, erotic, sad.

We went back to the house for a last glass of wine. Bill told us that he was leaving the country. There was, he said, no freedom for him here. Penny, who was not hearing this news for the first time, said nothing. She watched a spider walk along the wall. They had two daughters, both at boarding-school in Exeter. There would be no more Kellynch Elliots. A Shropshire Bridgewater Elliot was next in line, would inherit the title and the debts. Bill said he was off to Alaska, to a place called Anchorage. I asked why. 'Because it sounds safe there', he said, and we all laughed. He said that he had been there once, briefly, changing planes on the way to Japan. He had liked it. It was as far from Kellynch as you could get. It was all snow and minerals. He would study minerals there in the long nights. He had sold a couple of paintings – a flood-damaged Hudson, a doubtful Reynolds, to finance his expedition. You could live for ten years in Anchorage on a gentleman in brown velvet, a lady in blue satin.

I did not know whether he was being whimsical or speaking the truth. It is difficult to know the difference with that kind of person.

On parting, he kissed my hand. The gesture was more intimate than a peck upon the cheek. 'Dear girl', he said. 'Good bye. Wish me well.'

Rose was very quiet on the way home. I think she had once been a little in love with him.

I heard no more of Kellynch for seven years. I somewhat lost touch with Rose: she sold her farm and took off to the South Seas to do a book on tropical flora, and this broke the rhythm of our friendship. In those seven years much happened. My imprudent early marriage came to a final end in divorce, but my career prospered. I had been no more than a promising actress in those early days, and not even I had thought I would be able to do more than scratch a living: but a lucky break in the form of a film role – as Juliet in a freely adapted version of Fanny Burney's *The Wanderer* – had come my way and since then I had been able to pick and choose. Tragic heroines from rustic romances were offered to me regularly, and most of them I declined. I had become well-known and lonely.

I was sitting one evening in my flat off the King's Road reading a Thomas Hardy screenplay when the phone rang. I picked it up – which I might well not have done – and an unfamiliar voice said, 'Is that Emma Watson? Emma? You won't remember me, but this is Penelope Elliot. Do you have time for a word?'

Of course I remembered her. I could see her face as though it were yesterday – her silver-yellow hair, her pale high brow, her girlish Alice band, her freckled nose, her little breasts, her faded jeans, her long thin bare feet.

'Penny', I said. 'Yes, of course. How are you?'

She was well. The girls were well. Bill was well. She had left her fish man and married a lawyer. She knew I was well as she had seen me on TV. She was ringing about the Dower House. Bill's picture money – did I remember the picture money? – was running out, and he was thinking of letting the Dower House. They seemed to remember I was rather taken with it, and Rose had thought so too. Would I consider renting it for six months, for a year? Would I like to ring Bill in Calgary, or should she get him to ring me?

Whatever is he doing in *Calgary*, I asked. Oh, she said, he has fallen in love with the mountains and the everlasting snows. He says that Somerset is full of putrefaction.

We both laughed, and she gave me Bill's number. I tried to work out what time it might be in Calgary and what hours a man like Bill might keep, but I do not think I got it right because he sounded way out of all things when I spoke to him. Nevertheless we struck a bargain. I would take Kellynch Dower House for six months, renewable at six-monthly intervals. He said it had been done up slightly since my last visit. Not *too* much, I hoped. Oh no, he did not think I would find it over-restored. Any problems I could put through Penny and her husband. So useful to have a lawyer in the family.

This time I could detect the irony.

He was right in assuming I would not find the Dower House too much modernised. There had been attempts at improvement: the roses that had climbed in through the windows had been cut back, the roughly hacked dog-door had been blocked, the kitchen range had been given a coat of black lead, and loose covers had been fitted on some of the chairs. There were two new lavatories, though the bath still stood on claws in the centre of a three-doored bathroom. There was a second-hand refrigerator and a washing machine in an outhouse.

I was enchanted by my new retreat. How well I remember my first night there, as I stared at the flames of the log fire I had finally managed to light, and listened to some early Italian opera on the crackly radio. (Reception was never very good in that deep valley.) I was as safe as Bill in his snowy eyrie.

As I sat, a strip of wallpaper, disturbed by my presence, slowly unpeeled itself. A quarter of an hour later it began to rain and the chimney began to smoke. Rain fell down the chimney and on to the hissing logs. Smoke billowed at me. Coughing, I left the room, and found a rivulet of red water running through the back door, across the red tiles, through the hallway, and out again under the front door. I opened the door and saw the water disappearing into a grate partly blocked by twigs and moss. I cleared the grate, and watched with satisfaction as the bloody trickle drained away.

I was by now muddy, so thought I would take a bath. The hot water was boiling, and gushed forth bravely. But alas, the cold pipes had developed an airlock. I sucked and blew but to no avail. I had to wait for the water to cool. I assisted it with ice cubes. When I got to bed, I could hear the sound of scrabbling in the rafters. Rats, mice, pigeons, owls, squirrels, doves? I fell asleep, content.

Each day brought some new disaster. It is extraordinary how

many faults an old house can develop. I lived as in the nineteenth century. I became expert with bellows and stirrup pump, with mop and bucket, with toasting fork and balls of string and clothes pegs. Electricity cuts occurred almost daily. At times, tormented by the cooing of a hundred doves, I thought of buying a shotgun, but contented myself by throwing stones.

I arrived in a wet March, and stayed through most of the summer. My agent despaired of me and sent me threatening messages. Friends came to see me, were appalled by the discomfort, and went away. I wandered the hedgerows, climbed the hills, lost myself in the woodlands. I trod in the footsteps of the Wordsworths and Coleridge and Lorna Doone, I made my way through a thousand pages of *The Glastonbury Romance*. I studied the landscape and its history. I discovered that one of the oak trees in the avenue was the second tallest in Britain – *Quercus petraea*, thirty-six metres high, and more than six metres in girth. Once I went to Bath, but I did not like it there – it was full of young men drinking beer from cans, and the car-parks were crowded and expensive. I never got to Lyme. I made acquaintances – a young woman up the valley called Sophy Hayter who kept goats, a retired vet who told me where to watch for the red deer. I dined with the Wyndhams at the Elms, had a drink with Dominic the blacksmith, and spoke, once, to the vicar. I often called in the church to see the Elliot ancestors. One lay helmeted and cross-legged on his crumbling sandstone tomb. There was a plaque to the Lady Elliot who had been so ill for so long.

I was on good terms with the people who ran the Hall, who said I could take my guests round whenever I wished. The Elliot coat of arms, with a date of 1589, was engraved over the three-storeyed porch of the south front, and the great magnolia still blossomed. Occasionally I would wander in to admire the lofty plaster ceilings, the polished floors (which smelt more of the schoolroom now than of the country house), the quantities of gilt-edged looking-glasses, the paintings, the charming light rococo staircase. It was hard to think the house unworthily occupied and fallen in destination as one watched the peaceful pursuits of the students who came on botany or geology or painting courses. Some of them were very mature students, grey-haired, tweed-suited, rain-bonneted. They were usefully employed, and they kept the roof on, which was more than the Elliots had done. The whiff of carbolic and shepherd's pie was a small price to pay.

Sometimes I indulged a fancy that Bill Elliot was walking down the grand staircase with a new bride upon his arm, but this image derived more from Daphne du Maurier than from the house's own history. I could not help wondering how he felt about the place, and my proximity to it. Since I had become his tenant, he had taken to sending me enigmatic postcards. One mentioned the Chicken of the Woods, and drew me a little map of its whereabouts, so he too had remembered the details of our meeting. I did not have an address for him, so could not have responded had I wished.

There was a portrait of Bill in Kellynch Hall, by an undistinguished member of the St Ives school. He was wearing a sailor suit, and had gold ringlets.

In my Dower House, there was another portrait that interested me almost as much. It was of a woman dressed in the style of the 1820s, wearing a blue-and-yellow striped dress with a low neck. She stared out of the frame boldly and with a certain effrontery. Her hair was auburn, her smile slightly crooked. Her largish hands – not well painted – were clasped in front of her bosom, holding a posy of primroses. I liked her. I wondered if she had been banished from the big house, or stolen thence by one who loved her. She seemed to smile at me with encouraging complicity.

In August I wrote to Bill's agent in Taunton renewing my lease. I was growing more and more attached to my solitude. I dreamed of Bill quite often.

One fine evening in late September I took myself up to the deserted kitchen gardens behind my house in search of rosemary. Some of the more tenacious herbs still grew there, though the beds were overgrown, the espalier fruit trees untrained, and the glass of the greenhouses broken. Mr Shepherd at the Hall told me that once fourteen gardeners worked there, growing asparagus and beans and lettuces and peaches for the Elliots. Why did they not put the gardens back into cultivation, I asked, to provide food for the students? Nobody would do such work these days, he said. It was cheaper to shop at the supermarket. Why did they not run a course on kitchen gardening, I suggested, and let the students grow their own supper? A good idea, he said. But I knew nothing would happen.

So I was the only ghost who haunted the garden. I came down with my handful of herbs, watching the evening light slant and flatten over the cedar of Lebanon, the tall hollies, the yellow Bhutan cypress, possessed by a luxury of self-pity and self-admiration so intense that I was consumed by it. I almost ceased to exist. And as I stood there, in a trance, I heard someone speak my name. I started with surprise – yet I was not wholly surprised, for was I not always expecting an audience, and did I not know that I was, that autumn evening, after a summer of fresh air, in particularly good looks?

'Miss Watson?' I heard, from the terrace. There was a man standing there, my binoculars in his hand. I had left them on the little writing table in the outdoor alcove, along with my book, my pack of cards, and my glass of whisky – a glass covered, alas, inelegantly, by a postcard, to protect it from the flies. He had been watching my hawk.

'Yes?' I hazarded, a little coldly. Was he some intruder from the world of commerce, some angry messenger from my agent? But no, he was a gentleman.

'Miss Watson, I apologise for my intrusion. I could not pass without seeing the old house, and I was told I would find you here. And then I saw you, up in the walled garden. So I waited. Please' – he stretched out his hand – 'let me introduce myself. I am Burgo Elliot.'

'Ah', I said. 'You must be Burgo Bridgewater Elliot. From Shropshire.'

'Indeed, from Shropshire.'

We shook hands. I was in some confusion. For this was the heir, and I was the usurper.

In the circumstances – which included my glass of whisky – I felt obliged to offer him refreshment, to invite him in to see the improvements. Yes, he would like that, but perhaps we could sit first for a while in the garden? So we settled together in the alcove, I with my whisky, he with a sherry (he was lucky there, I do not often have sherry in the house) and a bowl of Bombay Mix between us. I inspected him, and he inspected me. He was, if anything, younger than Bill, so perhaps there was not much chance of his inheriting anything unless Bill fell down a glacier quite soon. Was he married, did he have sons, and would the estate be entailed to them when Bill died?

Such thoughts, which were quite unlike any I had ever had before I came to Kellynch, buzzed around in my head with as much determination as the wasps buzzed around the sherry. Where had they come from? Were they bred by the red earth itself, by the crumbling stone? They were not *my* thoughts at all. They had slept deep in the ancient masonry and had crept out at last into the late sun.

Burgo Elliot did not seem to hold me responsible for the neglect of the gardens, the peeling wallpaper, the smoking chimney, the laundry cupboard door. I was a paying guest, and apologies were due to me, not from me. But it saddened him to see how run down things had become. Did I not find it too melancholy?

No, I said. It was the melancholy I loved. I did not care for fresh paint. I was a romantic.

He smiled. This was fortunate, he said.

We moved indoors, and he made the tour, even glancing into my bedroom with its embroidered counterpane. He stroked the scarred kitchen table, patted the settee as though it were an old family dog, and sighed. He said he had not been to Kellynch for years, not since he and Bill were boys. Poor Bill, he said. Did I know Bill well? No, I said, hardly at all, though even as I spoke I knew this was not quite true. I did know Bill Elliot. I had invested in him, and he had lodged in me.

Burgo Elliot was, like his cousin, a handsome man, though in a different style. He was darker, he was taller, he had grey eyes, and a Roman – perhaps a Norman – nose. He was also very thin. His head was a fine skull of sharp planes and bone; he had worn thin with time like an antique silver spoon.

He was, it appeared, a bachelor. He denied wife and progeny. He also denied Shropshire: although he was indeed one of the Shropshire Bridgewater Elliots, he lived in London. As, he believed, did I?

We sat indoors and he spoke affectionately of the old days. Here they had played, he and Bill and Henrietta. He had been an only child, and had looked forward to his summer holidays, though Lady Elliot had been a sad lady, and the old man a monster. He it was who had let the Hall go to its final rack and ruin. He had stoked the fire with priceless manuscripts, buried the family silver in the pleasure gardens without marking the spot, and shot the local policeman. He had done nothing to restore the Hall after the war years, and in the bitter winter of 1947 the tanks had burst and the rococo staircase had been a cascade of ice. So Sir Henry and his lady had moved out to the Dower House, evicting old Boniface who had been squatting there as the sole remaining gardener, and they had camped like gypsies. The children had learned to fend for themselves. Bill had shot rabbits for the pot, and cooked them in the garden on an everlasting bonfire. They had made great cauldrons of oatmeal and nettle stew. The last of the staff had deserted, and the empty Hall had crumbled. When the old man died and Bill came of age, it was too late to rescue it. Lady Elliot had gone into a nursing home in Chard.

It was growing late, and my lamb cutlet would not feed two. So I fell silent, and he, being a gentleman, at once took his leave. He was on his way to see friends in Devon, who would be expecting him, he said.

He was lying. He would go no further that night than the Dalrymple Arms or the Egremont at Uppercross. But I accepted his fiction and let him go. I knew I would see him again. And I wanted time to think about his apparition.

How could I not have been stirred by it? It would have taken a dulled, nay deadened fancy not to have been stirred by Burgo Elliot.

Why, I wondered, had he remained single? In my experience there were two likely explanations – one, that he had liked those of my own sex too much, the other, that he liked them not at all. I pride myself on having a good eye in these matters, but Burgo baffled me.

He had spoken with great fondness of Bill. Had he been in love with the beautiful boy? Or had it been his own childhood that he mourned?

Bill, he said, had always loved the inanimate. He had thought it safe. When I had finished my cutlet, I went and knelt down by the little cabinet and looked at the weathered fragments of ammonite, the fossilised starfish, the swaying stone flowers of the sea, labelled in Bill's childish hand. And where was Bill now, perched on what ledge, huddled in what remote crevasse, while Burgo Bridgewater Elliot slept between clean sheets in a warm inn?

I became obsessed by Burgo Elliot. Had I dreamed him up? Even his name seemed false. Burgo – surely a name for a novel, not for real life. A name for a rogue and a villain?

Let me make this plain. Until I went to Kellynch I had no interest in what is called family. My own family – well, I have said they were lower middle class, but by the time I was born they were middle middle class. My father worked for an insurance company in Newcastle, my mother was a school teacher. He reads Trollope, she reads Jane Austen. They are sensible, hard-working people, but they have no connections and are proud of it. Nevertheless, my mother can never resist a temptation to tell the story of her meeting with the Duchess of Northumberland. It is a pointless story but she will tell it. My ex-husband, with more reason but as little excuse, likes to let it be known that his maternal grandmother was a Dalrymple. He reveals this fact in order to mock it. But nevertheless he reveals it. And am I not now letting you know that I married into the Dalrymples?

The Elliots and the Bridgewaters were much more interesting to me than the Dalrymples. How could I find out more about Burgo? I was too ashamed of my curiosity to ask anybody, and it was a happy moment when I remembered the books in my own back parlour. They were a deeply unattractive assortment of old bound volumes of *Blackwoods* and *Punch* and the *Spectator*, redolent of Sunday afternoons of ancient boredom, foxed and mildewed and spotted with birdlime – jackdaws often came down the chimneys and one of my occupations was to chase them away. I had never thought of browsing in this dull library, but now was its moment – and yes, indeed, there was exactly what I was looking for. There was the Baronetage, a heavy purplish folio volume with gold lettering on the spine.

I lugged it on to the kitchen table. I was not the first to consult it. The pages fell open, as I might have predicted, upon the Elliots of Kellynch Hall. It was clear that the entry had been much perused. There were two whole pages of Elliot this and that, but I could soon see that they were only of historical interest, for the last entry, added to the Gothic print in fine copperplate hand, read, 'Heir presumptive, William Walter Elliot, Esq., great grandson of the second Sir Walter.' We were back in 1810. This was no use to me. I needed something more modern.

I dug around, and at length found a 1952 volume of *Burke's Peerage*, which also fell open upon Elliots. And here they were, my very own Elliots. There was Sir Thomas, there was his son and heir William Francis Elliot and his daughter Henrietta. I read the names again and again, hoping to wrest some occult significance from the very words. There was no mention of Burgo Bridgewater Elliot. I could not find him anywhere. I needed a sequel, published after Sir Thomas's death.

In the morning I rang an old friend who I thought might help, and to whom I did not mind revealing my interest. He is himself a baronet, though he does not like this to be mentioned as he is also an actor and he hopes (so far in vain) not to be typecast. He was currently appearing in *Lady Windermere's Fan*. James seemed pleased to hear from me and delighted by the nature of my query. The Shropshire Elliots, I wanted? Well, first of all I must forget about the Shropshire bit. People do not come from where they say they come from. Does the Duke of Devonshire live in Devonshire, the Norfolks in Norfolk, the Bristols in Bristol? Certainly not. Now I am James Winch of Filleigh, he said, but I don't even know where

Filleigh is, I think it is the home of some cricket team where grand-father once got a hat-trick while touring with the Myrmidons. . . .

I checked his flow and asked him to look up the Shropshire Elliots, to see if they had any money left. 'Why, thinking of marrying one, darling?' he said, and went off to consult his reference library. He came back in triumph. I knew he would have the right books. People like that always do, however much they dissimulate.

Yes, he said, here were the Elliots of Kellynch. William Francis, m. Penelope Hargreaves, 2d., marriage dissolved 1978. And the heir was kinsman Burgo Bridgewater Elliot, of the Shropshire branch. He looked up Burgo, and told me that he was a company director of Felsham Metal Frame Windows. A very good prospect, said James. I should marry him if I were you, and not that other fellow. Or would you like to marry me and take a turn as Lady Filleigh?

I thanked him for his gallant proposal and rang off. I was shaking slightly and almost poured myself a vodka. I was shocked by my own curiosity. I could not shock you more than I shock myself.

Burgo reappeared in the spring. I had wintered in London, avoid-ing the dark nights and obliging my agent by doing some work. But in March I was back at the Dower House with the primroses, to find a postcard from Bill that had been waiting for me for weeks upon the red tiles. Rain had flowed over it, intruding cats had stepped inkily upon it, and its message was hardly decipherable, but I think it said, 'With love to my fair tenant. Have you yet heard the nightingales?'

On my first evening the phone rang. It was Burgo. This was not much of a coincidence, it seemed, as he said he had been ringing me all winter. Where had I been? In London, I said. Ah, so have I, he said. But now he was in Somerset. Could he call and take me out to dinner at the Castle Hotel in Taunton?

And so it was that Burgo Bridgewater Elliot re-opened negotia-tions. And, over his subsequent campaign, I remained as much in the dark as ever about his nature and his intentions. Never have I known so opaque an admirer. Never did he touch me, save in the way of courtesy – a hand at greeting, a hand to help me into the car or over a stile or to disentangle me from a bramble. Yet he was in his way translucent. He was worn thin with a lonely pain. One felt one could see through him and beyond. Like one of those elegant thoroughbred dogs that appear to have no space for normal bodily organs, he seemed to have nowhere within him to live a natural animal or emotional life. He was all stretched tenuous surface. Bill, in comparison, had been a solid man.

Perhaps, I sometimes thought, it was the place that Burgo came to see. It had cast its spell upon him, as it had upon me.

Was I falling in love with Burgo? I could not tell. I had nobody else to love, and at this moment in the history of my heart a second attachment, and to so eligible a gentleman, might have seemed a natural sequel to a somewhat unfortunate first choice. (Not that I entirely regret the cad. He had his points.) Did I *want* to fall in love with Burgo? Again, I could not tell.

It was impossible to reject his attentions. My vanity would not have permitted it. He was the perfect escort, who increased my consequence in my own eyes even when there were no others to watch, and he escorted me gallantly through all weathers. I dragged him up hill and down dale that spring, that summer, curious to see how far I could lead him. One day I decided to take him to Lyme.

I wanted to look for fossils. Bill had sent me a postcard of a dinosaur's egg from the Rockies, and I determined to try to find some small dull long-dead creature of my own to add to the Elliot collection. I informed Burgo of my plans, and we fixed a date for our excursion. I had bought a little hammer, and I told Burgo to bring his boots. I was becoming imperious with him, but he seemed to like it.

The weather did not look promising, and we wondered whether to cancel our trip, but out of stubbornness I would not. Burgo did not disobey. It rained as we set off. I insisted on going in my car. I said it would clear but it did not. We drove along twisting lanes, the windscreen wipers working, the windows misting, and on the high ground as we moved into Dorset there was fog and I had to put on the headlights. Burgo sat there without a murmur of complaint. What was he thinking of my folly and my obstinacy? I spoke to him of the Black Venn Marls and the Blue Lias and the Green Ammonite beds. I could not even tell if he was listening. I did not know what I was talking about. I wondered if he knew I did not know. Maybe, with Bill, he had searched those beaches as a child, had been there many times before. Why was he so docile towards me?

Lyme is a steep little town, not friendly to the motor car. Various signs ushered us towards parking places, and we ended up at the bottom, down by the Cobb. The rain had settled into a steady downpour, but despite this there were a few bedraggled persistent holiday-makers huddling their way along the streets. There was a smell of vinegar, fish, harsh false sugar and fried onions. There was even a pair of lovers embracing on the end of the Cobb. There is always a pair of lovers embracing upon the end of the Cobb. I made poor Burgo march along the Cobb, and we stood there and looked at the boiling water beneath us dashing against the rocks. It was very slippery underfoot. My trousers were soaked. Burgo, still looking every inch the gentleman, was wet through.

Even then I would not relent. I dragged the poor man off to the fossil cliffs – and you can guess the rest. We survived the Cobb, but the Black Venn Marls got us.

It was my fault. I was a bloody fool. But Burgo by this time was not behaving very sensibly either. There is something dementing about that landscape. The dark raw caked sliced earth, the ribbed ledges, the steaming fissures, the stunted trees sticking out of recent landslips, the dreary trickling of small black waterfalls, the dreary pounding of wave after wave upon the wet curve of the beach – I had never seen anywhere so desolate. As we walked along the beach, a great chunk of cliff the size of a packing case dislodged itself and fell with a mournful thud behind us. We should have turned back, but we went on. We both went on.

It was Burgo that saw the devil's toenail. His eyes are sharper than mine. He should never have pointed it out to me, but I should never have scrambled after it. I had not realised the black stuff was so friable. In short, just as I grabbed hold of the fossil, I slipped, and in slipping I dislodged a small avalanche, and thus it was that I did whatever I did to my leg.

I could not believe it. I am tough as well as stubborn. But I could not walk. There was nobody else in sight. Burgo would have to carry me back. I was covered in black mud, I was in pain, and I thought the tide was coming in. It was not a good surface for walking on at the best of times, and with the burden of a muddy lady Burgo must have found it agonising. I kept apologising. And still Burgo did not lose his temper.

I ended up in Weymouth General Hospital with my leg in traction. I was there for two and a half weeks. I had plenty of time to think. At the end of the first week Burgo asked me to marry him. I asked him why. He said it seemed to have been intended, and who were we to struggle against our destiny? If we found we didn't like it, he said, we could always get divorced. I was bold enough to ask him why he hadn't got married before, and he said that the black blood of the Bridgewaters had made it seem unwise, but maybe I wouldn't mind taking the risk? I seemed quite robust, he added.

I was quite pleased with myself, as you can imagine. Everything was going according to plan.

I told Burgo I needed time to make up my mind. He was far too much of a gentleman to retract his offer, I thought. I still did not know whether he wanted to marry me, thought he wanted to marry me, thought he ought to marry me, thought I wanted to marry him, or was in such despair that he didn't much care what happened. Or maybe he was up to some other game altogether?

My game by now is, I imagine, quite clear. I want the Dower House. I want it more than I have ever wanted anything. As I sit here, flying over the Rockies on my way to negotiate with Bill Elliot, I feel faint with desire at the thought of it. It is in my reach. Burgo says he will buy it for me, if Bill will let us have it. We shall see. If Bill won't let me have it, maybe I will marry Bill instead of Burgo. I feel such a sense of my own power as I sit here above the clouds. I can move mountains. A very small south-coast avalanche was enough to bring Burgo to his knees. The Rockies look more formidable, but I cannot believe that they or Bill Elliot are impervious to my intentions. Bill has been waiting for me for eight long years. He will have something to say, surely, when we meet on the shores of Lake Louise.

Love of person, love of property. It is not as simple as that. What if I were to substitute the romantic word *place* for that cold Augustan word *property*? Would you then think so harshly of me? For the Dower House is worthless, as property. It is its own history. It is Bill and Burgo and Henrietta eating rabbit in the garden. It is the hawk and the chicken of the woods and the red rain. It is the dead jackdaw in the book case, it is the avenue of oaks, it is the smiling woman with her primroses. She approves of my determination. So, too, incidentally, does Henrietta – she and Binkie and I get on *very* well. She thinks I should probably marry Burgo, but on the other hand she thinks it is time Bill came home, and I should try to get him back to the old country if I can.

I do not know what will happen. Emma Watson's story has no ending. Who knows what awaits me, down there on earth?

Works Cited

Aristotle, *The Nicomachean Ethics*, trans. H. Rackham, Loeb Classics edition (Cambridge, Mass.: Harvard University Press, 1982).

Auerbach, Nina, 'O Brave New World: Evolution and Revolution in *Persuasion*', in *Romantic Imprisonment: Women and Other Glorified Outcasts* (New York: Columbia University Press, 1986), 38–54.

Austen, Jane, *Catharine and Other Writings*, ed. Margaret Anne Doody and Douglas Murray (Oxford: World's Classics, 1993).

——, *The History of England: A Facsimile*, ed. Deirdre Le Faye (London: British Library, 1993).

——, *Three Evening Prayers*, ed. William Matson Roth (San Francisco: Colt Press, 1940).

Austen-Leigh, Richard, *Austen Papers, 1704–1856* (London: Spottiswoode, Ballantyne, 1942).

——, and William Austen-Leigh, *Jane Austen: Her Life and Letters, A Family Record* (London: Smith and Elder, 1913).

Babb, Howard S., *Jane Austen's Novels: The Fabric of Dialogue* (1962; Hamden, Conn.: Archon Books, 1967).

Baignent, Francis Joseph, and James Edwin Millard, *A History of the Ancient Town and Manor of Basingstoke* (Basingstoke: C. J. Jacob; London: Simpkin, Marshall and Company, 1889).

Bakhtin, M. M., *The Dialogic Imagination*, trans. C. Emerson and M. Holquist (Austin: University of Texas Press, 1981).

Barbauld, Anna Laetitia, ed., *The British Novelists; with an essay; and prefaces, biographical and critical* (London: Rivington, 1810).

Bertelsen, Lance, 'Jane Austen's Miniatures: Painting, Drawing, and the Novels', *Modern Language Quarterly*, 45 (1984), 350–72.

Bloom, Harold, ed., *Jane Austen: Modern Critical Views* (New York: Chelsea House, 1986).

The Book of Common Prayer (Oxford: Clarendon Press, 1803).

Booth, Wayne, *The Rhetoric of Fiction* (Chicago: University of Chicago Press, 1961).

Boswell, James, *Life of Johnson*, Oxford Standard Authors Edition (1791; London: Oxford University Press, 1969).

Bourdieu, Pierre, *Distinction: A Social Critique of the Judgement of Taste*, trans. Richard Nice (Cambridge, Mass.: Harvard University Press, 1984).

——, *The Logic of Practice*, trans. Richard Nice (Stanford, Calif.: Stanford University Press, 1990).

Bowen, Elizabeth, 'A Masterpiece of Delicate Strength', in Southam, 1976, 165–70; reprint of '*Persuasion*', *London Magazine*, 4 (June 1957), 47–51.

Bradbury, Malcolm, *Cuts* (London: Hutchinson, 1987).

——, '*Persuasion* Again', in Southam, 1976, 214–27; reprint of '*Persuasion* Again', *Essays in Criticism*, 18 (1968), 383–96.

Bradley, A. C., 'Jane Austen', in *Essays and Studies by Members of the English Association*, 2 (1911), 7–36.

Brissenden, R. F., *Virtue in Distress: Studies in the Novel of Sentiment from Richardson to Sade* (London: Macmillan, 1974).

Brontë, Charlotte, 'Charlotte Brontë on Jane Austen' [excerpts from letters], in Southam, 1968, 126–8.

Burke, Edmund, *A Philosophical Enquiry into the Origin of Our Ideas of the Sublime and Beautiful*, ed. J. T. Boulton (1757; London: Routledge and Kegan Paul, 1958).

Butler, Marilyn, 'History, Politics, and Religion', in *The Jane Austen Companion*, ed. J. David Grey (New York: Macmillan, 1986), 190–208.

——, *Jane Austen and the War of Ideas* (Oxford: Oxford University Press, 1975).

——, *Romantics, Rebels and Reactionaries: English Literature and its Background 1760–1830* (Oxford: Oxford University Press, 1981).

Chapman, R. W., 'A Jane Austen Collection', *TLS*, 14 January 1926, 27.

Cochrane, J. G., ed., *Catalogue of the Library at Abbotsford* (Edinburgh: privately printed, 1838).

Cohn, Dorrit, *Transparent Minds: Narrative Modes for Presenting Consciousness in Fiction* (Princeton: Princeton University Press, 1978).

Collected Reports of the Jane Austen Society, 1976–1985 (Chippenham, Wilts.: The Jane Austen Society, 1989).

Cooper, Edward, *Two Sermons Preached at Wolverhampton* (London, 1816).

Copeland, Edward, 'The Economic Realities of Jane Austen's Day', in Folsom, 33–45.

Cottom, Daniel, *The Civilized Imagination: A Study of Ann Radcliffe, Jane Austen, and Sir Walter Scott* (Cambridge: Cambridge University Press, 1985).

Court, Franklin E., *Institutionalizing English Literature: The Culture and Politics of Literary Study, 1750–1900* (Stanford, Calif.: Stanford University Press, 1992).

Cox, Stephen, 'Sensibility as Argument', in *Sensibility in Transformation: Creative Resistance to Sentiment from the Augustans to the Romantics*, ed. Syndy Conger (London and Toronto: Associated University Presses, 1990).

De Rose, Peter L., and S. W. McGuire, *A Concordance to the Works of Jane Austen*, 3 vols (New York: Garland Publishing, 1982).

Doody, Margaret Anne, 'Jane Austen's Reading', in *The Jane Austen Companion*, ed. J. David Grey (New York: Macmillan, 1986), 347–63.

Doyle, Brian, *English and Englishness* (London and New York: Routledge and Kegan Paul, 1989).

Duckworth, Alistair M., *The Improvement of the Estate: A Study of Jane Austen's Novels* (Baltimore: Johns Hopkins University Press, 1971).

Edwards, Ralph, *The Shorter Dictionary of English Furniture: From the Middle Ages to the Late Georgian Period* (London: Country Life, 1964).

Epstein, Julia, *The Iron Pen: Frances Burney and the Politics of Women's Writing* (Madison, Wisc.: University of Wisconsin Press, 1989).

Ermarth, Elizabeth Deeds, *Realism and Consensus in the English Novel* (Princeton: Princeton University Press, 1983).

Farrer, Reginald, 'One of Fiction's Greatest Heroines', in Southam, 1976,

148–50; pages 28–30 from 'Jane Austen', *Quarterly Review*, 228 (July 1917), 1–30.

Fergus, Jan, *Jane Austen: A Literary Life* (London: Macmillan, 1991).

Ferrier, Susan, *Marriage: A Novel*, ed. Lady Margaret Sackville (1818; London: Nash and Grayson, 1929).

Ferris, Ina, *The Achievement of Literary Authority: Gender, History, and the Waverley Novels* (Ithaca: Cornell University Press, 1991).

Folsom, Marcia McClintock, ed., *Approaches to Teaching Austen's 'Pride and Prejudice'* (New York: Modern Languages Association of America, 1993).

Foucault, Michel, *Discipline and Punish: The Birth of the Prison*, trans. Alan Sheridan (New York: Vintage, 1979).

Fowles, John, *Cinderella*, adapted from Perrault's *Cendrillon* of 1697 (London: Jonathan Cape, 1974).

Freud, Sigmund, *The Psychopathology of Everyday Life*, in *The Standard Edition of the Complete Psychological Works of Sigmund Freud*, vol. 6, ed. James Strachey, trans. Alan Tyson (London: The Hogarth Press, 1960).

——, 'Three Essays on the Theory of Sexuality', in *The Standard Edition of the Complete Psychological Works of Sigmund Freud*, vol. 7, trans. James Strachey (London: Hogarth Press, 1953), 125–243.

Gard, Roger, *Jane Austen's Novels, The Art of Clarity* (New Haven and London: Yale University Press, 1992).

Gilson, David, 'Auction Sales', in *A Jane Austen Companion*, ed. J. David Grey (New York: Macmillan, 1986), 13–15.

——, *A Bibliography of Jane Austen* (Oxford: Clarendon Press, 1982).

Gisborne, Thomas, *An Enquiry into the Duties of the Female Sex* (London, 1797).

Guillory, John, *Cultural Capital: The Problem of Literary Canon Formation* (Chicago and London: University of Chicago Press, 1993).

Hagstrum, Jean H., *Sex and Sensibility: Ideal and Erotic Love from Milton to Mozart* (Chicago: University of Chicago Press, 1980).

Handley, Richard, and Daniel Segal, *Jane Austen and the Fiction of Culture: An Essay on the Narration of Social Realities* (Tucson: University of Arizona Press, 1990).

Harding, D. W., 'The Dexterity of a Practised Writer', in Southam, 1976, 193–213; reprint of Introduction to *Persuasion* (Harmondsworth: Penguin, 1965), 7–26.

Heffernan, James A. W., 'Ekphrasis and Representation', *New Literary History*, 22 (1991), 297–316.

Honan, Park, *Jane Austen: Her Life* (London: Weidenfeld and Nicolson, 1987).

Howells, W. D., 'Great Honesty and Daring', in Southam, 1976, 142–7; pages 50–7 from *Heroines of Fiction* (New York and London, 1901).

Hume, David, *An Enquiry Concerning the Principles of Morals* (1751; Indianapolis: Hackett, 1988).

Johnson, Claudia L., *Jane Austen: Women, Politics, and the Novel* (Chicago and London: University of Chicago Press, 1988).

Johnson, Samuel, *A Dictionary of the English Language* (London: 1755).

——, 'Life of Milton', from *Samuel Johnson*, Oxford Authors Edition, ed. Donald J. Greene (1779; New York: Oxford University Press, 1984).

———, *Prayers and Meditations*, ed. George Strachan (London, 1785).

Kahler, Erich, *The Inward Turn of Narrative*, trans. R. and C. Winston (Princeton: Princeton University Press, 1973).

Kant, Immanuel, *The Critique of Judgment*, trans. J. H. Bernard, 2nd edn, 1931, in *Critical Theory since Plato*, ed. Hazard Adams (New York: HBJ, 1971), 379–99.

Kaplan, Deborah, *Jane Austen among Women* (Baltimore: Johns Hopkins University Press, 1992).

Kelly, Gary, *English Fiction of the Romantic Period 1789–1830* (London and New York: Longman, 1989).

Kermode, Frank, *The Classic: Literary Images of Permanence and Change*, corrected edition (Cambridge, Mass., and London: Harvard University Press, 1983).

Koppel, Gene, *The Religious Dimension of Jane Austen's Novels* (Ann Arbor, Michigan: UMI Press, 1988).

Krieger, Murray, *Ekphrasis: The Illusion of the Natural Sign* (Baltimore: Johns Hopkins University Press, 1992).

Lascelles, Mary, 'On *Persuasion*', in Southam, 1976, 154–63; pages 76–81, 203–8 from *Jane Austen and Her Art* (Oxford: Clarendon Press, 1939).

———, *Jane Austen and her Art* (Oxford: Oxford University Press, 1939).

Le Faye, Deirdre, *Jane Austen: A Family Record* (London: The British Library, 1989).

Lerner, Laurence, *The Truthtellers: Jane Austen, George Eliot, D. H. Lawrence* (New York: Schocken, 1967).

Lewis, C. S., 'A Note on Jane Austen', in *Jane Austen: A Collection of Critical Essays*, ed. Ian Watt (Englewood Cliffs, NJ: Prentice-Hall, 1963), 25–34.

Locke, John, *An Essay Concerning Human Understanding*, ed. Peter H. Nidditch (1690; Oxford: Clarendon Press, 1975).

Lockhart, John Gibson, *Memoirs of the Life of Sir Walter Scott, Bart*, 7 vols (Edinburgh: Robert Cadell; London: John Murray and Whittaker and Co., 1837–8).

Marshall, David, *The Figure of Theater: Shaftesbury, Defoe, Adam Smith, and George Eliot* (New York: Columbia University Press, 1986).

McKendrick, Neil, John Brewer, and J. H. Plumb, *The Birth of a Consumer Society: The Commercialization of Eighteenth-Century England* (London: Hutchinson, 1983).

McMaster, Juliet, 'The Secret Languages of *Emma*', *Persuasions*, 13 (1991), 119–31.

———, 'Surface and Subsurface', in *Jane Austen on Love* (Victoria, BC: University of Victoria, 1978), 28–42; reprinted in *Jane Austen's* Emma, ed. Harold Bloom (New York: Chelsea House, 1987), 37–44.

Mellor, Anne K., 'Why Women Didn't Like Romanticism: The Views of Jane Austen and Mary Shelley', in *The Romantics and Us: Essays on Literature and Culture*, ed. Gene W. Ruoff (New Brunswick, NJ: Rutgers University Press, 1990), 274–87.

Merleau-Ponty, Maurice, *In Praise of Philosophy and Other Essays*, trans. J. Wild, J. Edie, and J. O'Neill (Evanston, Ill.: Northwestern University Press, 1988).

——, *The Phenomenology of Perception*, trans. Colin Smith (London: Routledge and Kegan Paul, 1962).

——, *The Primacy of Perception*, ed. James Edie (Evanston, Ill.: Northwestern University Press, 1964).

——, *Signs*, trans. R. McCleary (Evanston, Ill.: Northwestern University Press, 1964).

Miller, D. A., 'The Late Jane Austen', *Raritan*, 10 (Summer, 1990), 60–4.

Miller, J. Hillis, *The Form of Victorian Fiction* (South Bend, Ind.: University of Notre Dame Press, 1968).

Milne, A. A., *Winnie-the-Pooh* (1926; New York: E. P. Dutton, 1961).

Mitchell, W. J. T., 'Eye and Ear: Edmund Burke and the Politics of Sensibility', in *Iconology, Text, Ideology* (Chicago and London: University of Chicago Press, 1986), 116–49.

——, 'Metamorphoses of the Vortex: Hogarth, Turner, and Blake', in *Articulate Images: The Sister Arts from Hogarth to Tennyson*, ed. Richard Wendorf (Minneapolis: University of Minnesota Press, 1983).

Modiano, Raimonda, 'Humanism and the Comic Sublime: From Kant to Friedrich Theodor Vischer', in *Studies in Romanticism*, 26 (1987), 231–44.

Moers, Ellen, *Literary Women* (Garden City, NY: Anchor Books, 1977).

Molan, Ann, 'Persuasion in *Persuasion*', *Critical Review*, 24 (1982), 16–29; reprinted in *Jane Austen*, ed. Bloom, 147–62.

Mooneyham, Laura G., *Romance, Language, and Education in Jane Austen's Novels* (New York: St Martin's Press, 1988).

Moore, Catherine E., ' "Ladies . . . Taking the Pen in Hand": Mrs Barbauld's Criticism of Eighteenth-Century Women Novelists', in Mary Anne Schofield and Cecilia Macheski, eds, *Fetter'd or Free? British Women Novelists, 1670–1815* (Athens and London: Ohio University Press, 1986).

Morgan, Susan, *In the Meantime: Character and Perception in Jane Austen's Fiction* (Chicago: University of Chicago Press, 1980).

Mudrick, Marvin, *Jane Austen: Irony as Defense and Discovery* (Berkeley: University of California Press, 1952).

Mullan, John, *Sentiment and Sociability: The Language of Feeling in the Eighteenth Century* (Oxford: Clarendon Press, 1988).

Mulvey, Laura, 'Afterthoughts on "Visual Pleasure and Narrative Cinema" inspired by *Duel in the Sun*', in *Feminism and Film Theory*, ed. Constance Penley (London: Routledge, 1988), 69–79.

——, 'Visual Pleasure and Narrative Cinema', in *Feminism and Film Theory*, ed. Constance Penley (London: Routledge, 1988), 57–68.

Nardin, Jane, *Those Elegant Decorums: The Concept of Propriety in Jane Austen's Novels* (Albany, NY: State University of New York Press, 1973).

Nolen-Hoeksema, Susan, *Sex Differences in Depression* (Stanford: Stanford University Press, 1990).

Oliphant, Margaret, '*Persuasion* Stands by Itself', in Southam, 1976, 140–1; pages 233–5 from *The Literary History of the Nineteenth Century* (London: Macmillan, 1882).

Ovid (Publius Ovidius Naso), *The Art of Love, and Other Poems*, trans. J. H. Mozley (Cambridge, Mass., and London: Harvard University Press and Heinemann, 1979).

Page, Norman, *The Language of Jane Austen* (Oxford: Basil Blackwell, 1972).

Phillips, K. C., *Jane Austen's English* (London: André Deutsch, 1970).

Pointon, Marcia, *Hanging the Head: Portraiture and Social Formation in Eighteenth-Century England* (New Haven: Yale University Press, 1993).

Richardson, Samuel, *Clarissa*, ed. Angus Ross (1747–8; Harmondsworth: Penguin, 1985).

——, *Sir Charles Grandison*, ed. Jocelyn Harris, 3 vols. (1753; Oxford: Oxford University Press, 1972).

Rifelj, Carol, *Reading the Other: Novels and the Problem of Other Minds* (Ann Arbor, Mich.: University of Michigan Press, 1992).

Rimmon-Kenan, Shlomith, *Narrative Fiction: Contemporary Poetics* (London: Methuen, 1983).

Rose, Mark, *Authors and Owners: The Invention of Copyright* (Cambridge, Mass., and London: Harvard University Press, 1993).

Roston, Murray, *Changing Perspectives in Literature and the Visual Arts 1650–1820* (Princeton: Princeton University Press, 1990).

Ryle, Gilbert, 'Jane Austen and the Moralists', in *Critical Essays on Jane Austen*, ed. B. C. Southam (London: Routledge and Kegan Paul, 1968), 106–22.

Sabor, Peter, ' "Finished up to nature": Walter Scott's Review of *Emma*', *Persuasions*, 13 (1991), 88–99.

——, 'The Strategic Withdrawal from Ekphrasis in Jane Austen's Novels', in *Icons, Texts, Iconotexts: Ekphrasis and Intermediality*, ed. Peter Wagner (Berlin: de Gruyter, 1995).

Sartre, Jean-Paul, *Being and Nothingness*, trans. Hazel Barnes (New York: Simon and Schuster, 1966).

Scott, Sir Walter, *The Abbot* (1820; London: Oxford University Press, 1912).

——, *The Antiquary*, 3 vols (Edinburgh: Archibald Constable and Co.; London: Longman, Hurst, Rees, Orme, and Brown, 1816).

——, 'Emma: a Novel', *Quarterly Review*, 14 (1815–16), 187–201.

——, *The Journal of Sir Walter Scott*, ed. W. E. K. Anderson (Oxford: Clarendon Press, 1972).

——, *The Lay of the Last Minstrel. A Poem* (London: Longman, Hurst, Rees, and Orme; Edinburgh: A. Constable and Co., 1805).

Seligman, Martin S., *Learned Optimism: The Skill to Conquer Life's Obstacles, Large and Small* (New York: Random House, 1990).

Sherlock, Thomas, *Several Discourses Preached at the Temple Church* (1754–97; Oxford: 1812).

Simpson, David, *Romanticism, Nationalism, and the Revolt against Theory* (Chicago and London: University of Chicago Press, 1993).

Smith, Adam, *The Theory of Moral Sentiments* (1759; Indianapolis: Liberty Press, 1976).

Southam, B. C., *Jane Austen's Literary Manuscripts* (Oxford: Clarendon Press, 1964).

——, ed., *Jane Austen: The Critical Heritage* (London: Routledge and Kegan Paul, 1968).

——, ed., *Jane Austen: The Critical Heritage, 1870–1940* (London and New York: Routledge and Kegan Paul, 1987).

———, ed., *Jane Austen: 'Northanger Abbey' and 'Persuasion', a Casebook* (London: Macmillan, 1976).

Spring, David, 'Interpreters of Jane Austen's Social World: Literary Critics and Historians', in *Jane Austen: New Perspectives*, ed. Janet Todd (New York and London: Holmes and Meier, 1983), 53–72.

Sterne, Laurence, *Tristram Shandy* (1759–67; Boston: Houghton Mifflin, 1965).

Tanner, Tony, Introduction to *Pride and Prejudice* (Harmondsworth: Penguin Books, 1975).

———, *Jane Austen* (Cambridge, Mass.: Harvard University Press, 1986).

Tave, Stuart, *Some Words of Jane Austen* (Chicago: University of Chicago Press, 1973).

Taylor, John Tinnon, *Early Opposition to the English Novel: The Popular Reaction from 1760 to 1830* (New York: King's Crown Press, 1943).

Thompson, James, *Between Self and World* (University Park and London: Pennsylvania State University Press, 1988).

Tillotson, Geoffrey, Paul Fussell, and Marshall Waingrow, eds, *Eighteenth-Century English Literature* (New York: Harcourt, Brace, Jovanovich, 1969).

Tucker, George Holbert, *Jane Austen the Woman: Some Biographical Insights* (New York: St. Martin's, 1994).

Varma, Devendra P., *The Evergreen Tree of Diabolical Knowledge* (Washington, DC: Consortium Press, 1972).

[Vickers, William,] *A companion to the altar: shewing the nature & necessity of a sacramental preparation in order to our worthy receiving the Holy Communion, to which are added Prayers and meditations* (London: Scatcherd and Whitaker, n.d. [1793?]).

Vickery, Amanda, 'Women and the World of Goods: A Lancashire Consumer and Her Possessions', in *Consumption and the World of Goods*, ed. John Brewer and Roy Porter (London and New York: Routledge and Kegan Paul, 1993), 274–301.

Weldon, Fay, *Letters to Alice on First Reading Jane Austen* (London: Michael Joseph/Rainbird, 1984).

Welsh, Alexander, *The Hero of the Waverley Novels* (New Haven: Yale University Press, 1963).

Whately, Richard, 'Whately on Jane Austen' [unsigned review of *Northanger Abbey* and *Persuasion*] in Southam, 1968, 87–105.

Williams, Raymond, *Keywords: A Vocabulary of Culture and Society* (London: Fontana/Croom Helm, 1976).

Wilton, Andrew, *Turner in his Time* (London: Thames and Hudson, 1987).

Wiltshire, John, *Jane Austen and the Body: 'The Picture of Health'* (Cambridge: Cambridge University Press, 1992).

Wolfe, Thomas, 'The Achievement of *Persuasion*', in *Studies in English Literature* 11 (1971), 687–700.

Woolf, Virginia, 'Jane Austen', in her *The Common Reader* (London: Hogarth Press, 1925); reprinted in *Jane Austen: A Collection of Critical Essays*, ed. Ian Watt (Englewood Cliffs, NJ: Prentice-Hall, 1963).

Index

Separate entries are provided for Jane Austen's works, by title, and for those of her characters and settings that receive significant mention. References to works by other authors are indexed under the author's name. A sustained treatment of a subject is indicated by page numbers in italics.